The LONG JOURNEY HOME

D0279298

Cecily Blench grew up in Herefordshire and studied English Literature at the University of York. She worked for an independent publisher for several years and is now a freelance writer and editor. *The Long Journey Home* is her first novel.

The LONG JOURNEY HOME

Cecily Blench

ZAFFRE

First published in the UK in 2021 by
ZAFFRE
An imprint of Bonnier Books UK
80–81 Wimpole St, London W1G 9RE
Owned by Bonnier Books
Sveavägen 56, Stockholm, Sweden

A CIP catalogue record for this book is
available from the British Library.

ISBN: 978–1–83877–381–6

Also available as an ebook and in audio

1 3 5 7 9 10 8 6 4 2

Typeset by IDSUK (Data Connection) Ltd
Printed and bound in Great Britain by Clays Ltd, Elcograf S.p.A.

Zaffre is an imprint of Bonnier Books UK
www.bonnierbooks.co.uk

For my grandmother
Mary Doris Norman,
1914–2016,
who was there

PART I
Burma, 1941–1942

1

Bagan, October 1941

Kate could hear her own breathing, fast and loud in the darkness. She tried to focus on the other sounds: the drip of water somewhere along the passage and a stone falling nearby. She could no longer hear the low roar of the Irrawaddy River; she had come too far into the tunnels.

'Hello?'

Her voice echoed. She touched the stone wall beside her and felt the deep carvings beneath her fingers.

I am not afraid, thought Kate. Any minute now the monks will realise they've left me behind.

She recalled wandering around the farm at night when she was a girl, following the dim illumination of the sky and the distant light of the stars. Here the darkness was a different shade. The tunnel had wound so far into the hillside that no light could enter and now she stood in absolute blackness, unable even to see her hand in front of her face.

I lost him in the darkness. The phrase suddenly emerged in her mind. It sounded familiar, a hushed, painful cry. *I lost him in the darkness.* Like a mantra she repeated it over and over, feeling her heart beginning to pound once again.

I never used to be scared of the dark, she thought. This is absurd. But the fear was primitive, ancestral, as though the ghosts of her past had been waiting here for her all her life.

I lost him in the darkness, came a whisper in the tunnel, and she knew that they were there.

✦

Kate had been cycling along a rough track, a few miles from the ancient city of Bagan, when two young boys munching on slices of green mango waylaid her. They had shaved heads and wore the ragged yellow robes of novice monks.

'Good morning, lady. You want see temple?'

She laughed. 'I've seen quite a lot of temples in the last few days. I'm not sure I need to see another one.'

The younger of the boys, swallowing his piece of mango, said, 'No, no, this temple very special. Nice . . .' and here he paused to confer in Burmese with his brother, 'nice cat cones.'

'Cat cones?' said Kate.

'Very nice cat cones,' confirmed his brother. 'Very big, very old.' They looked at her expectantly.

'Ah – do you mean catacombs? Are there any?'

'Yes, lady,' said the younger boy, now examining her borrowed bicycle with the air of a professional dealer. He squeezed the tyres, nodded sagely at the frame, and rang the bell.

'All right,' said Kate, 'how much for the tour?'

'For you, lady,' said the older boy, sucking his teeth, 'five annas.'

'Two,' said Kate.

'Four.'

'Three.'

4

'Done,' he said. 'Your name?'

'Kate. And yours?'

'Nyan. This my brother, Shwe.'

'Pleased to meet you,' she said, shaking hands solemnly with each of them, then leaned the bicycle against a fence.

'This way, Miss Kate.'

Nyan walked beside her, looking with interest at her clothes and the knapsack she carried. 'Why you come Bagan?'

'I work for the government,' said Kate. 'In the education department in Rangoon.'

'You are teacher?'

'No, but I visit schools and write reports about them. This week I've been visiting some of the schools near Bagan. What school do you attend?'

'Ananda monastery school,' said Nyan, pointing vaguely to the east.

'Do you like it there?'

He nodded enthusiastically. 'Is good school. Teachers very nice.' Kate decided not to point out that he and his brother were obviously playing truant.

They went through an archway and joined a path that led steeply downhill between grassy rocks. Kate saw that they were descending slowly into a gorge and thought they must be near the river; sure enough, a moment later she saw the Irrawaddy glinting through the trees at the bottom of the hill.

'Where's this temple?' she asked, pushing damp hair off her forehead.

'Here,' said Nyan, pointing at the slope beneath their feet.

Squinting against the sun, Kate moved closer to the rocks and pulled off a creeper. Beneath it she saw intricate carvings

5

and words in curling Burmese script. In the quiet of the afternoon a bell rang out down in the gorge, somehow muffled. She felt the hair stand up on her arms even in the heat.

'This way,' called Nyan, beckoning. Kate followed the boys, clambering down steep stairs, and saw the stone walls of a temple emerging from the hillside. Panting slightly, she reached the bottom and found herself on a sunny paved terrace above the river. Pink and yellow orchids bloomed nearby and, on the riverbank, fig trees trailed their leaves in the limpid river. She wiped her sweating palms and waved ineffectually at the insects that buzzed around her face, noticing that her shirt and shorts were damp with humidity.

The boys were sitting on a step, grinning, and at the back of the terrace she saw the entrance to the temple set into the rock. A little old woman squatted in the wide arch, making a garland of white flowers. She looked up with a red, betel-stained smile as Kate approached and held out a candle, her other hand holding up one thin finger.

Holding out three coins, Kate took the candles, giving one to each of the boys and keeping one for herself. The old woman picked up a flaring taper and lit the candles with an unsteady hand.

Kate and the two boys stepped inside the temple doorway and instantly she felt the temperature fall. The only light came from the door and from a couple of guttering candles that stood either side of a statue of the Buddha, smiling beatifically in his niche. His neck was draped with flower garlands and the floor nearby was crunchy with dried petals. Two great pillars held up the terraces above. The whole place smelled strongly of incense, enough to make her light-headed.

'Welcome,' said a soft voice and an elderly monk appeared. The boys spoke to him in Burmese and he bowed low before picking up one of the lit candles. She wondered how long it had been since his last visitor and had the fleeting impression that he had been waiting for her for a long time.

The monk bowed again to Kate, his face craggy in the candlelight, and slipped through a roughly carved narrow doorway. Kate followed cautiously, watching her feet as she passed through into the tunnel, where a single thick candle, almost burned down, was stuck to the floor with wax. Looking up, she saw the monk disappearing around a corner into the darkness and felt a chill.

The tunnels of Kyaukgu Umin, the boys whispered to her, were the oldest in Burma. 'Millions of years old,' said Shwe confidently. Hundreds, certainly, thought Kate. The walls – and here they gestured upwards, Nyan raising his candle – were carved with scenes from the life of the Buddha.

Ahead of them, the old monk paused and stood patiently, the candlelight flickering on his face. He spoke softly to the boys, his free hand tracing lovingly over the carvings on the wall.

'He say this one birth of Buddha,' said Nyan, and Kate saw what might be rays of light emanating from a round object that was perhaps once a baby, although centuries of eager hands had worn the carvings almost smooth.

The monk continued down the corridor, the boys following in a small pool of light. The tunnels seemed to go back for miles into the hillside. The main passages were wide and obviously well-used, their floors polished by the bare feet that must have ranged over them for centuries. Somewhere out there the war was raging, but the ghosts of Kyaukgu Umin knew nothing of the world outside. How extraordinary to think that this scene had not changed: a monk in a worn saffron robe pacing through the timeless tunnels.

Ahead, the monk and Nyan were examining another carving, talking quietly, and then they moved around a corner and were out of sight, Shwe trailing behind them. As Kate held up her candle to see the wall, a draught made it gutter and go out, and suddenly she was alone.

꙳

I lost him in the darkness. I lost him. I lost him.

'Miss Kate?'

From somewhere ahead she heard a voice and this time she was sure it was real.

'Shwe, is that you?'

'Here, Miss Kate.'

She sensed him coming back along the tunnel, although she could see nothing, and at last she heard his breathing, felt his small sticky hand take hers.

'Where's your candle, Shwe?'

'Wind blow down.'

'Mine too.'

For a moment they stood silently and then she felt him tug her hand, leading her carefully forward, his bare feet silent on the stone floor.

'All right, Shwe,' she said, swallowing. 'If we keep moving we'll probably see the light from Nyan's candle.'

'Yes, Miss Kate,' he whispered, sounding subdued. Running their hands along the walls, they inched around the corner.

Hoping at any moment to see a friendly glow, Kate kept her eyes open, peering into the blackness.

'They too far,' said Shwe beside her.

'Then we just have to keep going,' said Kate firmly, though her legs were like jelly.

They shuffled along, feeling the gnarled rocks under their hands. A dreadful thought struck her. 'Shwe,' she said, 'does this passage split into two anywhere? We don't want to go down the wrong path.'

'No, Miss Kate,' said Shwe, although he sounded uncertain. 'Stop, lady. Stop for moment.'

She felt him touching the wall carefully, laying a cheek against the stone, running his fingers over whatever carvings were to be found there. Then he knelt and touched the floor, feeling the texture of the ground beneath him.

'Do you know where we are?'

'Yes, lady. I think. Come.' He took her hand again and tugged her along, still moving gingerly in the darkness but with more purpose.

Suddenly there was rock in front of them and Kate realised they were at a junction. Without hesitating, Shwe pulled them along the right-hand tunnel, then took another turning and another.

'Are you sure . . .' Kate began, but she didn't finish, because ahead of them was light, flickering around a corner. It proved to be the last inch or so of a candle, burning in an alcove. Two more bends of the passage brought them to an opening where a different, whiter light was spilling into the tunnel.

'Daylight!' exclaimed Kate and felt relief flooding through her. They emerged into the entrance chamber of the temple, on the opposite side from where they had entered the tunnels. Nyan and the monk were standing by the Buddha, the old man muttering prayers.

Kate strode past them and out through the front door, down the steps, past the old woman, until she was standing at the front of the terrace, looking at the river and taking huge gulps of clean air. The bell chimed again behind her, the sound ringing out across the valley.

2

Rangoon, October 1941

Kate closed the front door of her flat and made her way along Pagoda Road, clutching a stack of folders. She was heading for the Secretariat Building on Dalhousie Street and was already too warm in the hot breath of the morning. She stopped to buy sliced pineapple for breakfast and waved to the woman who sold flowers outside the Sule Pagoda.

The steamer down the Irrawaddy to Rangoon had taken two days and Kate spent the hot midday hours sitting in a patch of shade, watching the arid landscape of Lower Burma slide slowly by. People sat all around her on the deck, playing with their children and eating grilled corn and fresh fruit.

Her field trip was over and she was due back at the government office where she had worked for two years. The war had barely touched Burma during that time, but now it was creeping closer. Japan had invaded Indochina a few weeks earlier and there were rumours of troop movements all across Asia, of submarines in the Bay of Bengal.

The Secretariat, when she reached it, looked as complacent as ever, with neatly kept formal gardens and well-scrubbed brickwork. Servants trotted about cleaning and repairing, taking messages, while men in suits passed to and fro, cogs in the well-oiled machine of Empire.

The ground floor was thronging with staff and she stopped to speak to a few people as she passed through. The noise decreased as she made her way into the depths of the building, which sprawled over acres of ground. Several flights of stairs and a long corridor took her to the education department, where a pale young man hovered outside her office door.

'Hello,' he said, visibly relaxing as he saw her.

'You must be Edwin,' she said. 'I heard they'd found someone to fill the vacancy.'

'That's right. Miss Girton, I presume?'

He was a few years older than Kate, perhaps in his mid-thirties, tall and slender with straw-coloured hair and a melancholy expression. She noticed he was sweating heavily in his light cotton suit, like all new arrivals.

'Call me Kate. They told me downstairs that you're staying at the Strand and that you've come from England via Bombay. Word gets around fast here. Come on in.' She elbowed the door open and he followed, looking around at the small, messy office.

'What do you think of the Strand?' said Kate, thumping her pile of papers onto the nearest desk. 'It's a dreadful old heap, isn't it?'

'I hadn't really thought about it,' said Edwin. 'Someone in India told me it was the only hotel in Rangoon so I made a reservation. Silly, really, now I think about it.'

Kate shrugged. 'It's one of the few hotels suitable for people who travel on Cook's tours and like everything to remind them of home.'

'Do you live nearby?' asked Edwin.

'I've got a flat not far from here. Belonged to the dear and departed parents of a chap who works downstairs so he's letting it to me for now.' She gestured to a seat. 'When did you arrive?'

'Oh – Friday, I think,' said Edwin, frowning. 'I got to the Strand in the afternoon and slept for most of the weekend. It was a long journey from Bombay.'

He looked with interest at the photographs on the wall, little boys and girls sitting in neat rows, sometimes with a teacher or a monk in the centre. 'Did you take these?'

'Most of them,' said Kate. 'Visiting schools is my favourite part of the job, but I don't get a chance to do it often these days. I've just been up to Bagan – it was a rare chance to visit a few schools and fit in some sightseeing too. We've been understaffed for so long that I end up buried in a mountain of paperwork.'

'Well, I'm here to work,' said Edwin earnestly. 'Talk me through everything you're doing and I'll get stuck in.'

Kate showed him a list of projects that needed to be completed soon and meetings that were planned with other members of the department. On seeing the little scrap of torn paper and her messy handwriting, he winced and quietly wrote it out neatly on a clean sheet.

'You're going to be useful,' she said, glancing up as he pinned the sheet of paper to the wall opposite. 'Organisation isn't my strong point, as I expect you can see.'

'I like tidiness,' he said, smoothing the paper. 'I'd be very happy to organise all of this, if you'll let me.' He gestured around at the desk.

'Be my guest.'

Kate hadn't known what to expect of Edwin, but she liked him immediately. He reminded her vaguely of a boy she had known in the village at home: clever, bespectacled, shy around women, uneasy with the boisterous banter of the other boys. He had gone away to university and flourished by all accounts. Douglas, that was it. She wondered if he had been caught up in the war.

Frowning at the page before her, she pushed her thick dark hair behind her ears and was aware of Edwin watching her for a moment before he turned away. She shifted in her seat, feeling her cotton dress sticking to her legs, and went to switch on the ceiling fan.

At one o'clock, after she had introduced Edwin to the people in the neighbouring offices, a delivery boy brought two packed lunches and they stopped to eat. Edwin sniffed the parcel of curry and rice cautiously.

Kate moulded a ball of rice with her fingers and dipped it into the curry. She noticed Edwin tentatively copying her and laughed at the alarm on his face when he first tasted the spicy curry.

'Here, have some water.'

He mopped his face and took another bite. 'It's rather nice, actually.' For a moment she felt that she'd overstepped – some men didn't like being laughed at, especially not by a woman they'd just met. But he was laughing too, now, although he seemed out of practice, and she wondered how long it was since he'd laughed at all.

'So, what's your story?' asked Kate, licking her fingers and taking a gulp of water.

'You mean, why am I not in the army?' said Edwin, with a half smile.

14

'I suppose that is what I mean. I expect you've got some dreadful medical problem that will make me feel bad for even asking, haven't you?'

'Sort of,' said Edwin. 'It's my eyes. I'm blind as a bat.' He took off his glasses and waved them and she saw immediately that his eyes were unfocused as he squinted at her.

'How unfortunate. At least your specs aren't those awful thick milk-bottle bottom lenses. My sister Laura has those and she looks like a mole. A very *nice* mole, though.'

Suddenly vulnerable without his glasses, Edwin put them back on and adjusted them, looking embarrassed. 'Anyway, I went to sign up, back in the first year of the war. But I didn't meet the minimum requirements, what with a weak chest too, so that was an end to it. Lucky me, I suppose.' But he looked doubtful.

'I gather you were teaching in London.'

'Yes,' he said, fiddling with his glasses again and looking down at the half-finished meal before him. 'A grammar school in Lambeth. Not a brilliantly well-paid job but it was pleasant and easy. The boys were cheeky but rarely troublesome.'

'What made you chuck it all in and come out here?' asked Kate, mopping up the last remnants of her curry.

He had obviously been expecting the question. 'My wife died. In May.'

'Oh. I'm sorry.'

He looked down. 'I thought coming out here would be a good distraction. I was about to take up a position in Bombay when they said I'd be more useful here.' He smiled feebly again and finished eating his curry, before folding the banana leaf carefully and putting it in the wastepaper bin. 'And what brought *you* out here?' he asked.

'It was just chance, really,' said Kate, standing to pour tea from a large thermos into two little cups. It was Chinese tea, thin and yellow, with leaves floating here and there. 'My friend Christina wanted to visit – her uncle works for Burmah Oil somewhere in the north – and we decided to come out together for six months. I was working in a very dreary job in Birmingham so I was thrilled to chuck it all in. I'd always liked the idea of Burma.' She passed him one of the steaming cups and he looked uncertainly down at the pale tea.

'Anyway, Christina got engaged to a wealthy Scotsman after about two months here and is now living in Delhi. I meant to go home, but when the war came . . . well, I cancelled my ticket and got this job. And here I still am.'

'Do you miss England?'

'Sometimes,' said Kate. 'I miss my mother – she's been alone since my father died a few years ago. And I miss the country-side, the cool spring weather. But for a long time I'd felt this sense of being trapped there. I wanted to escape.'

She looked at her hands. 'Everyone who comes here seems to be running away from something.' She glanced up and saw Edwin's expression. 'Oh – I didn't mean—'

He shook his head. 'Perhaps you're right.'

The door opened and another young boy came in, carrying a bowl of warm water, a cloth, and a bar of soap, which he took first to Kate, who washed her hands thoroughly.

'Hello, Cho. Capital of France?' she said to the boy.

'Paris!'

'Italy?'

'Rome!'

'Iceland?'

'Too hard!' complained the boy laughingly. 'No one knows that.'

He carried the bowl round the table for Edwin to wash his hands, then bowed and shut the door gently behind him.

3

Worcestershire, November 1922

'*D*id you have to fight in the war, Daddy?' asked Kate when she was seven years old, as they ranged across the common together. He was quiet for so long that she thought he hadn't heard her.

'Yes, darling,' he said at last.

'Mummy said your lungs were hurt.'

'It was mustard gas.' He called to the dogs. 'Harry! Ginger! Don't get too far ahead!'

'Mustard gas?' said Kate, puzzled. 'Is it made of mustard?'

'Not exactly,' her father replied. 'It comes from some of the same chemical compounds, I believe. I don't know the science, I'm afraid.'

The two spaniels sprinted back, panting and eager to please, pushing their wet noses at Kate until she knelt to fuss them. 'Good boy, Harry. Good girl, Ginger.'

'We ought to be heading back,' said her father, glancing at the sun, which sat low on the horizon. 'It'll be getting dark soon.'

'All right,' said Kate, and they walked on across the common, watching the light draining slowly from the sky. A herd of ponies stood some way off, silhouetted against the skyline.

'Daddy?'

'Yes, Kate?'

'Does it make you sad to talk about the war?'

'It does, rather.'

'Was it very scary? Were you afraid?'

'Often,' said her father, sounding suddenly dreamy. 'It gives you a strange clarity, knowing you might be killed at any time.'

She thought he had probably had enough and decided not to probe further. But he was still thinking, and at last he said, 'I was lucky to get away with only minor health problems. Mustard gas is incredibly toxic. Many men weren't so lucky.'

'Does it kill people?'

'Oh, yes.'

'When they breathe it in?'

'Yes, but it also causes a lot of damage to the outside of the body if you're exposed too closely to it.' He glanced at her. 'I oughtn't to tell you all this, darling, it's not a pleasant subject.'

'It's all right,' said Kate, taking his hand. 'It's interesting. Why didn't you get more hurt?'

'I was a mile or so from the worst of it,' he said. 'There were men much closer who . . .'

He closed his eyes and Kate watched him curiously.

'Anyway, there was a gas attack and it drifted,' he said. 'I inhaled some as I was putting my mask back on—' He coughed, the deep painful cough that Kate heard every night, echoing from his room at the top of the house. 'And this was the result.'

'Did they send you home?'

He shook his head, his eyes still watering. 'No – they didn't realise it was bad. I was back in action a week or so later.'

They had nearly reached the herd of ponies and her father reached out a hand, slowing Kate's pace so as not to alarm them.

'Are you still angry at the Germans?'

'The Germans?' He laughed. 'Good heavens, no! I never held a grudge there. They weren't responsible.'

'Then who was?'

'It was a British gas attack,' he said at last. 'The fools managed to gas us, their own men – released it too early and it drifted back to the British trenches on the wind.'

A grey pony nudged gently at his hand. Kate, beside him, timidly touched the side of the pony's nose and felt the velvet softness.

'We lost a lot of men that day,' he said. 'And all for a stupid mistake. I'll never forgive that.'

Her father turned to look out at the view. They were higher than anything else for miles, and woods and fields stretched out to the horizon where shadowy grey mountains rose in the distance.

'Nothing will ever equal this view,' he said at last, and she heard him take a deep breath before coughing again. 'The heart of England.'

4

Rangoon, November 1941

It was a year of unseasonable weather in Rangoon. In the midst of the dry season the heavens opened one Saturday and the rain poured down.

Kate made her way along Pagoda Road, jumping across puddles and dodging around equally hurried pedestrians, cursing all the while. In one hand she carried a red silk umbrella and with the other she clutched a stack of books to her chest.

A boy wearing little more than a loincloth galloped past her, hauling a rickshaw that held two well-dressed women sitting bolt upright under one parasol. The boy was drenched and muddy and Kate felt chastened, although at the same time cheered to think that someone else was having a worse time of it.

Turning a corner, she scurried along for a few yards more and then darted in through an open doorway. Mr Myint's shop was tiny even by Rangoon standards. It was a cubicle opening onto the street, not much bigger than a London telephone box. Books were piled high all around, right up to the ceiling, and Kate sometimes felt that if she looked at the floor for long enough it too would be made of books.

'Good morning!' she called and, sure enough, a smiling face appeared between the stacks.

'Ah, Miss Girton, very nice to see you,' said Mr Myint. 'Still raining? Here,' and he handed her a length of cotton to dry off with. He was a little elderly Burman, wrinkled and dusty.

'Thanks,' said Kate, pressing it to her face and hair. 'Definitely still raining.'

'What have you brought for me this time?'

'Well,' she said, putting down the pile of books she carried, 'here are the four I got from you last month, the three from the month before, and a couple of new ones my sister sent that arrived last week.'

Mr Myint shook his head. 'All finished already? You read too fast, madam. It is not good for you.'

'Good for business, though,' said Kate. 'Anyway, what deal can you do for me?'

The old man looked through the pile, examining the condition of the books, running a finger along the spines. Most of them had seen better days. The hot Burmese sun and the grubby fingers of dozens of eager readers had turned them yellow and brittle in the years since they had made their way east.

He looked with interest at the new books from London, which stood out – the pages still white and uncreased, the covers glossy.

'Hemingway – I know this name.'

'He's all the rage back home,' said Kate. 'Bestseller.'

'He is English, yes?'

'American, I think, but very well respected. I thought it was rather good, although at this stage my judgement isn't to be relied on. Spanish Civil War, love story, religion, lots of guns. Something for everyone.'

The old fellow tipped his head to one side, assessing the pile before him. 'You can choose . . . three books.'

Kate laughed. 'Oh, come on, you can do better than that. Those two are brand new! I'd say six is a better number.'

'Six? Madam, you will bankrupt me. Four is my final offer.'

'How about five and I promise to get my sister to send more from London? Brand-new editions, the first in Burma.'

The old man sighed and raised his eyes to heaven. 'Very well, madam. Choose your five and be gone.'

But he was careful to wrap Kate's haul in an old newspaper and, looking out at the still heavy rain, added a couple of banana leaves as an extra layer before tying the whole parcel up with string.

※

Throwing down her umbrella, Kate picked up the letter that lay on the mat at home. It had a London postmark and the handwriting told her it was from her sister Laura.

Dearest Kate,

It's been months since we've heard from you, do write to Mother soon, won't you? She says she doesn't mind – she knows you're busy – but I know she'd like to hear from you more often.

Things are rather awful here. Of course I don't see much of it on the maternity ward, but all around I know there are men hurt and dying, and essential supplies are often hard to come by. I feel useless.

There may be an opportunity to transfer soon, and I am inclined to do it. They are looking for theatre nurses. The work will be harder and I expect I shall hate every minute, but at least I'll feel that I'm doing something useful while Will is in North Africa. I can only pray that he doesn't have cause to pass through my care.

They say that the East will soon be at war. I do so hope that Burma will not be caught up in it. Perhaps you ought to come home?

Kate sighed. How could she explain to Laura that going home was what she most dreaded? And that, even if she wanted to, the journey back would be too dangerous? Rumours of war were flying about but there seemed little that she could do at this stage. I'll stay, she thought – until the bitter end. Whenever that might be.

✷

Standing in the street as carts and rickshaws rolled past him, Edwin looked uncertainly at the scrap of paper in his hand. He had been given a list of potential landlords by Miss Soe at the Secretariat.

His room at the Strand, white and empty, was too quiet and it felt so far removed from the reality of life in Rangoon that he might as well have been in England.

'No Burmese names?' he had murmured, looking at the list.

Miss Soe smiled apologetically. 'Landlords in Rangoon are mainly European and Indian. Most Burmese are not wealthy enough to own extra properties.'

'Of course.' He was distracted by the flower that bobbed in her hair and caught its scent, disturbingly feminine.

'If you like I can ask someone here to make enquiries for you?'

'Oh, no,' said Edwin. 'It's quite all right, thank you. It's a good opportunity for me to explore.' She smiled and left, but the scent took some time to fade.

Now, a week later, he was rather regretting his decision. It was always so hot in the streets of Rangoon, although the rain seemed to have stopped, and his task had been thankless; the first four landlords on the list were no longer letting rooms out.

'The war,' said an elderly Indian businessman, waving a hand regretfully. 'I am selling everything.'

Edwin wondered, fleetingly, what Kate did with her weekends. The day before she had taken him out to lunch, showing him how to eat tealeaf salad and writing down a few useful Burmese phrases phonetically. Most of the European women he had met since coming to the East had been finely dressed and rather reserved, and everything they said was tinged with resentment that they were stuck in colonial exile. Kate dressed casually and she was bright and enthusiastic about her work and about Burma. She rarely spoke of the life she had left behind in England and he sensed in her a kindred spirit, although he could not have said why.

The fifth name on his list of landlords was Mr D. Haskell, and he stood now outside a busy factory, with 'Haskell's Imports and Exports' emblazoned on the wooden frontage. He stepped into the shade of an archway that led into a courtyard, where several large lorries were parked. Men were heaving crates and boxes around the yard, surprisingly agile in their cotton *longyis*, their bare chests gleaming.

'Can I help you, sir?' A Burmese servant had appeared – obviously the gatekeeper, for his belt held a hoop of heavy keys and a large knife like a machete hung at his side in a leather sheath.

'I'm looking for Mr Haskell. I was told he might have rooms to let? He's not expecting me, sorry. My name is Edwin Clear.'

'Of course, sir. I will ask Mr Haskell if he can spare a moment. Wait here, please.'

Before long he was shown into an office and a tired-looking young man in a white shirt and slacks stood up to greet him. He was tall and thin and Edwin saw that he wore a black skullcap.

'Mr Clear. Good to meet you. Daniel Haskell. Have a seat.'

'Thank you,' said Edwin, shaking the proffered hand and sinking into a chair. He wiped his forehead, trying to be discreet.

'It takes some time to adjust to the heat,' observed Haskell with a smile. 'Or so I've heard. I don't know anything different.'

'You were born here?'

'My family has been in Rangoon for generations. There's a fairly large Jewish community – my father's grandparents were Polish and Iraqi and my mother's family are Cochin Jews from India.'

'I saw the synagogue on my way here.'

'But you're not Jewish yourself?' A servant placed two small cups on the table and Edwin caught the smell of strong coffee.

'No. My wife Emilia was, though.' He paused and, feeling that it was better to get it out of the way, said, 'She died. The war, you know.'

26

Haskell shook his head. 'I'm very sorry. It isn't easy. I've cousins in Poland and – well, you can imagine. I haven't heard from them for two years. I fear greatly for them.'

Edwin nodded. A door slammed somewhere and there was a spluttering noise as an engine turned over. There were calls back and forth, then at last the engine started with a roar. The lorry idled for a moment before pulling away and gradually the commotion faded.

'It is a catastrophe,' said Haskell, sipping his coffee. 'Not just for the Jews, of course. But we're dying out here, too. One day soon there will be no Jews left in Rangoon.'

Edwin, his mind still on Emilia, nodded silently again.

'Anyway,' said Haskell, 'they told me you were looking for a room.'

'Yes, I'm at the Strand at present.'

'You're with the government, I presume?'

'Yes. At the Secretariat.'

Haskell looked thoughtful. 'I have a little apartment next to my house. It's very simple. You are welcome to it.'

'That's—'

'But I don't think you should take it.'

'Why not?' Edwin stared at him.

'They say that Japan will soon attack the Empire, Mr Clear. How long do you think the government will keep its foreign staff here once that happens? Save your time and trouble and stay at the Strand.'

Haskell walked Edwin to the gate, a sheaf of paperwork in one hand, occasionally calling instructions or greetings to workmen who passed by. The sun was high in the sky and out on the street it was baking. The morning's puddles had already dried up.

'I'll get you a rickshaw,' said Haskell, and soon Edwin was climbing into the little contraption, pedalled by a boy who could not have been more than twelve.

'Take a couple of weeks to think about it,' said Haskell. 'If you want the apartment it will be waiting for you.'

'Thank you,' said Edwin, shaking his hand. 'I'm obliged to you.' And then, because it seemed the only thing to ask, he said, 'Will you stay?'

'Yes,' said Haskell, although he looked melancholy. 'This is my home.' He raised a hand and walked slowly back under the archway into his factory, vanishing among the crowds of workers who thronged the courtyard.

5

London, August 1938

Edwin met Emilia's parents a week before he asked her to marry him.

He had met her first in Hampstead library, beginning with a conversation in which it transpired that each believed the other to be a member of the library staff.

Once they had it all sorted out they parted, but he was hopeful of seeing the shy girl with fair hair again and was rewarded the following week. After a few weeks Edwin plucked up the courage to ask her to join him for a cup of coffee.

Edwin had reached the age of thirty without any romantic experience, and he was surprised at how straightforward it all seemed. Emilia was pretty and kind, if painfully shy, and he knew at once that he wanted to marry her. It was time to settle down. If he was ever aware of a lack of physical attraction between them he did not acknowledge it, not to himself and certainly not to her. They talked for hours about books and he could imagine them growing into old age together, in a little house lined with bookcases.

In passing she had mentioned that she was Jewish – she did not practise herself – and now, on the way to meet her parents, Edwin was tying himself in knots, worrying that they would disapprove of him and that he was on a hiding to nothing.

'What is it?' asked Emilia, seeing his anxious frown as they stepped down off the bus at the end of her road.

'Oh – nothing.'

'Don't be silly,' she said, taking his arm. He noticed how pretty her hair looked, plaited back like that. 'Mummy and Daddy will love you.'

'I'd settle for like,' said Edwin, squeezing her hand in the crook of his arm. 'Let's not get carried away.'

And of course her parents had been charming – friendly, kind, generous, and genuinely interested in the suitor their daughter had brought home. It was easy to see where Emilia had got her cleverness and her love of reading. The Rosens were academics and their house was crowded with books, paintings and unfamiliar objects.

'My mother's,' said Mrs Rosen, seeing his eyes fall on the small menorah on the mantelpiece. 'But we do not practise now.' She had a faint accent, the last remnant of a childhood in Belarus.

Mr Rosen had poured Edwin a glass of wine and gently interrogated him about his life and his prospects. He asked probing questions about Edwin's upbringing and seemed puzzled but gratified at the attachment that had formed between his daughter and this young teacher.

'When do the Hoffmans arrive?' asked Emilia as they ate lunch.

Her mother looked gloomy. 'They were supposed to be in England by now. We have heard nothing from them.'

'German friends,' said her father to Edwin. 'The windows of their shop were smashed a few months ago by fascists so they decided to bring the children to England.'

Later, much later, when the war had begun, Edwin thought to ask after the Hoffmans. 'They never arrived,' Mr Rosen told him, his shoulders now hunched with sadness and fear. 'They must have been imprisoned – or worse. What a godawful time this is.'

After lunch, when Emilia and her mother had disappeared into the kitchen, her father turned to Edwin once again as he gestured to an armchair by the fire.

'Well, young man – what does the future hold for you? What are your plans?'

'I want to marry Emilia,' said Edwin abruptly, flushing scarlet as he said it.

Mr Rosen stared at him, taken aback. 'You do?'

'Yes, sir. With your blessing, I hope.'

'Well . . .' He looked faintly surprised again, as if trying to unravel some mystery. 'It's a pleasant thing for a father to hear. But don't you think it's rather soon? You've only known each other a few months. There's no harm in waiting, is there?'

Edwin shook his head. 'I'm sure. I haven't asked Emilia yet, of course – but I feel certain that this is the right time.'

Mr Rosen nodded. 'Very well. You have my blessing. Ask her. Only . . .' He stared hard at Edwin. 'Look after her, won't you? She's a better person than you or I will ever be.'

'Of course,' said Edwin, 'of course.'

The following week, walking on the Heath, Emilia accepted Edwin's proposal. Like her father, she hesitated for a moment, holding Edwin's gaze intently.

'Are you sure?'

'Of course I'm sure!' said Edwin. Wasn't this what people were meant to do? Get married, settle down, have families? Wasn't it expected? Wasn't this the best way to quell the sense he had always had of not quite belonging?

31

'Then I accept,' said Emilia, squeezing his hand. 'I know you'll look after me.'

'I will,' said Edwin, and at that moment he had never meant anything more. 'I will.'

6

Rangoon, November 1941

A month after his arrival in Rangoon, Edwin sat scribbling, still in the office at six o'clock, as Kate gathered her things to leave.

He looked a little more relaxed, she thought. He had spent time wandering around the city both with her and occasionally alone, and he talked with something approaching enthusiasm about the temples he had visited and the food he had tried. But his brow was often furrowed and he looked as though he carried a great weight much of the time, as he did now, peering down at the densely filled pages before him.

'Why don't you come to the party?' said Kate impulsively. 'There's a St Andrew's Day celebration tonight at the Scottish church.'

Edwin looked up and hesitated. 'Will we be welcome?' he said. 'Not being Scottish, I mean.'

Kate laughed. 'Of course. They do it every year. There are more Scots in Rangoon than you would believe, but they always invite the English and the Americans too. Come hell or high water, they have their party.'

'Well, it sounds very jolly,' said Edwin unconvincingly.

She smiled. 'Do come. Really. You don't have to stay all evening if you don't want to. But it's a good chance to meet some of the European community – quite a lot don't live in Rangoon and just come into the city at this time of year. They'll be so glad to see a new face.'

'I'll think about it . . .'

'Oh, don't – please just come. Meet me at the Sule Pagoda at seven and we can walk over there together, I know the way.'

Edwin looked as though he had deep misgivings, but said at last, 'All right, then. See you there.'

✴

The Scottish Presbyterian church had been built seventy years before to serve the needs of the growing foreign community and on this night it was filled with dancing Scots. The sound of bagpipe music spilled out from the doorway, where it mingled oddly with the smells of Burmese food cooking in the streets nearby.

'I wonder what the locals think of this music,' said Edwin over the din as they entered the crowded church.

'They probably think it sounds like caterwauling!' said Kate, waving at one or two people she knew. 'Bit of an acquired taste, really, isn't it?'

She introduced him to various acquaintances. 'Mr Edwin Clear, just out from England, new entry at the Secretariat.'

'Delighted to meet you,' said Mrs Campbell, a well-built woman in a gold-trimmed tartan evening gown, with a gentle Edinburgh brogue. 'This is my dear friend Mrs Hamilton, from

Devon, and little Sam,' she said, gesturing to the woman beside her, who cradled a large blond baby.

'He's a fine fellow,' said Edwin, tweaking the baby's toe. 'Hello, Sam.' The baby gurgled delightedly and bounced in his mother's arms.

'How are your schools, Miss Girton?' enquired Mrs Hamilton.

'Doing very well, thank you, Mrs Hamilton.'

'It's a great thing that we've been able to introduce some of the principles of British schooling.'

'Well, that's not exactly—'

'I do like seeing those sweet little monks in their robes,' said Mrs Hamilton with a chuckle. 'The Church of England would be thrilled to attract such devout schoolboys.'

'It's an economic choice, rather than a matter of faith,' said Mrs Campbell dismissively. 'They don't learn any decent subjects. Just chanting those funny poems over and over.'

'Well, in fact . . .' Kate began, and then closed her mouth firmly. 'I suppose Sam will go to school in England?'

'Oh yes,' said Mrs Hamilton, jiggling the baby. 'His two older brothers are at Eton and my husband was an Eton boy. It's the sensible choice, really.'

Kate escaped as soon as she could, sweeping Edwin off to meet more people. For him it was rather an ordeal, but everyone he met was kind and he found himself drawn into conversation with a homesick Englishman with a glass eye who wanted to talk about pubs. He saw Kate greeting a young, ruddy-faced Scotsman in a kilt, who kissed her hand and led her onto the dance floor.

'It's so hard getting a decent pint out here,' lamented the Englishman, with a wave that captured the subcontinent. 'I dream of the places I used to go – the Lamb and Flag near Covent Garden, that was a favourite, and that marvellous place with the stained glass on Fleet Street – the Bell, is it?'

'I'm afraid I don't know it,' said Edwin apologetically, racking his brains to think of a London pub he had been to, but his new friend didn't seem to need any input and was happy to ramble quietly on, spilling the warm, substandard beer in his glass as he reminisced.

Edwin watched Kate dancing with the young Scotsman. It was a fast reel and she hurtled across the floor with more enthusiasm than skill, flushed and laughing. He wondered if this was a boyfriend, but before long she was dancing with someone else, another tall fellow with dark hair and two left feet.

Eventually the pub bore found someone else to rhapsodise to and Edwin found himself talking to a procession of middle-aged women, who seemed delighted to have a new face in their midst.

'Mr Clear, you must meet Mrs Dashwood, she'll be so glad to see you. She has two marvellous daughters, where are they tonight?'

'And Miss Peters, you must meet her, she's just arrived from Aberdeen, lovely girl!'

They swirled around him, bringing friends and husbands over and processing a string of young women past him. It was at this point that Edwin, rather bemused by all the attention, suspected that his status as a widower had gone before him. It had happened in London; a voluble matron, on hearing he was widowed, would suddenly show great interest and drag over some poor girl she was trying to marry off.

The eligible young women of Rangoon were all charming, friendly girls, and while they were obviously pleased to have someone new to talk to, he realised he had little to fear from them. In the not-so-distant past it must have been very hard living somewhere like this if you were on the hunt for a husband, but the community now was big enough to allow matchmaking, and any girl who desperately wanted to be married could simply set sail for Bombay, or London, and try her luck elsewhere.

Feeling that he had done his duty, Edwin took his beer over to a quiet, dimly lit corner, where he sat for a while, glad to be alone.

He found himself nodding off and several times jerked his head up to find that a new dance had started. Finally, he was awoken by a nudge to his shoulder, as Kate appeared beside him, looking flushed.

'Don't you want to dance?' she asked as she sat down.

He shook his head. 'Not really a dancer, I'm afraid.'

They watched the swirling couples. 'It's not so bad,' she said. 'I just try to avoid treading on anyone's toes and cling on for dear life.'

'Who were those fellows you were dancing with?'

'Oh, just friends,' she said with a shrug. 'I don't know them well.'

She rubbed the waistband of her green silk dress and sighed. 'I knew wearing this was a mistake. It's too tight, isn't it?'

'I think you look very nice.'

'The seamstresses find it hard to gauge European sizes as Burmese women are all so tiny. I feel like an elephant when they measure me. Lovely workmanship, though.'

The young Scotsman she had danced with first now materialised before her and bowed, his kilt flapping. 'One more dance, Miss Girton?'

✳

'You're getting better at this!' said Hamish above the din, watching approvingly as she twirled in the right direction.

'Do you think so? I need more practice really, classes or something.'

'I'd offer to assist,' he said, a smile crinkling his ruddy face, 'but I'm leaving tomorrow.'

'Leaving Rangoon?'

'Aye.'

'I thought you'd always lived here?'

'I joined up last week.'

'Oh, I see,' said Kate. Somehow all the men she danced with seemed to go off to war eventually. Hamish had almost kissed her once and she had supposed that eventually they would go to bed together, but now it would never happen. 'Where are they sending you?'

'India, first, for training. Then who knows?'

The music sped up and the bagpipes and the fiddles played on, the red-faced players stamping the floor.

This party had taken place every year for forty or fifty years, but there had been lonely Scotsmen in Burma for much longer, for one reason and another. The first had come a century or more before, seeking timber and oil, crossing the hot plains and climbing high into the rugged mountains. They had found oil and teak, and their fortunes besides, and many had stayed and made homes for themselves, from the Gulf of Martaban to the Chinese border.

The song finished with a thumping of feet on the floor and everyone cheered and raised glasses. Kate sagged into Hamish's arms, feeling his laughter above her head – but something was wrong, for the thumping noise carried on and everyone stopped talking to listen intently to the distant thunder.

'Is that . . .?'

'Bombing,' said Hamish quietly. 'Yes, I think so.'

She pulled away from him and stood tensed, her head craned towards the sound. The gaps between the thuds grew longer, but always there was another and a murmur of conversation broke out. The musicians had put down their instruments and were talking excitedly to one another. The elderly master of ceremonies, Mr McLeod, now hurried to the stage.

'Excuse me, ladies and gentlemen. I think we must end the party there. It's after midnight anyway.'

'What was that?' someone called.

'I cannot say for sure,' said McLeod, 'but it sounded very much like bombing to me, as I'm sure it did to you.'

'From Siam?'

'I don't know,' he said. 'But I suggest you all take your families home and make yourselves safe. We'll know more tomorrow. Go home – and God speed you all.'

The crowds began to disperse. Kate turned to Hamish.

'Do you think that sound was really from Siam?'

'Perhaps,' he said, 'but it sounded very close. Too close.'

She nodded.

'I must go,' he said, looking around. 'I need to get ready to leave.'

'Of course,' she said. He gave a little bow and then picked up her hand and kissed it.

'Silly boy,' she said and pushed his shoulder. 'Go.'

'It was very nice to see you,' said Hamish. 'I'm grateful that my last night as a civilian was spent dancing with a pretty girl. If I don't see you again . . .'

'Good luck,' said Kate. 'Be careful.'

She found Edwin sitting where she had left him. He looked even whiter than usual and was staring into the middle distance. A beer glass lay shattered on the floor beside him, the pooled liquid already attracting flies.

'Are you all right?' she asked.

'Yes, fine,' he replied jerkily. 'It was just . . . the bombs, you know.'

She sat down beside him and wondered if he was going to faint. 'They were rather a shock.'

He cleared his throat. 'My wife was killed in the bombing in London.'

Kate had not asked what had happened to her; it seemed too close, too personal. She might have been ill. But of course it was the war. Even in London, no one was safe.

'There were hundreds of bombs,' he said quietly. 'That morning the whole of North London was burning, the air full of smoke . . .'

'But you survived,' said Kate.

'I wasn't there.' He said it quickly, as though confessing to something dreadful. 'I was away. I came back to find the house blown to bits.'

'Oh,' she said. 'Oh, Edwin – I'm sorry.'

He sank back in his seat, as though all the air was gone from him, and stared bleakly at her.

She wondered what his wife had been like – how long he'd known her and how he would survive without her. He sounded distraught still, scarred by what had happened. But there was more to it than that, she thought, as she watched his trembling hands.

She wanted to tell him that she was bitterly sorry for him and that she, too, had experienced the guilt that came with losing someone you loved, but the hosts were calling for the hall to be emptied and they joined the surge towards the door, emerging at last into the warm night.

'Shall I escort you home?' said Edwin, looking ill at ease. The thumping sound had stopped, and all that could be heard were the soft noises of the city.

'No need, but we're going the same way,' said Kate. 'Let's get a rickshaw, I'm too tired to walk.'

She gently woke a youthful rickshaw driver who had fallen asleep waiting outside the church and negotiated a price for him to take them home. Blearily he climbed into the saddle and pedalled dreamily off.

They glided slowly through the suburbs of Rangoon, gradually heading south into the city. Despite the lateness of the hour there was still activity everywhere, the lights of teashops glowing invitingly through the darkness. The inhabitants of

Rangoon must all have heard the explosions, if that was what they were, but life carried on as normal for now.

'The Strand first, please,' said Kate to the boy, glancing at Edwin. He was sitting very still again, his fingers white with tension.

Outside the hotel Kate climbed stiffly down from the rickshaw and gently helped Edwin to alight, leading him up the steps to where a doorman waited, looking concerned.

'He's had a bit of a shock,' she said. 'Look after him, will you?'

'Of course, madam,' said the doorman, holding out a hand to steady him. He opened the door, letting a pool of warm light flood the steps.

Kate patted Edwin's shoulder. 'Will you be all right?'

Edwin shook himself, seeming suddenly to realise where he was, and stood up a little straighter. 'I'll be fine.' He blinked. 'Goodnight. And thank you.'

He watched as Kate climbed back into the rickshaw and the boy pedalled off again, heading for Pagoda Road.

7

Rangoon, December 1941

Kate padded around her flat, occasionally moving things from one room to another. Officially she was tidying up, but really she was just enjoying the space – her space. A fortnight had passed since the Scottish party and Japanese forces had started bombing targets in the far south of Burma, while ground troops invaded Malaya and Singapore. Asia was suddenly at war, but in Rangoon things were oddly calm and Kate tried not to think about what was to come.

Having a whole flat to herself still felt like a luxury. In the busy house of her childhood, dominated by her father's sickroom, there had rarely been time to be alone. Occasionally she would run out into the fields, brushing her hands in the dew of the early morning, or stand out at dusk in the summer listening to the birds, before going back inside.

The day she got the keys to the flat she had waited until the footsteps of her kindly landlord had died away before lying down on the cool wooden floor, her arms and legs outstretched, listening to the murmur of the street outside and the chiming of a clocktower.

Every day, coming back from work at the Secretariat, she was delighted to see the place again, to sit in the chair by the window with a drink and read or watch the city. She did not dwell on the fact that she was lonely; it seemed a fair price to pay for the solitude she craved.

Of the occasional lovers she'd had in Rangoon, none had been invited back to the flat. She couldn't have said why. It seemed too private. Perhaps, if she had fallen in love with one of them, it might have been different, but they were short-term flings, usually with men who were passing through, equally uninterested in lasting arrangements.

'You can be very cold,' said Paul, the most recent, the last time she saw him, as she buttoned her dress in front of the mirror in his room.

'Cold?'

'Detached. You're not very loving.'

'But you're not in love with me,' said Kate, surprised.

He looked back at her appraisingly. 'No, I suppose I'm not.'

'Ah. You want to be loved, but not to have to do any loving yourself. Don't you think that's rather selfish?'

He shrugged. 'It's what I'm used to.' His honesty had been one of the things that had attracted her in the first place. Now she wanted to slap him.

'And how does that usually end up?'

He sighed. 'I get bored and move on.'

'Well, don't let me stop you,' she said, pulling on her shoes. She picked up her bag and looked around for anything she might have missed.

'You'll fall in love with someone eventually,' said Paul, leaning back against the headboard and lighting a cigarette. 'I wonder if you'll be as cold to them?'

Kate stared at him, feeling a rush of fury tempered by indifference. Who was he to pass judgement on her, as if he knew her? He knew nothing about her – had never asked about her family, her background, or wondered why she might be unable – or unwilling – to open her heart. She would not give him the satisfaction of knowing.

'Goodbye,' she said, and went to the door. She was angry at him, but also oddly relieved that things could end with such finality. It was clean and she need feel no remorse.

'Kate,' said Paul, in what she knew was meant to be a conciliatory tone, 'I'm leaving next week. I'd like to see you before I go.'

She hesitated. Then, without turning back, she said, 'No, I don't think so. Good luck.'

She could hear him calling something as she went down the hallway, but she kept walking, her legs carrying her automatically home.

✦

Edwin sat under a shady awning outside the teashop nearest to the Strand, slurping the last dregs of a bowl of noodle soup. He had brought a book, but it lay untouched as he watched the activity on the street outside.

'Hello,' said Kate, appearing beside his table. He squinted up at her. 'I thought you'd be here. I've been tidying and now I'm much too hot. Want to go swimming?'

'Yes,' said Edwin at once. 'Where can we go?'

'The India Club pool,' said Kate. She jerked her head. 'It's a mile or two that way.'

'All right,' said Edwin. 'I'll get my things.' He laid some money on the table before disappearing back to the Strand. Kate looked around for a waiter, feeling vaguely that she ought to buy something, but the only person she could see was a boy who lay curled up on a table, fast asleep, his head covered by a cloth.

A plump man at the next table leaned over and placed a tiny cup of weak tea in front of her, poured from his own jug.

'Thank you,' she said, and he bowed his head before going back to his newspaper.

What a decent man, thought Kate, sipping the tea. She hoped that he had offered it out of kindness rather than obligation. The Burmese were proud and treated the British as equals. If only we treated them that way in return, she thought uneasily, recalling the things she had heard Europeans say when there were no 'natives' around.

Edwin emerged wearing a pair of shorts and carrying a bag over his shoulder. She noticed how pale his legs were but that his face had picked up a healthy colour over the last few weeks. She drank up and they started off through the hot streets towards the India Club.

'It's my birthday today,' she said.

'You should have said,' exclaimed Edwin. 'Many happy returns.'

'Thanks.'

'Don't you celebrate it?'

'Not really,' said Kate. 'I've always been too busy and there was never time or money when I was a child. I almost forget it these days.'

'The older you get the less you want to remember,' said Edwin. 'I shall be thirty-four soon. It seems rather old. I shan't ask you to tell me how old you are.'

Kate laughed. 'Today I turn twenty-seven.'

'So you must have been born just after the first war started,' said Edwin after a moment.

'My poor mother, can you imagine? Having a baby twelve days before Christmas, not long after the outbreak of war, in one of the harshest winters on record.'

Edwin shook his head. 'She must have been very stoic.'

'She was. My father hadn't yet been called up, so at least he was able to spend a few months with me before he was sent to France. My sister Laura would have been four, I suppose. And my grandparents were still alive then, so I expect they helped, too.'

'Were you living on the farm?'

'Not at that point – we lived in a village nearby. In 1917 my grandfather died, so Mother, Laura, and I moved onto the farm to help Grandma. Then the following year Grandma was carried off by the Spanish flu and Father came home unable to work much, so the only thing to be done was for Mother to run the farm.'

Kate thought of those early years, when she and Laura had ranged through the fields and outhouses, discovering eggs still warm in the hen boxes and stroking the soft noses of young lambs. Her father had gone back to work in his office three days a week, which gradually decreased to two and then one as his health declined. Her mother, understanding that the farm would have to support them all eventually, had spent long days outside, learning from the elderly farmhands who had been there since she was a girl.

'How old were you when he died?' said Edwin.

'I was twenty-one. Spring, 1936.'

Edwin said nothing, but she knew he was listening intently as they approached the Scott Market.

'He came home from the war with gas damage,' she said. 'He was all right for a few years, physically at least, but it was a gradual decline.'

'That sounds very difficult.'

'It was, for all of us. My mother was strong but I know she was unhappy for a long time.'

'What about you?'

'I felt trapped,' said Kate in a low voice. She looked up, frowning slightly. 'I know that sounds awful.'

Edwin shook his head. 'You were young. It's natural to feel that way.'

'Is it?'

'Of course. No one would choose to witness the decline of someone they love.'

'I felt dreadfully guilty – still do, I suppose.'

'Kate, believe me when I say that you have nothing to be ashamed of,' said Edwin earnestly. 'I know all about shame—' He broke off suddenly and looked flustered.

Seeing his discomfort, Kate cast around for a change of subject. She led him on through the crowds, talking automatically about the India Club, but her mind was elsewhere. She wondered what Edwin was so ashamed of – what had happened to him? It was hard to imagine that this kind, gentle man could ever have hurt someone.

But that's probably what he thinks of me, she said to herself, feeling chilled even under the hot sun. Perhaps we're more alike than we think. She turned back to look at him, pushing through the crowd behind her, his glasses slipping down his nose as he rummaged in his pocket for a coin to give to a small child. What sins had Edwin Clear committed?

✦

The India Club lay a few streets back from the Scott Market. It was solidly built of teak, the gardens still immaculate, and Kate wondered if she was imagining the slight whiff of decay as they walked up the driveway between quivering jacaranda trees.

'You don't strike me as a club sort of person,' said Edwin, looking at the sign that heralded the entrance.

She laughed. 'I'm a swimming sort of person. The Pegu Club is the fashionable place to go for drinks, but there's no pool and anyway, they're odd about women going in alone. This place is charmingly chaotic and considerably cheaper.'

The huge front doors were closed and though Kate rattled the handle and called, no one came. Squatting down, she peered through the latticed glass; the vast and empty hallway stretched away and a broom lay abandoned on the floor, evidence of its last half-hearted journey etched into the dust nearby.

'They must have closed because of the bombing,' said Edwin. 'That's a pity.'

'The swimming pool is at the back,' said Kate, and marched off along the side of the building, stopping now and then to look in through a window.

'But we can't . . . can we?' Edwin dashed after her, trying to keep his hat on with one hand and gripping the bag that contained his swimwear and water bottle in the other.

Kate disappeared around the corner ahead and he emerged to find her standing before a high wooden fence, eyeing it appraisingly.

'Look,' she said, and pointed to a knothole. Dropping his things, he peered through.

On the other side he could see a whitewashed swimming pool, surrounded by neat lawns, with trees overhead to shade it against the cobalt sky. Wooden sun loungers lay on either side of the pool, each with a little table beside it, and he imagined uniformed waiters bringing cocktails to pink sunbathers as they rested between dips.

'There's still water in the pool,' said Kate. Putting down her bag, she turned to him. 'How are you at climbing?'

'What?'

She was off before he knew it, clambering briskly up the fence, feeling out each foothold with her rubber-soled shoes. Before long she was at the top and turned briefly to look back down at him, laughing.

'Good thing I wore shorts today!' She swung over the top and then paused. 'Aren't you coming?'

For a second he saw her silhouetted against the sky, almost unbearable in its brightness, and then she was out of sight.

'Oh – all right,' said Edwin, and began to climb. At one point he looked down and regretted it; it would be a long way to fall. He had not climbed anything since he was a child.

He reached the ground on the other side, panting slightly, to find Kate peering at the water while untying her laces.

'It's fairly clean,' she said. 'They can't have been closed for long.' A few palm fronds floated on the surface.

'I've left my swimsuit on the other side,' said Edwin in dismay, looking back towards the fence.

'Me too,' said Kate, shrugging. 'Never mind.' She pulled her shoes off, looking down at the cotton shorts and blouse she wore.

'You're not—'

With a splash, Kate leapt into the water. It was cool, and for a moment everything was gloriously quiet and calm. She opened her eyes and saw the eerie green expanse of the pool stretching away, free of the dozens of pairs of plump legs that would usually be kicking lazily below the surface. She swam down as close to the bottom as she could. It was odd to be alone here. She wondered where the patrons had all gone and if they would ever return.

There was a muffled splash over at the deep end and she watched Edwin diving down, his hands neatly pointed. He looked even paler than usual, and she remembered the Burmese legends that Miss Soe had told her about green ghosts, souls doomed to wander. Edwin, she thought, the ghost trying to find his way home.

Later, they lay baking on sun loungers and Edwin told her about his parents and his happy childhood in Kent, about how much he had enjoyed teaching. In turn, Kate told him about her mother, who ran the farm single-handed and was tougher than anyone she knew, and her sister Laura, who was a nurse and worked terribly hard, and how she had read Kipling's poem about Mandalay as a young woman and had thought of Burma ever since.

'I would have liked siblings,' said Edwin, fanning himself with a banana leaf. 'I was rather a lonely child. It must have been fun.'

'I suppose it was when we were little,' said Kate. 'But Laura was four years older than me, so she left home when I was twelve to go to secretarial college and later went in for nursing.'

'And she got married?'

'Yes,' said Kate, wrinkling her nose. 'To Will. A perfectly amiable solicitor's clerk.'

'You don't like him?'

She shrugged. 'He's a nice enough chap. Just a bit boring. I was disappointed in her lack of imagination. Although I suppose I was also envious that she'd escaped. We grew apart a lot when I was stuck at home and after Father died it got even worse. She didn't approve of me coming here. She thought it wasn't fair on Mother. I suppose she was right.'

Kate stared at the surface of the water, which twinkled as it was gently ruffled by a breeze, thinking of Laura in cold, wet London. She looked up at Edwin, who was still watching her. 'The war seems to have done wonders for our relationship. Will signed up immediately and Laura went to nurse in London. She started sending me great stacks of books.'

'A peace offering?' said Edwin.

'I suppose so, yes. We don't talk much about the past, but I'm glad to be friends again. I wonder when I'll next see her.'

'I wonder that about my parents,' said Edwin, frowning slightly. 'I know they're safe enough in Kent but one can't help worrying.' He stood up and stretched. 'I think I'll have another dip.'

Kate watched him practise diving, his thin arms surprisingly muscular, and wondered for a moment what it would be like to fall in love with him. No, she thought firmly, surprised at the strength of feeling. Don't mistake friendship for romance, for it is far more rare and precious. It occurred to her that Edwin was probably the first man who had not treated her as a potential conquest: the first real friend that she had had.

She knew that they were both carefully avoiding the painful territory they had encountered before. Edwin's loss was still raw and the weight of it sometimes made him maudlin and prickly. Eventually, she supposed, they would talk about it properly. Perhaps she could tell him about her own grief, the tragedy that had sent her away from home.

It was a long, hot, strange afternoon and the war was a world away. They talked and laughed, comparing suntan lines. Edwin pretended to be a waiter, serving her half a coconut shell he had found on the ground, and she showed him her spluttering impression of the ageing colonels who usually used the pool. They swam again and finally, when the shadows were lengthening, they climbed over the fence and made their way back towards Pagoda Road, their clothes drying quickly in the warm evening.

8
London, June 1941

*E*dwin had consumed most of a bottle of whisky on the night his father found him. He was curled up on the floor of the temporary lodgings he had rented after the bombing, weeping into a scarf of Emilia's, the empty whisky bottle rolling nearby.

'What do you want?' he slurred, seeing his father enter the room. 'How did you . . . get in here?'

'The landlady let me in,' said his father, shaking his head a little. 'Oh, Edwin. You're a mess.' He leaned for a moment on the door frame, wincing as he stretched out his bad leg.

'Leave me alone,' Edwin said, struggling up to lean against an armchair.

'No can do. Sorry, son.' His father went to the sink and filled a glass with water. 'Drink this. Come on.'

Silently Edwin drank while his father pottered around the room, humming an irritatingly cheerful tune, picking things up here and there from the messy floor. He barely looked at his son and Edwin had the sudden painful realisation that his father was ashamed of him.

'What do you want?' he said again.

'I've come to take you home.'

'My home is gone,' said Edwin and felt the tears start again. 'It's all gone.'

'I mean our home. Your mother's and mine. You're coming back with me.' His father came at last to look at him, his face creased with pity and discomfort. 'Poor lad.'

Edwin thought of refusing, but he could barely summon the energy. With his father's help he struggled to his feet and noticed that the scarf was still in his hand. He pressed his face into it.

'It's not fair,' he said, his voice muffled. 'It's not fair.'

'I know,' said his father, helping him out of the room and down the stairs to where his old car waited to take them home. 'I know.'

'It was my fault . . .' mumbled Edwin as he clambered into the back seat. 'My fault.'

'Of course it wasn't,' said his father beside him, holding his arm firmly. 'It was an accident, a tragedy.'

'I'm guilty. I've done . . . dreadful things.'

'Don't be absurd, Edwin,' said his father and closed the door gently. He got into the driver's seat and peered at Edwin in the rear-view mirror before shaking his head and starting the car.

✦

The rest of the night was a blank. They must have got home to the house in Kent, for when Edwin awoke, his head aching, he was back in his narrow childhood bed, a cup of tea cooling on the nightstand, an aspirin beside it.

He drank some of the tea with the aspirin and slept again. A little later his mother came in, smoothing his bedclothes and kissing him on the forehead. She had been fond of Emilia and had been subdued since her death. He smiled weakly up at her and felt sleep approaching again.

'I've telephoned the school,' she said as she left the room. 'I said you're ill. They won't expect you until Monday.'

55

A little later he was awake, staring at the wall, when his father came in, shuffling in his carpet slippers. They had never been close; not through any dislike, but simply because they were too similar – shy, reserved, uneasy talking about matters of the heart.

His father had done well for himself; born a coalheaver's son, he had excelled at grammar school and ended up working for a bank, saving enough to send his son to a decent school. Edwin's mother, a teacher herself before marriage, had had high hopes for him, a headmaster's post perhaps, but if they were disappointed to find Edwin still a lowly schoolmaster at thirty-three, they had never shown it.

His father sat down at the end of the bed, a little awkwardly, and proceeded to give him the first dressing-down Edwin could remember since he was a boy. He told him, in effect, that he could not go on this way and must pull himself together or ruin his life.

Edwin, who felt his life to be ruined quite enough already, listened carefully, full of shame and resentment, but he knew his father to be right, and wasn't sure whether to hit him or hug him. He did neither.

'Did I ever tell you about my pal Jeremy?' his father asked suddenly and cleared his throat. 'We were school friends. He had a twin sister, Diana, and the three of us were a little club, thick as thieves we were. I stepped out with Diana for a time – it didn't last, and of course later I met your mother, but we stayed friends. Nice girl, she was. Jeremy loved animals and trained to be a vet.'

'I remember him, I think,' said Edwin, dredging up a memory from his childhood, shortly before the first war, recalling a big jolly man with a huge St Bernard that went everywhere with him. He had let the infant Edwin ride the dog around the sitting room, squawking with laughter.

56

'Jeremy died at Passchendaele. Did you know that? I didn't see it happen. A great loss.' His father was staring at him. 'And Diana never spoke to me again. She resented me, you see – for surviving. Twenty years of friendship, thrown away just like that. The last I heard she'd left her husband and was busy drinking herself to death. Not what Jeremy would have wanted, of course. She let the grief win.'

Edwin wondered, inexplicably, what had happened to Jeremy's dog and felt tears coming again. Somehow he had never thought to ask why he had stopped coming to visit, had barely remembered his existence until today. Why had his father never talked of Jeremy? Hadn't he, too, let grief rule his actions?

His father was silent now, staring at the floor, and then seemed to make an effort to look at his son.

'I don't say any of this to chastise you, Edwin, but to help you. You must learn to deal with the grief. Not for my sake, or your mother's, or even for your own, but for Emilia's. Do you think she'd have wanted this? Of course not. She'd want you to pick yourself up and learn how to live again.'

The next day Edwin applied for a job in India.

9

Rangoon, December 1941

Taking a deep breath, Kate knocked on the door and heard Mr Carlton's reedy voice say, 'Enter.'

She went in and saw the old man hunched behind his desk. She had seen him only a few times since he had offered her the job in 1939. He evidently had little interest in education and tended to let his section of the department run itself.

'Miss Girton,' he said, peering up over his spectacles. She saw a stack of closely typed printed pages in front of him, but he moved his hand to cover them and put his pen back on the inkstand.

'Well? What is it you want?'

'I wondered if you have any information, sir,' she said, trying not to sound impatient, 'about the war. People are afraid and no one seems to know anything.'

He frowned. 'What sort of information?'

'Well – when the Japanese are going to arrive, for one.'

'Don't be foolish,' he said, looking cross. 'You'll cause a riot with that kind of talk.'

'Everyone says it's coming,' she said.

'We do not anticipate an attack on the city in the near future,' he said firmly, scribbling furiously on the paper before him. 'The Japanese are far too busy targeting Singapore, which is unlikely to fall.'

'So why has the city introduced a blackout?'

'It's a precaution, Miss Girton,' he said, standing up. 'Rest assured, you will be given instructions in ample time if there is any danger to the civilian community.' He marched over to the door and wrenched it open, glowering at her. 'Now please leave.'

Reluctantly she went back into the corridor and the door slammed behind her.

'Anything useful?' asked Edwin when she reappeared in the office.

'No. Nothing. Everyone I speak to either pats me on the head and tells me not to worry or bleats on about bloody Singapore.' Fuming, she sat down heavily.

'If I were the Japanese Imperial Army,' said Edwin, 'an unlikely turn of events, I grant you – I'd say this was the ideal time to invade Burma, while everyone's eyes are on Singapore. It seems the obvious thing to do.'

'Try telling that to Mr Carlton,' she said. 'The thing is, they probably know much more than we do. It's just that they won't tell us.'

'People ought to be leaving the city,' said Edwin, fiddling with a pencil. 'It's not safe here.'

'I think some are,' said Kate. 'Apparently a lot of Europeans, Mrs Campbell for one, won't be coming back from India after Christmas. And a lot of the Indian merchants are making plans to get out.'

'Evidently no one believes the official line,' said Edwin, drumming his fingers on the table. He watched a flock of parakeets dive past the window, before they skimmed across the lawns and off into the distance. They circled around a tall stupa, their green wings reflecting the sunlight, before they flew away.

✦

A few days later Japanese troops came ashore at the southern tip of Burma and began inching their way north towards Rangoon. Two days before Christmas the first aerial attack on Rangoon came. The wireless crowed about a Japanese plane that had been shot down, but hundreds of people were dead and whole streets lay in ruins.

Trying to maintain a semblance of normal life, Kate spent Christmas Day with some of the staff of the Secretariat, who held a picnic in the nearby park. Most of them were Buddhists and she felt grateful to be spared the absurdity of an English Christmas.

'Where is Mr Edwin?' asked Miss Soe, ladling fish soup into bowls as they sat on the dry grass, the sun high in the sky above them.

'I don't know,' said Kate. 'I reminded him yesterday. Perhaps he doesn't like Christmas.'

'But all English people like Christmas!' said Miss Soe. 'It is very important for you, yes?'

Kate shrugged. 'Very important for children, although I think that's mostly because they get presents. I've always found it a bit tedious. This is much nicer!'

She looked around at the dozen or so people who sat on mats, some of them playing with babies and small children, others chatting quietly and offering around platters of food.

It was very hot in the park and the slender palm trees over-head did not afford much protection. Europe, she had heard, was suffering a punishing winter, but she could hardly imagine the snow and ice.

At 11.30 that morning the air-raid sirens had gone off across Rangoon, but the all-clear went out two hours later, and people seemed remarkably relaxed about it all. Perhaps this is the only way they know how to cope with such horror, thought Kate, seeing people setting up stalls once again in the street near her flat. Perhaps we all close our eyes because we don't want to see.

Late in the day, as the sun was going down and the children were playing a lazy game of football, Kate looked up to see Edwin strolling across the park, swinging a cloth bag.

'Mr Edwin is here!' said Ohmar, who worked in the office beside theirs, and quickly a plate of leftovers was made up.

'Hello,' said Kate, squinting up at him.

'Merry Christmas,' said Edwin, squatting down beside her. 'Oh, thank you,' he said, as the food was passed to him. 'Look, I've brought some fruit for everyone. It's not much, but . . .'

With exclamations of delight the children dived at the bag and held up its contents one by one for everyone to admire. Out came several guavas, a giant pineapple, a heap of tiny oranges, and three warm papayas.

As the fruit was efficiently sliced up by Miss Soe and her friends, Kate looked at Edwin. 'Had a good day?'

'Yes, busier than expected,' he said. 'I got roped into helping the teachers at the boarding school down the road. They were loading all their belongings into trucks and getting the children ready to board a ship tomorrow morning.'

'They're leaving?'

'Seems so. I'm surprised they've left it this long, really.'

'Where are they going?'

'India, at first. After that, who knows. Maybe they'll come back when the threat is gone.'

Kate looked thoughtful and watched the platters of fruit making the rounds. 'Do you really think they'll come back?'

'No. Would you?'

'God, I've no idea. It could be ages – months or years. And anyway . . .' She stared absently at the game being played nearby. 'I'm not sure it would be the same.'

'Mr Edwin, you play football with us?' called one of the boys.

'Oh, no, I'm useless,' Edwin said shaking his head. 'Really. You're better off without me on the team.'

'Please, Mr Edwin!'

After the demand was repeated several times, Kate was surprised to see him struggling to his feet and brushing the grass off his shorts.

'Don't say I didn't warn you,' he called, and within moments he was off, dashing around among the boys as though he were ten or fifteen years younger than he was.

'He is pretty fast!' laughed Miss Soe beside her.

'Pretty terrible, too,' said Kate as she bit into a slice of warm pineapple, the juice trickling down her chin. 'He wasn't joking.'

At last, when he could take no more, Edwin collapsed, puffing, on the ground. 'I haven't done that much exercise since I was at school.'

'You are very hot!' exclaimed Miss Soe, pointing to where the perspiration ran down his face. 'It is too hot for you in Rangoon, I think.'

'It must be cooler up in the hills, or on the coast,' said Kate. 'Where would one go?'

Miss Soe looked thoughtful. 'There is a place far to the west – my family took me there when I was a child. Two days' journey from here perhaps if you went by motor car. It is called Chaungtha. A beautiful place. One night we ran to the sea and put our hands in and suddenly there were little lights everywhere, under the water.'

'What was it?' asked Kate breathlessly.

Miss Soe shrugged. 'I do not know the English word for it. Tiny animals in the water, shining like stars.'

'Sounds like what we call bioluminescence,' said Edwin. 'I've heard of it – it's plankton or something like that. How extraordinary.'

'So beautiful,' said Miss Soe dreamily. She turned away to help the children to more food, spooning out aromatic tealeaf salad.

'Little stars in the water . . .' said Kate. 'How I wish we could go there.'

'Two days' journey,' said Edwin regretfully.

'But think of swimming in that sea.'

She pictured the place, imagining a strip of palm-fringed beach where the waves gently whispered and, through the darkness, an unearthly glow under the surf.

'I'm going to go there one day,' she said. 'There are so many wonders in Burma and I've hardly seen any of them.'

'All right,' said Edwin agreeably. 'I'll come with you.'

'You will?'

'Of course. When the war is over.'

＊

Late that evening Edwin sat silently in a corner of a capacious cellar, surrounded by smartly dressed strangers. The air-raid siren had gone off an hour before and with very little fuss the Strand's guests were shepherded safely out of the main building.

Most of the people around him were familiar, now – he had passed them on the stairs or exchanged nods in the break-fast room. Uniformed staff moved among the guests, calmly distributing blankets, pillows, drinks and trays of canapés.

'Anything I can get for you, sir?' said a young waiter, looking at him with some concern. 'Would you like me to call the doctor?'

'I'm quite all right,' said Edwin, knowing he was pale and clammy. 'Just a bit tired.' He jumped as he heard another distant thud and caught the boy's sympathetic look. 'Thank you.'

He could see a red-faced man berating the night manager on the other side of the cellar, his voice getting louder, and was filled with admiration at the manager's diplomatic concern. Most of the guests, however, were sitting coolly with cocktails, reading their week-old newspapers by the light of oil lamps, and he had the impression that they were rather enjoying them-selves. The British upper classes loved this sort of thing, he reminded himself. Give them a disaster and the chance to keep up appearances and they were in heaven.

He wondered how Kate was coping, imagined her sitting with her neighbours, laughing at some joke and practising her Burmese. She's the strongest person I know, he thought suddenly, and remembered how she had brought him home without fuss after the Scottish party. She was unlike any woman he had ever met, but she seemed to know him better than anyone else. She was dismissive of convention, refreshingly opinionated, and she made him laugh. She would survive anything. He hoped that she was safe.

But nowhere is safe now, Edwin thought bleakly, feeling the distant vibrations under his feet. He wondered how much of the city would be left in the morning.

10

Rangoon, January 1942

The office door banged open and Kate appeared, flinging a sun hat and white gloves onto her desk. She perched on the edge of the desk and pulled off her shoes, wincing as the stiff leather pinched her bruised ankles.

'Where have you been?' said Edwin, looking up from his work. 'Anywhere nice?'

'The hospital. Visiting.'

'Oh – how was it?'

'Awful,' said Kate, pursing her lips. She collapsed into a chair. 'God, I could do with a drink.'

'There's only water, I'm afraid,' said Edwin, but she shook her head.

'I so wanted to be useful. I heard that Lady Dorman-Smith was looking for volunteers to sit with wounded people at the Rangoon General so I thought I'd offer my services. But it was simply dreadful.'

'Are you squeamish?'

'Oh, no. I can cope with any amount of that. It was just . . . the atmosphere. That awful sickbed smell that pervades everything. It took me back to the years of looking after Father. There were dozens of miserable people lying in narrow beds, and troupes of absurd English women twittering around with chocolate and card games. I couldn't bear it so I got out as fast as I could.'

Kate slumped in her seat for a moment. Then she sat up, reached for a handful of hairpins, and set about tidying her hair. 'My first great test of the war and I've failed it,' she said wryly.

'You haven't failed,' said Edwin. 'Visiting in gloves and high heels and talking brightly about the weather – well, it isn't your style, that's all. You're more – practical.'

'I hope so,' she said, pulling a pile of papers across the desk. 'I'd rather do something useful.'

She started to read the report in front of her, a thick wad of pages that had taken weeks of work, comprising her earnest suggestions for improvement in the schools of the Irrawaddy Delta, some of which she had visited the year before. They would surely not stay open for long now that the Japanese were moving ever closer. She had barely even started her report on the schools of the Bagan area and knew with a heavy certainty that it would never be written.

The afternoon wore on and she found her concentration slipping. The Secretariat was quieter than usual, and the occasional sound of hurrying footsteps or a slammed door in the distance made her jump. Many of the most experienced staff had left to join the army and others had departed altogether for the safety of their families.

'It's chaos out there,' said Edwin, and she looked up to see him standing at the window, peering down at the traffic. From their high office at the Secretariat, it was possible to see right along Dalhousie Street, where a mass of cars, bicycles and rickshaws fought for road space with stallholders and slow-moving bullocks.

The other window looked out over Fraser Street, where a row of houses had been hit by the Japanese. Kate knew that Edwin walked to work the long way round to avoid the bombed-out houses. He had seen enough destruction.

'The streets are rammed,' he said, shaking his head. 'Hundreds of people with luggage piled on carts.'

'I don't blame them for wanting to leave.'

'Half of the typing pool downstairs seems to have disappeared,' said Edwin, sitting down and staring at the dusty typewriter in the corner, which he had tried and failed to get to grips with. 'Do you think anyone's getting any work done?'

'I'm certainly not.' Her abandoned pen had begun to leak dark ink across the report. She watched the stain grow bigger and thought vaguely about looking for blotting paper, but it hardly seemed worth it. The work had already been made irrelevant by history and she felt rather cross at having spent so much time on it. 'Are you going somewhere?' she asked, seeing a suitcase under the table.

'What? Oh, that. The Strand is closing in a couple of days. They've booked me in at Minto Mansions.'

'You could have stayed with me.'

He laughed. 'Don't you think people would talk?'

'I'm sure they do already,' said Kate with a shrug. 'I don't let it bother me.'

'I didn't think of it.'

'I suppose you'll be more comfortable at Minto's,' she said. 'I can't offer much more than a wooden floor and a couple of rugs.'

'I don't suppose we'll be here for much longer anyway,' said Edwin. 'Thanks for the offer, though.' He frowned. 'Do you ever think that we ought to just leave?'

'What – get on a plane?'

'Something like that.'

'I think it's a bit late for that. At this stage we may as well see what the government tells us to do.'

'They still seem to think we'll drive the Japs out before long.'

'Drive them out with what? Where are the armies that ought to be coming to protect Burma?' said Kate, scrunching her report into a heavy ball and throwing it into the bin. 'That's what I don't understand.'

Edwin did not reply. She saw that he had tensed and at the same time heard the distant, familiar sounds of bombing once again. In the last few weeks he had been forced to live with the noise, but she knew that it haunted him. He would never be free.

11

Rangoon, February 1942

In mid-February they sat in the office amid a sea of crates, hunched over the wireless, no longer pretending to do any work.

'I wonder what will happen to it all,' said Edwin, gesturing to the trunks on the floor. The day before, a government missive had decreed that all schools were to be closed. They had spent the morning packing up files so that the Japanese would not gain any advantage when they took the city. Some had already been carted away to a mysterious destination.

'It's supposedly all being flown out to India,' said Kate. 'But I expect there are more important cargoes to be taken. It'll probably just get thrown on a bonfire.'

'All your work.'

She shrugged. 'The safety of the children is what matters – and there isn't much I can do about that either.'

There was a knock on the door and Miss Soe peered around it. 'Ah, Miss Kate, Mr Edwin.'

'Come in,' said Kate, pulling out a chair. 'Join us. We were just discussing the futility of trying to save all of this.'

'I cannot stay,' said Miss Soe apologetically, holding out an envelope. 'I have been asked to hand these out.'

Kate ripped the envelope open and breathed in sharply.

'What is it?' said Edwin.

'We're leaving. It says that all European staff must go north to Mandalay as soon as possible. What about everyone else?' asked Kate, looking up at Miss Soe. 'Aren't you coming with us?'

Miss Soe smiled wryly and spread her hands, the flowers quivering in her hair. 'Who knows? Perhaps we go later. You should leave without delay. I will miss you, Kate.'

'I wish there was something I could do,' said Kate, grasping her hands. 'It's not safe here. I could write to someone—'

Miss Soe shook her head. 'My parents live a long way out of the city. I will go to them soon, I think. Do not worry for me.'

She kissed Kate on the cheek. 'I must go. I wish you luck. Good luck as well, Mr Edwin – I hope you will both be safe.'

'And you, Miss Soe. Be careful.'

※

In her small flat, Kate gazed around at the piles of her belongings. She saw the books and the basket of laundry, the wicker chair her landlord had given her, the little carved table she had carried home from the Scott Market, the silver jewellery box that Christina had sent from Delhi. All her life was laid out on the floor and suddenly it seemed no more than baggage, insignificant in the shadow of the crisis that was unfolding.

Moving through the stacks of belongings, she sifted through them, making new piles for 'staying' and much smaller ones for 'going'. It would all be lost and in a few weeks a Japanese officer might be sitting in her chair and sipping her gin. She decided to take the gin, decanting it into the old leather-bound hip flask of her father's that had accompanied her all the way from the farm.

She stuffed clothes into her knapsack – a couple of shirts and dresses, shorts, plimsolls, a jumper, a shawl. There was also a small pile of underwear, socks, her toothbrush, a penknife, a sewing kit, a hairbrush, a little drawstring bag with a few cosmetics and what her mother termed 'female essentials'. She had already withdrawn her modest savings from the bank, asking for silver coins instead of notes, and they were packed tightly at the bottom of her knapsack.

Her heart ached at the thought of leaving. In the years since her arrival, Rangoon had become home. She thought back to the first difficult months, when the heat and the loneliness had threatened to overwhelm her. It had been slow progress to acceptance and familiarity. The only bright thought was that now Edwin would be coming with her – Edwin, who was just as lonely and regretful as she was, but who had a spark of humour that matched hers, and whose company she enjoyed more than anyone else's. He listened to her and she felt no judgement from him.

Kate stood still in the middle of the sitting room. The sun was going down and the room was filled with a warm light. Not far away, over the rooftops, she could see the stupa of the Sule Pagoda, burning orange and as beautiful as it had ever been.

Everything seemed quiet. Then, through the still night came the chiming of the clock tower on the High Court. The bells had chimed for decades, comforting to the ears of homesick colonists, planters and diplomats. Now they rang out over a city almost emptied of those who had made Rangoon their home. The Empire couldn't last forever, she had always known that at some level. But the bells seemed to say more clearly than ever before that it was doomed.

Shouldering her knapsack, she closed the door and went down the stairs. In the warm night the street was strangely empty. Occasionally someone would rush past, looking pre-occupied, and in the distance she could hear vehicles, but the normal hubbub had been replaced by a tense quiet.

Kate started on hearing a rustle in the shrubs to her left, then relaxed as she saw it was just a mangy-looking cat. It darted across the road and disappeared down an alley. The houses she passed mostly appeared empty but, in one or two, candles flickered.

She reached the crossroads and paused for a moment, looking back along Pagoda Road. I have been almost happy here, she thought. Then she slipped her arms through the straps of the knapsack and started walking, heading for the railway station.

12

Worcestershire, March 1929

'*H*ow's your chest?' asked Kate, placing the tea on the bedside table and sitting down with her book.

'Cough's still rough,' said her father. 'I think it's these new pills. I told Dr Thwaites that they were only making things worse but he insisted I carry on.'

'What about the nightmares?'

'Worse,' he said briefly. 'Didn't get much sleep last night. Now, what about that book?'

They were halfway through Three Men in a Boat, which Kate had read to him before, and when she got to the bit about the tin of pineapple, they were both laughing so hard that she had to put the book down.

'Gets me . . . every time,' wheezed her father, his laugh turning into a spluttering cough.

She watched him chuckling intermittently as he coughed into his handkerchief, his forehead gleaming with the effort. He looked old, she realised suddenly, although he was not yet fifty. Since coming back from the war his face had grown lined, and the brief moments of levity could not make up for the fact that he was dying.

He looked up at her, as though sensing her thoughts. 'I do appreciate you reading to me, Kate,' he said, his voice hoarse. 'It's the high point of my day.'

He sat back against the pillows, pale in his striped pyjamas, and looked weary.

'Shall we leave it there?' said Kate. 'Mother says not to tire you.'

'No, no,' he said, waving at the book. 'Carry on. It'll do me far more good than resting.'

She picked up the thread of the story, but her mind was not fully on J and his adventures on the river. She wanted to ask her father what his nightmares were about, but in the past all he would say was, 'Tunnels.'

He fell into a doze as she read to him, and jerked suddenly awake, staring with wide eyes at the window.

'What is it?' she asked. 'What do you see?'

'The dead,' he croaked, gesturing at the window. 'They're all out there.' His breathing slowed and he focused on her again. 'I'm sorry. Go on with the book.'

'But—'

'Please. Where were we? The bit about the pie?'

She lifted the book again and then paused. 'I'll be able to keep reading to you next week.'

'What about school?'

'I'm not going back after the holiday.'

He shook his head. 'I thought we'd talked about this . . .'

'We have. And my mind's made up. Mother says that it will be hard to afford a nurse and to pay the school fees, so this is the best solution. There'll be more money for the doctor and for the farm.'

'I don't want to keep you here.'

'It's not a very good school, you know,' said Kate firmly. 'They don't teach anything useful. The most highly valued class is deportment. Does that sound like something I'd be any good at?'

Her father laughed, as she hoped he would, and she turned to the book. 'Here we are, Chapter Thirteen. The strange disappearance of Harris and a pie.'

13

Lower Burma, February 1942

Kate awoke shortly after dawn, her neck uncomfortably stiff after a night spent on a hard wooden bench, hearing the train wheels rattling below her. Edwin was nowhere to be seen.

After many hours spent at Rangoon central station, surrounded by crowds of people all frantically trying to leave the city, they had found seats on the only direct train going to Mandalay that night, and had wedged themselves into a corner opposite a party of three exhausted children travelling with a schoolmistress.

The train had not been due to leave for hours and soon Kate was surrounded by slumbering passengers, including Edwin, the feet of the little boy next to him resting on his knees. When the train had at last begun to move, sometime in the middle of the night, she had shifted and tried to get comfortable, but her heart was racing from the anxiety of the last few weeks and she felt wide awake.

At last she had slept, an uneasy sleep. At one point she saw a herd of bullocks being chased by a tiger, their eyes rolling in panic, steam rising from their gasping mouths. Then she jerked awake and realised it had been a dream, before falling back into a fractured slumber.

When she woke again, she watched the countryside roll slowly past the glassless window. The train was only travelling at a few miles an hour and every so often it would stop briefly and then move off again. In every direction she could see billowing spires of white smoke, evidence of the night's bombing raids; it seemed that the whole country must be ablaze.

Edwin reappeared, carrying a big thermos flask and smiling broadly.

'You look pleased with yourself,' said Kate. 'What have you brought?'

'Tea,' said Edwin, setting it down gently. 'I took the flask to find water but there was an old fellow outside the window up there selling tea, so I got him to fill it up. No sugar but it'll do.'

He passed a cup around to the children who sat nearby.

'That's very kind,' said Miss Woodford, the schoolmistress, and in return offered biscuits from a box in her basket.

'What else were you doing?' asked Kate, as they watched the children drinking. 'Any news?'

'I talked to some soldiers further up the train,' said Edwin. 'Apparently the rumour is that in a week or so the army will leave Rangoon too and go north. We're just in time.'

'You mean they'll abandon the city?' asked Miss Woodford incredulously. 'And just let the Japs overrun it? Why not stay and fight?'

Edwin shook his head. 'I think we're beyond that stage. The idea is to regroup in the north and then march back to take the city.'

Kate sat back in her seat, trying to absorb this. The idea that Rangoon would fall had been abstract; now it seemed a certainty.

The day passed slowly. The train would travel for a few miles and then stop and stand for an hour with no explanation. There was nothing to do except talk to the other passengers, read, try to amuse the children, and take occasional expeditions up the train to the filthy toilet compartment, where the track could be seen through the hole in the floor.

'My colleagues are waiting for us in Mandalay,' said Miss Woodford to Kate, watching as Edwin played noughts and crosses with the children. 'We're supposed to fly to India in three days. Suppose we don't get there in time?'

'We'll get there.'

It was late on the second night when they finally came to a station. As they pulled in, Kate saw electric lights and a sign saying Pyinmana. They were not even close to Mandalay.

At dawn the train was still stationary. She left the carriage and stepped out onto the platform, stretching her aching limbs. The air was cool but the sun was already rising and she knew it would be hot soon. Kate made her way through the station, passing large groups of people who seemed to be camping there, perhaps also waiting for transport north. They all looked tired and anxious.

'Good morning, madam,' said the Pyinmana stationmaster, looking up when she knocked gently on his door. He was a young Indian man with round glasses that emphasised the dark circles under his eyes. He had clearly been working through the night.

'Can I offer you a cup of tea?' he said, starting to pour from a flask on his desk.

'Thank you,' said Kate, reaching for the cup he offered. She drank deeply and felt a little better. 'I was hoping you had some information about what's going on, and also if you know of any transport we might take on to Mandalay. We came on the train last night.'

He smiled. 'As to the first, I had a telephone call to say the line north of here was buckled, perhaps due to the unusual number of trains passing by. I don't think it's anything to be concerned about.'

'I thought it might have been bombed.'

'I wondered the same, but apparently not. Just the usual wear and tear. That is life in Burma, I'm afraid, madam.'

'I know,' said Kate wryly. 'I've never been on a train here that got to its destination on time.'

'My recommendation is that you try to hire a truck of some sort to take you to Mandalay. This train might move on, or it could be here for days. You could be in Mandalay by tomorrow evening if you find a decent vehicle.'

'All right,' said Kate, 'I'll do that.'

'If you go outside the station you'll find several chaps on this street who may be willing to take you. I would recommend that you choose one of the older drivers. And don't pay more than ten annas per person. They will try to take advantage of the circumstances.'

❋

The truck that Kate eventually found was driven by a kind old man named Mr Maung. As the three children scrambled up onto the truck he made animal noises to make them laugh and fussed about tucking them in with old rugs.

It was a truck with an open back, which he had bought third or fourth hand, but he claimed it had once belonged to Lord Mountbatten. There was a padded front seat, only slightly torn, which Kate insisted Miss Woodford should have, while she and Edwin climbed into the back with the children.

'Are you sure you wouldn't like a turn?' Miss Woodford said when they stopped for lunch after several hours.

'I'm fine in the back,' said Kate. 'The children are teaching me travelling games.'

'We're playing "Count the elephants" at the moment!' said Bobby, clambering down out of the truck to sit on the grass.

'How many is that now?' said Edwin.

'Seven,' said Louise, holding up six chubby fingers.

'Eight!' called Bobby, pointing to a track running parallel with the road where a female elephant was ambling along carrying a large load of timber on her back, and another smaller bundle in her trunk.

'They are rather amazing,' said Edwin, watching the creature move. 'You know, I'd never seen an elephant until a couple of months ago.'

'Never?' said Sarah, the oldest girl, busily eating a mango they had bought en route. 'How odd!'

'Well, I didn't grow up in Burma like you, you see,' said Edwin. 'There aren't any elephants in England.'

'My father was from England,' said Sarah thoughtfully. 'He was going to take me and Mummy back there but she died and then he died too. She was Burmese but her family didn't want to keep me.'

'Now, Sarah, that's not true,' said Miss Woodford. 'But your Burmese grandparents are very old and poor and it would have been difficult for them to look after you.'

The girl shrugged and made a face at Kate. 'I don't mind. I don't know them and I'm not really Burmese or English. I don't belong anywhere.'

✦

The road to Mandalay wound through low hills. They were parched and dry at this season but in a few months the monsoon would come and all would be green. Every now and then they passed a pagoda at the roadside, most of them humble, but occasionally a dramatic edifice would appear over the horizon, its golden spire gleaming in the hot sun.

The road was fairly quiet, but what little traffic there was was heading north. Besides the occasional car and bus, there were vast numbers of bicycles and rickshaws on the road. At regular intervals they would also pass a party on foot.

'All go to Mandalay!' said Mr Maung, gesturing at a large family plodding along on the verge, clutching bundles and cases. 'Everyone go that way!'

'I wonder what they'll do,' said Kate quietly to Edwin. 'They can't all leave the country.'

'Perhaps Mandalay will hold,' he replied.

They arrived in the city at dusk on the second day. The streets swarmed with people and everywhere there were homeless families, refugees from the south. Kate stepped out of the truck into the warm heavy night and breathed in deeply. The air smelled of sewage, spices, and something metallic that was oddly familiar: the smell of war.

14

Mandalay, February 1942

The weeks in Mandalay seemed, later, like the calm before the storm. Battles raged in the south of Burma and refugees came north in a steady stream. Some of them had walked all the way to Mandalay; many others came by train, car, and by steamer along the Irrawaddy. A ring of refugee camps had sprung up around the city.

The morning after their arrival, Kate and Edwin reported to the government office at the central fort.

'I wasn't expecting things to be this bad,' said Edwin, stepping gingerly over a pile of rubbish. 'It feels like a battlefield already.'

'Too many people, I suppose,' said Kate. 'I hope they can find something for us to do.'

Fort Dufferin was a massive enclosure, at least two miles square, with high stone walls. As they approached, Kate saw that the wide grass verge beside the road had been turned into a camp, with tents and rudimentary wooden shacks huddled on the narrow strip and people cooking on open fires.

Between the walls and the road was a moat. Once, perhaps, it had been calm and beautiful, carpeted with water lilies; now it lay green and stagnant, with rubbish floating on the surface.

Children from the camp played in the water, churning up the filthy sludge with their bare feet. Kate shuddered to think what else that water was being used for and of the infections they might pick up.

The government headquarters was the usual hive of activity and at first no one seemed to know what to do with them now that their jobs no longer existed.

'You've two options,' barked a brisk moustached man at last. 'You can sign up as volunteers with the Evac. Department and make yourselves useful, or you can make arrangements to get the hell out of Burma. There are still planes leaving. Your choice.'

'I'll stay,' said Kate, after a brief pause and Edwin nodded.

'Me too. We want to help.'

'Very well.' He frowned at the ledger in front of him and drummed on it with a pencil. 'Miss Girton, I'll send you to the medical team as they're short of female staff. You'll report to Dr Mosby and Dr Singh. Mr Clear, you'll be best in the main Evac. Office – we've just lost a couple of staff there. There's a lot of work to be done, not least in planning ground routes out of the country. I think that's everything.'

✦

Kate found that her new role suited her, although the work was hard and draining. Thousands of people lived in the camps and many of them would not make it out.

She was given a rusty old car to use for transporting medical supplies to the camps and, occasionally, patients back in the other direction. Accommodation was provided, a small bungalow close to the clinic that had belonged to a British family. Edwin, meanwhile, was staying in a requisitioned hotel, which he said reminded him uncannily of family holidays at Eastbourne. He was just as busy as she was and she saw him only occasionally as she hurried around the city.

One of the enormous advantages of the bungalow was that it had a bookcase. Browsing through it, she found herself wondering what the owners were like and whether they would ever be able to return to Mandalay. She didn't feel guilty about helping herself to their books, but she felt a sadness looking at their possessions, thinking of her own dear flat in Rangoon.

This family, the Faulkners, had had a taste for the classics – there were leather-bound volumes of Shakespeare, Austen, and Dickens, which they must have shipped out from England at huge expense. The books had not been served well by the humidity of Mandalay and were mottled and discoloured.

Then there were brightly coloured picture books that Kate imagined a loving grandmother selecting in a far-off English town and parcelling up to send to her relatives on the other side of the world.

They might be in England already, the Faulkners – if they had made it to India they could have taken a ship or even flown. If England survived the war they would settle into a new routine there, although, she supposed, for the rest of their lives they would think occasionally of their lost home in the East.

✦

Returning late one afternoon to the clinic, after a long day spent inoculating people against cholera, Kate found a young

Burmese woman efficiently folding bandages, the sleeves of her white blouse carefully rolled up.

'Hello. I'm Kate.'

'My name is Myia Win.' The woman smiled. 'It is nice to meet you.'

'Are you from Mandalay?' Kate went to the cupboard and examined the contents, looking down at the list in her hand.

Myia nodded. 'I have worked for the government here for several years.'

'I thought you might be a teacher,' said Kate. 'Your English is very good.'

'I used to be a teacher. But my father worked for the government and when he died I was offered a job.' Her expression clouded.

'I'm sorry,' said Kate, and hesitated. 'I lost my father, too,' she said at last.

Myia inclined her head. 'It is very difficult.'

'Do you live here alone?' said Kate.

'My mother and little brother have just left for India,' said Myia, closing the box in front of her and placing it on the floor. She reached for a new supply of bandages. 'They decided Mandalay was not safe.'

'But you're still here.'

'I wasn't ready to leave,' she said, and looked out of the window at the silhouetted shapes of pagodas, which rose in the distance. 'I know I shall have to eventually. But . . . well, this is my home.'

'I suppose if you have worked for the British you're not safe,' said Kate.

'That's why my mother wanted to leave,' said Myia. 'She believes that if the Japanese take over they will punish those known to have associated with the British. My father worked for the Mandalay office all his life and even my grandfather worked for the British around the turn of the century. He was old enough to remember when they arrived here and deposed the last king of Burma. Things are much better now,' she added, as though to reassure Kate that she bore no grudge. 'Are you married?'

'No,' said Kate. 'Are you?'

Myia shook her head. 'I was engaged, but . . . well, he's gone.' She closed her eyes for a moment and sighed. 'Sometimes people let us down.'

Kate watched her for a moment and then turned away to continue sorting the supplies that she would need to deliver tomorrow. There was something strange about Myia, something brittle underneath the friendly exterior. She seemed unusually independent, but at the same time reserved, as though she had spent a long time repressing her feelings.

It was only much later, driving home by the light of the flames engulfing whole streets, the latest evidence of the Japanese advance, that it occurred to Kate that Myia reminded her of herself.

15

Worcestershire, September 1931

*K*ate stood outside the bedroom door. On the tray in her hands was her father's breakfast and she looked down at the scrambled eggs, taking a deep breath. Every day it grew a little harder to see his decline, but she knew he needed her company. She plastered on a smile and knocked gently, hearing his faint voice answer.

'Did you sleep?' she asked, putting down the tray.

'A little,' he said. He was sitting back against the pillows and looked exhausted. 'These dreadful dreams come every night and then I lie awake for hours remembering it all.'

'The war?'

'Yes. Mostly.'

'You've never talked about it much,' said Kate.

'It's . . . hard,' said her father. His breathing sounded shallow. 'It was easier just to lock it all away. I don't want to remember.'

'But the nightmares keep coming.'

'I hoped they might fade, with time. But the same scenes keep on running through my head.'

'Are they . . . things that really happened?' asked Kate tentatively.

He nodded and she saw the sweat glisten on his forehead. 'The whole damn day. I remember it all, beginning to end.'

'The day you were gassed?'

88

He stopped and stared intently at something she couldn't see. 'The boy comes back every night. I see him waiting for me.'

'The boy?'

'He was young,' said her father. 'Only eighteen or so.'

'Who was he?'

'I never knew his name. He came stumbling into my part of the trench, crying and afraid. He'd heard the bombing and thought we were next. "They're coming!" he kept sobbing. He didn't have a gas mask.'

Kate was silent. She could imagine it vividly and wondered how her father had managed to keep all this inside him for fifteen years.

'I started leading him through the tunnels. I knew there were a couple of masks left by men who'd already been killed. I told him to stick with me and we'd find a mask.'

'What happened?'

'The gas was rolling in. I could see it. "Hurry," I said, "and cover your mouth and nose." Useless, really. We ran through the tunnels and I thought he was close behind me. I got to the main dugout and looked back and he wasn't there. I'd lost him, somewhere, in the darkness.'

'It wasn't your fault,' said Kate, laying a hand on his in a bid to stop the trembling. 'It wasn't your fault.'

'I went back for him,' said her father, speaking faster now. 'Found a torch and started back through the tunnels. I could barely see anything, what with the mask. At last I found him on the ground.'

'Dead?'

'Not quite. The gas had rolled over and he was choking – drowning, you might say. Clawing at his throat. I ripped off my mask and pushed it over his face, but it was too late, he'd breathed in too much.

I came to my senses pretty fast and put the mask back on. There was nothing else I could do.'

He stared dully at Kate, his forehead lined. 'I lost him in the darkness. He shouldn't have been alone.'

'You're not to blame,' said Kate, and she found herself saying it over and over as her father pressed his face into the counterpane, making her feel, not for the first time, that they had swapped roles and that she was comforting a small, fearful child.

16

Mandalay, March 1942

Kate heard the howls of pain long before she could see where they were coming from. As she looked frantically around between the crude huts that filled an area of scrubland on the outskirts of the city, it was hard to tell who was making the sound.

A young man appeared from a hut and saw her. 'Please! You help us? My wife!'

'Of course.' She heaved her bag of supplies higher onto her shoulder. Following him into the dark hut she saw a young woman lying on the floor. She was heavily pregnant, her knees bent, her dirty *longyi* hitched up around her waist. She was groaning with pain, the sound sometimes turning into a scream.

Kate found herself frozen. She had assisted at a birth at the hospital a week before, but she had never had to deliver a child on her own. In that case the woman, already a mother of four, had quickly pushed out the baby and grabbed it from the doctor with a proprietary glare before wrapping it in her shawl.

This woman was obviously in a great deal of pain, her back arching up off the floor. Her eyes were wild and she was muttering and yelling between the screams. Her husband, in tears, gripped her hand and looked beseechingly at Kate.

She dropped the bag and knelt between the woman's knees, gently pushing the *longyi* up. On the floor under her buttocks was a pool of blood. Kate felt her heart plummet. The howls had now turned to guttural groans. The dark curls of hair under the *longyi* glistened with blood and sweat, but she could see no sign of the child yet.

'She's bleeding badly,' Kate said, looking up at the husband. 'She needs a doctor.'

'You are doctor, no?'

'No, no. I'm sorry,' she said, feeling as though she had tricked him. 'I'm a volunteer. But I will try to fetch a doctor here.'

'You have motor car,' said the man, gesturing imploringly. 'Take her to hospital. Please.'

Kate hesitated. The hospital was so full already. But this woman was in so much pain and was perhaps losing her baby. She needed help.

'All right. Yes.'

She backed the car up to the hut and somehow they got the woman onto the back seat, every movement causing her to scream. Her *longyi* was now soaked with blood. Her husband, terrified, got into the back with her and held her head on his lap, stroking her hair and singing gently.

Kate drove as fast as she dared towards the city, drumming on the steering wheel when the traffic slowed. Her heart was pounding and she felt afraid. The howls in the back had quietened into moans and she glanced back to see the woman shaking, obviously in shock. Her husband was crying enough for both of them.

She saw the walls of the central fort ahead of them. The Civil Hospital was only a mile or two away and she knew that

Dr Singh would be there. She pulled onto the busy road that went around the fort and as she did so the car made a clanking noise, as though something had fallen out of place.

✦

Edwin sat on a high stool behind his desk, scribbling a memo. He pushed back the hair that fell over his forehead and wondered vaguely if any barbers would be open.

'Blast,' said Patrick, who sat opposite, reaching for a sheet of blotting paper and dabbing at the map in front of him. 'This map won't be much use if I add an unnecessary leg of twelve miles.'

'Which one are you working on?'

'The Hukawng Valley. It's a very tough route. Pure jungle, all the way to India.'

'Let's hope most of them find a safer way out.'

The office door was flung open and Kate appeared. Edwin looked quickly from her white face to the blood that covered her hands and felt his heart constrict. For a second he was back in London, just after the bombing, and there was nothing he wouldn't do.

He went to her, ignoring Patrick's curious glances, and took her hands, feeling them tremble in his. 'Kate – what's happened?'

'I need your help,' she said rapidly, each breath heaving out. 'My car's broken down and there's a woman dying. Have you got a vehicle here?'

'The deputy commissioner has one,' said Patrick, eager to help. 'It's out in the yard.'

'Of course!' Edwin looked at him gratefully. 'Good idea, Patrick.'

'Is he here?' she asked.

'No, and he doesn't have a driver any more,' said Edwin, 'but I know where he keeps the keys.'

As he and Kate ran outside, Edwin felt his heart beating fast and knew that she was compelled by the same urgency. 'Over here,' he said, pointing to an elderly Rolls Royce.

Between them they got the car started, sweating as the stiff handle resisted, but at last the engine coughed into life. Kate hurried to open the gate as Edwin backed the old car round, then she jumped in.

When they reached Kate's car, all was quiet. The woman on the back seat was unconscious, but her chest was rising and falling gently. Her husband, his eyes swollen, was huddled over her, stroking her face, his tears falling into her thick black hair.

They transferred the patient to the Rolls Royce and this time Kate sat in the back, holding a folded blanket between the woman's legs, trying to stop the flow of blood. Edwin drove like a man possessed; she thought once or twice of telling him to slow down, as the rough road was bumping the patient, but she was not sure that he would even hear her. Beside him sat the woman's husband, leaning around the seat to clutch his wife's hand.

The grass that surrounded the hospital was crowded with refugees. With difficulty, Edwin got the car into the courtyard and Kate ran ahead.

Pushing open the swing doors, she paused. The reception was empty and none of the usual nurses ran about carrying supplies; Dr Singh, of whom she had become very fond, was nowhere to be seen. Several of the cupboards had been left with their doors open, showing empty shelves.

'Oh, God.' She stood irresolute for a moment and wondered what to do next. She jumped as the doors behind her banged open again and, with a swell of relief, she saw Dr Singh, looking weary, his eyes bloodshot and his thinning hair plastered to his scalp. She wondered when he had last slept.

They got the woman out of the car and inside the hospital on a stretcher and Dr Singh led the way into the operating theatre. From somewhere he summoned two Burmese nurses and suddenly Kate and Edwin were no longer needed. Kate saw the doctor in urgent discussion with the nurses and the husband weeping again, then the door closed and she and Edwin were left outside in the whitewashed corridor.

'Are you all right?' she said. Edwin looked up at her in surprise and then down at his unsteady hands.

'Oh – yes. I'm fine.' But he sank to the floor and closed his eyes, taking deep breaths. She sat beside him, her head tilted back against the wall.

'Whatever happens,' she said, 'thank you for helping.'

'She deserved better,' said Edwin. His voice was muffled and she thought he was crying, but did not want to embarrass him, so she linked her arm through his and squeezed.

'Yes, she did.'

Kate thought vaguely that she should go back to work, but her limbs were heavy and her head pounded. Instead she sat listlessly on the floor of the corridor, listening to the distant buzzing of flies and drawing shapes with her fingertip in the dust. An hour passed this way, perhaps two.

Dr Singh emerged quietly from the theatre, his overall bloody. He had not had time to change his shoes and his sandals were stained. Scrambling up, Kate saw at once what he had to say and her stomach churned.

'She's gone,' he said. Edwin, still on the floor, glanced up blindly and then looked away.

'And the child?'

'Dead. She'd been bleeding for too long – eight hours at least, possibly all night.' He sighed. 'It wasn't your fault, Kate. You did what you could.'

'Not enough,' she said. 'What will happen to her husband?'

He shrugged. 'He'll survive, for now. He's in shock.'

'We should help him.'

'How? Money? Unless you can bring his wife back to life, dear Kate, you must leave him be. He's not the only one, you know. Soon the Japanese will be here – and then we will all have bigger problems to worry about.'

She looked at the doctor for a moment. 'Why are you still here?'

'It's my job.'

'But the others have all gone.'

'I have no wife, no family, and there's no one waiting for me in India. I am old. Where should I be if not here, working in my hospital?' Dr Singh smiled, his face kindly. 'Do not forget how privileged you are, Kate. You have the means to get away and a bright future. Many of these people have neither. Take the chance you are given with both hands and leave this city.'

She watched him disappear down the corridor and realised that the bombing had started again somewhere nearby, a distant thunder that went on and on.

Edwin stirred on the floor beside her and she knelt down. There were tear tracks down his cheeks and she knew that he was thinking of Emilia.

'What happened?' said Kate, and suddenly everything became silent; the whine of aircraft overhead, the crunch of collapsing buildings and the low roar of the fires that were sweeping through the city all somehow ceased to matter. It was just her and Edwin, sitting on the floor in a hospital corridor, an ocean of silent calm.

Edwin did not reply for a long time. At last he said, 'I betrayed her.' He chewed his lip and she had a sudden glimpse of the man he must once have been.

'She died because of me,' he said in a rush, and Kate heard the tremble in his voice.

'It wasn't your fault,' she said, remembering how she had said those words to her father, long ago.

'I was to blame,' he said with a shrug. 'Without my actions she would not have died.' He shook his head, looking weary. 'You don't understand.'

'Perhaps I do,' said Kate, watching him.

'Why? What have you done?'

A door banged open nearby and three nurses spilled out, talking intently. All three looked overworked and exhausted, with dark shadows under their eyes and stains on their *longyis*.

'We ought to leave,' said Kate, pulling herself up. 'We're of no use here.'

They walked slowly out of the low building, avoiding the crowds of anxious people who were waiting for attention. A few harried-looking staff were making their way through the masses, taking down details.

'I suppose I ought to return this,' said Edwin as they reached the car.

'Thank you for helping me,' said Kate.

'We're friends,' said Edwin, patting her shoulder. He looked drained. 'It's what we do, isn't it?'

17
Mandalay, April 1942

Late at night, Kate paced restlessly around the house, opening and closing cupboards and peering at the things the Faulkners had left behind.

She went through Mrs Faulkner's wardrobe, holding up evening dresses and stroking the smooth silk. She tried on a pale yellow floor-length number, quite unlike anything she would normally choose, and laughed on seeing herself in the mirror. It was cut on the bias and evidently made for a much slimmer, taller woman, but she liked the soft fabric and the way it clung to her hips.

Still wearing the dress, Kate drifted barefoot into the kitchen and opened the cabinet where she knew the alcohol was kept.

There was a tentative knock on the door and she opened it to find Edwin hovering outside. He hardly seemed to notice what she was wearing.

'Hello,' she said. 'Drink?'

He looked at the bottle of whisky in her hand. 'Please.'

She slopped two generous measures into glasses and brought them out to the veranda, where he perched on the edge of a tattered wicker sofa.

'Thanks,' he said, and breathed in deeply over the glass. He looked up at her. 'I heard the hospital was bombed.'

She nodded. 'Completely destroyed. Hundreds dead.' She gulped at the whisky, feeling the numbing heat spread slowly through her chest. 'I left at around nine – there was nothing else to be done.'

'What about your friend – Dr Singh?'

Kate shook her head. 'No sign. Presumed dead.' She collapsed into a chair. Her head hurt from the crying and the endless awful sounds of the bombing raids.

Edwin looked around the veranda, at the smart furnishings now covered in dust. 'This place must have been quite nice once.'

'I think they left just after Christmas. There are bits of wrapping paper and so on inside. Probably far away by now.' He was watching her as she spoke. 'What?'

'Nothing. You look tired.'

'Thanks. So do you, actually.'

'I haven't been sleeping,' he said, rubbing his forehead. 'I hate this waiting.'

'We'll know soon enough,' said Kate. 'I suppose we'll have to leave.'

'And then what?' said Edwin. She saw that he was gripping his glass tightly.

'I expect we shall be sent to India,' said Kate, sounding more confident than she felt. She had no idea what they would do next and the empty future that rose up before her was enough to fill her with panic.

'In a strange way, I was starting to feel at home here,' said Edwin with a half smile. 'I was so unhappy when I arrived, and of course it's awful knowing that people are suffering, but these last few weeks in Mandalay I've felt . . . needed, I suppose. Useful, for once.'

'Me too. Perhaps we've both got some sort of saviour complex.'

He shrugged. 'When you've lost someone, I think it's natural to want to make amends.'

She watched a bat flit across the darkening sky. People in the houses nearby were beginning to light candles. Somewhere far away a siren was howling.

'Kate,' said Edwin, taking another long drink, 'can I tell you something?'

She eyed him curiously. 'About your wife?'

'I don't know how . . .'

'You were unfaithful to her,' said Kate, and she saw him close his eyes, his face crumpling. 'I guessed. Sorry.'

'Then you know what a wicked person I am,' he said, his face haggard. 'I was out that night. With – with someone else. She died alone because I wasn't there.'

They sat in the silence and Kate realised it was almost dark. She looked around for the lamp and the box of matches she kept above the lintel. The warm glow of the oil lamp quivered at first, then, as she turned it up, burned bright and strong.

'Reminds me of home,' she said, putting the lamp back on the little table. 'We didn't get electricity on the farm until a few years ago. My father was afraid of naked flames after the war so we all carried safety lamps up to bed.'

'How old were you when you started taking care of him?' said Edwin.

'I always did, really. He got worse as the years went by and my mother had enough on her plate running the farm. Laura had already moved away, so at fourteen I left school and became a full-time nurse.'

She frowned, picking at a thread on her dress. 'I swore I'd never be a nurse again – and here I am in Mandalay and it's all I'm good for.'

'Your father must have been very grateful to have you there.'

'He felt so guilty that he was keeping me back from the world, kept telling me we'd hire someone and I could go back to school, but I knew we couldn't afford it. I just kept plodding along, never admitting how miserable I was.'

'We all do that. It's hard to admit things, even to yourself.'

'I suppose I understand what you mean about Emilia,' said Kate, 'about not being there.' She poured out more whisky, seeing her hand tremble slightly. 'I wasn't there when my father died.'

Edwin listened, his thin face in the lamplight, kind, friendly. She felt that she could tell him anything, although it was hard to find the words.

'I was at the cinema,' she said, 'watching a new picture with a friend. I shouldn't have gone. I came back and he was dead.'

'But you couldn't have known,' said Edwin. 'You have nothing to feel guilty about.'

'It's not that,' said Kate, and now she could feel her heart thumping, and the blood, or the whisky, roaring in her veins. It was a comfort to talk about it finally with someone who understood.

'I felt relieved,' she said at last. 'I could see the world changing around me, my schoolfriends growing up and having lives of their own while I was stuck at home. I loved my father dearly, but I was so miserable, so fed up with the nursing, the smell of the sickroom, the hideous memories of the war. I was relieved that he was gone – for him, partly, relieved that his suffering was over – but also for myself.'

She looked over at Edwin, afraid of what she might see, and to her surprise he took her hand, very gently.

'Oh, Kate,' he said, 'dearest Kate.' He sat still for a moment, his hand warm, holding hers tightly. He shook his head. 'You are not alone. It's quite normal to feel that way.'

'Is it?' she said.

'We're human,' said Edwin. 'We can't be selfless all the time.'

'I was never selfless,' she said wryly. 'I was the grumpiest, most inept nurse anyone could have asked for. My poor father.'

'What about your mother, your sister? They must have felt the same.'

'Perhaps they did,' said Kate. 'It was so hard for Mother. All those years when she was fighting to keep the farm afloat, working long hours and dealing with an ill husband. When he was gone she was grieving, I saw that, but I sensed that she felt relieved, too, although she'd never admit it. She's very tough – doesn't take any nonsense from anyone.'

'You sound quite alike,' said Edwin, smiling.

'I suppose we are. Laura looks more like her – I got Father's nose – but Mother and I respond to things in the same way. Neither of us were natural carers, but we got through it.'

'But you decided to leave.'

'After that, home wasn't home any more,' said Kate. 'Even after all those years of unhappiness, I looked back with a sort of nostalgia to the time before my father died. Without him the place seemed empty. So I moved to Birmingham, took my exams, did my teacher training. Went to bed with a lot of unsuitable men. Then eventually the idea of Burma came up and I ran away again.'

Edwin lay back on the sofa, cradling his glass of whisky in both hands. 'It's odd, isn't it? You can have a good life, a loving home, and still not feel quite as if you belong.'

'Is that why you came out here?'

He swilled the whisky around his glass. 'I suppose it is. I was looking for something – different. When Emilia died, I knew I'd never find it in London.'

For the first time in a long while, Kate found herself thinking about the home she had left behind. It was spring once again, the season in which her father had died, and she knew her mother would have her hands full on the farm, anxiously watching over the ewes who were due to lamb any day.

She saw her, in her oversized rain coat and wellingtons, pausing to talk with the farmhands before driving into town with one of the dogs in the back of the car. Later she would sit at the kitchen table, writing letters and frowning over unpaid bills.

They talked on, hardly noticing the hours passing, and eventually the whisky bottle was empty. At last Kate saw Edwin nodding off and found that she too was starting to doze.

She jerked awake and realised that it was starting to grow light. They had been on the veranda all night.

'Look, Edwin,' she said, prodding his outstretched foot. 'It's morning.'

He groaned. 'My head hurts.'

'Drink some water. I've got an idea.'

'An idea?'

'The sun will be coming up soon. Get in the car.'

'I thought yours was broken.'

'Mrs Farnham bequeathed hers to me when she flew out yesterday. I don't suppose she'll be coming back for it.'

She drove them through the quiet streets. Smoke was rising in the distance from the night's raids and already there were sweepers and teashop boys going to work.

'Are you safe to drive?' said Edwin. 'Where are we going?' His clothes were crumpled and there were dark circles under his eyes. Kate realised that she was still wearing the yellow silk dress and her feet were bare.

'I'm fine,' she said. 'Wait and see.'

She drove out along the trunk road, away from the city. On all sides there were broken-down vehicles, people sleeping rough beside the road, the ruins of bombed buildings.

'We should just make it,' said Kate.

'What are we looking for?'

'That,' said Kate, and pointed. The spire of a huge white pagoda rose up ahead of them. The first rays of the rising sun were catching the golden tip, making it sparkle in the early morning.

The Irrawaddy snaked around the base of the great temple, mist scudding gently across the surface. A lone monk walked across the causeway leading to the temple, his saffron robe glowing against the pale, clouded mountains that rose in the distance.

'What is this place?' said Edwin, as the car rolled to a stop by the riverbank. She switched the engine off and the silence was suddenly deafening.

'This is Amarapura,' said Kate. 'One of the old capitals of Burma. This was once the centre of a great kingdom.'

They walked down to the water and Kate saw a rowing boat pulled up under a tree. She unhooked the rope and pushed it down to the water.

Edwin, still slightly drunk, didn't question her for once, and climbed in. They took an oar each and sculled out from under the trees, until they were far out on the river, drifting gently in the lazy current.

Kate paused in her rowing and watched the sun come up. All my life I have dreamed of seeing something like this, she thought, and soon I must leave. The pagoda, glowing white in the morning sun, the mist on the river, the birds flying low over the paddy fields on the far side – all seemed suffused with beauty, and she knew with a perfect clarity that she would never return.

'It's extraordinary,' said Edwin, and she heard his voice catch.

'I've wanted to come here for ages. I didn't think we'd get another chance.'

'I'm glad you brought me here.' He watched an ibis standing silently in the water close to the bank, its long curved beak occasionally darting down to fish below the surface.

Perhaps that's why we were drawn to one another, thought Kate, as the sun rose fully above the horizon, and they began to row gently back to the shore. He, too, is looking for something like home.

She sensed that Edwin had not told her everything. There was something nagging at her, an idea of what the secret might be, but it was not something she cared to put into words, not yet.

18

London, May 1941

*A*t eight o'clock in the morning, Edwin stood twenty yards from the wreckage of his home. The bomb had ripped straight through between his house and the next one in the terrace, half-demolishing both and killing Emilia where she hid under the kitchen table.

A policeman was talking to him, but he could take nothing in. He watched the house intently, as though she might suddenly emerge unhurt from the wreckage.

'I want to go in,' he said suddenly.

'I'm sorry, sir,' said the young officer. 'You can't. It's too dangerous. The rest of the house might collapse at any moment.'

'What else have I got to lose?'

The policeman looked down at his notebook. 'I'm sorry. The demolition fellows are working in there.'

The elderly couple who lived next door, whose names he had forgotten, had been fast asleep in their room on the far side of the terrace when the bomb hit, and had emerged to find half of their house gone. He had seen them being helped into an ambulance, trembling but alive.

'I'm sorry to ask, sir, but – you and your wife lived alone?'

'What? Yes. Just the two of us. Why?'

'Just procedure, sir. We need to know how many people were in the house.'

'Just one,' said Edwin, the words bitter on his tongue.

'You weren't here, then, sir? Were you away all night?'

'Yes. I was – staying with a friend.'

'All right, sir.'

Edwin looked along the street, back towards the city, and for the first time noticed the smoke rising from numerous other sites nearby.

'Lot of other bombs,' said the officer, following his gaze. 'They say this is the heaviest night yet.'

In the distance he could hear the clanging of bells, as fire engines and ambulances raced all over the city. Dozens of others must have died. But what did he care for the rest of them? Almost immediately he heard Emilia's voice rebuking him, telling him not to be so selfish.

Since their marriage two years before they had rarely argued. Neither of them were any good at confrontation, so when a difference of opinion reared its head they simply avoided the subject. Emilia had wanted to have a baby as soon as possible but he was reluctant, although he couldn't quite say why. 'I need to be earning more,' he said to begin with and, a little later, 'They say there's a war coming.' Their lovemaking, which had never been frequent, became rarer and rarer.

'I must get going,' said the policeman. 'Will you be all right, sir? Have you got somewhere you can stay?'

'Oh – yes. I'll be fine.'

The young man noted down Edwin's parents' address and put his notebook away in his pocket. 'You'll be notified if there are any developments. Once again, sir, I'm very sorry for your loss.' He hesitated – he looked so young – and then turned towards his car.

'Thank you.'

The car rattled off down the road and Edwin sat down on the pavement, staring at the remains of the house. He could see activity inside and occasionally saw a billow of dust or smoke rising. He could taste it.

He found himself weeping suddenly, sobs choking out of him, making him retch into the gutter. He knew he would have to go and tell her parents. Emilia was dead, and he was to blame.

19

Mandalay, April 1942

The end, when it came, was quick. Late in April, early in the morning, Kate was awakened by a bang on the door. A boy on a bicycle handed her an envelope and sped off down the street, his *longyi* flapping as he stood up on the pedals.

Kate opened the envelope with a sense of resignation. The typed announcement had obviously been prepared in advance, the date scrawled in.

GOVT EVACUATION OFFICE
MANDALAY
E. O. No. 1639 dated <u>19 April 42</u>

You are required to evacuate from Mandalay today. No exceptions will be made. Your assigned meeting place is Mandalay Race Course. You should be there no later than 11 a.m. and await further instructions. Bring only essential luggage and practical clothing.

ALL GOVT EMPLOYEES AND BRITISH CIVIL-IANS ARE REQUIRED TO FOLLOW THIS ORDER. REPEAT NO EXCEPTIONS WILL BE MADE.

It was much as expected. Once again Kate found herself picking through the belongings in the house. She had travelled light from Rangoon, so there was little enough that was actually hers. But the house was full of things that had once been loved dearly by the Faulkner family and it was sad to imagine the toys and shoes and books being left behind.

After packing her own things, and as much portable food as she could find, there was a little space left in the knapsack. Kate spent a few minutes browsing the bookshelves, debating what she would most appreciate. In the end she chose the Thomas Hardy omnibus edition that she had been meaning to start and a little book of translated Burmese poetry.

She wondered if Edwin had received the same summons. She knew he would not be sad to see the back of his faded lodgings but being sent away would surely be just as much of a blow to him as it was to her.

The yellow silk dress still lay crumpled on the floor where she had flung it. Feeling guilty, she picked it up and stuffed it into the side pocket of the knapsack. With a last look around, she closed the door.

As she passed the humble houses of her neighbours she glanced through open doors and saw people going about their lives: cooking, doing laundry, playing with children, singing, making tea, sitting and staring contentedly into space.

She wondered if they were scared. They had to know that war was coming nearer and that there was no escape for them. Perhaps they felt that exchanging the British for the Japanese would make no difference to their lives.

But not everyone was as calm. The streets were busy and the flow seemed to be going in a northerly direction. Clearly people were leaving at a greater rate than before. Each day, going around

the refugee camps, she had found that many huts had new occu-
pants and knew that the previous inhabitants must have struck
out for somewhere else, further from harm.

She wondered whether to call in at Edwin's hotel, but it was
out of her way and she guessed that he would have left already.
She emerged onto North Moat Road and joined a noisy flow
of people, many on foot, others on bicycles and horse carts.
Occasionally a motor vehicle, tooting madly, would approach
and the crowd would part to let it through before closing in
again around it. A tumult of voices swirled all around her and
she felt faint in the sticky heat of the morning.

'Are you well, miss?' asked a young man, looking kindly at
her as he held his children's hands to pull them through the
throng. He wore a ragged *longyi* but his little girls were neatly
dressed, their dark heads crowned with flowers.

'Oh, yes, thank you,' she said. 'It's just so busy, and so warm.'
They walked together for a moment and then a current in the
crowd pulled her away; she looked over her shoulder to see him
smile and bow his head.

'Good luck!' he called.

She could see Mandalay Hill in the distance, its lone golden
stupa twinkling in the sunlight. The racecourse, which lay at the
foot of the hill, was heaving with people and vehicles, and the
once green turf had been churned to dust.

Kate wandered uncertainly through the crowd. She could
see familiar faces here and there, but most of them were
strangers. There were groups of army wives and their children, government staff, and a few civilians. She was much too
warm, and stopped to wipe her brow, trying to see over the
heads of the crowd.

'Kate!' called a voice, and she looked around to see Edwin, his hair plastered to his forehead, carrying his suitcase.

'Hello,' she said, relieved to see him. 'What's going to happen now? I suppose we need to find transport.'

'I was just talking to Evans, over there, the ginger fellow. There aren't any planes going from Mandalay. He says the government has put on vehicles to go north.'

Kate looked around at the masses of people. Only a few of them worked for the government. What would happen to everyone else? What about the thousands camped outside the city?

'They're sending the women and children first, then the men will go another day. Apparently there was a mix-up with the announcements.'

Kate looked at him in surprise. 'You mean we won't be able to go together?'

'I suppose not. You'll be all right, though.'

'Of course I'll be all right,' she said irritably. 'I was thinking of you. What if you get left behind?'

'I'm sure I won't. I'll just get a truck or something in a day or two – as soon as I can.'

'Where to, though?'

'I suppose we'll head for wherever flights are still leaving from.'

Kate sighed and looked around. The hot sun made her head ache and the thought of getting into another bumping, baking truck for a journey to who-knows-where filled her with gloom.

'I just wish I knew where any of us were headed.'

'Oh, Kate! There you are!' Myia appeared at Kate's side, looking anxious. 'I was hoping to find you.'

Kate thought how young Myia looked, although she too was approaching thirty. As usual her black hair was swept up in a gleaming knot and she wore a crisp white blouse tucked into her cotton *longyi*. She carried a canvas bag over her shoulder.

'Did you get a letter, too?'

'Yes,' said Myia. 'I was not expecting it. Do you know where we are going?'

'No idea. I wish I did.'

'Perhaps I should stay,' said Myia, twisting the pendant that hung around her neck. 'This is my home. How will I get back?'

'It's not safe,' said Kate gently. 'The Japanese will know that you work for the government. You can't stay here.'

'There's a truck over there with space for two,' said Edwin, reappearing. He gestured to where four army trucks were lined up next to each other. Several young soldiers, sweating and stressed, were helping European women and children climb into the back, calling out instructions and lifting toddlers and babies up into waiting arms. Kate hesitated.

'You'd better go,' said Edwin. 'Take the chance while it's there.' He took her elbow for a moment. 'Kate . . .'

'What?'

'Nothing. Just that – well, thank you. Your kindness has meant everything to me and—'

'Don't be absurd, Edwin,' she said. 'I'll see you again soon. Just be careful, all right?' Instantly she regretted not saying more, for it was true; she could not remember a friendship quite like this one. There was so much that they still had to talk about.

There was a shout and they hurried over to the trucks. The driver of one, an Indian soldier, emerged to confirm that he had space for two. 'But you must get in straight away, please.'

'Where are you taking them?' asked Edwin.

'I've orders to head for Katha,' said the driver, getting back into the front of the truck. 'Once there, I'll await instructions.'

'There's nothing at Katha,' said Edwin, but the driver was already closing his door. Edwin helped Myia into the truck, and then looked at Kate. 'Listen, whatever happens keep heading north. There's an airfield at Myitkyina – if you can get there then you'll be safe. I'll try to find you there. Or in India.'

Kate clambered up and squashed down beside Myia in the back of the truck, which was already occupied by four women and their numerous young children.

The metal of the truck burned against her skin and she felt light-headed. She looked at Edwin and thought that she ought to say something, find the words for a fitting goodbye, but she was neither his wife nor his lover, and all she could do was to raise a hand as a friend and wave to him, standing there in his wrinkled suit, an anxious smile on his face, as the truck pulled jerkily away and out through the gates, heading north.

PART II

Burma and India, 1942

20
Mandalay Region, April 1942

For Edwin, the last days in Mandalay were a blur of heat and anxiety. After watching Kate's truck disappear, he went back to work and waited for the command to leave. He considered paying for a place in a vehicle, but some vague sense of duty kept him at his post.

Civilisation in Mandalay had all but broken down. Every day the city was strafed by Japanese planes and fires raged all around, the air filled with a noxious blend of smoke and dust. Leaflets were dropped by the enemy, urging the populace to abandon the city. Chinese and British casualties were arriving in trains and on the back of trucks, but few medical staff remained to treat them. Those doctors who stayed were overworked and one by one they vanished, either to move their surgeries further north, away from the Japanese advance, or to save themselves.

A week or so after Kate had left, Edwin was woken by the tooting of a horn outside his lodgings. Stumbling out onto the dusty street he saw his colleague Patrick rearranging luggage strapped to the back of an ancient two-seater motor car.

'Morning, Edwin. Time to leave!'

'What?'

'A message came round. Didn't you get it? They're abandoning the city. I thought you might like a lift.'

'Give me five minutes,' said Edwin and hurried back inside. For a few seconds he leaned against a wall in the dark hallway and closed his eyes, breathing deeply, before gathering a few possessions.

Soon they were on their way, crawling through the suburbs of Mandalay in a stream of cars, cyclists, and pedestrians. It seemed that all the world was on the move.

'Where did you get this car?' said Edwin. 'It's seen better days.'

'I looted it,' said Patrick, watching the traffic with a frown. 'Well, found it. In a garage near my digs. Took ages to start, but she's going all right now. The owners are long gone.'

Slowly they moved south, winding through the tightly packed streets. Occasionally they passed a bomb site, flattened buildings and black ash showing where the Japanese had dropped their incendiary bombs.

'God, what a mess,' said Patrick, shaking his head. 'These poor people. They don't deserve any of this.'

Soon Edwin saw that they were passing Amarapura. Only ten days ago he and Kate had been out on the water in the early morning, and he wondered, with a pang, when he would see her again. The strange intensity of their friendship had crept up on him and, as the sun rose over Amarapura, he had felt closer to her than ever before. The peace of that morning was gone, but the pagoda itself still stood out, white and brilliant. It had outlived the kings of old and now the British imperialists. He wondered if it would outlast the Japanese, too.

Occasionally by the roadside they saw British sentries, armed with guns, but they didn't seem to be stopping anyone and waved the cars and walkers through. Finally they reached the great Ava Bridge, which crossed the Irrawaddy south of Mandalay. A group of soldiers guarded the toll gates, but they stood open and Patrick drove slowly through.

'They're blowing up the bridge tonight,' said Patrick, gesturing at the metal struts on either side of them.

Edwin peered down at the river and saw it stretching away on either side, gleaming like copper. 'This really is a retreat, isn't it? What about those who don't get across in time?'

'Too bad, I suppose,' said Patrick. 'It's the only bridge across this part of the Irrawaddy. After tomorrow it'll be boats only. Or swimming, although I wouldn't want to try that.'

Just before they left the bridge Edwin looked back for the last time. Smoke rose high above the ruins of Mandalay and sorrow gripped him. Some of it was for Burma, but it was so tied up with Emilia and London and Kate and her father that he couldn't be sure who, or what, he was grieving for.

꙳

They drove for several hours under a blazing sun, passing streams of people walking and others piled into rickshaws and on bicycles. After examining his maps, Patrick turned off the main road onto a little-used lane, just after a crumbling pagoda.

'If I've got it right this will save us some time,' he said. 'We just need to keep going west. We're bound to hit an airfield eventually. And of course India's over there somewhere if we drive for long enough.'

'How did you get those maps?' asked Edwin, glancing at the rolls in the back. 'We were told to destroy everything.'

'I liberated them,' said Patrick. 'It seemed a shame to burn them when they might be useful. There are three or four airfields marked. We'll just have to hope they're not already in enemy hands.'

A little later the car started to make alarming noises, juddering and clanking, while steam rose from the engine. The sound made Edwin think of Kate and the woman they had tried to save. He would never forget the cries of pain and fear, the misery in her husband's eyes.

'Know anything about cars?' asked Patrick as they rolled to a stop on a dusty verge.

'Not really,' said Edwin apologetically. He had seen the Rolls Royce again a few days before, a burned-out shell on the road near Fort Dufferin. 'Don't you?'

'Not a thing,' said Patrick.

Together they opened the bonnet and peered down at the unfamiliar arrangement within. It was red-hot to the touch and steam still hissed.

'Could we be out of petrol?' asked Edwin.

Patrick frowned. 'We shouldn't be, I filled it up with all that I could find. It should take us much further than this.'

'Perhaps there's a leak,' said Edwin and squatted down to peer under the car. 'I may be wrong,' came his muffled voice, 'but I'd say that's a leak. Quite a bad one.'

Patrick knelt down and looked to where Edwin was pointing. In the dust was a dark puddle, formed by a rapid dripping of liquid from the car's undercarriage.

'Oh, Christ.'

Edwin sniffed. 'It's oil.'

'I've nothing to fix it with,' said Patrick, sitting back on his haunches.

In the end there was nothing to do but go on, leaving a trail of drips on the dusty road. The noise of the engine grew worse all the time and the light faded as they drove west, talking of what they would do when they found an airfield and got away to India.

'I expect I shall join up,' said Patrick, frowning at the sky, where an aeroplane flew in the distance, heading north. 'I'd like to be involved when they run the Japs out of Burma.'

'Do you have family at home?'

'Just my parents,' said Patrick. 'The minute I get to Calcutta I'll write and tell them I'm safe.'

Edwin wondered what he ought to do. He had no picture of the future or what he should do with it. In the short term, his concern was with finding Kate and making sure she was all right. He imagined exploring the new city with her. But what then? What would he do with the rest of his life? Try as he might, he could not see what he would be doing in five years, or ten, or twenty. The future was blank.

The engine began to smoke and the car got slower and slower. At last Patrick heaved a deep sigh and stopped the car on a narrow road between two fields of sugar cane. Smoke poured out from under the bonnet. They salvaged what they could of their possessions and pushed the car as far off the road as possible.

'Heap of junk,' said Patrick, but he patted the bonnet of the car and looked regretful. 'Well, she gave us a head start.'

'How far back do you think the Japanese are?'

'They could be anywhere,' Patrick said. 'They may be sneaking around the countryside in small groups. On the wireless it just said that they were moving north . . .'

It was completely dark by the time they reached the edge of a village. Patrick was all for knocking on a door and asking for refuge, but Edwin was anxious about being seen by anyone, or being mistaken for a hostile force and attacked.

In the end they slept in a tumbledown barn and drank murky water from a tank outside. Reluctant to eat the minimal supplies they had brought, they broke lengths of sugar cane from the neighbouring field and sucked the sweet juice.

The next day they walked on, heading west.

21

London, October 1940

In the Blitz, nothing was as it seemed. The streets of the West End were darkened, but behind closed doors, if you knew where to look, the life of the city went on, sparkling brighter than ever.

When had it begun? Edwin had been caught in an air raid in Leicester Square. He'd had a drink, two drinks, and when in the flickering darkness of the Underground station he became aware of the advances of the man who stood pressed against him, furtive but determined, he'd frozen for a moment before disgust set in. He shoved the fellow away and pushed through the crowds. Glancing back, he saw the face of the man in the lamplight – handsome, with a knowing smile that lingered and seemed to say, 'You'll be back.'

But no, that wasn't the first time. More than once, in the streets, he'd been whispered to, importuned.

'I'm looking for somewhere to stay,' said a handsome young officer with a cut-glass accent. 'Might you . . .?'

'No. Sorry!' And he'd scuttled away, wondering what kind of signal they were reading in him.

✷

Another night, weeks later. He'd been drinking late with colleagues at a pub not far from the school. It had been a difficult day; they'd had news that another of the young teachers had been killed in the Western Desert, a fellow of Edwin's age with a wife and children. Edwin drank more and faster than ever before, and suddenly it was time for last orders and he was stumbling out onto the street. His colleagues, all men too old for the war, patted his shoulder and pointed him towards a cab rank.

There were no cabs, so he wandered to the station, but he'd missed the last train. Emilia would be worried, he knew, and he felt a pang of remorse. He would get home to her somehow. He knew the city well and it was only a few miles, after all. He was drunk, but the streets were familiar and he felt as though he was flying as he strode towards central London. Even in the darkness he could dimly see the massive shape of St Paul's looming like a ship, the centre of the city drawing him on. Occasionally he heard the drone of a plane overhead.

In no time at all, it seemed, although it could have been hours, he was strolling through the West End. Passing a doorway, he heard the distant sounds of music and thought enviously of the party that was taking place somewhere below the street, the dancers moving fast in each other's arms, the pouring of drinks, the dimmed lighting.

He was standing now in the middle of the road, in a trance, and it was not until he saw people spilling out of doorways all around that he realised an air-raid siren was howling. He watched them run, feeling detached from it all, and walked on.

Edwin noticed that the street was almost empty. Everyone had gone to the shelter, but where was it? He tried to picture the area from above to work out where the nearest Underground station was, but it was a blur. It occurred to him suddenly that Emilia was away for the night, staying with her parents. His home would be dark and empty.

The man who appeared before him looked unruffled. He had been standing in a doorway, watching Edwin approach.

'Hello,' he said.

'Where's the shelter? Aren't you going to it?'

'No.' The man shook his head. 'I always just stay at home and have a drink. Why bother?'

'You could be killed.'

He shrugged. 'Always a possibility.' He was young, his dark hair falling in messy curls around his ears. He wore an expensive suit, and Edwin could see that he was a gentleman – of sorts. 'I'd rather enjoy myself while I can. Wouldn't you?'

'I don't know,' said Edwin. The drink had worn off a little now, but he still felt distant, as though he was observing the scene from above. The man had a louche look to him, his shirt untucked, his waistcoat half-buttoned. The siren was still shrieking but it had become background noise.

He was watching Edwin with a sardonic smile. 'Why don't you come in for a drink?'

Later, Edwin would replay that moment again and again in his mind, turning over all the different ways in which he might have said 'No', the excuses he could have given, then the journey home, and a different outcome.

Instead, he said, 'All right,' and followed the man into his house. As the door clicked shut, the bombs began to fall.

22
Upper Burma, May 1942

A rumour went around that a ferry would shortly be calling at Katha. Kate and Myia took their luggage down to the jetty and sat hopefully on the edge, dangling their legs over the water and peering downriver. They had been awaiting onward transport for days.

The Irrawaddy at this point was as wide as ever, and the current, though sluggish, was clearly powerful. They watched young boys diving off the jetty and being carried downstream before scrambling back up the bank.

Much of Katha's commerce centred on the river and all around people were living on it or by it. Wrinkled old fishermen in tiny sampans bobbed around in the shallows, while larger boats fished upstream.

At the edge of the water women stood washing clothes or themselves, their *longyis* pulled up demurely to cover their bodies, the water dripping from their long black hair. After drying their hair, they helped one another to style it, always tucking in a bright orchid or spray of cherry blossom, before painting on thick *thanaka* paste to protect their cheeks from the sun.

In the distance came the low bellow of a horn and Kate squinted at the haze over the river. A few minutes later a large steamer appeared around the bend, belching smoke and approaching at a stately pace. The deck was crowded and people were pressed against the railings. As they watched, one or two young men, keen to be home, jumped over the rail and swam briskly for the shore.

'We'll never get on,' said Myia, and as she spoke a swell of hopeful passengers surged past them, hurrying along the jetty in the hope of getting a place. There were far more people trying to get on than off, and the men working on the boat were pushing people back.

'What now?' said Kate.

'We could try the train station again.'

'What's the point? None of the trains have any space. We're stuck here.'

As the day wore on they bought cups of tea from a stall by the dock and approached a number of officials, but no one seemed to have any information about how they might leave Katha.

'I find you truck to China,' offered one young man, gesturing to the east. 'Is not difficult.'

'China?'

'I do not want to go to China,' said Myia, looking at Kate. 'We'll just get stuck there instead.'

'Let's keep it as a last resort.'

Later they had bowls of fish soup, purchased from another stall, and sat watching the river. A European man arrived and ordered the same. He was around fifty, stocky, with sun-browned skin and dressed in faded khaki. An English teak merchant, Kate supposed, or perhaps an oil worker.

'Afternoon,' he said, catching her eye and nodding.

'Hello.'

He busied himself accepting the soup and then sat down nearby on a log and ate it unhurriedly, watching the boats and the people come and go.

'Heading north?' he asked.

'Trying to,' said Kate. 'We're aiming for Myitkyina.'

He nodded. 'The airfield. Me too, actually. Fred Thompson.' He held out a strong hand to each of them in turn.

'Kate Girton.'

'Myia Win.'

He spoke to Myia in Burmese, and she laughed and said, 'And you.' She turned to Kate. 'You know that phrase, I think.'

'Oh – pleased to meet you?'

'That's right.'

'The lads I work with tend to laugh at my pronunciation,' said Fred. He lapsed back into silence, looking a trifle embarrassed. Kate sensed that he was used to being on his own a lot. His voice had a northern lilt and she wondered where he was from.

'How are you getting to Myitkyina?' he said.

'We're not sure yet.'

'Would you like a lift?'

'A lift! Yes, please!' said Kate, adding as an afterthought, 'In what?'

'I've got a little boat,' he said, jerking his head upstream. 'She's moored over there, out of sight. Room for a couple more. I'll be going as far as Bhamo – the river's too narrow for boats after that and there are rapids. You can get a truck from there to Myitkyina.'

⁕

The boat was a small paddle-steamer, her name written in looping Burmese script on the prow. Underneath, in English, it said 'Irrawaddy Flotilla Company'. On board was a mixed crowd of refugees, several of them ill or wounded, and the smell of gangrenous wounds permeated the boat. They looked without curiosity as Kate and Myia came aboard. Many of them had evidently been travelling for some time and looked wretched.

Fred soon cast off and the steamer made its way up the river. At last he handed over to his young apprentice, a boy in a maroon loincloth, then went around the ship checking knots, patting luggage, and checking that all was well.

'Thank you,' Kate said as he passed. 'For taking us.'

'No trouble,' he said, with a faint smile. 'Helping a few people is all I can do at this stage.' He looked around the boat, surveying his empire, then gazed upriver, where the sun was starting to descend towards the hills. 'Her last voyage.'

'Last?'

He nodded. 'She'll be scuttled once we get to Bhamo. Can't risk her falling to the Japs, you see.'

He caressed the wooden rail and then was gone, hurrying off to whatever business awaited him, and Kate felt a glimmer of sadness. It was clear that he loved this boat, and its impending loss was yet another small tragedy in amongst all the others.

They watched Katha disappearing around the bend, and now all that could be seen was the wide brown expanse of the Irrawaddy, although the smoke from fires rose in the distance. Birds waded in the shallows and gentle waves lapped against the sides of the ship.

They slept that night on deck, surrounded by people. The boat was anchored close to the bank, palm fronds quivering overhead as the river flowed by. Kate noticed Fred curled up

131

next to the rail, a coil of rope under his head, and realised he must have given his cabin to someone who needed it more. She liked him even better for that.

It was cool outside, but pleasant after the heat of the day and, wrapped up in her shawl, Kate felt almost comfortable. She lay on her back for some time watching the stars and listening to the sounds of the boat, and eventually fell asleep.

✳

The day dawned hot on the boat, which was already moving by the time Kate woke up. She and Myia ate some of the fruit they had bought at Katha and dipped lukewarm water from a barrel in the middle of the deck. It tasted slightly of tar.

At around midday, as Kate dozed in a patch of shade beside the cabin, a commotion on board made her eyes fly open.

'What is it?' said Myia groggily beside her.

'Aeroplanes,' said someone in the crowd nearby, and at that moment she heard the roar of an engine somewhere to the south.

At last the plane passed over. It was too high to see the markings, but she knew instinctively that it was not a British plane. They watched it roar away, until it was almost out of sight, and then something black fell to earth, followed a couple of seconds later by a distant rumble.

Smoke could be seen rising from whatever target it had hit and Kate felt her breath catch in her throat.

Myia let go of the sack she had been gripping tightly. 'I wonder what they hit?'

'Something military,' said Fred, who had not moved from the wheel. He was scanning the skies with binoculars. 'There's a base not far from here, the King's Own, I think. The Japs are very far north. We must get to the airfield as soon as possible.'

Later that day they stopped to take on food and water at a village from which smoke was rising. The men told Fred that the village had been looted and burned by Chinese soldiers.

'Aren't the Chinese on our side?' said Kate later.

Fred smiled cynically. 'In theory. But they're badly paid and short on rations, or so I understand. Desperate men, desperate times.'

She watched him steering the boat, his strong hands resting lightly on the wheel. 'Have you lived in Burma for a long time?'

'I came out from Liverpool in 1920,' he said. 'Seems like yesterday.'

'It must be hard to leave.'

'It doesn't seem real yet,' he said. 'How can I leave all this behind?' He gestured at the glimmering water and the misted hills, and she understood at once what he meant. There was beauty all around them, but he was also giving up a whole way of life. He would have to start again, as she would. I've done it before, thought Kate, but it was hardly a comforting thought, and sometimes it seemed that she would be running forever.

23

Upper Burma, May 1942

Early on their third day aboard Fred's ship, Bhamo hove into view in a heat haze. People began to clamber wearily off the boat, helping the sick and injured passengers off first, piling their belongings on the jetty.

'Any news?' said Fred to a harassed official on the dock.

'The Japanese have crossed the Shweli Bridge. They'll be in Bhamo by tomorrow.'

'Aren't you coming?' said Kate, seeing Fred start back up the gangplank.

'Got to scuttle the boat. It'll take me a couple of hours to get sorted out. You should go on ahead, there are bound to be trucks going north.'

'All right. See you at Myitkyina, perhaps. If not, thank you again.'

'I'd advise you to get on the first plane you can,' he said. 'Don't hang about too long, it's not safe here. I'll be along later, once I've taken her upriver.' He hesitated and smiled. 'Good luck.'

He nodded again and then vanished into the cabin.

'It seems a dreadful waste,' said Kate. 'Imagine having to sink that lovely boat. It's his livelihood.'

'Better than letting it be used by the Japanese,' said Myia. 'They are very close, now.'

They stood by the harbour for a moment, watching the crowds come and go. In the distance a queue of trucks and cars were at the centre of a mob of people.

'We'd better get over there, I suppose,' said Kate, shading her eyes. 'How much do you think a lift to Myitkyina will cost?' She turned to see Myia staring off into the crowd. 'Myia?'

'Sorry?'

'Are you all right?'

Myia turned to her, looking startled. 'I thought . . . I saw a familiar face. Here of all places.'

'Who was it?'

But Myia was scanning the crowds again, frowning, and shook her head. 'I think it was a mistake. It doesn't matter. Let's go.'

✳

It took over twenty-four hours to drive to Myitkyina, in the back of a rattling truck that had to take long detours to avoid numerous broken bridges. But they had come so far already that it seemed no time at all before they were slowing down. It was another dusty nondescript town, the northernmost end of the railway line in Burma. They had seen a broken-down train abandoned a few miles from the town.

They bumped through the outskirts and onto a rutted road leading west, along which people were drifting in a steady flow. As they drew closer they could see a plane already parked on the runway, surrounded by a swarm of people, all trying to get on board. Many others were sitting in small groups on the parched grass.

'Heavens,' said Kate, feeling panic rising as they alighted from the truck, exhausted and unsteady from the long drive. 'What shall we do?'

Myia was staring at the distant chaos and shrugged distractedly. 'I don't know. We'll never get on there.'

They sat down on the grass, in the partial shade of a scraggly bush, and watched the scene before them. People were still thronging around the plane, but someone seemed to have taken charge and several men with flags were fanning out, gradually moving the crowds back.

A man ran out of the crowd and tried to mount the steps to the plane's door, but he was immediately tackled by one of the soldiers and knocked to the ground. The prone body was dragged away and the runway cleared by the soldiers. There was a long pause, the crowds restlessly watching the plane preparing for take-off, its doors now closed. The engines started and built up to a low roar. Kate saw people in the crowd clutching hats and scarves as the wind from the engines buffeted them.

Finally the plane began to move, and after the usual slow start it pelted off along the runway and then rose sharply into the air. It circled once above the airfield and then, heading west, was soon out of sight.

The crowds around them were mostly women and children. Occasionally Kate looked around, hoping against hope to see Edwin pushing through the throng towards her, but he was never there and eventually she stopped looking. She had not expected to find him here, not really. He could still be in Mandalay, or at some other airfield. Perhaps he had been lucky and was already in India.

The day wore on. At last Kate went looking for someone with information and, in a wooden hut, she found an over-worked British soldier, leafing through lists and crossing out names. Crowds of people were waiting to speak to him but at last she fought her way to the desk.

'Are there any seats available?'

'We can find you one,' he said, swatting at a fly.

'You can?' she said disbelievingly.

'Later today, or tomorrow perhaps – once the old and sick have gone – as far as Dinjan or Dibrughar in Assam. Are you travelling alone?'

'No, with a Burmese woman, a government employee. Shall I write our names down?'

He shook his head. 'The only seats available are for Europeans, I'm afraid.'

'But surely—'

'I don't make the rules, miss,' he said wearily. 'Your friend will have to stay here for now – she may get a seat when all the Europeans have been taken. Could be a while, though. If you want the seat, fill this form in.'

Kate stared at the paper in his hand and found herself backing away. 'I'll come back later.' He shrugged and turned to the next person in the queue.

As she strode out of the hut, Kate felt a bubbling rage seeping through her body. Most of her anger was directed at herself; she should have foreseen this. It was how things had always been, yet suddenly it seemed an outrage that Myia's life might be worth less than hers simply by a chance of birth. For a brief moment she had been tempted to take the seat but knew that she would not be able to live with herself. There had to be another way.

'What is it?' said Myia as she returned.

'No seats,' said Kate shortly. 'Not for some time, they say.'

Myia nodded, observing her closely, but said nothing. The next plane approached not long after. Once again the runway was cleared as it circled and finally came in to land; again the crowds of people flocked around it.

Kate watched a tall young man run towards the plane, carrying a baby and pulling a small girl along behind him by the hand. The child was stumbling and lolling and was obviously sick. They vanished into the crowd.

It looked like chaos from a distance, but there seemed to be some sort of organisation to the madness. People were shuffling around, presumably being given orders, and occasionally figures could be seen ascending the steps and entering the aeroplane, many of them carrying or dragging others.

She saw the man emerge from the crowd. He was now alone. Were his children crammed into that little plane without their parents, bound for a mysterious country? How would he find them again?

He waited alone on the edge of the crowd until the engines started and then slowly walked away, glancing back often at the scene behind him, sometimes waving, in the hope that his children might see. As he passed a few yards away from her, Kate saw that he was wiping his eyes on his sleeve, his face scrunched with misery and relief.

The noise of the plane grew louder and the crowds were once again moving away from the runway, knowing that their time had not yet come. Kate, still watching the young father with pity in her heart, felt a nudge from Myia.

'Look.'

'What?'

She peered towards where her friend was pointing. In the sky to the south a black shape was growing larger by the second, a whining noise getting louder.

'Is it the Japanese?'

'I think so,' said Myia, squinting, and Kate looked around wildly at the people on the airfield. Others were starting to notice and shouts broke out as frightened people began to stream in all directions, running this way and that as they sought to guess where the first attack might fall. The airfield had no shelter except for a few ramshackle huts in the distance and a series of protective trenches, set well back from the landing strip.

There was hardly time to panic. In less than a minute the plane was upon them, followed swiftly by another, and Kate and Myia crouched instinctively as the shadows passed over them. The sound had stopped; they seemed to be gliding silently, like birds of prey.

There was a wail nearby, and Kate saw the young man looking around in horror and disbelief, clutching his face as he watched the plane above him heading towards the runway where his children sat. Then he began to run.

'It's too late,' said Kate, 'it's too late!' Looking up, she saw the shape of the plane almost directly overhead. There was the faint sound of gunfire now – the soldiers on the airfield had obviously started firing, but the plane was huge and it seemed absurd that men with guns could do anything to stop it.

As if in a dream Kate saw the man running hard towards the runway, could almost feel the straining of his lungs as he hurled himself along, the blood beating in his ears. He was twenty yards from the British plane when the firing started, a furious rattle of machine gun fire that instantly punched holes in the wings and body of the aircraft. People all around were running, mostly away from the plane, but he and a few others went towards it, their grief and anger driving them on.

But it was already beginning to burn, a thick plume of smoke rising into the air, a creaking noise coming from somewhere. The man was almost upon it when the plane exploded, sending smoke and burning metal into the sky, making the earth tremble.

Kate found herself thrown backwards, the force of it like nothing else she had known. Winded, she lay on her back, her ears ringing, and idly watched the smoke drift upwards.

24

Magway Region, May 1942

Edwin sat in darkness in the back of the truck as it bumped along, feeling another man's shoulder jolting against his each time they hit a rough patch in the road. He could not remember the faces of the men around him.

A few days into their walk he and Patrick had fallen in with two Indian families, also heading west. One night, sleeping in a damp barn a hundred miles west of Mandalay, they were violently awoken by a great shouting and the door banged open. His heart beating wildly, he watched as a dozen Japanese soldiers appeared.

They had been betrayed by nearby villagers who had seen them arrive the night before. Edwin and the three other men were taken outside, hearing the howls of fear from the women and children left behind. The soldiers tied their hands, pushed them into a truck that was already half-full of prisoners, and suddenly the escape from Burma was over.

How long they drove for, none of them could say. They were allowed out of the van occasionally to relieve themselves and given water but no food. At last the truck stopped and they were left for hours, listening to muffled voices in the distance.

Finally, after nightfall, they were released. Edwin clambered out of the truck, his eyes struggling to focus. They were in a dusty yard, edged on one side with rough buildings and on the others with a tall wire fence.

They were locked in an empty room with a high ceiling. Water was brought, and then a platter of glutinous rice to share, which they wolfed down. Then they were left in darkness.

'What do you think they will do to us?' asked one of the men in the blackness of the room.

'They will kill us,' his friend replied flatly, his voice sounding strained.

'I'm not sure,' said Patrick, somewhere to Edwin's left. 'I think they will keep us prisoner.'

'To what purpose?'

'They may make us work. When Singapore fell they took thousands of men prisoner. The rumour is that they are using forced labour to build new roads and railways in Siam.'

'But will they do that in Burma?' asked the first man doubtfully. 'What use is Burma to them?'

'It's the road to India.'

'What of our families?' the questioner asked. No one replied and he said heatedly, 'Perhaps they are already dead!'

'No,' said Patrick. 'No, they can't be.'

But Edwin thought of the rumours he had heard about the fall of Singapore and Malaya and felt a surge of horror. He recalled the story of a group of Australian nurses who had been ordered by the Japanese to walk out into the sea, away from the shore, and who were then shot in the back as they struggled through the surf. For a moment he thought of Kate and was reassured to think she was probably somewhere safer by now, though his dreams that night were of blood washing up on a sandy beach, a woman's shoe bobbing empty in the shallows.

✦

Edwin was already awake when the Japanese returned early the next morning. The door was opened with a scraping of bolts and he saw two young soldiers standing outside, another group further along the corridor.

He recognised the nearest one as the translator of the day before. He looked more like a student than a soldier, his eyes gentle behind round spectacles, his black hair parted in the middle. He stepped forward and grasped Edwin by the shoulder.

'You come with us, Mr Clear.'

Too tired and frightened to resist, or to wonder why he was being singled out, Edwin found himself being marched through corridors between the soldiers, who did not speak any further.

They reached a door and, after knocking, the men pushed Edwin into the room. Behind a large desk sat another soldier. The man, close to middle age, sported a row of medals and was clearly deeply respected by the younger men, who had both bowed upon entering.

He spoke in Japanese, and the translator immediately relayed his words in English.

'Major Sakai says welcome, Mr Edwin Clear. He hopes you had a pleasant journey and good sleep.'

Edwin looked incredulously between the two men, but the only thing he could say was, 'How does he know my name?'

He half expected someone to hit him, but the young translator bowed his head and spoke to Sakai in Japanese.

The older man shrugged and lifted a suitcase onto the table. Edwin recognised it as his own.

He watched Major Sakai lift his belongings out of the case and lay them out on the table. There was little of interest in there, he thought, until he saw the map being unrolled. He remembered shoving it in there when he and Patrick had abandoned the car. Sakai examined it for a moment and held it up.

'Major Sakai says what is your profession?'

'I'm a teacher.'

'That is why you are in Burma?'

'Yes,' said Edwin. It was not quite the truth, but somehow being a teacher seemed safer than being a government employee – and after all he had been a teacher once. It seemed a long time ago.

'You are soldier?'

'No – a teacher. As I said.'

'Have you ever been soldier?'

'No.'

Major Sakai shook his head and looked irritated.

'Why you have this map?'

'We were trying to get to India.'

'It is government map. Why you have it?'

'I borrowed it.'

'Why?'

'So I could get to India.' Edwin felt himself sweating heavily. He had no idea what they wanted of him and he worried that even with few secrets to tell he would somehow say the wrong thing.

The major growled something in Japanese and the translator said, 'You are spy.'

'What? Of course not. I'm a civilian. I don't know anything.'

'Who are the other men with you?'

'Friends.'

'More spies?'

'Civilians. Men with wives and children. You saw them.' Edwin felt his heart thudding. 'Where are their families?'

'That is not your concern. They are safe.'

'Is that true?'

But they would say no more on the subject. They questioned him further and Edwin could see they were dissatisfied with his answers, but he knew he didn't look much like a spy. It was only the map that had made them suspicious.

When they grew impatient, he was pushed face first against a wall, his heart pounding, hearing shouting behind him, then he felt the agony of a heavy stick slashing down, over and over, against his back. More questions were barked at him, but he could not provide any different answers and at last the beating stopped. His back throbbed and stung and he could feel blood seeping into his shirt.

He was sent back to the cell and, a little later, Patrick was taken out. He reappeared after two hours, hobbling, his nose broken and bleeding profusely.

'What happened?' whispered Edwin, aghast, as Patrick sank onto the floor beside him.

'They found my papers,' he muttered. 'There wasn't much of anything useful, but it was enough to make them suspicious. They beat the back of my legs and my spine, trying to make me give something up. I asked them if they'd heard of the Geneva Conventions but that just made them angrier.'

The next day they were put in separate rooms. Edwin heard the two Indian men being taken away for interrogation, but he did not hear them return to their cells. The day after that he was taken outside by one of the soldiers, who manacled his hands.

Squinting in the bright sunlight, he was led across the yard and made to climb into the back of a waiting truck, where an elderly priest and two young British soldiers already waited. His manacles were chained to the floor and they were left alone.

'Where are they taking us?'

'South,' said the old man. He was short of breath and looked unwell. 'One of them told me we were going to a labour camp somewhere south of Rangoon.' His accent was Scottish.

'What about the others?'

'What others?' said one of the boys.

'I came with three other men.'

'They'll probably be sent elsewhere,' said the boy. 'We arrived with half of our battalion last week and we've all been separated.'

Edwin slumped against the side of the truck, hardly feeling the pain of the raw wounds on his back. More prisoners arrived, but he recognised none of them as they were pushed into the truck to join the rest. He watched three Japanese soldiers conferring and then two of them climbed into the front seats and the engine started.

'I wonder what will happen to them,' he said, almost to himself.

The young soldier who had spoken shrugged, but the other leaned forward earnestly. 'Sorry to say, mate, but I think you'd better forget about the others. Think of yourself. That's all any of us can do now.'

Edwin hardly knew anything about Patrick, knew nothing of the other two men except that they had families, and it suddenly seemed horribly unlikely that he would ever see them again. The truck rattled along. Through the glare on his spectacles he could see distant hills and, closer to the road, a patch of bright flowers in a field nearby. He closed his eyes and felt the metal burning the back of his neck.

25
London, April 1941

It had been six months since the man in the West End had taken him inside and handed him a drink before getting down on his knees and reaching for Edwin's trouser buttons. Edwin had stayed until the early hours, until the drink had begun to wear off, as had his desire.

But he had gone back, once, twice, three times each month, prowling the dangerous, darkened streets of the West End and Soho, going further and learning more about himself each time. It was urgent, fumbling, sometimes rough, but more often surprisingly tender.

It was astonishing to find this hidden world, populated by men just like him. Most of them wanted sex and nothing more, but occasionally he met a man who wanted to talk. They would share a few brief confidences and, in the dark, he heard the longing, the guilt about their families, the regret at having always to stay hidden, heard it mirrored in his own voice. Then the shame descended and he would hurry home.

He had told Emilia that he was teaching extra classes for university applicants on the nights he was out and he wondered how much of it she believed.

'How are the boys doing?' she asked, as they sat opposite one another, eating the supper she had made. Edwin thought of the

previous night's liaison, with a boy who could not have been more than twenty, and felt a surge of nausea.

'Oh, fine. Fine. How was your day?'

'A bit horrid, actually,' said Emilia, taking a forkful of fish pie. 'Someone shouted at me in the street.'

'Shouted at you?' Edwin could hear the sound of sirens in the distance. How quickly they had become used to this new normal. London was under attack and here they sat, eating supper.

'The usual abuse. He'd obviously come to Golders Green to find Jews to shout at. I heard him bellow at someone else further down the street. The war seems to be bringing home-grown fascists out of the woodwork.' She paused, waiting for a reply, and then shrugged and went on with her meal. 'I suppose they'll be delighted when Hitler has bombed London out of existence.'

Edwin thought of the end of the war. In his mind there was no doubt that the Allies would win. But what will happen to us, he wondered, now watching Emilia quietly eating her supper. What will we do? She sipped from the glass of wine by her plate. She was drinking more these days. Wine was scarce, but Emilia's father sometimes brought them a bottle, and while previously it might have lain untouched for weeks, now she opened it almost immediately.

'I had a letter from Adam. He's in Port Sudan now. The fighting sounds rather fierce there at the moment but I suppose he'll be all right . . . Edwin?'

He tried to wrench his thoughts away from the secrets that were piled up inside him and thought of Emilia's brother, far away, fighting in the desert. Adam would do more to protect her than he ever could.

She had put down her knife and fork and was watching him. Her eyes looked red. He took her hand and squeezed it.

'Edwin, what is it? Won't you talk to me?'

'I'm sorry. I feel anxious and distracted all the time. I suppose it's the bombing.' He kissed her cheek, feeling her relax a little against his shoulder. 'I'm sorry.'

He wanted to tell her, more than anything, but knew he never could. Sometimes the guilt rose in his throat and he felt that he must say something or burst, but he could think of no words that were adequate for the task. He wondered if she was happy. He loved her, but it wasn't enough.

Sometimes, as he wandered through Soho at midnight and heard the sirens begin to howl, he wished that a bomb would fall and kill him and save both of them from a life of loneliness and deception.

But over and over he escaped the gaze of the Luftwaffe and went home tired and ashamed, until suddenly there were no more nights left and he was standing in a quiet street in Golders Green as the smoke rose above what had once been his life.

26

Upper Burma, May 1942

The jungle seemed alive with voices. All around them people were walking north, children and old people and families and groups of young men and women. Kate noticed that the vast majority were Indian and wondered how many of them had ever even seen India. They too had left their homes and were walking towards an unknown future.

She and Myia had slept restlessly under a tree, listening to the sounds of crying and arguing all around them as people began to grasp that there would be no more aeroplanes. She had known from the moment the plane exploded that she would not get to India that way and felt oddly calm about it. The only thing to do was to start walking.

Fred Thompson had appeared after breakfast, as though it had been arranged, carrying an army knapsack and with a *kukri* hanging in its sheath at his side. With little discussion they shouldered their bags and started walking north. Fred said they should head towards Fort Hertz to begin with, but the name meant nothing to Kate; all she knew was that they were walking towards India, an incomprehensible distance away.

To begin with it felt crowded, but as the hours passed people spread out more as the slower walkers fell behind. Eventually they found a rough dirt track that wound through the trees, sometimes emerging to pass fields and, in the distance, villages.

All around, bright yellow and white orchids bloomed and broad ferns drooped onto the edge of the track. A bird called somewhere nearby, a long and piercing sound, and was answered by its mate in the distance.

'Look,' said Fred, pointing back the way they had come. Kate turned to see thick smoke rising a few miles away above the treeline.

'They've bombed Myitkyina,' he said, watching intently. 'The whole town must be ablaze.'

'Then they have won,' said Myia. She stood staring at the smoke, her face a pale mask, twisting the silver pendant at her throat.

'It's not over yet,' said Fred, but he sounded unconvinced.

As they paused to drink from a stream, Kate saw a European boy of fifteen or so scooping up water in a thermos flask, which he passed to a woman sitting nearby. She drank deeply from it. The boy, watching her anxiously, looked up and caught Kate's eye fleetingly. He raised a hand in greeting.

'Hello,' said Kate. 'Going to India?'

'I'm not sure. I don't think my mother is strong enough,' he said, looking worried again. 'She's been very ill.'

'Don't be absurd,' said his mother. 'Do you think I'm going to stay here and get tortured by the Japs? Your father would have been very disappointed in me. Now, pull me up.'

She looked as though she had lost weight recently; her skin hung loose around her neck and on her arms, and the cotton dress she wore was far too big. She was around forty, Kate thought, but looked older, her grey hair in dishevelled curls.

With her son's help she heaved up off the ground, grabbing his arm for support once she was upright. Her skin looked clammy and her breathing was fast.

'I'm Christopher Bryant,' said the boy as an afterthought, 'and this is my mother. We don't know the way.'

'I do,' said Fred, handing his walking stick to Mrs Bryant. 'Stick with us.'

✦

That first day their group covered six miles. They were slower than before and Kate had noticed that Fred had a slight limp, which increased as the day wore on, but she knew that she and Myia were better off in a group than alone, even if they were faster walkers. Mrs Bryant trudged painfully on, leaning on her son, while the others took turns carrying her bag.

The road was only a road by Burmese standards; it looked more like a farm track to Kate's eyes. The column of refugees was strung out over a huge distance. There were many people ahead of them and many more behind. In a fifteen-minute break they might be passed by twenty or more people, although the numbers seemed to be getting fewer as the day went on.

The straps of Kate's leather sandals rubbed her toes and every step on the dusty road brought gravel and dirt under the soles of her feet, where it scraped uncomfortably. Her shoulders ached from the hours carrying her knapsack.

A truck appeared in a cloud of dust on the road behind them. As it approached they saw that it was driven by an elderly Kachin farmer and was stuffed to the rafters with refugees, with more perched on the roof of the cab.

At the next rest stop Christopher came over to where Kate sat beside Fred. The boy was tall but skinny as a rake. He looked anxious.

'Can we stop for the night soon? My mother's feet are terribly painful and her breathing's getting all funny.'

Fred patted the boy's shoulder. 'All right, son, don't fret. I'll go ahead and scout out a decent place to camp, shall I? We'll need to get off the road and find somewhere under the trees, near water, ideally.'

'Yes, thanks,' said Christopher gratefully. He sat down next to Kate and wiped the sweat from his forehead as Fred marched back onto the road and out of sight around a corner.

'He's a good chap,' said Kate. 'We're lucky to have met him.'

'Didn't you know him before?'

'No, we met a couple of days ago.'

'It's a strange situation,' said Christopher rather solemnly. 'I expect we shall all know each other well when this is over.'

Kate smiled at him. 'I expect so. Tell me about your family. How long have you been in Burma?'

'Oh, ages,' he said. 'We live in Maymyo. My father was in the police there but he was killed on duty just after the war started. Car accident.'

'Your mother's very brave,' said Kate, looking to where Mrs Bryant sat dozing against a tree, her swollen legs stretched out before her.

'She likes it in Burma. She didn't want to leave but we were told we had to. They made us get a train from Maymyo to Hsipaw and then a lorry took us to Myitkyina. She's got cancer, you know.'

Chewing his lip, Christopher sat watching the road where Fred had vanished.

'Where are *your* family?' he asked.

'My mother is back in England, on a farm in Worcestershire, and I've a sister in London.'

'Are you married?'

'No,' she said. 'Probably for the best. All the young men have gone to war.'

'I wish I was old enough to join the army,' he said.

'Don't wish too hard,' said Kate. 'You and Fred are the only men we've got if there's any danger.'

Christopher thought about this, obviously pleased to be counted among the men. 'I don't have any weapons, though. Fred's got that Gurkha knife and a revolver – I saw him cleaning it earlier.'

Myia emerged from the trees, holding out a handful of unfamiliar shiny purple fruit, which looked to Kate a little like plums, although the taste was quite different.

'What is it?' said Christopher, after trying one.

'I do not know the English name.'

'It's a star apple,' said Mrs Bryant. 'Your father bought them for me at the market once or twice.'

'The leaves are good for stiff joints,' said Myia. 'I picked some of those for you. We can boil them later.'

Fred returned shortly before sunset and led them to the campsite that he had found, beside a trickling stream. While the others were laying out blankets he made a fire and Mrs Bryant stirred a pot of rice that she had seasoned with a pinch of precious salt. They had agreed to ration the food they carried, and when the rice was finished they all looked mournfully at one another. Kate thought of the sweet cakes she had bought sometimes in Rangoon and felt her mouth water.

The camp was only twenty yards from the road, and in the gathering dusk they occasionally saw flickering lights passing.

'Silly fools,' said Fred. 'Daft to go wandering about in the dark. We ought to have stopped to camp even earlier.' He lit a pipe and sat down on a log as the others were preparing to sleep.

'This isn't so bad,' said Kate quietly as she lay next to Myia on a thin blanket, feeling twigs underneath her spine and looking up at the stars. 'Reminds me of camping trips with my father when I was little. A long time ago.'

'It's all right for now,' whispered Myia, rolling over to look at her. 'But I'm worried about when the monsoon comes. It's not due for a few weeks but the monks said it would come early this year.'

'I hope they're wrong,' said Kate.

In the early hours she woke and found herself unable to get back to sleep. She got up and paced in a slow, wide circle around the campsite, every nerve alert to strange noises and rustling in the undergrowth. Once she heard a shout in the distance and twice a vehicle crunched its way along the road nearby.

She threw more wood on the fire and lay down again, tense and still. She slept a little more, but it was fitful, and when the sun rose a few hours later she felt unrested.

27

Worcestershire, September 1933

'*W*hat did the doctor say?' asked Kate's mother as she drew the curtains in her husband's room.

'Oh, the usual,' he said, sighing.

'No improvement?'

'Not that he mentioned.' She reached for the cup on his bedside table, and he took her hand. 'The outlook isn't bright, my love. I don't know what I'd do without you.'

Kate, passing on the landing, saw her mother lean to kiss his head. 'Don't be silly,' she said, folding down the collar of his nightshirt. 'Perhaps we might get another opinion?'

'Thwaites knows what he's talking about. And besides, it's an unnecessary expense.'

'We can find the money.'

He shook his head. 'No need. I'll keep taking the stuff he gives me and we'll keep plodding on.'

'We always do.'

He smiled up at her wearily. 'Have those logs been brought up from the wood, yet? I heard the trees coming down yesterday.'

'Kate brought them up with the donkey this morning. She and I are going to put them in the woodshed later.'

'She's a good girl.'

Kate tiptoed quickly down the stairs and went to look for her thick gloves.

✳

'How do you manage to be so brave?' said Kate, feeling the heavy axe between her hands and lining up the next log.

'About what?'

'Everything.'

Her mother thought about it. 'It doesn't feel like bravery to me,' she said at last. 'This is just – life. Often difficult but with moments of joy. Those moments are what keeps me going, I suppose.'

'But you've drawn the short straw,' said Kate. 'It's been hard, hasn't it?'

Her mother shook her head. 'Do you know, I often feel as though I'd got the long straw. I feel lucky.'

'How can you?'

'I married your father in 1909,' said her mother, throwing split logs into the corner of the woodshed. 'Most of my friends married around the same time. Several of them had their first children in 1910, the year I had Laura. And then the war came. How many of their husbands do you think came home?'

Kate was silent, knowing that no answer was required. All through her childhood they had visited friends of her mother's, who sat in their drawing rooms, bright and intelligent as they discussed schooling, holidays, friends.

She did not see them properly until later; only her mother noticed how carefully made up their fragile faces were and how their voices cracked when they spoke of the future, and how it was always the help's day off when people happened to call.

'Of the six who were bridesmaids at my wedding, only Jenny and Victoria have living husbands,' said her mother. She pulled off her thick gloves for a moment and looked critically at the calloused palms of her hands. 'And Jenny's is in a wheelchair.'

'It's not fair,' said Kate as she thudded the axe down, feeling a sense of satisfaction as the log split perfectly in half. She picked up another and carried it back to the block, positioning it carefully. 'On any of you.'

Her mother shrugged. 'Nothing to be done.'

'Do you ever wish things had been different?' said Kate. 'That you'd not married at all, or at least married someone who wouldn't have to fight?'

'No,' said her mother simply, shaking her head. 'I wonder, sometimes, but I don't wish. The only choices we can make are those we're meant to make.'

'What choices did you make?'

Carrying an armful of logs, her mother looked thoughtful. 'Did I ever tell you about Rupert?'

'No. Who was Rupert?'

'We were very nearly engaged,' said her mother. 'This was – oh, about 1907, I suppose. He was an Irish landowner's son, staying with friends somewhere near here, and they brought him along to a Hunt Ball. We danced together every night for two weeks. He was very open about pursuing me and I fell head over heels for him, although I don't suppose he knew that we were poor. In those days one tried to hide it. He was going back to Ireland and invited a big party of us to join him for a week in Limerick with lots of Irish friends. I was all set to go with them.'

'What did Grandfather think of that?' said Kate, flexing the stiff muscles in her arms.

'He wasn't too impressed, as you can imagine, but he was persuaded that it would all be very respectable. Several friends were going and all of Rupert's aunts and sisters would be there. What I didn't tell him was that I knew Rupert was going to ask me to marry him.'

'And what happened?'

'I stayed with friends in Fishguard the night before the ferry. The others had gone on ahead, so it was just me. They took me to the harbour. We were running a bit late, but I would just have made it.'

'And?' Kate prompted. She had stopped chopping, waiting to hear the end of the story.

Her mother laughed. 'And I didn't get on the ferry. I watched it steam out of Fishguard Harbour and away towards Ireland without me on it. Then I got on a train and came home.'

'But – why?'

'As I got out of the carriage I had this sudden feeling that the future waiting for me over there wasn't mine. It would have been more materially comfortable, but it wasn't the right one. It's not often in life you get such a clear choice: to get on the ship or not get on the ship. So I didn't, and watched that possible life disappear for good. I met your father the following year when he came to the farm to see your grandfather about insurance.'

'What happened to Rupert?'

'Oh, he got engaged to someone else – a girl he'd met that week in Limerick, as a matter of fact.' Kate's mother shook her head and threw another log into the corner. 'We lost touch after that. I don't even know if he survived the war.'

She dusted down her overalls and pointed. 'Look, there are just a few left. Get those split and then we can finish off here and have some tea with your father.'

Kate lined up a gnarled log, eyeing it carefully, and then lifted the axe, feeling the smooth wooden handle under her fingers, and brought it down sharply. The two halves of the log fell neatly to either side.

'Perfect,' said her mother, gathering them up. She looked kindly at Kate. 'What I mean is that life is a series of choices. There's no way around it, although sometimes they are taken out of your hands. And every big decision you make leaves a life unlived, a sort of alternative life, that disappears.'

'A ghost ship,' said Kate.

'Exactly,' said her mother. 'You can't make it turn back and you can't get another ship to the same place. It's gone. All you can do is wave from the shore.'

28

Upper Burma, May 1942

The second day was worse. Blistered feet and aching leg muscles affected everyone, particularly Mrs Bryant, and progress was slow.

They stopped for lunch in a clearing, where an Indian family sat grouped around their heavy bags, looking exhausted. Their young daughter had been stung by an insect and her ankle was swollen.

'You'd better lift that up as high as you can,' said Fred. 'It should help to reduce the swelling.' He pulled out an army first aid kit and rummaged through it while Kate introduced their party.

'How far have you come?' she said.

'From Prome,' said Sameer, the father, coughing painfully. 'We've lived there for many years.'

'We've never been to India,' said the little boy, Satish, watching as his mother Nabanita took the battered tube of ointment Fred had found. She looked at it rather dubiously but applied it liberally to Shreya's ankle.

'Where are you heading?' asked Mrs Bryant.

'I have cousins in Bombay,' said Nabanita. 'We will go to them. We had to leave everything behind.' She gave the ointment back to Fred and looked anxiously at the swelling, smoothing her daughter's hair.

'I had a small business in Prome,' said Sameer. He coughed painfully, and his thin body shook. 'I've lost everything. I do not know what we will do. You have left your homes, too?'

'We live – lived – in Maymyo,' said Mrs Bryant, gesturing to Christopher. 'My late husband brought us to Burma for his work and we stayed on.'

'Will you go back to England?' asked Sameer.

'I suppose so,' said Mrs Bryant. 'Do you know, I haven't really thought about it.'

'Let's take it one step at a time,' said Fred. 'There'll be plenty of time for making plans once we get to Fort Hertz.' He looked at the sun, which dazzled through the trees. 'We ought to be getting on.'

'So should we,' said Sameer.

'Shreya cannot walk,' said Nabanita, looking imploringly at her husband. 'Let us stay here for the night.'

'You ought to keep moving,' said Fred. 'The Japanese may only be a day or two behind us.'

'What about Shreya?'

'I'll carry her,' said Fred, and took off his knapsack. He looked at Shreya appraisingly. 'Why, I've carried lunch bags heavier than you!'

'I should carry her,' said Sameer, standing up. 'I'm her father, it's my duty.'

Fred laid a hand on the younger man's shoulder. 'You don't look well yourself. She will make you much slower, which is no use to any of us. Let me take her – I promise I will be as gentle with her as if she were my own.'

✦

They camped that night in an abandoned animal shelter, a little way off the road. As she chewed steadily at her watery rice Kate realised that from now on every night would be the same, every day the same, and each step would take her further away from the country that she had grown to love. Leaving meant surviving, she knew that, but it was a bitter pill to swallow.

'Are you all right?' she said quietly to Myia, watching her fiddle once again with her necklace. 'Did your fiancé give you that?'

Myia nodded. 'It was a promise. I can't bear to let go of it yet.'

'Where is he?'

'For a long time I didn't know,' said Myia. 'He told me he had business to attend to and then just . . . disappeared. I thought he no longer loved me. But I had a letter.'

'A letter from him?'

'Yes. From Denpo. He had been in Japan.'

Kate stared at her as the implications of this sank in. 'Did you know he was going there?'

'No. I supposed that he and his friends would be working to undermine the British somehow but I never supposed that they would join forces with the Japanese.'

'What was he doing there?'

'He didn't say.'

She understood now why Myia had seemed so preoccupied, almost since the day they had met. 'Was he alone?'

Myia shook her head. 'He follows another young man, a rebel leader called Aung San. I am sure he went with him to Japan, perhaps many others too. I had not heard from him for over a year when the letter came.' She chewed her lip. 'He said he still loved me.'

'Oh, Myia.'

'I didn't know what to do. I wrote back but heard nothing.' She looked up at Kate. 'He's not a bad person. It hasn't always been easy, under the British. These men believe that Burma should be ruled by the Burmese.'

It's hard to argue with, thought Kate, although she recoiled at the thought of Denpo collaborating with the enemy. Was he, even now, marching through Upper Burma with a rifle in his hand, rounding up the Britons and Indians who were left behind? How far would he go in his desire to rid Burma of the British imperialists?

'Did he know your family worked for the British?'

'Oh yes,' said Myia, smiling ruefully. 'I think he hoped to convince me one day that they were not my friends. I would never betray those I care about, though – in fact, I hoped to change *his* mind. I suppose we were a very poor match.'

'How did you meet him?'

'Through friends, in Mandalay. He was part of a *Yoke thé* troupe – a puppet show. He was so clever and so kind. I loved him at once.' She smiled, her eyes full of tears.

'He sounds like a good man.'

'He is,' said Myia, although she looked uncertain. 'I hope he will remember it before long.' She looked down at the silver crescent and tucked it back into her blouse. 'I do not think I will ever see him again.'

✦

The monsoon and the army arrived on the same day. Six days of walking had passed, each much like the last, a monotonous trudge along a rough, dry track that seemed to go on forever. The middle of the day was gaspingly hot, the nights sticky and humid. At each camp they kept a fire burning to deter tigers.

Now and then they passed an abandoned car or truck that had broken down or run out of fuel. Each time Fred tried to get it going again, but to no avail. Also littering the roadside were bags of clothing, personal belongings and even occasional items of furniture.

One morning it began to rain and soon the drizzle became a deluge. They walked on. Kate felt her feet being rubbed raw and her clothes were suddenly soaked and heavy. The children scampered around at first, delighted to catch the first raindrops, but by afternoon they looked miserable and exhausted.

At a crossroads they found an army jeep with four young Indian soldiers perched on the bonnet. They looked as though they would rather be anywhere else.

'The road to Fort Hertz is closed,' said their leader, gesturing with his rifle. 'We expect a Japanese attack there any day.'

'Which way should we go instead?' asked Fred, pulling out his sodden map.

They pointed to a turning a few miles ahead that would take the group westwards. 'This route will take you via the Hukawng Valley and Shinbwiyang towards Assam. The Indian government is setting up aid camps in the hills. If you keep going that way you should join up with them.'

'I had hoped to avoid the Hukawng Valley,' said Fred.

'It's a dangerous route,' said Myia. 'It will be very risky. Especially in this season.' The rest of the group, already sunk in the misery of sore feet and wet clothes, said nothing.

*

They followed a precipitous path through the hills for two days, and at last the ground began to slope away, although the shadowy outlines of other mountains rose nearby.

'This must be the valley,' said Myia. They stood on a high promontory in the trees, looking out at the dense forest before them.

'How far is it to India?' asked Satish.

'A long way, my boy,' said Fred heavily. 'Hundreds of miles.'

'It sounds very far,' said Nabanita, her voice quavering. 'I am worried.' She gripped her husband's hand and stared out at the curtain of rain that fell over the valley. Her children looked anxiously up at her.

'We have no choice,' said Sameer.

'Mrs Bryant, take my arm,' said Fred. 'This bit's going to be steep.' He looked back at the group and jerked his head. 'Come on, everyone. Let's just take it day by day.'

They scrambled slowly down, clinging on to shrubs and vines, following a winding path. Kate looked around. The jungle seemed sinister, with gnarled evergreens and giant ferns looming out of the mist. For a moment she remembered lying beside the pool in Rangoon with Edwin, laughing and gazing up at the blue sky. It seemed another world, and she pushed the thought of him away. At least Myia, who knew the country, was here, as well as Fred, so strong and dependable. She felt already that she would trust him with her life.

The trees closed overhead, and soon the only sounds were the rustling of leaves and the heavy falling rain.

29

Tavoy, June 1942

Edwin was woken by a banging on the cell door, the same as every day. Fumbling for his glasses, he pulled on his tattered shoes and followed the other prisoners out into the yard, the air already sticky in the early morning.

They stood in rows, heads bowed, as Japanese officers ticked off their numbers on a list. The captain stood at the far end, watching impassively.

Hundreds of men stood in the yard. Some of them were Burmese, but there were also many Indians and Europeans, soldiers who had been captured as the Japanese tightened their grip on the countries of Asia. Edwin had heard Australian voices in the distance, and also what he guessed was Dutch, spoken by men who were rumoured to have been brought from Java. He had been a prisoner for weeks; he thought five or six, but the days merged into one another and he could only guess at the date.

One of the lieutenants called to the captain and he marched over to where the officer stood in front of a young Burmese man. The two Japanese conferred and then both looked at the prisoner, who was visibly trembling, his hands knotting and unknotting the ragged *longyi* that was all he wore. The officer grabbed the man by the shoulder and dragged him forward out of the line to a clear spot.

'Kneel!' he barked, and the man knelt in the dirt. The captain studied him carefully and then lashed out with the back of his hand, sending him reeling.

'You are thief,' he said. It was a statement of fact, not a question.

He slapped the man again, drawing blood from his nose and cheek and he knelt again and cowered.

'This man,' said the captain, looking around at the assembled lines of men, who watched with trepidation, 'this man steal. He steal bread from kitchen, and we think not first time. He steal from *you!*'

Before the man could move the officer beside him kicked him, hard, and he rolled over onto his side, groaning. But they were not finished. Taking turns, the two Japanese men kicked him in the side and head. He curled into a ball but there was no escaping the onslaught.

'Stop!'

The shout came from an Indian man in the row nearby. He was young, twenty-five or so, with dark hair curled around his cheeks and a thick beard. He was much taller than the Japanese men and towered over the Burmese. His fists were clenched.

'He was starving. His rations were cut because his shovel broke.'

'Quiet,' said the captain, and approached the Indian man, staring impassively at him.

'But—'

'If you speak again, you die.'

170

The man was silent. On the ground the prisoner lay whimpering, blood running from his head. He tried to sit up but the pain was too much and he slumped back down.

The captain barked an order in Japanese. The officer lifted his rifle and stood over the writhing figure, taking his time, walking around him to find the best angle. He held it aloft, the blade of the bayonet glinting. Then it was thrust down with a sickening crunch, once, twice, three times, until the ground was swilling with blood.

Edwin felt his underarms prickling with sweat, disgust rising in his throat.

'And him,' said the captain, jerking his head at the Indian and speaking briefly to his men in Japanese. He looked at the man and frowned. 'You will be punished.'

Looking around at the lines of prisoners, he raised his voice. 'This what we do to men who steal. Thieves will die. Men who speak out of turn will be beaten. If you do again,' he said, turning to the Indian man, 'then you die.'

They dragged the unprotesting man out of the line, making him kneel, and the captain took his narrow sword from its sheath, handing it to the officer. He watched calmly as the officer lifted the sword high and then brought it down, the flat of the blade connecting with the man's back with a stinging slap.

The man flinched but immediately tensed again, his body bent over. More strokes came and Edwin could see his fists clenched on the ground, his whole body absorbing the blows. The surrounding men watched silently.

Finally, when blood began to show through the man's khaki shirt, they stopped. He was pulled up and shoved back into the line.

'Next time,' said the captain, 'you die.'

Orders were shouted, and the lines of prisoners marched out of the yard. The Indian man passed where Edwin stood, his handsome face rigid with pain. Watching him go, Edwin saw his back, where bloody stripes seeped through his shirt.

✦

All that week they toiled on the hillside, where the new road towards India snaked slowly north. Each day, after a breakfast of rice gruel, they were taken by truck to the worksite where they shovelled earth and stones for ten hours before being taken back to the camp as darkness fell.

Edwin felt stronger and yet more wretched than ever before. There were times when he felt that he could not go on, when it seemed that his body could not take any more. Sometimes he stood and gasped for breath between shovel-loads and wished to collapse and die there on the road. But a shout would come from the over-seer and he would find, somehow, the strength to go on again.

At night he looked with surprise at the muscles that were suddenly visible, though his body was thinner than ever, and his hands and feet were blistered and bloody.

Keeping sane was his priority, although he had no idea how. Sometimes he recited poems in his head, and often found himself trying to recite whole books that he had known and loved, a thousand years ago. *Oliver Twist* had been his favourite book as a boy, and each night before sleep he found the opening lines coming to his mind.

Occasionally one of the work groups would not be needed on the road, and they were put to work chopping wood, sweeping the yard, folding sacks, or one of a hundred other tasks.

On these days Edwin found that he was able to think, something that on the road he barely had the time or energy to do. He could hardly remember the faces of those he had known before Burma, although Emilia's voice sometimes echoed in his dreams. Kate came often to his mind, and he hoped that she was safe. He remembered the strange moments they had shared and wondered where she was. He imagined that she was in India already, trying to make herself useful. Kate, who hated to sit still, would not be content to wait the war out.

✦

Raking gravel one day in the drizzling rain, Edwin saw the tall Indian man who had been beaten by the Japanese. He was shifting sacks of stones, his strong arms lifting them on and off his shoulder with ease. He wore shorts and a ragged shirt, and battered army boots.

'I saw what you did that day in the yard,' said Edwin. It felt strange speaking, after so long almost silent. 'I thought it was very brave.'

The man looked at him and shrugged. 'It was foolish, I think.' He looked too young and mild to be a soldier, but his arms were thickly muscled and his shoulders broad.

He heaved the sack off his shoulder and dropped it with a thud on the ground. 'The man died anyway.'

'At least you tried.'

'Would you do the same?'

Edwin was taken aback. 'Me? Oh, no. I'm not brave at all.'

They worked in silence for a while. Edwin felt his shirt sticking to his back and a terrible dry thirst in his throat. He swallowed and wondered if he could drink the rain that pooled in the mud around his feet.

'Yet here you are,' said the man.

'I'm sorry?'

'You're here, in this camp. Which means you stayed on in Burma when the rest of your people had gone.' He looked over at Edwin and gave a small smile. 'You have been brave.'

Edwin cleared his throat and looked away, discomfited, busying himself with the spade. He shovelled hard, feeling the blisters on his hand burst as he dug.

'I'm Edwin,' he said as an afterthought.

'Rama,' said the man and smiled again. 'Like the wolf in your Mr Kipling's stories.'

⁘

The next day Rama worked beside him again and at lunchtime, as they ate their pathetic ration of rice, they sat side by side in the dirt.

'How did you come to be here?' asked Edwin, but he immediately regretted the question, for the young man beside him looked depressed.

'They killed my friends,' he said at last.

'I'm sorry.'

'We were separated from our unit. We came across a village in the jungle where the inhabitants had all been killed. Men's tongues cut out, women and girls raped and then killed with bayonets.' He gave a shuddering sigh. 'We started to bury them. Then a group of enemy soldiers came back and found us.'

Edwin felt the hairs on his arms stand up as he listened. How was it possible that such horrors could take place?

'They put the others in a row by a ditch and made them kneel,' said Rama, his hands kneading the forgotten rice to a sticky pulp. 'Then they killed them.' He shook his head. 'I thought they were going to kill me, too, but instead they took away my turban and used it for target practice, laughing. Why did they let me live?'

'I ask myself the same question every day,' said Edwin hesitantly. 'For over a year I've wondered why I am alive.'

'A year?' said Rama. 'What happened to you?'

'Last May,' said Edwin, swallowing the last bit of rice with difficulty. 'I suppose you know that London was bombed by Germany?'

For a moment he wondered why he was telling Rama this, but he felt an affinity with the young soldier and knew instinctively that he understood the pain and the grief of being left behind.

'Yes,' said Rama.

'My wife was killed. Our house was hit. I wasn't there.'

'But you might as well have been,' said Rama.

'Exactly. I failed to protect her. When the Japs caught me I thought my time had come. I was so scared, but I had this feeling that God was simply catching up with me. That it had been an oversight that I'd survived and that now the debt was being collected.'

'Did they hurt you?'

'A bit. It was a stick, though, not a sword. Not like your—' He gestured at Rama's back, remembering how the Japanese had struck him.

Rama lifted his shirt and half-turned. The thick welts on his back were red and raw, showing livid on his dark skin.

'Does it still hurt?'

'Yes.'

'Mine are mostly healed,' said Edwin, and pulled up the frayed cotton of his shirt, twisting to look at the thin silver lines that crossed his back.

Rama leaned forward to examine them. He lifted a hand and for a moment his warm fingers touched Edwin's pale skin. Edwin started at the strange intimacy of it and stood quickly, his shirt falling back down to cover the scars.

30

The Hukawng Valley, June 1942

They were now deep in the Hukawng Valley, following paths that led gradually west. The weather was cool and wet and they all suffered from colds, malnourishment, and the unpleasant effects of constant dampness. Kate watched the skin on her feet starting to peel away, initially with disgust and then, as time went by, with a detached interest.

The food they carried was mostly rice, and when it was too wet to make a fire they rationed the remaining tinned food, pulled up forest greens, or simply went hungry.

Often they slept in huts that were dotted through the jungle. Some of them were abandoned native huts, which Fred called bashas, but many more had been built from bamboo and plantain leaves by other refugees who had passed that way. Once they found the dead bodies of two men in a hut and moved swiftly on, making an excuse before the children saw.

Somewhere in the depths of the Hukawng Valley they camped one night, repairing a battered hut that lay a few yards from the path. In the morning the little boy Satish started a fever, so they stayed for another day, and then another, the others using the time to rest and scout for food as he lay sweating and shivering under a rug.

'We ought to push on,' said Fred, peering at his map. 'I think we're only a few days' walk from Shinbwiyang. It's meant to be one of the biggest villages, there might be a doctor there.'

'My son is too sick to travel,' said Sameer anxiously. 'We cannot move him.'

Fred folded up the map and put it away, catching Kate's eye as he did so. He beckoned, and she followed him a little way out of the camp.

'What should we do?' she said.

'The boy needs medicine,' said Fred, looking back at the shelter. 'If they won't bring him I think I'd better try to get to Shinbwiyang, bring back some quinine or whatever they have.'

Kate stared at him. 'Leave us, you mean? You can't go off alone!'

'I'm not worried about being alone,' he said, shaking his head. 'Will you be all right, though? You and Myia will have to look after the others.'

'Of course,' she said. 'I wish there was another way, though.' She imagined nights in the forest without Fred's comforting presence, knowing that she would jump at every crack of a twig.

'It's got to be done.' He observed her intently for a moment. 'You look as though you might have a slight fever, too.'

She touched her forehead and felt it hot under her hand. Her skin was damp with sweat and she realised that she had been exhausted for days, even more so than usual.

He patted her shoulder and, without thinking, she reached up to take his hand in hers.

'You'll take care of them. You're stronger than you think.' He looked up at the sky, which was darkening. 'I'll leave first thing in the morning.'

✦

Kate sat up late with Myia, talking quietly and watching over little Satish while his parents took turns trying to get some sleep. Eventually Nabanita gave up the attempt and took over, holding his clammy hand as he slept fitfully.

Kate curled up nearby, but she felt as though a weight was pressing down on her chest, making her breathing shallow. Sleep seemed impossible. She was afraid of what would happen when Fred left; afraid that the fragile normality they had constructed would shatter. She recalled the way she had touched his hand earlier and her cheeks flushed in the darkness. It was odd, this closeness she felt to him, and she had no wish to examine it too closely, but she was afraid that once he vanished into the jungle he would never return.

Eventually she slept and dreamed of fire raining down on London. She saw Parliament ablaze, black smoke coating the city, and a woman in a yellow dress running frantically. She saw that it was her sister Laura and that she was carrying a baby. Smoke rose from the buildings all around. There were dozens of people looking through the wreckage and they were all searching for someone, but a voice said firmly, 'He is gone.'

Kate awoke from her short sleep as it was getting light. All was silent, and then came the gasping, heaving sound of crying just a few yards from her head. Sitting up blearily, she saw

Nabanita crouched over, her arms clasped around her son's body, pressing it to her breast and shaking with sobs.

✶

It seemed to Kate later that that moment had been a turning point; the point at which her old life had ended and the new one had begun. She had seen death before, but now it was everywhere. In the Hukawng Valley anyone could get sick and die, and no one would come to save them.

Fred abandoned his plan to leave for Shinbwiyang and she felt shamefully relieved. Late in the afternoon, he knelt down beside the grieving parents. 'Tomorrow we must continue our journey. I know this isn't easy.'

'What about Satish?' asked Nabanita, looking at him with swollen eyes. 'We can't just leave him!'

'We must bury him,' said Fred sombrely.

'That is not our way,' said Sameer as he cradled his son's body.

Fred knelt beside him and laid a hand on the young man's shoulder. 'I'm afraid cremation will be impossible – the wood is too wet and the rain keeps falling.'

He and Christopher helped Sameer to dig a shallow grave at the edge of the clearing, using sticks and cooking implements and finally their hands, as Mrs Bryant stitched a shroud from a bedsheet, her swollen hands clumsy. Shreya sat beside her, silently passing her pins and scissors.

'What are Indian funerals usually like?' asked Christopher, when Sameer and Nabanita had retreated to the shelter to prepare Satish's body, their weeping audible.

'Sameer's family are Hindus, but it varies between religions,' said Fred. 'I went to a Hindu funeral in Varanasi. It was rather wonderful, actually. The father of a man from my regiment. They burned him for hours and then took the ashes down to the Ganges and flung them in as the sun began to set.'

✳

It was almost dark by the time the funeral began. They held what candles and torches they could muster, and stood in a ring around the grave as the body was lowered in.

Nabanita began to sing a Hindu song, unfamiliar to Kate, but she thought it very beautiful in its melancholy. It made her think of the funeral that Fred had described, and she pictured the crowds of mourners in white, the embers burning low, and the elation as the loved one was cast into the sacred Ganges, blood-red under a setting sun. She remembered her father's burial, and the numbness that had overcome her, standing in the cold churchyard, gripping her mother's hand as the vicar droned on. This seemed far more real, and more final.

It was the strangest funeral that Kate had ever been to, and the saddest, she thought, as she watched the grave being filled in and all that was left of little Satish disappeared under the black earth.

31

The Hukawng Valley, June 1942

After the funeral they travelled west for several days. They came to a river, where the remains of a log bridge perched uselessly on each side as the water rushed past, muddy and laden with sticks and leaves. The river was wide and the whole main section of the bridge was gone.

'Must have come down in a storm,' said Fred, surveying the torrent. The banks were high and the trees went almost to the edge. Peering down, Kate could see that the river was deep here, and that the cliff was too steep to get down to it safely.

'How are we to get across?' said Nabanita, gripping Shreya's hand tightly. There were dark circles under her eyes and she walked as if she was in a dream. Her jewelled sandals had come almost to pieces and the frayed hem of her sari was stained black by mud.

'We could build a new bridge,' said Christopher, but Fred shook his head.

'It's too big a job. These bridges are usually built with the help of elephants.'

'If only we had an elephant,' said Shreya.

Mrs Bryant was leaning heavily on Christopher's arm and he helped her to sit down on a fallen tree. She winced, and Kate saw how swollen her ankles were.

'We'll carry you over, if necessary,' said Christopher, patting his mother's shoulder.

'Don't be silly, darling.'

'I mean it!'

'I'll get across the same way as everyone else. Walking, I expect.'

'I'm going to look for a crossing,' said Fred, heaving his bag onto the floor.

'I'll come with you,' said Christopher quickly, and they scrambled off along the bank.

Kate laid her head back against a tree and closed her eyes. Fever had been threatening for days, but she had pushed through it, reluctant to slow or worry the others when there were much weaker members of the party. Fred, she knew, could see through her bravado.

'Which river is this?' she heard Mrs Bryant ask.

'I think it's the Chindwin,' said Myia, who was pacing on the bank. 'It starts in the mountains somewhere near here. Or perhaps this feeds into the Chindwin.'

The roar of the water was so deafening that Kate could hardly hear herself think, and it was almost a relief. With her eyes closed the rest of her senses seemed heightened, and focusing on the noise of the river she began to identify the different sounds that made it up: the trickling over rocks near the bank, the splashing of waves at a sharp bend, the shifting of pebbles, and under it all, the low murmur of the current in the depths.

'Mama?'

Kate's eyes flew open. Nabanita was standing on the broken section of bridge that projected over the river. She had taken off her shoes but her knapsack was on her back. She was very close to the edge, staring down at the rushing water below.

'Come down, Nabanita,' said Sameer sharply. 'You're scaring Shreya.'

She looked back at him, as though waking suddenly, and stared at him and their daughter.

'Please come down,' he said, and now he sounded more gentle. He pushed Shreya wordlessly towards Mrs Bryant, who took her into her arms and stroked her hair, holding her hand tightly. They watched as he scrambled up and Kate could hear him talking quietly to Nabanita.

For a moment she was quite sure that Nabanita was about to jump into the river and was frozen, knowing that there was nothing to be done. She looked so hopeless, standing there in her filthy sari, the golden chains around her ankles caked in mud. The misery emanating from her was almost visible and Kate imagined a great black cloud of grief that would smother them all.

Then it was over and Sameer was helping Nabanita down, both of them trembling, and Christopher appeared, running, to let them know that he and Fred had found a crossing a short distance away, a ferry run by a group of Kachin boatmen, who took the group across in twos and threes on a sturdy raft, their bare feet deft on the knotted wood. Kate fumbled in her bag for coins and watched Sameer holding tightly to Nabanita and Shreya as they were taken across.

They climbed off into the shallows, holding hands unsteadily. Nabanita staggered out of the water and sat down on a rock, her tears mingling with spray from the river as they ran down her cheeks.

✦

'Do you believe in ghosts?' said Kate the next day, looking at Fred as they walked side by side.

He shrugged. 'I don't know if I believe in classical ghosts, white misty figures in castles and all that. But I saw things during the war that made me think there was something else. Why do you ask?'

'I was thinking of the green ghosts that the Burmese talk about. Restless spirits.'

'You sound sceptical.'

She thought of the human remains they had seen littering the route. The dead were with them, sure enough, but it was impossible to connect the physical remnants with whatever else might be left behind.

But perhaps she did know about ghosts. After all, hadn't she felt her father's presence on the farm until she moved away? Those early mornings, watching the sun come up over the meadows, mist billowing, when she had been sure he was standing just out of sight under the eaves of the barn, keeping an eye on her. In Burma he might have been a green ghost.

'Ghosts mean different things to different people,' said Fred, as though she had spoken aloud. 'I think the dead stay with us – to remind us.'

'Remind us of what?'

'Not to waste it.'

I wish I knew how, thought Kate, looking down at the thick mulch of leaves beneath her feet. I have spent so long grieving that I barely remember what it was I wanted to do with my life. Is there still time to salvage it, to make something worthwhile?

'Who are your ghosts?' she asked. It was an intimate question, she knew, and for a moment she thought he wasn't going to answer.

'My brother died on the *Lusitania*,' said Fred. 'You won't remember it, of course, you're too young. I forget how much time has passed.'

'During the last war, wasn't it? I was just a baby,' said Kate.

Fred nodded, frowning slightly. 'Graham was on the crew, working in the engine room. He'd been in trouble with the law, petty stuff really, but our parents thought he'd be safer at sea, find some discipline.'

There was a chattering in the trees as some unseen animal leapt from branch to branch, shaking down a heavy patter of raindrops. Kate peered into the foliage for a moment, but whatever it was had already moved on.

'I wouldn't have known what happened to him, except that a friend of his who'd survived came to find me in Liverpool later that year when we were both home on leave. Tom, his name was. He told me about the torpedo and the sinking, about the mad panic that spread through the decks when they realised the Germans had got them. It all happened so fast – they were only a few miles off the Irish coast.'

'What happened to Graham?'

'As the ship was going down, people were fighting to get on the lifeboats. Graham spent the last minutes of his life helping people into the boats – frightened women, screaming children. This fellow Tom was with him, but he said he'd have bolted for a place himself long before without Graham's example. The two of them, and doubtless many others, stayed on board until all the lifeboats were full. Hundreds more were trapped below deck.'

'And what happened then?' asked Kate, not sure if she wanted to hear the rest.

'They jumped overboard – the ship was sinking fast beneath them and they had to swim hard so they weren't sucked down. They got separated in the crush, and by the time Tom was rescued by a ship from Cork, my brother must have been long dead.'

Fred glanced back at the rest of the party, who were some way off. 'Tom survived by using the bodies of the dead as a raft. He was shaking and crying as he told me all this, although of course I didn't blame him. We all do what we must to survive. They'd died as they hit the water, most of them, and the others froze to death pretty quickly. He hauled himself up onto the bodies and kept mostly above water.'

Kate felt a chill even in the sticky afternoon heat. Through a gap in the trees she could see a mountain range in the distance, just visible under a bank of heavy clouds. They were capped with snow and spears of sunlight fell from the unseen sun, making the white tips gleam.

'He had hypothermia and when he got to Dublin he was a wreck. Once he came out of hospital he went home for a bit, but he was called up not long after, poor lad.'

'It was good of him to find you.'

'He wanted me to know how Graham had behaved when the ship was sinking. He guessed, rightly, that it would help the family to know that his last actions had been selfless and kind.'

He stared absently at the dripping jungle that flanked them on all sides. 'That was Graham all over, of course. He was always kind. He made some mistakes, but when it came to the crunch I imagine he knew he was going to die and used his time wisely. I suppose that's what I'm trying to say. I think – or hope – that there's always time for redemption. Graham is with me whenever I start to worry about doing the right thing, hovering somewhere nearby.'

It was a startling thought and Kate considered the idea. Was her father with her? She wanted to believe that something, anything, remained. Fred must have been only a young man when his brother died. He had carried Graham with him for nearly thirty years.

'I hope it gave your parents some comfort to know what he did at the end.'

'I think it did,' said Fred, 'although my mother was never quite the same. She didn't want me coming out here, thought she'd never see me again. Rightly, as it turned out. They're both long gone now.'

'What became of Tom?' asked Kate.

'The war,' said Fred, heaving a sigh. 'Killed at Ypres in 1917, I gathered.'

'My friend Edwin,' said Kate, hearing her voice tremble, 'this chap I met in Rangoon. He had done something that he was terribly ashamed of – his wife died, you see, and he wasn't there. He seemed lost, didn't know what he wanted, but I suppose that was it: he was looking for redemption, too. A chance to forgive himself.'

'He'll get it,' said Fred, sounding certain. 'He might not know it, but he will. We're not defined by our mistakes. It's what we do next that matters.'

'I hope you're right.'

'You've spoken of him before,' said Fred quietly, with a half smile. 'He sounds like a good friend.'

She sensed the question behind the words. 'More like a brother, really,' she said. 'I worry about him.'

'He'll be well out of Mandalay by now,' said Fred. 'It sounds as though the city has been completely overrun.'

'I hope he's safe.'

'There are other routes than this one. If he's lucky he may have fallen in with the army as they retreat west. Or perhaps through the Taungup Pass – it may still be possible to get to Chittagong.'

'What stories we shall all have to tell when we get to India,' said Kate. She saw Fred glance at her. 'What? You don't think we'll get there?'

'We'll get there,' said Fred steadily.

'What, then?'

He shrugged. 'I admire your optimism.' He shifted the heavy load and she heard his back click as he stretched it. 'You're a good sort of companion for this journey, Kate.'

'I was just thinking the same.' She watched him as he turned back to wait for the rest of the group. The rain began again, gentle at first, but soon heavy raindrops were bouncing off leaves all around. Looking back towards the mountains, she saw that the clouds had descended and the snowy peaks were out of sight.

32

The Hukawng Valley, June 1942

The road towards Shinbwiyang was ankle-deep in mud and progress was slow as they trudged along it the following morning, shoulders hunched in the pouring rain. Often, now, they saw among the trees the remains of travellers who had not survived the journey – decaying bodies, half-covered by leaves, and sometimes bones that had been picked clean.

After lunch the rain stopped abruptly and the jungle began to steam. Finding a decent campsite in the early afternoon, with a tumbledown hut left by other travellers, they decided to camp early and take advantage of the sun's brief rays.

'We'd best get as many clothes laid out as possible,' said Fred, flinging down his knapsack. 'This could be the last sun for days.'

Within ten minutes every damp and mildewed article of clothing and bedding had been pulled out and now lay steaming in a wide patch of sunlight in a clearing among the trees.

Kate rinsed out her shirt and shorts and laid them to dry, then washed herself, standing knee-deep in the stream, out of sight of the camp. Without soap it was impossible to get all the dirt off her skin, but she was cleaner than she had been in weeks. She retrieved the yellow silk dress from her knapsack and put it on, feeling self-conscious, but it was the only clean thing she had left. The thin silk felt alien against her skin as she wandered back to camp.

'Look, Mother – I've made you a seat, come and sit down.' With Christopher's help Mrs Bryant lowered herself stiffly onto a folded sack and leaned back against a tree.

'Thank you, darling.'

'I'm going to make a swing for Shreya.'

'That's a lovely idea.'

Kate saw how exhausted Mrs Bryant looked. Her feet were swollen and barely fitted into her tattered shoes. The leather had started to come apart and the filthy stockings were in shreds. Her grey hair, which must once have been carefully styled, was pulled back in a limp bun. She looked old and it was hard to imagine her getting to the next village, let alone to India.

They watched Christopher at the edge of the woods, show-ing Shreya how to tie sailors' knots. He set her to plaiting vines together to use as a rope and began looking for a suitable seat for the swing.

'Your son is a good boy,' said Nabanita abruptly, sitting down beside Mrs Bryant. Her cheeks were thinner than ever, and she watched as Shreya ran about, picking up sticks for examination. She still plaited Shreya's hair carefully each morning, brushing it over and over until it gleamed.

Mrs Bryant reached out carefully, taking Nabanita's small brown hand in her puffy white one. 'So was yours.'

Nabanita nodded. 'It is very hard for Shreya. I'm glad Christopher is able to make her laugh. It allows her to forget for a little while.' She swallowed. 'I worry that I am failing her.'

'You could never do that.'

'I feel paralysed since Satish died. How will I start again when this is over? I don't want Shreya's whole life to have this shadow over it.'

'She knows that you love her,' said Mrs Bryant. 'That's all they need.'

Kate closed her eyes. She thought of her parents, of how often she had privately raged at them in her youth, frustrated by the constraints of the house and the farm and the feeling that the years were slipping away. But they had loved her unconditionally – that was enough.

Some time later she awoke suddenly. Mrs Bryant was fast asleep against the tree, snoring gently, Nabanita and Sameer were curled side by side on a rug, and Myia was lying gracefully on a patch of warm rocks, her long hair, newly washed, spread out to dry.

She could hear Christopher whistling somewhere nearby, the heavy dripping of water off leaves, and the faint trickling of a nearby stream. The air felt thick and humid. It was late afternoon.

Stretching her stiff limbs, Kate wandered into the jungle, pausing every now and then to examine a plant growing among the trees. Bamboo shoots were usually the only edible things available. She saw Christopher stalking through the undergrowth, carrying a catapult and scanning the trees for wildlife. He saw her and waved before darting away.

The jungle looked quite different when the sun was out. Instead of the usual dark and brooding atmosphere, it felt almost friendly. Birds sang high overhead and once she heard the chattering noise of a monkey as it swung somewhere nearby. Bright flowers bloomed in the distance.

The further away from camp she went, the easier it was to believe that she had dreamed the last few months, and that she was simply taking a walk in the woods. She sat on a low branch and closed her eyes, imagining that she was in the woodland that bordered the farm at home. She remembered an early summer evening, not long after she had left school, when she and her father and mother had walked into the woods to listen to the nightingales.

He walked slowly, leaning on her mother's arm, his breathing laboured, and when they stopped he sat down on a tree stump. Kate stood a little behind them, feeling superfluous. Her mother's hand rested lightly on his shoulder, both of their heads tilted to one side as they listened, just as she imagined they had done when they were courting in the years before the war.

'Do you hear it?' Her mother was smiling as she looked back. Kate tilted her head too, listening intently, and heard the distant sound of the nightingale, a high, sweet song. She smiled back, unaware of what was to come, seeing only her parents – her mother, happy, her father, his eyes closed, looking more at peace than she had ever seen him.

As a child she had pressed flowers, layering pansies and rosebuds carefully between sheets of tissue paper before twisting the screws at the four corners of the press, only opening it when all the moisture had gone and the flowers were dry and flat, their beauty suspended in time. Somehow she had done the same with her memories, pressing them safely away. For a moment the scene was as vivid as it had ever been, and she could have reached out to touch her mother and father, waiting patiently in the wood for the first nightingale of summer.

'Kate? Do you hear it?'

There was a rustling sound nearby. She looked up to see Shreya running towards her.

'Are you all right?'

'Do come and see,' said Shreya, tugging her hand. 'It's the most wonderful thing!'

'What?' said Kate, laughing at her urgency. 'Oh, all right. What is it?'

They ran along the path, leaping over roots and fallen logs, pushing back the vines that dangled overhead, and Kate felt suddenly carefree.

'What – oh!'

She slowed and cocked her head, astonishment dawning on her face. For coming clearly through the trees was music, a tinkling tune that sounded more familiar than her own heartbeat.

'This way,' said Shreya.

The tune went on, growing louder now, and despite the heat Kate felt the hairs on the back of her neck stand up.

They reached a clearing. The sun was sinking and long shadows extended across the grassy meadow. And there, in the middle, was a grand piano. One of its legs was broken, weeds were growing around the others, and there were leaves and twigs all across the lid, which tilted towards the ground. The varnish had begun to bubble and crack from the intense heat and heavy rain.

Fred was standing at the keys, his eyes closed and his shoulders relaxed, playing a wistful melody that soared up and down.

'I know this tune,' said Kate, and she felt tears pricking.

He played on, his fingers moving across the keys without hesitation, his body swaying gently with the tune. Time seemed to pause as they listened, and despite the weeds and the vines that threatened the piano, and the warping of the strings, and

194

the death and pain that hovered just out of sight, Kate had never heard anything more beautiful.

The tempo sped up and she saw Shreya dancing, pretending, perhaps, that she was in a far-away ballroom as she moved gracefully across the clearing. Tears were rolling down her cheeks.

At last the melody soared up once more and then ended, the last high note fading gently away. Fred glanced up and looked suddenly bashful, closing the lid gently then stepping briskly away from the piano.

'Fancy finding this here,' he said. 'In awful condition, of course – you heard the missing strings and the flatness? Such a pity, it must have been a beautiful instrument.'

'How did it get here?' asked Shreya, still swaying dreamily, her long black lashes wet with tears.

Fred shrugged. 'I imagine one of the silly memsahibs thought she could take it with her and then found that no one was keen to carry it. Coolies ditched it, I expect. Who can blame the poor devils? It weighs a tonne.'

'What's that song? Is it British?'

'It's by an English composer, Vaughan Williams,' said Fred. 'It's called "The Lark Ascending". You need a violinist, really – or an orchestra, if you've got one. It's not meant for a solo pianist.'

'Strange hearing it here, of all places,' said Kate. 'It's beautiful.'

'I found it sad,' said Shreya.

'To me . . .' said Fred, and he smiled, 'it's England. All of it, contained in that one tune. A lost world. That's why it's so beautiful. And so sad.'

'Where did you learn to play so well?' asked Kate. His playing had been so sure, so instinctive. She remembered his hands on the wheel of his boat as they steamed up the Irrawaddy, deft and reassuring.

'Once upon a time,' said Fred, 'I was a music student, just before the last war. I had a scholarship to the Royal College in Manchester. I joined up in 1914, planning to go back and finish when it was all over. I never did, of course. I heard that tune at a concert after the war and I've never forgotten it.'

Neither will I, thought Kate dreamily, noticing flecks of dust suspended, glowing, in the dappled light that shone all around them, billowing as Shreya danced again across the clearing. She wondered, not for the first time, why Fred had left England.

'It was my father's favourite, too,' she said, her voice unsteady. 'He played it over and over when we got a gramophone. Then we played it at his funeral. I haven't heard it since.'

Fred nodded. He dusted the lid of the piano ineffectually and ran his hand over the wood. 'I'm sure your father would be very proud of you,' he said at last, catching her eye, and she felt an ache of longing, although she could not have said what she was longing for.

Shreya waltzed back over and looked curiously between them, sensing the strangeness that had fallen.

'Come along,' said Fred, patting Shreya on the shoulder. 'Better get back to camp. Your mother will worry.'

'She won't,' said Shreya. 'She knows I'm tough.'

'All mothers worry,' said Fred. 'And fathers.' He looked at Kate and smiled, as if noticing how she was dressed for the first time. She felt rather foolish in the yellow silk, but Fred said nothing.

Kate followed them out of the clearing, looking back once more at the piano. It would never leave these woods, she knew, and she imagined it sinking slowly into the weeds. Within a few years it would be lost to time, and no one who passed this way would know it had ever existed.

33

Shinbwiyang, June 1942

They reached Shinbwiyang a few days later. What had once been a small village, nestled in the trees, had now been turned into a sprawling refugee camp.

Walking between the ramshackle buildings, flinching at the smell, they immediately saw one of its causes. Mass graves had been dug around the edges of the village, soil piled high, the occasional wooden cross stuck into the earth.

People milled around or sat silently in the entrance to one of the huge dormitories. Children were playing in the distance, but the adults talked quietly; most of them looked miserable and unwell. They glanced at the newcomers without interest.

Kate walked with Fred and Myia through the camp. Among the trees, the thud of hammers could be heard, and voices rang out clearly. As they approached they saw the wooden frame of a building being lifted gently off the ground by several people, as others stood around, watching anxiously.

When it was stable, the English soldier who had been directing proceedings turned to them, wiping his forehead, and introduced himself as Jim. He was skinny and sallow and evidently not well at all.

'If you think it's bad now you should have seen it a couple of weeks ago,' he said. 'People fighting over rations, pushing and shoving the elderly and children, men hitting women. It was anarchy.'

'Everyone looks very sick,' said Myia.

He nodded. 'Cholera, I'm afraid. Plus dysentery, malaria, etcetera.'

'How many people are here?'

'Oh, I couldn't say. Perhaps two thousand.'

'And have you any doctors?'

Jim shook his head. 'There was one, an Indian fellow, but he moved on last week. Before that they tell me there was a French chap, but he didn't stick around either. Funnily enough, no one wants to stay here.'

'So who's in charge?' asked Kate, nodding her head at the camp.

'There's a handful of British chaps running things day to day and trying to keep order. But we've very little food. We've had the occasional drop of supplies from the RAF but it's never enough.'

'The army know you're here?' said Myia. 'But why don't they help?'

Jim looked at her cynically. 'You may well ask. We assume it's because they're overstretched elsewhere. It's impossible to land planes in this jungle so they couldn't airlift everyone out, not by any means, but they could do better than a sack of rice.'

'Is there any help coming?' asked Kate.

'Apparently the army are building camps along the route to India,' said Jim. 'It may be true, but they haven't reached us yet.'

Kate looked glumly at the others.

'How many in your group?' Jim asked, running a hand over his forehead. 'Are they sick?'

'Eight of us,' said Fred. 'Some sickness, mostly malaria.'

'If there was anywhere to go I'd advise you not to stay here,' said Jim. 'I'd get as far away as possible.'

'Some of our party can't go any further,' said Fred.

'Conditions in the hills are atrocious,' said Jim. 'A scout came back yesterday from a reconnaissance mission. The terrain up there makes the valley look like Kew Gardens.'

Kate looked helplessly at Fred. 'We must get to India.' But her limbs felt heavy, and suddenly the idea of walking to India was laughable; it might as well be on the moon.

'That building over there is the clothing exchange,' said Jim. 'They'll give you whatever you need, within reason. Shoes, certainly,' he said to Kate, and with surprise she looked down at her filthy bare feet. She had lost her shoes somewhere along the way but could not have said when or where.

*

A week passed. For Kate it was a time of fever and confusion, as she slept much of the time in the hospital ward and felt oddly distant even while conscious. One night she awoke and thought she heard singing. It sounded like the Indian song that Nabanita had sung at little Satish's funeral. She saw Satish playing in the aisle by her bed, throwing a ball to his father, and knew she was dreaming.

Her fever reached its climax a day or so later and she woke one morning to find that the malaria had receded. Her hair was damp with sweat and she felt weak, but her head was clear for the first time in weeks.

'How do you feel?' asked Myia when she came a little later. She looked tired and pale. Her *longyi* had been replaced by a long cotton skirt and she wore a man's shirt that was much too big for her.

'Better. No more hallucinations. I saw all sorts of things.' Kate hesitated. 'How are the others?'

Myia looked down. 'Sameer is dead.' Kate felt her heart lurch. 'It came on very fast. He had dysentery – there was nothing they could do.'

Kate stared at her. 'What about Nabanita? And Shreya?'

'You can imagine. They won't speak to anyone.'

'Oh, God.'

Left alone, Kate lay looking up at the bamboo ceiling. The ward around her was dirty and noisy, with feverish patients calling out, and children clustered around the immobile forms of their parents. English voices were mixed with the sounds of Hindustani and Burmese. Perhaps they were people she had known back in Rangoon, in another world. She thought of Nabanita and could almost feel the force of her grief radiating through the camp. She had lost too much.

Christopher shuffled in the next day. He looked a little healthier than before, but his young face was lined with anxiety.

'My mother's dying,' he said conversationally as he sat on the end of her plank bed, pulling at a loose thread in the cuff of his shirt.

'Where is she?'

'In the next hut. She's asleep most of the time. Better that way, I suppose.'

Kate squeezed his hand. 'She's been so strong, Christopher. She might make it.'

He shook his head. 'Not this time. The cancer's really taken hold of her, it's all through her body now. And the malaria won't go.' He looked up with a sigh and his eyes were gleaming with tears. 'She won't leave this place.'

✦

Kate felt stronger each day and soon she was able to move out of the hospital into a dormitory. It was a gloomy place where rats scuttled in and out, looking for scraps of leftover food, of which there were few.

Across the room a little Burmese girl played with an empty box, as her mother lay asleep beside her. The woman was thin, and her round face looked worn beyond her years, but she had once been beautiful. She wore a faded *longyi* and was covered by a thick blanket. She coughed occasionally and winced in her sleep.

The little girl caught Kate's eye where she sat reading and came over to look curiously at her book, a silver bracelet sliding down her small wrist.

'Hello,' said Kate, smiling up at her. 'What's your name?'

'Mi Khin,' said the little girl. 'And you?'

'Kate. Is your mother sick?'

'I do not know,' said Mi Khin, looking anxiously back to where her mother lay asleep. 'She says not. But she sleeps a lot.' Mi Khin's English was confident, and Kate wondered where she had learnt it.

'Do you have any other family?' she asked.

The girl's lip trembled. 'Papa. I do not know where he is.'

'Who looks after you? Does your mother bring you food?'

'No,' said Mi Khin, shaking her head. 'Ah May sleeping. The kind man brings food.'

'He sounds very kind.'

'He says I remind him of someone.' She pointed to the doorway. 'There he is.'

It was Fred, carrying a bag of rice and another of army-issue tinned food. He saw Kate and smiled, passing one of the bags to Mi Khin, who eagerly unpacked it.

'You look much better.'

'Thanks. I feel better. Still a bit feeble, though.'

'I came to see you in the hospital, but you were asleep,' he said. 'I didn't want to wake you.'

Mi Khin saw another girl pass by the open window and scampered away, calling to her.

'Poor little thing,' said Fred. 'She attached herself to me a few days ago. Her father's an Englishman, I gather, or perhaps Anglo-Indian – name of Smith – but he went off to India and hasn't been heard of since. Her mother doesn't seem well but won't go into the hospital ward as she doesn't believe they can help her.'

He nodded his head towards the woman who slept on the floor. 'She barely eats. I think she's dying. The little one may make it, though.'

'It's all so awful,' said Kate, staring at the prone form. 'I can't believe so many are dying.' She looked up at Fred. 'What can we do?'

He shrugged, looking tired. 'We can't leave just now. The paths are too bad in the hills, so they say. It would be reckless in the extreme. And Mrs Bryant is very ill. I think we must bide our time and do what we can to help these poor people.'

'I'll go and volunteer tomorrow.'

'In the hospital?'

'I suppose so. It's all I know how to do.' She sighed. 'I wish I was good at something else. I don't want to spend the rest of my life nursing.'

Fred touched her on the shoulder. 'You won't, Kate. When this is over, there's a whole world out there. You can do anything you want – anything.'

He sounded so certain. For a moment she believed him wholeheartedly.

34

Tavoy, July 1942

The days crawled by, each one like the last. Edwin registered occasionally, with dull surprise, that he was still alive.

On bad days he silently shifted rocks, fell down, picked himself up, watched other men collapse by the roadside, and witnessed the casual cruelties meted out by the Japanese. They were not monsters, he saw that now; just hardened and trained not to feel remorse. They had a sense of ruthless efficiency that divided the world into 'useful' and 'not useful'. Edwin expected every day to slip from one group to the other.

The work was monotonous and he drifted into reveries. They were shrouded in mist, somehow, and he could not be sure if he was remembering something or simply daydreaming. A girl lying on a rug, a book in her hand, leaves in her dark hair. *Kate, is that you?* But she was gone, and only the road remained.

On better days he found himself working near Rama. Sometimes they heard the thunder of dynamite being used to carve out a way through the hills ahead, but Edwin no longer jumped at the sound. Explosions had become part of the background noise of his life. Often they were put to work breaking rocks with pickaxes, exhausting work that left little breath for talking.

On easier days they were given rakes and ordered to smooth long stretches of gravel and sand.

At first they talked mostly of books, and the world outside became a little more real. Edwin told Rama about *Oliver Twist* and how he recited the start each night, always falling asleep before he got to the third paragraph.

'I was twelve when I first read Dickens,' said Rama. 'A little barefoot boy marching into the Delhi city library and asking for a card – can you imagine?'

'Is that where you grew up?'

'No, I was born in the Punjab. My brother was working in Delhi as a cook's assistant and so I went there too to find work when I was eleven.'

'Did they let you join the library?' asked Edwin, leaning on his shovel for a moment, imagining the ragged child and the suspicious librarians. He saw a guard in the distance and started shovelling again. It had begun to rain and the dusty road was already turning to mud. He could barely see through his smeared spectacles but could not find the energy to wipe them.

'No,' said Rama. 'I had no papers or money, nothing but the clothes I wore. My parents only spoke Punjabi and I knew very little English.'

'So what happened?'

'I stole the books,' said Rama with a chuckle. 'Well, borrowed without permission. I returned them all.'

'Did you get caught?'

'Never. I worked as an errand boy, so I would carry a great basket into the library, pretending I was delivering lunches to people working there. Then I would dash into the fiction room, take the next volume of Dickens and hide it under the banana leaves in my basket before leaving, and return it the next time. I got through all of his novels that way. It took me months to read the first one and a week to read the last – I can say that Charles Dickens taught me to read English.'

He smiled and continued his work, using a heavy rake to level the surface of the road where Edwin had been shovelling stones. Black mud splattered across his boots.

'I read his novels at school,' said Edwin. 'We wrote essays about some of them.'

'A boarding school?'

'Yes. Not one of the famous ones. My parents weren't really wealthy.'

'Wealth is relative,' said Rama mildly.

'Of course. But in England – well, we were middle class I suppose. My father started out poor but managed to achieve some success. He never felt he'd really made it, though.'

'Your caste system is interesting to me,' said Rama. 'It's not so different to India, really. Everyone has their place.'

'Perhaps you're right,' said Edwin. 'There was a boy at school with me – Jenkins. He was there on a scholarship and they never let him forget it. The richer boys bullied him mercilessly for being poor.'

'And you?'

'I didn't join in, but I let it happen.' Edwin wiped his sweaty forehead. He recalled the afternoons in the library, watching out of the window as Jenkins hurtled along the driveway, pursued by a flock of jeering boys in tailcoats hurling stones.

Another memory followed, of dark corridors, a tall figure holding a candle, whispers in the darkness, an empty bed beside his. He shivered in the heat of the afternoon.

'What happened?' said Rama, watching Edwin curiously.

'There was a master who none of the boys trusted. God, I haven't thought about any of this for years. Memory is so fickle. He was cruel and there were rumours that he – you know – interfered with boys.'

Rama listened impassively, his skin glistening with rain and sweat as he raked. It was still very hot and Edwin felt light-headed.

'I can't imagine why I'm telling you all this. One night he came to our dorm and took Jenkins away. I was pretending to be asleep, but his bed was next to mine and I saw them leave. It happened again and again, once a week at least. Jenkins stopped speaking and got all thin and spotty, which made the bullying even worse.'

Licking his dry lips, Edwin thrust the spade into the ground and it clanged against a stone. 'Eventually Jenkins must have told an adult. There was a big fuss and his parents came to the school. He was made to repeat the accusation in front of all the masters and they asked if he had any witnesses. He said I had seen him being taken away each night and would swear to it.'

'And did you?'

'I couldn't do it,' said Edwin. 'I was terrified that if I said anything the master would start on me as well.' He shook his head. 'I betrayed Jenkins. It was crueller than anything the other boys had done. I felt so terribly ashamed.'

'What happened?'

'He was expelled for lying. I'm sure he was relieved to get away, but the shame for his family was dreadful. He'd lost his scholarship so there was no chance of another school place. I heard later he went to work in a factory and was killed in a machine accident. My fault.'

Rama shook his head. 'You were a boy. You were scared. What happened to the master?'

'He didn't touch me. I think he found other victims, though. He was dismissed from the school after I left – he'd been caught with a boy and they couldn't turn a blind eye after that. It was hushed up, though. The last I heard he was working in another school.'

'The world is full of terrible men,' said Rama. 'What happened was not your fault.'

'I didn't start it,' said Edwin. 'But I should have protected Jenkins. I have always been a coward.' Emilia's face came to his mind and the guilt rose up in his throat and threatened to choke him.

'I'm sorry to tell you all this. I just needed to get some of it off my chest.'

'You have carried the guilt for too long,' said Rama seriously, looking at him directly. 'Let it go.'

'It's not just that,' Edwin said, and felt his voice quaver, tears threatening to fall. 'Emilia, too. I betrayed her. I sometimes feel as though I've let down everyone I ever cared about.'

He blinked and felt his eyes blur. There was a clang nearby as a tool was dropped on the ground, and he felt his free hand being taken in a larger, warmer one that squeezed and held on tight.

'They are beyond forgiveness,' said Rama. 'You must forgive yourself.'

After long seconds his hand was released and Edwin wiped his eyes. He saw Rama going back to work, the shovel almost light in his strong arms. Edwin looked around but the nearest prisoner was a dozen or so yards away and he was paying no attention to them, fully occupied by the misery of his task.

Edwin started shovelling again, his mind reeling, feeling the sweat pooling on his back as he watched the gravel scatter across the road.

35

Shinbwiyang, July 1942

Sweeping the dormitory one day, Kate heard a gasp from the pile of blankets nearby. She looked up and realised that Mi Khin's mother was watching her out of half-closed eyes. She was lying on the floor, her breathing laboured. Kate approached and knelt beside her, taking her hand gently. It felt hot and limp.

'Can I bring anything for you?' she said. 'There's water here.'

The woman shook her head but allowed Kate to drip a little water between her lips, running her tongue slowly around her mouth to catch the drops.

'Where is my daughter?'

'She's outside, playing with some other children,' said Kate, putting the flask down. 'Shall I go and get her?'

The woman shook her head. 'No, leave her please. She is happy.'

Her voice was very low, and Kate had to crane to hear what she was saying. The woman looked exhausted.

'Won't you come to the hospital?' Kate said. 'We could take better care of you there. It's basic but they have some medicine . . .'

She shook her head. 'It is not necessary. I know I will die here. I'd rather be with Mi Khin than in a place full of sickness.' She heaved a sigh and pulled the blanket closer around her.

'Don't say that,' said Kate, feeling a sense of dread. 'You'll be all right.'

'No,' said the woman, and she stared intently at Kate, 'I was told that I would die here.'

'Told? By whom?'

'By a *nat*.'

'A *nat*? A spirit?'

She nodded and closed her eyes. 'I cannot fight it. I am sure it sounds strange to you as a foreigner but it is very simple to me.'

Kate listened, a thousand questions racing through her mind, but she suppressed them. Somehow she believed the woman implicitly; she would die here.

'What is your name?'

'Hla Pemala,' said the woman, reaching out a hand to touch Kate's gently. 'And yours?'

'Kate.'

'Who is the man? The old Englishman?'

'That's Fred.'

'He is kind to Mi Khin.' She smiled a little. 'My husband Joseph's father was English. Perhaps Fred reminds her of her grandfather.'

'Where is your husband now?' asked Kate hesitantly.

'I do not know,' said Hla Pemala. A tear rolled gently down her cheek. 'India, perhaps. I do not want Mi Khin to be alone.'

'She won't be alone, I promise,' said Kate, feeling her throat constrict.

✦

A day later she saw Fred emerging from the dormitory with Mi Khin cradled in his arms. She was crying, her face pressed against the rough fabric of his jacket.

He caught Kate's eye and nodded towards the dormitory. 'They're taking her mother into the hospital.'

'Is she . . .?'

He shook his head, and gently put his hands over Mi Khin's ears. 'But she won't last the night.'

Kate saw two men come out of the dormitory, carrying Hla Pemala on a stretcher as a nurse hurried alongside, anxiously watching the woman's face. Her eyes were closed and it seemed that she had already gone.

'I ought to be with her,' said Kate.

Fred nodded. 'I'll take the little one away.'

So Kate went with the dying woman into the hospital ward and held her hand, listening to her shallow breathing. She knew very little about Hla Pemala's life or how she had ended up in Shinbwiyang. She had married an Anglo-Indian man some years before and had tried to flee to India to be with him, but the rest of her story was a mystery. Kate wondered about her childhood, where her parents were, what had made her so sure that she was doomed.

Hla Pemala died shortly before midnight but Kate stayed beside her bed until the sun came up. Mi Khin had lost enough already, she thought, and knew that one way or another she would feel responsible for the child for as long as the journey to India might last.

✦

Kate stood in the rain, watching Christopher dig his mother's grave. Mrs Bryant had been unconscious for some time, and though she woke occasionally she had not seemed to recognise Kate when she visited. Her breathing became slower and slower and at last she slipped away.

'How do I go on?' Christopher had said blankly as he held his mother's cold hand. I don't know, thought Kate now, as he flung mud and stones onto a heap, his face a mask of misery. How do we go on when we're left behind?

Looking around, she saw Nabanita nearby, watching them. She was standing under the dripping trees, her dark hair plastered to her head. Kate wondered whether to go over to her, but Nabanita turned and walked briskly away without looking back. I have let them all down, thought Kate.

When the rain began to ease she heard an engine in the distance, and looked up to see a small plane flying low over the trees. There were shouts from the camp, and she saw half a dozen men including Fred hurrying into the jungle, two of them pulling a rough wooden sledge over the muddy ground.

'What is that?' said Christopher, leaning on his spade. 'Is it the army?' His face and clothes were splattered with mud.

'Just a supply drop, I think,' she said, peering through the trees. The plane was out of sight now, and the sound of the engine was growing fainter.

'Why can't they rescue us? If they know we're here?'

'They can't land the planes,' said Kate, feeling helpless. 'There's no way out except on foot.'

He shook his head. 'I just feel that there must have been *something* we could have done to save her.' He looked down at the empty grave. Puddles were forming at the bottom.

'You did all you could.' She hesitated. 'I'll do everything I can to help you, Christopher – I hope you know that. Fred will too.'

He nodded, his mouth pressed tightly closed, and she knew that he was trying not to cry.

'I'm due at the hospital,' she said, noticing the light beginning to fade. 'Are you sure you don't mind doing that alone?'

'It's my duty,' said Christopher, and with an effort he smiled. 'Thank you. Good luck on your shift.'

Kate hurried away. She looked back and saw him digging frantically again, flinging earth over his shoulder onto a pile that grew steadily bigger. He no longer looked like a boy; whatever vestiges of childhood remained had been swept away, lost somewhere in the mud of the Hukawng Valley.

✦

Weeks went by, although Kate did not count them. She worked long hours in the hospital, sharing shifts with the few others who had medical experience. Most of them were amateurs, and she knew that they could not provide anything like the level of care required.

More people arrived at the camp every day, and every day more people died. Those who were not sick already often succumbed within days. It was not a healthy place, but for most of them there was no other option. The mountains beyond Shinbwiyang were such impossible terrain during the monsoon that the place had become a bottleneck, as many of the people who had trudged slowly towards India now became trapped there.

Kate assisted with operations, bandaged wounds, dispensed medicine, emptied bedpans, and laid out the bodies of those beyond help. Sometimes whole days went by when she could barely recall what she had been doing and she realised, with alarm, that she had somehow detached from it all.

One night she was called to assist at the bedside of a child with a fever, a little Indian boy who tossed and turned, his forehead burning hot. He was around the same age Satish had been and she felt gripped by despair. Was she condemned to see him die again and again?

'Will he die?'

The boy's father, curled on the floor beside the bed, had awoken and was now watching through half-closed eyes as Kate pressed a wet cloth to his son's forehead.

'It's not a certainty. But he is very ill.'

'Is there no one who can save him?'

'The staff are doing all they can.' She could not bring herself to tell him that they were running low on supplies.

The boy murmured faintly and his father grasped his hand, stroking the little fingers as tears coursed down his cheeks.

'That poor man,' said Mrs Abernathy when she went to the dispensary a little later. 'Did you know he's already lost four children? That boy's the last of them.' Mrs Abernathy, wife of a minister in the Church of Scotland, had been at Shinbwiyang since March.

'I don't know how people survive losing a child,' said Kate. She thought of her family and suddenly felt deeply homesick.

'At first it seems that the world must end,' said Mrs Abernathy, her voice gentle. 'But slowly and surely the light comes back. It's thirty years since my daughter died. The pain never leaves, but in time it becomes transformed, and love is what remains.'

'What was your daughter's name?'

'Catriona. We were ambushed by *dacoits* in the far reaches of the Shan State. My husband was wounded and she was killed, along with two of our men. She was six.'

Kate swallowed. 'I'm sorry.' She had always been ambivalent about the idea of motherhood, but the events of the last few months had turned her firmly against the prospect. I have buried too many children already, she thought.

'Afterwards, I wanted to leave Burma,' said Mrs Abernathy, absently folding a bandage again and again. 'My husband said that it was more reason than ever to stay and spread God's word. I was very angry with him at first, but in time it softened and I began to love him again, to love Burma.'

'Did you ever get justice?'

'They caught the men who did it. My husband intervened and asked that they be shown mercy, but the authorities wanted to make an example and hanged them. I couldn't regret that they were dead, but I felt deeply sorry for their families – it wasn't their fault. One of the wives ended up being baptised into the church. She was a great help to me. I wonder now what will become of her?'

Kate listened with increasing admiration as Mrs Abernathy fretted about the congregation she had left behind. What extraordinary strength of character the woman must have to have forgiven the people who had killed her only child, and to be working here alone while her husband remained with his flock to face the venom of the invading Japanese. If she can do this, then I can too, she thought.

The little boy's fever broke near dawn and his father looked on hopefully as Kate and Mrs Abernathy sponged his small limbs and helped him to drink from the jug of tea beside the bed.

'He's not out of the woods yet,' said Mrs Abernathy, speaking softly to the boy's father. 'But he's better. I promise you we'll do all we can. He's lucky to have you by his side.'

Impulsively the man took her hands and they stood together, heads bowed, as if they were praying. Kate slipped away, realising that her shift should have ended an hour before.

It was beginning to grow light outside and the rain had stopped. Kate stood in the grass outside the hospital, breathing in the cool air and listening to the first birdsong. She walked slowly around the edge of the village. Mist was rising from the grass and everything seemed imbued with its own special light.

Somewhere high overhead an engine droned; automatically she looked up. She could not see a plane, but far above two parachutes were descending, silhouetted against the pale blue sky, like angels coming to earth. She watched them get lower and lower until they were swallowed by the trees.

36
Worcestershire, August 1935

'*W*hy don't you go to the pictures?' asked her father, watching her folding clothes. 'Go with Mabel or someone, why don't you?'

'I'm quite happy here,' said Kate. She opened the sock drawer and flung a few strays in.

'It's not healthy for you, Kate,' he said. 'You're a good girl but you ought to go out sometimes. I hate to think of you locked in here with me – just because I'm stuck at home doesn't mean you have to be.'

'I'm fine, Dad,' she said, shaking her head. 'I know I can go out if I want to.'

'Such a waste,' he said, lying back heavily.

'What is?'

'All of this. You. Me. Your mother.'

Kate went and sat on the foot of the bed. 'Don't say that. It's hard, but it's not a waste. We're all right, aren't we?'

'It's getting worse,' said her father quietly. 'But it won't go on forever. You'll have your freedom one day.'

'Don't!' said Kate, standing up. She felt suddenly angry and it was all that she could do not to shake her father. 'I won't have you saying things like that! It's not fair!'

He closed his eyes. She saw a tear trickle down his cheek and felt a rush of love and despair and fury at the unjustness of it all. His skin was mottled, his hair nearly white, his arms lying thin across the bedclothes. She would not let him go, not yet.

37

Shinbwiyang, August 1942

The men who had arrived by parachute were doctors, sent by the Indian government. They brought huge bags of medical supplies and suddenly the situation in the camp hospital seemed a little less dire.

'I don't envy them,' said Mrs Abernathy. 'It's a huge task they've got.'

'Two aren't enough,' said Kate, gesturing hopelessly at the ward and at the camp beyond, where hundreds lived in cramped, diseased conditions.

'It's better than none, my dear. Let's be grateful that God has sent them to us.'

Kate knew that planes couldn't land in the jungle, but it did not stop her from illogically wishing that the government had also sent transport to get everyone to India.

One afternoon as she trudged towards the dormitory, her feet and back aching, Mi Khin ran out, clutching something. 'Look!'

'What is it, Mi Khin?

'A train!' She opened her small hands to show a toy steam engine, carved carefully from a block of wood.

'How lovely, where did you get it?'

'Fred made it! I will show my friends!'

She dashed away, cradling the train, and Kate looked up to see Fred emerging from the doorway, smiling tiredly.

'Should keep her busy for a bit.'

'It's a very kind thing to do.'

'I loved trains when I was that age. I kept meaning to carve one for little Satish, on the journey here.' He looked after Mi Khin, his expression melancholy.

'You're fond of her, aren't you?'

He shrugged. 'We're all she's got now.'

'I'll do everything I can.'

Fred nodded. 'At some point soon we'll have to think about leaving. The weather's improving every day and those doctors are here now. People are starting to slip off into the hills.'

'I've almost forgotten we're still on the way somewhere.'

'Yes. I see you, sometimes, on your rounds – as if you're in a dream.'

'It's the only way I know to survive.'

'We all do what we must.' He hesitated, as though there was something else he wanted to say, but then he looked at the fading sky. 'I'd better get on.'

She watched him hurry away and felt the usual flutter in her stomach. They had been through so much together, but she still knew very little about him. He's a good friend, she said to herself, but what she had with Edwin was friendship; this felt different. She shook her head. It would not do to get attached. That way lay only heartache.

✦

Late one night, Kate sat reading by candlelight in the hospital ward. Most of the people who slumbered around her had malaria, and sometimes she heard a cry or a murmur. She dabbed their foreheads, brought water, and when all was quiet again returned to her seat to see out the long night. Things were better than they had been for weeks, but always there was more sickness, more sorrow.

The door creaked open and she saw Myia peer around it.

'Hello. Are you all right?'

Myia came in and sat down on the floor. She was pale, and for once her glossy hair was dishevelled. It had been weeks since they had spoken properly and Kate felt guilty that she had been too busy to check on her friend.

'Myia?'

'I don't know what to do,' she said, almost whispering.

'What's happened?'

'I have had news of Denpo.'

Kate stared at her. 'News? Here?'

'He and his friends are now in Rangoon. They have been fighting alongside the Japanese. Denpo is leading a company of soldiers.'

'How do you know this?'

'I've been helping to register people when they arrive. I ask them for any news they have and note it down. Usually they have nothing. Today a man arrived who had been working as a driver for the army in Rangoon and other places. It was he who told me about Denpo.' She looked up. 'There's something else. Do you remember in Bhamo, I thought I had seen someone I recognised near the dock? I thought I saw Denpo. Well, apparently he was in Bhamo at that time – they were trying to set up an army training school.'

'So it *was* him?'

'I think so, yes.'

'What would you have done? If you had known?'

'I don't know.'

Kate rubbed her eyes and folded down the page of her book. 'Why is this man – the driver – here now?'

'He became afraid for his family and decided it was not safe. He was going to China but somehow has ended up here.' Myia twisted her hair. 'It feels like – what is it you say? Destiny?'

'It's a coincidence, surely,' said Kate, although she felt on edge. 'It can't be anything more.'

Myia stared down the ward and then looked up at Kate. 'I feel so confused.'

'Has anything really changed?'

'Perhaps not. I just thought that . . . I might change his mind. I am the only one he really cares about. I could stop him before he betrays his country.'

Kate shook her head, feeling impatient. 'Isn't it a bit late for that? He's already betrayed Burma, and you, by allying with the Japanese. There's nothing you can do.'

'Kate, you know so little about Burma. You do not understand us, not really. This is not a simple matter of good and bad. Denpo thinks he is doing the right thing for Burma.'

They were both silent. The candle flickered and the quiet ward was a sea of darkness around them. A child whimpered somewhere nearby.

'I must check on her,' said Kate, getting up. She put the book down on her chair and looked at Myia. 'Perhaps when we get to India you can write to Denpo. Please don't do anything rash. What can you do from here?'

'Nothing,' said Myia.

'How can you possibly change his mind? You'll end up being used, just as he is. Don't let love blind you, Myia – think about what's right.' She felt like a hypocrite at once. Who was she to say what was right?

Myia stood up and brushed down her skirt before going to the door. She turned back to Kate, looking angry for the first time in the months that they had known one another. 'What do you know about love?'

Nothing, thought Kate later, as she sat staring at the candle flame. I have loved until my heart cracked from side to side, and still I know nothing at all.

✳

The next afternoon Kate found a note folded on her pillow.

My dear Kate,

I'm so sorry that I have to leave. I have spent months mourning the fate that has befallen my country and I can no longer run away. You said that this was more about Denpo and perhaps you are right. I have never loved anyone the way I love him. All I know is that I cannot go to India. The journey we have made together is one of the hardest things I have ever done. We have endured too much already. But I will never forgive myself if I turn my back on him and on Burma now.

You are much stronger than you think. Go away to India, to safety, and try to forget the terrible things you have seen. One day when the war is over I hope that we can see each other again.

Your friend,

Myia

Kate ran out into the half-light and found herself at the edge of the jungle. Myia was nowhere to be seen; she was probably long gone. She has made her choice, thought Kate, but listening to the dripping of the trees, and the distant shouts of children playing, she felt more alone than ever.

She walked in a daze through the camp and saw Nabanita and Shreya leaving the hut where rations were distributed.

'It's not enough,' Nabanita said, frowning at the bag of supplies. 'How are we supposed to live on this?'

'Hello, Kate,' said Shreya. Her mother looked up and her mouth hardened at once as she reached for Shreya's hand.

'How are you?' Kate asked, looking tentatively between them.

'We are coping,' said Nabanita, although she looked exhausted. She wore a tattered second-hand dress. Kate remembered the gold sandals and embroidered sari she had worn when they first met. 'Despite the meagre rations.'

'Is that just for this week?' said Kate, looking at the bag she was holding. It held a few pounds of rice and a small selection of dried food packets.

'No. For a fortnight.'

'That doesn't seem right – I'm sure the standard ration is more than that.'

'For you, perhaps,' said Nabanita. 'Haven't you noticed that they have different rations for Indians and Europeans? It's the same old story – one rule for whites and one for everyone else.' She sounded weary but spoke without malice.

Kate flushed. She hadn't noticed.

'We'll survive,' said Nabanita. 'Come, Shreya – we've got to go.'

'Apparently conditions in the hills have improved,' said Kate quickly. 'Fred is making plans for us to leave.'

'He's mad,' said Nabanita. 'I'm not going to risk Shreya's life. She's all I have left.'

'I'd be all right,' said Shreya, looking up at her mother, but Nabanita shook her head fiercely.

'No. The army will rescue us. It's just a matter of waiting.'

'It could be a long time,' said Kate.

'Then we'll wait for a long time,' said Nabanita, tight-lipped.

'Is Christopher going with you?' asked Shreya.

Kate nodded.

'Will you all go back to England?'

'I don't know. If you change your mind . . .' said Kate, and she hesitated. 'We're leaving in three days,' she went on at last. 'I think we have to try.'

'We're staying,' said Nabanita firmly.

'I understand,' said Kate. 'I'm sorry. For everything.'

They stared at one another for a moment. 'I wish you good luck,' said Nabanita at last and turned away.

38

Shinbwiyang, September 1942

They left Shinbwiyang on a grey day in early September. 'We won't go too far today,' said Fred, looking around at Mi Khin, who marched steadily behind him. 'Just as far as the first relief camp. Your little legs will get tired.'

'I can walk a long way,' said Mi Khin indignantly. 'Ah May and Papa walk with me for long distance. Papa says I am strong!'

'You are strong,' said Christopher. 'I suppose you don't want a piggyback, then?'

'What's a piggyback?'

'It's when I give you a ride on my back,' he said, taking off his knapsack and squatting down. 'Want to try it?'

Mi Khin scrambled onto his back and Kate laughed to see her triumphantly riding along, nudging him with her heels.

'Christopher is my horse now!'

At dusk they arrived at a rudimentary camp that had been built on a steep slope and were welcomed by a hearty British soldier who was cooking sausages and fried potatoes over a roaring fire. Other travellers sat nearby.

They were given large cups of sweet, scalding tea and Kate sat cradling hers, feeling her stomach rumble as they waited for the food to cook. The scent of sausages on the air was unbearably familiar and she smiled to see a moth-eaten Union Flag draped over a branch, like a souvenir of a lost civilisation.

'Keep still,' said Fred, kneeling down beside her.

'What? Oh.'

He had a lit cigarette in his hand and used it to prod the leeches that had collected on her legs one by one. They fell off immediately, black and swollen, and she looked down at them with mild interest.

'I'd forgotten all about leeches.'

'The fellows here have cigarettes but no spare salt. They've given me a tin to take with us – best leech treatment available. Plus I'm out of pipe tobacco.'

One of the leech bites was bleeding and Fred pressed his handkerchief to it gently, frowning slightly. 'Better wash that carefully and keep it covered so it doesn't get infected.'

'Thanks for taking care of me.'

He looked up and caught her eye, his hand warm on her ankle.

At last dinner was served. Mi Khin prodded uncertainly at the food at first, but soon she was shovelling it down. She and Christopher sat side by side on a log, joking as they ate, both clearly pleased to be on the way somewhere at last.

Kate wondered where Myia was and thought suddenly of Edwin for the first time in weeks. I may never see either of them again, she thought. She looked around at the little group and prayed that she could keep them all safe.

Fred, at Christopher's urging, began to tell them stories of his years in the army as a young man. He had fought at the Somme, and then later in Mesopotamia, where the Ottomans rode elephants across the desert and he himself had fought on camel-back.

'The Turks had occupied Baghdad for months and had grown cocky. Their armies were overstretched elsewhere and they thought they could hold the city without many troops. But they underestimated the Arabs. They'd twigged, by this point, that we were their best hope, so they were on our side.'

'Did you ever go in disguise as an Arab?' asked Christopher breathlessly. 'The fellows in my books always do.'

'Oh yes, several times. I wore robes and a great big turban – you wouldn't have recognised me.'

'And you got away with it?'

'Sometimes,' said Fred with a half smile. 'Eventually I was stabbed in the bazaar during the Battle of Baghdad.'

'What happened?' asked Christopher, looking deeply impressed.

'I picked myself up and went on fighting, of course.'

'That's terribly brave.'

'Not really,' said Fred. 'Stupid, more like. I lost so much blood I collapsed and had to be invalided home not long after. Weeks on a dreadful ship, dodging submarines all the way across the Med, and then months in hospital back home. Then I was sent back to the front until the war ended.'

'What did you do after that?' asked Kate, although she suspected that the road that had brought him to the East had not been a happy one.

'Well, I settled back in Liverpool for a bit,' said Fred. 'I tried, anyway. But somehow . . . It wasn't the same, you see.'

'What wasn't?' asked Christopher.

'I'd spent three years fighting with barely a break, all for this idea of an England I wanted to defend. I'd think of the fields and the woods and the beaches and the pubs and that was what kept me going, even after my brother had been killed. But once I was home . . . it was gone. All of it, somehow, turned to ash. So I came out here. That way I could preserve the memories of how it used to be.'

He smiled bleakly. Kate thought of the thousands more like him who had returned from the war, their ideals as well as their limbs shattered. They had come home to a country that seemed no longer to want them, and which forgot their sacrifices with unseemly haste. She thought of her father, who had seen no place for himself in this new world and had turned his face to the wall.

When Mi Khin began to nod off, Kate urged her to bed and tucked her under a blanket in the driest part of the shelter. She yawned and turned over, her dark hair splayed on the bag that served as a pillow.

'What happened next?' asked Christopher, looking over to where Fred leaned against a tree stump. 'When you got to Burma.'

'I didn't come straight here,' said Fred, drawing on his cigarette. 'First I went to India and spent a few years in the army there. Good years, they were, and good people. But the crowds and the poverty began to get me down and finally I thought I'd come East to see what was happening. In Rangoon I got a job with the Irrawaddy Flotilla Company – and the rest is history.'

'Did you never marry?' said Christopher. There was a small silence.

'As good as,' said Fred finally. 'There was a woman, a young Shan.' His eyes flickered towards Kate and he seemed reluctant to say more.

'What was she like?'

'As lovely as the days were warm,' said Fred, and Kate heard the longing in his voice. 'She stayed with me for ten years and bore me four children. The oldest would be not much older than you, my boy. The smallest must be about Mi Khin's age.' He glanced over to where she lay sleeping.

'But you don't see them?'

'Their mother was the daughter of a Shan chief, up in the mountains. He tolerated our relationship, but when he died she was called back to take his place. She took the children and a marriage was arranged for her soon after with another chief. The children were young and it would have been cruel to confuse them, so I let them go.'

Christopher shook his head. 'You should find them,' he said.

'It's too late.'

'When my father died, I would have given anything for another day with him. Same with my mother. *Anything.*' They heard the break in his voice and his fractured breathing as he wept in the darkness. Fred's smoke rose in a wavering stream, silver on the night air, and Kate found herself crying silently too for all that she and her companions had lost.

39

Worcestershire, March 1936

'*What* are you going to see?' asked her mother, crunching across the driveway, her boots encrusted with mud. She looked tired and Kate felt guilty at once.

'The Mill on the Floss,' she said. 'Perhaps I shouldn't go – you look exhausted. You ought to have a rest.'

'Don't be silly,' said her mother, pushing her shoulder lightly. 'I'm quite all right. I'll have a cup of tea with your father shortly. The men are having a break too.'

'How many more to go?'

'We're over halfway,' said her mother. 'Fifty-six lambs so far from thirty-five ewes. About another thirty due to pop any day now.' She looked out across the fields, squinting slightly in the glare of the low sun, and breathed in deeply. 'It's rather a lovely evening. Spring is coming.'

'I hope so,' said Kate. 'It's been a miserable winter.'

'Look at this,' said her mother, pulling a branch delicately away from the hedge. 'The hawthorn is starting to come out.' Kate saw the tiny pale green leaves that were beginning to sprout here and there.

'Laura and I used to eat hawthorn leaves, do you remember?'

'I do,' said her mother, laughing. 'They didn't do you any harm. Some old country people swear by them for cooking. Very nutritious, apparently.'

'They just tasted of leaves,' said Kate, wrinkling her nose. 'I'd better go, the bus won't be long.' She hesitated. 'Sure you'll be all right?'

'Of course,' said her mother, and kissed her cheek. 'Enjoy the picture. See you later.'

Kate buttoned her coat and started towards the road, hands deep in her pockets. She glanced back and saw the light come on in the kitchen. Her mother bustled around, filling the kettle, hanging her coat on the back of the door, taking things out of the larder for supper.

Looking up, Kate saw that a lamp was glowing in her father's room too, and as she watched, he appeared at the window in his dressing gown and blew a kiss.

40

Tavoy, September 1942

The camp at Tavoy ran smoothly and there had been little violence since the incident at roll call. Occasionally a prisoner would be taken away and interrogated, and even more occasionally someone would simply disappear, his absence only noticed at night when the man's cellmates saw that they were one fewer.

Edwin realised that the Japanese hardly needed to use violence to enforce their will. The fear of what might happen was enough to keep most of the prisoners in their place, and there was little hope of rescue while the Japanese held dominion over Burma.

The guards disliked too much camaraderie among their prisoners and regularly a truck would pull into the main yard, offloading a dozen or so men, and taking away a similar number. Where they went, no one knew. Of the many prisoners at Tavoy, the chances of being picked were slight, but they were there all the same.

A few days of sickness had given Edwin a respite from working on the road, but the dysentery had retreated all too quickly, and before long he was sent back to work, the Japanese doctor silently ticking the box that declared he was fit enough. Now the monsoon was over and the dry heat had returned, leading to sunburn and heat rashes.

Edwin sometimes looked back at his old life and could hardly believe that he was the same man who had taught schoolboys in Lambeth, overhearing their jokes about his shyness and his spectacles; now he laboured each day under torrential monsoon rains and baking sun, heaving earth and stones to build a road that would one day link up with the railway that now stretched from Bangkok to the Burmese border.

But something else had changed, too, although he did not yet have the words to speak of it. Almost every day, when it was possible, he worked with Rama, and the days that they were not together seemed to drag at a glacial pace. He could hardly recall the old, shameful lusts that he had indulged in London, in that other life. This was real.

He often wondered what Rama was thinking. There were days when a guard was stationed too near for them to talk, so they worked quietly, heads down, content just to be near one another. On other days they were able to talk and did so, of everything under the sun, except the most important things.

Edwin longed for something to change so that they could be alone, just to talk, but the camp was set up so that no one was ever really alone during the day, and at night he was locked into his cell with three others, hearing snores and the occasional grunts of a lonely man in the darkness.

✦

'Do Sikhs believe in God?'

'Of course,' said Rama, without pausing as he raked sand across the road. 'We do not see him like your God, though.'

'What is he like?'

'He is not male or female,' said Rama. 'But for simplicity in English we say "He", as you do. He is an immortal being, without physical form, supreme, and all-seeing. We are all equal before him.'

Edwin listened as he worked, spreading thick red sand before him. 'I read about Hinduism and Buddhism before coming to Asia but your religion sounds quite different.'

'There are a few similarities,' said Rama. 'We all believe in the cycle of life and rebirth.'

'Do you believe you'll be reincarnated?'

'Of course,' said Rama. 'The only way out of the cycle is to achieve total union with God – and I do not think I'm there yet.' He laughed.

And I could not be further away, thought Edwin, feeling the blisters on his palms rubbing painfully against his rake. He leaned on its handle for a moment and flexed his fingers, hearing the stiff knuckles crack.

'What do you believe?' asked Rama.

'Very little, these days. I was brought up as a Christian but I haven't been to church for a long time. I suppose I still believe there is a God,' he said doubtfully. 'But he's probably given up on me.'

'Not if he is a loving God,' said Rama. 'God does not give up on anyone.'

'But I'm a sinner.'

'We're all sinners, Edwin. What is your sin?'

Edwin swallowed. How could he tell Rama? What if he had misunderstood the connection between them? Even if he hadn't, Rama was honest and decent. He would be disappointed.

'My wife,' he said, forcing out the words.

'Emilia,' said Rama, and her name was soft on his tongue. 'Ah. You deceived her. Did she know?'

'No. At least, I don't think so.' He remembered sneaking home in the early hours, trying not to disturb her, but knowing that he smelled of cigarettes and alcohol. Perhaps she did know. The thought of her hurt and anger made his stomach lurch.

He did not know how to form the words for the rest of it – that it was not a woman he had been meeting, but a series of unfamiliar men, and sometimes he was terrified he would never be normal. But meeting Rama had changed all that, for he suspected that Rama knew exactly what he was because he was the same. And if Rama, so wise and trustworthy, was the same as him, then perhaps he wasn't so abnormal after all.

He remembered Rama touching his back and the hand that had clasped his. Was it possible? Could he dare to hope?

'You're not alone, Edwin.'

✦

As the season changed, the duties they were given became more varied and Edwin was given the task in the evenings of ferrying water to buildings around the camp, in exchange for a half day away from the road each week. Since the rains had stopped, water was rationed, and washing was supervised. It was almost pleasant to wander around in the dusk, speaking to no one, alone with his tormented thoughts.

'It's doing you some good,' observed Rama one day. 'You look a little less sunburned.'

Edwin felt his forehead. 'Working at night is a lot more bearable. I wish we could do this at night too.' He gestured at the road, which was almost shimmering in the midday heat.

'It must be nice to be alone for a while.'

'I'd rather be here with you.'

Rama smiled at him, and suddenly all that needed to be said passed between them in a bolt of understanding. The sun was high overhead and Edwin felt faint. He could see a Japanese guard in the distance looking their way, and forced himself to keep working, feeling his neck burn and wondering how he had lived a whole life without experiencing this sense of divine elation.

'If only we were somewhere else,' said Rama, his usually calm face restless. 'I can't bear it here. We'll never be alone. There's so much I want to say . . .'

'Yes.'

Rama paused, leaning on his shovel. 'What if we were to escape?'

'From the camp? Is that possible?'

'I don't know. Perhaps not, although I've thought of it again and again. It would be hard to get past the guards unless we can think of a way to distract them.'

Edwin looked around and saw the soldier walking towards them, his rifle resting on his shoulder. 'The guard's coming.'

They both began to shovel faster, heaping the sharp gravel and then smoothing it out. The guard, a few yards away, paused and watched them suspiciously but they did not catch his eye.

'No talk,' he said at last. 'You work, no talk.'

He watched for a few more minutes and then strolled back up the line, pausing to shout at a Burmese prisoner who sat on the hard ground, his legs having given way. The man scrambled to his knees and began digging that way. The guard kicked him hard and the man fell over, then picked himself up again.

Edwin watched all this and then turned towards Rama, his voice low. 'I'll come with you. If you think of a way to get us out of here, then I'll come with you.'

41

Nagaland, September 1942

The journey now entered more challenging terrain. From the moment they left camp the next morning, the path went firmly upwards, winding through steep jungle slopes and leading them along the edges of deep ravines. Steam billowed on all sides as the temperature rose.

Back on the road after some weeks, Kate noticed once again all the things she had grown accustomed to on the way through the Hukawng Valley. The straps of her knapsack bit into her shoulders and, while she at least had shoes again, they rubbed constantly. There were many streams to be forded, which they crossed by holding hands in a chain, and after the first few it seemed pointless to remove footwear before entering the water.

Before leaving Shinbwiyang she had sorted through her possessions. The books, mildewed and damp, were thrown away, along with most of her clothes. She had debated briefly whether to keep the yellow silk dress, but it was torn and stained now and she could not foresee a time when she would need it. Her silver rupees, all the money she had in the world, lay heavy in the bottom of her bag. The only sentimental item she allowed herself was her father's hip flask, in which she could carry water. Very little else remained of her old existence, and she knew that if she ever reached India she would have to create a new life from scratch.

Often, throughout the day, they would see other travellers, but there were various routes through the hills and they could only have seen a fraction of the total. Occasionally they walked for a mile or two with another group, but generally their walking speeds did not match and other travellers overtook them quickly.

They walked for a day with a man named Fielding, an eccentric and well-spoken Englishman who said he had come from Taungoo and had been separated from his friends.

He seemed curious about their mixed group, and teased Mi Khin until she scowled and retreated to walk with Christopher.

'What were you doing in Taungoo?' asked Fred.

'I own an oilfield there,' said Fielding. 'Been in the family for donkey's years.'

'Oh, really?'

'My old man died last year and I thought I ought to come and check on the natives, make sure none of the oil's being appropriated, and all that. I've club fees to pay.' He grinned, then blew his nose on a monogrammed handkerchief. 'Wasn't expecting to get caught up in all this.'

He told them of his childhood in Hong Kong, the prestigious schools, and the career in the City. Fred asked innocuous questions and looked thoughtful.

'He is a bit daft,' Kate conceded later, having seen Fielding solemnly trying and failing to light a fire before Fred took the flint away.

'He's either daft or a liar,' said Fred, glancing over to where Fielding was now fiddling with a pair of binoculars, occasionally holding the wrong end up to his eyes. 'I say liar.'

'Why?'

'There aren't any oilfields at Taungoo,' said Fred. 'The only one that's remotely near is owned by an old chap who I happen to know, and he's alive and kicking. This fellow's talking nonsense.'

'Perhaps he's just got mixed up.'

Fred grunted, sounding unconvinced, and none of them were sorry when Fielding announced the next morning that he was pushing on alone.

'Cheerio, kids,' he said, clapping Christopher on the shoulder and waving at Mi Khin, who darted away. 'Good luck to you.'

As he disappeared, Christopher snorted. 'Kids! What a stuffed shirt. He reminds me of Bertie Wooster.'

'I do not like him,' said Mi Khin solemnly, looking up at Fred. 'His clothes are silly. And he stares at me.'

'I didn't like him either,' said Fred, taking her hand.

Kate didn't think Fielding had been much stranger than some of the other travellers they had met: the Punjabi businessman in a pinstriped suit who rode a pure white bullock, the British soldiers who carried a bag that they claimed contained a Japanese head given to them by a Naga tribe, and the monk they had seen being arrested at an aid camp on suspicion of spying.

'Are we in India yet?' said Christopher suddenly.

'I don't know exactly where the border is,' said Fred. 'It's somewhere in these hills. We may be crossing it right now.'

They decided to make a ceremony out of it and, linking hands in a line, they all took a big step forward together, Mi Khin swinging her legs as Fred and Christopher lifted her up between them. She looked back wistfully. 'Not Burma any more?'

'No, sweetheart,' said Fred. 'We're in India now.'

'Closer to Papa?'

'I hope so.'

The food supplies they had collected at Shinbwiyang dwindled quickly and the extra rations they were given at camps along the way were not enough to slake their ravenous hunger. Most meals still consisted of rice and bamboo shoots and the occasional *daal* provided by the army. There was never enough protein to make up for the energy they expended each day.

One evening, out to collect water, Kate gazed into a deep, still pool. After years spent half-heartedly dieting, she hardly recognised the sharp-cheeked stranger who now stared back at her. At some point, perhaps at Shinbwiyang, she had stopped bleeding each month, and despite being grateful to avoid having to deal with it she couldn't help feeling that the last vestiges of womanhood were being stripped away from her.

She remembered standing in a tiny room that smelled strongly of jasmine, in one of Rangoon's smaller markets, a few months after her arrival in Burma. She had been careful, but not careful enough. The shrivelled proprietor, an ancient Chinese man, dug through drawers full of traditional remedies, selecting this and that, grinding the herbs in a mortar, and finally handed her a little paper bag.

'Hot water,' he said, with a pouring gesture. 'One pinch. Drink three time each day until all gone.'

'That's all?'

'Yes. Drink it. You bleed later.'

When he saw that she understood, he accepted the payment of ten rupees and then bowed deeply and saw her out. He had asked no questions and appeared completely uninterested in who she was or in excuses for her predicament.

Kate took the bag home and followed the instructions. It tasted much like herbal tea and was not unpleasant. She finished the herbs and waited anxiously for two more days. When the blood came on the third day, thick and vivid, she cried with relief in the bathroom at the Secretariat. Then she went back to work.

It all seemed a long time ago, and she could barely remember what it was like to go to bed with a man. That was part of the old life, when she had been a person with physical desires. Now her entire existence was taken up with survival. Eating, sleeping, and walking took all her body's energy, and every day she detached from it a little more.

In the pool her eyes looked dark and sunken and she could have wept for the plump, healthy girl she had once been. She imagined going home to England like this, seeing the shock on her mother's face.

No, she would not go back like this. If she got to Calcutta – *when* she got to Calcutta – she would write to her mother at once, telling her she was still alive, and then . . . then what?

She thought of going home. The pale sun of autumn would be saturating the corn fields, and the leaves on the trees burnished copper. She thought of walking over the common and stopping to sit on her father's bench to look at the view, the heart of England laid out before her.

※

One day they emerged from dense jungle, panting after ascending a steep trail, into a small clearing. Fred, who was in the lead, stopped abruptly, holding an arm out to one side to halt the others.

In the centre of the clearing stood a Naga tribesman. He wore a black loincloth and a heavy beaded necklace. He made no immediate attempt to communicate, simply studied them carefully, his gaze moving from Kate and Fred to the children, who stared back at him with equal interest.

He was a young man, only twenty or so, but there was something so wise in his expression that Kate trusted him at once. Even the realisation that he carried in one hand a spear, and in the other a rifle, did not alarm her. He was slight and his ribs were visible, but his arms and legs were noticeably muscular.

Fred, beside her, laid his revolver carefully on the ground. The tribesman inclined his head slightly and placed his rifle on the ground before laying his hand flat to his chest.

'What language do they speak?' murmured Christopher.

'None that we'll understand,' said Fred softly. 'There are dozens of Naga languages.'

The man cocked his head slightly, listening to them.

'I don't suppose you speak any English, do you?' said Fred, stepping forward a little way.

The man said nothing but picked up his gun. 'Oh dear,' said Fred, but he paused, watching what the tribesman was doing. He was holding the gun out before him, as if for inspection.

'May I?' said Fred. Approaching slowly, he did not touch the weapon but examined it from all angles. Then he stepped back and bowed his head, smiling at the tribesman. 'Lee-Enfield. English!' he said.

The man inclined his head in return. He recognised the word and understood what it signified. If he knew any more of the language he was not inclined to let on.

He took a few steps to the right, holding out the gun before him, and then stopped to gauge their reactions. He pointed again with the gun.

'I think he wants us to follow him,' said Fred.

'Is it safe?' whispered Christopher. 'Aren't they headhunters?'

'He doesn't look as if he wants to harm us,' said Kate. 'He seems rather sweet.'

'I'm not sure sweet is the word,' said Fred, looking around, 'but we're on their land. If they wanted to hurt us they'd have done it by now, one night when we were all asleep.'

Twenty minutes' walk took them to the edge of a village, where wooden houses thatched with palm leaves were arranged closely together. At the centre was a larger building, with a curved gable like the prow of a ship, and a roof that sloped steeply almost to the ground.

A small group of tribesmen stood waiting for them, and in the distance Kate saw several women peering out from the doorway of a hut. They talked quietly among themselves, but no one made any effort to talk to the strangers and somehow it seemed natural to sit down on a bamboo mat in silence, exchanging smiles now and again with the bolder women.

Fred sat beside her, his legs crossed with more ease than most British men of his generation. She was aware of his stillness, sensing the strong muscles in his back completely relax for once. He had encountered the Nagas before, she realised, and knew that he trusted them.

'Look, there are more rifles,' said Christopher, pointing at the men, several of whom carried identical Lee-Enfields. 'Perhaps they took the heads of the Englishmen who carried them.'

'It's possible,' said Fred, 'I don't think so, though. They're not anti-British as long as they get left to live independently.'

A meal was brought out for them: freshly steamed rice and long strips of dried meat, tough but indescribably delicious, tasting strongly of woodsmoke.

The Nagas watched them eat. When the leaves on which the food had been served had been taken away, two men appeared from inside the main building, carefully carrying a wooden box. They placed it down on the mat, and from inside one of them lifted out a familiar object.

'What is it?' asked Mi Khin.

'A Gladstone bag,' said Fred, sounding astonished. They laid it down before him and gestured at him to open it.

'What's inside?' said Christopher, peering over Fred's shoulder.

Fred lifted out a sheaf of papers, followed by a little book, written in English, a collection of children's stories.

Kate took this and opened the cover. An inscription inside read, in a quavering hand, 'To Darling Nicholas on your 7th birthday, with love from Grandma. Lashio, 1940.'

She stared at the page, mulling the implications of the careful inscription. Nicholas, whoever he was – just a little boy – had evidently made it this far, but no further. Was he with his parents, she wondered? Which of them had succumbed first?

Wordlessly she pushed the book to Fred and looked at the pile of papers. On the top was an unused air ticket from Lashio to Calcutta. Underneath was what looked like the deed for a house, and a number of financial documents that she hadn't the heart to examine. Then there were a few carefully folded items of clothing and a pair of shoes.

'Look,' said Fred, and showed her a British passport, the cover blotched with white specks of mould. Inside the pages were blurred by water, but the photograph was still visible: a man in his forties, dark-haired, bespectacled.

'Herbert Jones,' read Christopher. 'Who's he?'

'Nicholas's father, I expect,' said Fred. He looked up at the tribesmen who stood nearby, watching the unpacking, and pointed at the passport and then at the huts.

Their leader observed him closely for a moment, then beckoned. Kate stood up with him.

'Stay here,' said Fred to Christopher. 'Look after Mi Khin.'

'But—'

'We'll just be a minute.'

Kate and Fred followed the man in silence as he led them between two of the largest huts and out into a patch of jungle on the other side. They came to a clearing in the trees. The Naga pointed and Kate saw two branches bound tightly together to form what was unmistakably a cross, leaning slightly, in the middle of the clearing.

'Look,' said Fred, and below it she saw the graves, four recently dug earth mounds.

'Adults?' said Fred, gesturing with his hand to his own height. And then, nodding back to where Christopher and Mi Khin sat in the village, 'Children?'

The man laid his spear carefully on the ground and then pointed one by one at Kate and Fred, his hand raised just above his head, and then pointed again, this time lowering his hand to a little below shoulder height.

'A man and a woman,' said Kate heavily. 'And two children. A boy and a girl. I suppose Grandma must have died on the way here, or perhaps she never left Lashio.'

'The Jones family.'

'What do you think happened?'

'The usual,' said Fred. 'Malaria. Dysentery. Despair.' He sounded more hopeless than Kate had ever heard him. 'What a damned waste.'

'There are other crosses,' she said, looking around the clearing. Much older graves were visible, although they had faded into the grass. 'Can they possibly be Christians?'

'Christian,' said the Naga, and pointed to the crosses, then to himself. He recited something in his own language, and then said, unmistakably, 'Ourfatherwhichartinheaven.'

He smiled, looking shy, and then turned to lead them away. As they returned to the clearing, Fred tried to find out where the English rifles had come from, but the answer was opaque. The man pointed at Kate, and then made a gesture as though aiming a rifle.

'English,' he said.

'I think he's saying he got the guns from a woman,' said Fred. 'A white woman. Sounds as though someone's been arming the Nagas. Perhaps they are joining the war against the Japanese.'

They found Christopher and Mi Khin hooting with laughter as they tried to talk with a group of curious young Nagas, who seemed equally amused by these strange visitors. The youngsters all had scraps of English that they had picked up, perhaps from whoever had converted them or armed them.

The graveyard in the jungle was on Kate's mind as they left the Naga village. Fred had stowed the passport and the other papers in his pack and Kate slipped the story book into hers. They also took the bag and its contents, at the urging of the men in the village.

'We'll ditch it somewhere later,' Fred said quietly. 'They obviously want it off their hands.'

The Nagas seemed relieved to have acquitted themselves of this responsibility. Kate wondered how long the Jones family had stayed with them and knew they had done all they could. These people lived remote lives, far from the war rooms of London and Berlin and Tokyo, and deserved to be left alone. Instead, the war had come to them.

42

Nagaland, September 1942

Late one night Kate was woken by a rustling. She looked blearily at the spot a few yards away where Fred had made his bed, but he was nowhere to be seen. She could see the shapes of Christopher and Mi Khin nearby, silent bundles wrapped up on the jungle floor under a crude roof.

Perhaps Fred had just gone to answer the call of nature. But the sound came again, this time on the other side of the camp. There were people in the trees, she was sure of it.

Kate stood up as quietly as possible and looked around. It was too dark to see much; a crescent moon was dimly visible behind a layer of cloud but its light did not penetrate to the jungle floor.

Fred's *kukri* lay in its sheath on the ground by his bed; quickly she picked it up, drawing the blade and measuring its weight in her hands. She took a few steps away from the camp, straining to see in the darkness.

She thought she could hear whispering some distance away and tiptoed towards the sound, her heart hammering as she went further from the camp. In a gap between the trees she could see a figure standing motionless.

'Fred?' she called softly, then someone leapt out of the under-growth to her right and crashed into her, pushing her painfully to the ground and clutching her wrists tightly as she flailed. He was taller and stronger than she was and in a moment she had dropped the *kukri* and lay helpless, her eyes welling with fear and anger.

'Quiet!' the attacker exclaimed, his voice hoarse.

She could not see the man above her, as he had her pinned on her side with his knee, but she could feel the rough cloth of his sleeves against her skin, and smelled his sour breath somewhere above her head. It took all she had not to cry for help, but she could feel the cold barrel of a gun pressed against her neck.

Over the pounding in her ears she became aware that someone else was now standing nearby and they spoke together in words she could not understand. The other man crouched down beside her and she was startled to hear that he was English.

'So sorry for the inconvenience, madam,' he said sardonically, and she would have spat in his face if she'd been facing the right way. 'Don't mind Li Wei here.'

His voice was familiar and she realised with a jolt that it was Fielding, the English aristocrat who had walked with them a few days earlier. He sounded more serious now and his accent was less refined than it had been.

'You! What do you want?'

'Money. Food. Guns. And whatever else you've got.'

'We haven't got anything.'

'Liar. I saw the old fellow had a pouch stuffed with rupees, not to mention a Smith & Wesson. Then there's that pretty little girl with the silver bracelet – it, and she, might fetch a good price. And what about you?' He ran a hand over her backside and laughed quietly. 'Maybe I'll keep you.'

A gunshot rang through the night, somewhere over their heads. Kate tried to turn over but could see nothing, until suddenly the man pinning her down stood up and she rolled away from him. Looking back she saw Fred advancing across the clearing, his revolver pointed steadily at Fielding, who just as steadily aimed back. The man above her, she now saw, was Chinese, and wore an army uniform.

'Put down the pistol,' said Fred. 'And let her go.'

Fielding barked an order in Chinese and Li Wei stepped away from Kate, gesturing at her to stand up. He put the gun down on the ground and stood watching. Fielding moved sideways so that he was standing almost in front of her.

'What do you think you're doing?' said Fred.

Fielding laughed. 'Taking what we can get, old man,' and for a moment he lapsed back into the aristocratic accent he had had when they first met him. 'You mustn't mind old Fielding, he's an *awfully* good sort.'

'I knew you were talking claptrap,' said Fred, shaking his head. 'That story about the oilfield. Should have known.'

'Don't feel bad,' said Fielding sardonically. 'Everyone else I've robbed has fallen for it, why not you?'

'Desperate people. Spinning them a tall tale so you can steal from them. You're despicable,' said Fred. Kate heard a rustling in the trees and wondered if there were more accomplices nearby.

Fielding shrugged, looking bored. 'Perhaps. Who cares?'

'Was any of it true?'

'Some of it. I really was born in Hong Kong, but instead of sitting on my arse in a club in Mayfair I've spent most of my life travelling and gaining rather more useful skills and interesting acquaintances.'

'Criminals.'

'Some of them. Doesn't matter. Some of the most useful people are criminals. Like Li Wei here – he was a deserter from the Chinese army when I met him and he's been most helpful.'

'You're—'

'Enough,' said Fielding, and his voice was suddenly serious. 'Enough questions. What's your aim like, old man?'

'Good enough,' said Fred. 'How's yours? Feeling confident?'

'No need,' said Fielding. 'I'm—'

There was a yell as Christopher leapt out of the trees and onto the back of Li Wei, who staggered and pitched forward, trying to get the boy off him. Kate knelt quickly and picked up the *kukri*, and stood again, her heart hammering.

At last Li Wei stood up and flung the boy off his back, and suddenly he had the pistol in his hand, pointed at Christopher's head, and everyone was standing very still.

A shot was fired, and for a moment nothing seemed to happen. Then Li Wei fell and Kate realised that Fred had shot him. She felt the blood roaring in her ears and the cold weight of the blade in her hand.

'Drop it!' Fred shouted at Fielding, coming nearer. For a moment Fielding did nothing and then, imperceptibly, she saw him turn towards Christopher, his hand tightening around his pistol.

Kate lifted the *kukri* with both hands and stabbed Fielding as hard as she could in the lower back, feeling rather than hearing the crunch as the blade went in. He staggered forward and she let go of the knife, staring as though her hands belonged to someone else. Fielding sank to his knees and looked around mutely at her, then collapsed into the dust.

His hand was outstretched and she saw the fingers loosen around the pistol until he lay still. Fred picked up the gun and, in a businesslike way, collected the one that Li Wei had held, placing the weapons on the ground. Quickly he searched the soldier's body, finding a knife that he threw onto the pile. Finally he put a foot on Fielding's back and pulled out the *kukri*, wiping it quickly on the dead man's shirt.

Blood was soaking into the jungle floor and Kate watched the darkening patch with a distant curiosity, as though she were hovering somewhere overhead.

'Are you all right?' asked Christopher, who was suddenly beside her, looking with concern at her trembling hands.

'I'm fine,' said Kate, although she did not feel it.

Christopher helped Fred to drag the bodies away and conceal them in the woods, heaping damp leaves and sticks over them. Kate watched, as though from afar, as the gaunt white faces of the dead men disappeared under the leaves. I have seen them in my dreams, she thought.

'We won't hear any more of it,' said Fred, brushing his hands on his trousers. 'There are plenty of other bodies about.'

Kate nodded numbly. As they neared the camp, she let Christopher go on ahead, putting out a hand to steady herself on a mossy tree. She closed her eyes.

Her whole body was trembling and she felt for a moment as if she might faint as the blood roared in her ears. The ridges of the tree bark under her fingers felt oddly reassuring and for a moment she was at home in England, perched in the thick branches of an old oak tree. Soft rain. Wind on leaves. The crack of a twig.

Someone came towards her and she felt strong arms holding her tightly, pressing her to his chest.

'You did a brave thing,' Fred said quietly. 'I'm sorry it came to that.'

'I'm fine.'

'No, you're not,' he said, and stroked the back of her head. 'You will be, though. I promise.' She could smell woodsmoke and blood on his shirt.

She looked up at him, and for a moment he held her gaze, his expression half wary, half longing. Then he leaned forward and kissed her, his arms tightening around her, and she felt a pulse of desire. She became acutely aware of the thumping of her own heartbeat and the sighing of the wind in the trees.

A call came from nearby and they pulled quickly apart as Mi Khin appeared, trailing a blanket, her eyes wide in the half-light. 'A noise woke me up. Christopher says men fighting!'

'It's all right, sweetheart,' said Fred, tucking the blanket firmly around her shoulders. 'Let's all go back to bed.'

He looked up at Kate with a shy smile and then looked away again, as they made their way back to camp. She knew, with a sense of inevitability, that in the morning he would be stiff and formal with her. He had kissed her because she was there and he was fond of her, but she knew that his heart lay elsewhere, that she would be a poor replacement for the woman he had lost.

The children took some time to get to sleep and long after the others had drifted off, Kate lay listening to Fred's slow, heavy breaths somewhere nearby. She was no longer trembling, and gradually she felt her heart rate return to normal. Eventually she slept, as the first pale fingers of dawn began to appear through the trees.

43
Worcestershire, March 1936

*T*he bus dropped her off at the turning and she watched it rattle away down the hill, the lights receding until she was standing in darkness. Her eyes gradually adjusted until she could see the outline of the hedges against the dark blue sky.

She felt elated, her steps light, and realised what a tonic it had been to leave the house. The cinema had been warm and softly lit, the dramatic plot and loud music of the film a wonderful distraction. *I should do this more often*, thought Kate.

She had walked up this lane more times than she could recall and she could pick out familiar shapes formed by the stars above her head. Soft rustles came from the fields on either side of the lane and occasionally she saw something small dart across the road.

The quiet was broken by the sound of a car coming along the lane behind her; instinctively she pressed herself into the hedge, wondering who was going to the farm at this time of night, at such a speed.

The headlights flooded the lane for a moment, dazzling her as she looked back, and then the black car raced past her and up the lane. As it receded she recognised it and began to run.

The quarter of a mile home seemed to take forever and no time at all. Everything shrank down to the bodily sensations – the rasping breath, the cold night air on her cheeks, the burning calf muscles, and the rubbing of shoes that were not made for running.

At last, reaching the main gate, she slowed, and saw with dread the police car parked beside the house, just beyond it an ambulance with its back door open at the entrance to the barn, the headlamps throwing light across the cobbled yard. There were three or four men talking intently in a group beside the police car.

'Where's my mother?' she said loudly, and they turned to her, gaping. No one replied at first, and then Ben, the oldest farmhand, came hobbling towards her, taking his cap off.

'Miss Kate – oh, my dear – there's been an accident.'

'I know,' said Kate, feeling suddenly calm, as though someone else was speaking with her voice. 'I understand.' She laid a hand on his arm, feeling vaguely sorry for him, seeing the tracks of tears down his old whiskery cheeks. 'Do you know where my mother is?'

'She's in the kitchen, Miss Kate,' he said, his voice quavering. 'With the young lady constable.'

'Thank you,' said Kate, and went towards the back door. Before she got there it opened and her mother emerged, looking pale.

'Kate.'

'Mother?' She ran to her at once, and put her arms around her, feeling the slight body beneath the thick jumper.

'I saw you come into the yard,' said her mother, her voice low and unsteady. 'Oh, Kate – I can't bear to tell you.'

'It's all right, Mother,' said Kate, and held her tighter. 'I know. It's Father. I knew as soon as I saw the police car.'

She felt her mother crumple as sobs heaved through her body, saw past her to where a young policewoman stood anxiously by the back door, twisting her hat in her hands and looking as if she would rather be anywhere else.

Her mother breathed in deeply. 'He borrowed a shotgun,' she said quietly. 'Ben found him in the barn.'

Kate looked over to where old Ben now sat on a pile of logs, the ankles of his worn overalls tied about with twine. One of the other farmhands lit him a cigarette and she saw his hand shake as he took it, staring wordlessly into the distance.

'We knew it was coming,' she said, hating the words as she spoke them.

'Not like this,' said her mother, shaking her head violently. 'Not yet.'

The policewoman tried to get them to come inside, but they gently shooed her away. People milled about and occasionally the sergeant appeared to ask questions or offer condolences. The farmworkers stood about in groups, talking quietly.

Kate looked at the stars again, tracing the lines of the Plough over and over as the night wore on. At last the doors of the ambulance slammed and it moved off. Two policemen spoke to her mother while Kate stood silently by, watching their mouths move, wondering why everything seemed so quiet.

They were asking if the policewoman should stay at the farm, but Kate's mother said no, that wouldn't be necessary, and thanked the girl for the tea she had made. Looking rather relieved, she patted them both on the shoulder and got into the car with her colleagues.

The car rattled out through the gate, and then old Ben appeared before them, apologising and trembling in equal measure, and they embraced him and thanked him for his loyalty, and eventually the other farmhands came over and led him away to his cottage.

'Don't leave him alone, will you?' said her mother anxiously.

*'No, ma'am,' said young Tim. 'He'll be right. Good night to you.'
He hesitated. 'Very sorry for your trouble.'*

And suddenly the yard was empty, the door of the barn locked tight, and all that remained was the usual pungent animal aroma, and the lingering smell of cigarette and gun smoke.

44

Margherita, October 1942

It was autumn when they reached Margherita. The deep jungle of the Naga hills had given way to the tea fields of Assam. Camps were operating every few miles and by travelling from one to the next Kate, Fred and the children found at last that their long trek was nearly over.

'I can't believe we're in a town,' said Christopher, looking wonderingly at the humble buildings that surrounded them as though he was in some great city.

Margherita was a small and pleasant town in the colonial mould, with attractive views across rolling hills and terraced fields of tea. On the outskirts they were greeted at a reception camp, where a pair of young men took their names and sent them directly to the makeshift hospital that had been set up in a series of large tents. Bright pink bougainvillea flowered all around.

'Look how smooth the grass is,' said Christopher as they walked across the field. 'This doesn't feel like India at all.'

'It's a golf course,' said Fred, pointing. 'See that sandy patch? It's called a bunker.' He strode steadily across the immaculate turf and Kate noticed that his leather boots had rotted almost to pieces, although he had carefully mended them with twine.

'Look, Mi Khin,' said Christopher. 'Perhaps we can build a sandcastle. Have you ever been to the seaside?' She shook her head blankly.

In the hospital they were registered and sent to separate wards. 'Look after her,' called Kate, as Mi Khin was carried off by a pair of kindly nurses, clucking over her and promising baths and toys.

'What about you, madam?' said the elderly Indian doctor who supervised their admission. 'You are ill.'

'Yes, I suppose I am,' said Kate, feeling her hot, clammy forehead. She had barely noticed the return of what she guessed was malaria, but now that they were safe she felt close to collapse.

'Nurse?' called the doctor, and soon Kate was led away to a cubicle to undress and bathe.

Nurse Basu had clearly dealt with many refugees and did not flinch when she saw the state of Kate's body. Her feet, under the layers of mud, were bleeding and rotten, and her legs and arms were covered in infected leech bites and swollen welts from mosquitoes.

The nurse made her stand in a deep tub of warm water and Kate, who had barely removed her clothes for weeks, looked on with macabre curiosity at the washing process, lifting her limbs now and then to assist. She noticed, without surprise, her protruding ribs and deflated breasts, feeling by now wholly detached from her body.

'Your feet are quite bad,' said the nurse. 'They will heal but it will take some time.'

'I had no shoes for a while. I found some more but they didn't fit properly.'

'I've seen children who walked the whole distance with no shoes,' said the nurse, gently sponging Kate's legs. 'Several of them had lost all their toes.'

'Poor little things,' said Kate. 'The children who came with me are all right, I think, apart from a few cuts and lost toenails. And of course they're so thin.'

'The boy isn't yours, then?'

'Oh, no,' said Kate. 'I just sort of found them both. Their mothers died in the Hukawng Valley.'

She thought desolately of the misery she had seen. How would these children ever live normal lives?

'What about the gentleman who came in with you?' said the nurse, turning Kate around to wash the back of her legs. 'Your husband? Or father, perhaps?' She giggled a little.

'Neither,' said Kate. 'He's just another friend made along the way.' Since the night that she had killed Faulkner, Fred had been distant – regretting, she supposed, their moment of closeness. For a moment she had wanted him badly and it was impossible to go back to their usual easy friendship when so much lay unsaid between them.

When no more dirt would come off, Kate stepped out of the now brown water of the tub and was given a towel. It was threadbare but felt like a wonderful luxury, and she wrapped it tight around herself. When she was dry, the nurse gave her a cotton gown to wear and led her along a corridor with rough wooden partitions.

The sounds of the hospital murmured all around – distant crying, urgent conversations, the creak of trolleys. Her feet, in light slippers, made no sound on the floorboards.

The nurse led her through a door at the end of the corridor, which said 'Princess Elizabeth Ward'. Inside were eight beds, all of them empty.

'It's so quiet,' said Kate. 'Why so few patients?'

'This ward is just for European ladies,' said the nurse, busily plumping the pillows on the bed nearest the door.

'Oh, I see,' said Kate, suddenly embarrassed. 'Are the other wards full? For Indian ladies, I mean?'

'Yes, mostly.'

Kate climbed into bed, the white cotton sheets brushing against her skin. This world felt alien but somehow horribly familiar.

'You know,' she said tentatively, 'you could bring others in here if they need beds – I mean . . .'

'There's a rule,' said the nurse, looking a little shocked. 'You mustn't worry about it. Now lie down and I'll be back shortly with the doctor.'

'Nurse – can I send a telegram from here? I must let my mother in England know that I'm all right. I have money.'

'Of course. I'll get some paper so you can write it down. Someone will take it up to town.'

When the nurse was gone, Kate lay looking up at the fan spinning lazily above her. She felt as if she was up there on the ceiling, looking down at a pink figure in white sheets. Surely she would wake soon to find herself curled in mud in some wretched stretch of jungle, her body starting to decay, with nothing to fill the time but more walking.

✶

One evening Fred limped into Kate's room, escorted by Nurse Basu, who watched him like a hawk from her seat in the far corner as she darned socks.

'My chaperone,' he said, nodding his head in her direction with a smile. 'She wouldn't let me come in at all to begin with. She says five minutes only.'

'She's sweet,' said Kate. She looked at Fred, who stood with his hands behind his back, looking around the ward. 'You look well.'

'Oh, I'm fine,' he said. 'A few square meals inside me, even if they do serve the most insipid curries I've ever eaten. Better than rice and leaves.'

'I'm still on porridge. I look forward to something more substantial.'

He looked Kate over, taking in the sweaty hair on her forehead and her flushed cheeks. 'You still look peaky.'

'I know.'

'Feverish, are you?'

'Yes. I can't sleep . . .' She wondered whether to tell him that her nights were disrupted by visions of ghostly figures and decided against it.

Fred looked at her. 'Nightmares?'

'Yes.'

'I get them too,' he said wearily. He sat down on the cane chair by the bed, wincing as he sat back. 'I used to get them years ago as well, after the last war. The odd thing was that they didn't start until I was back in London, safe and sound. Now they're old friends.'

'My father did, too. I think that's why . . .' She hesitated.

'He killed himself?'

'Six years ago. How did you know?'

He sighed. 'I pieced it together. Happened to a friend of mine. The memories of the trenches wouldn't go away.'

'Mother was so relieved when the war ended,' said Kate. She remembered her mother running across the garden to where she and Laura were playing with the old sheepdog, still wearing her apron and her slippers. 'She kept saying, "Daddy's coming home!" But he never did come home. Not really.'

Fred laid a hand on hers and looked intently at her. 'What do you see in your nightmares?'

'The dead.'

He nodded. 'I used to think it was a punishment.'

'For what?'

'Surviving.'

She found herself blinking back tears. 'But you've done so much good. You fought in the war. I've never done anything useful.'

Fred was silent for a moment and then looked at her. 'Didn't I tell you about my brother Graham, and what he did before he died? You can't change the past. All that matters is what you do when things are falling apart. And here you are.'

'What do you mean?'

'You've brought those kids through hundreds of miles of rough country. You killed a man to save their lives. You could have left long before but you didn't. You stayed. You did something good. Don't you know how rare that is?'

'Why did you bring Mi Khin?' asked Kate abruptly, knowing the answer. 'Above all the others?'

Fred shrugged, but she saw tears glistening. 'She reminds me of my children. It's too late for me to get them back but I might be able to do something for her.'

'Redemption?'

'Yes. Of a sort.'

She sighed. 'What will happen next?'

'When they discharge us? We'll travel to Calcutta, I suppose.'

'The nurses say it's a long journey.'

'Three days by train, at least,' said Fred. 'Nothing to what we've been used to.'

'What will you do once we get there?'

'My first task will be to make arrangements for Mi Khin. She deserves a real home and a family, even if her father's dead. I'll do whatever I can for her. And Christopher, of course.'

'And then?' Kate found her heart was beating fast.

'I've spent a long time looking for a home,' said Fred quietly. 'I think you have, too.' He took her hand and squeezed it gently.

Nurse Basu cleared her throat and began rattling medicine bottles in a meaningful way. Fred smiled wryly and pushed back his chair.

'Time's up. I must go.'

Kate looked up at him and suddenly the future seemed much brighter. 'I'll see you tomorrow.'

'Sleep well,' he said, and lifted her hand quickly to kiss it before hurrying out under Nurse Basu's stern gaze.

45
Birmingham, September 1936

*L*aura's voice sounded anxious as it echoed slightly down the line.

'Kate, are you sure it's wise to leave Mother like this?'

'Like this?' said Kate, raising her eyebrows.

'Well – you know. So soon.'

'It's been six months.'

'That's hardly any time,' said Laura earnestly. 'Not when you've been married for twenty-five years.'

'Mother's fine,' said Kate stiffly. 'She wanted me to go. She urged me to, in fact.'

Laura sounded unconvinced. 'Of course she'd say that . . .'

Kate shook her head. 'You ought to know her better than that, Laura. She says what she feels. She's doing fine. Of course she's sad but—'

'What?'

'I expect,' said Kate carefully, 'she's also rather relieved.'

There was a silence. 'Kate, that's a dreadful thing to say!'

'Not if it's true.' Kate took a deep breath. 'It's been tough for her. She's had to run a farm while also looking after Dad and trying to scrape a living.'

'They loved each other,' said Laura, sounding defensive.

'Of course,' said Kate, surprised. 'Mother will always love Dad, just as we will. But she's been exhausted and overwhelmed for years and years. Can't you see that it's a weight off her shoulders?'

'Certainly sounds like it's a weight off yours!'

'Christ, Laura, don't be so sanctimonious,' said Kate sharply. She heard her sister start to protest but she suddenly felt angry and hurtled on. 'You have no right to judge how Mother or I might be feeling. We spent years in that house, waiting on him, hearing his nightmares, watching him slowly die before our eyes.'

'Kate, I didn't mean—'

'You weren't even there! You sailed off into the sunset as soon as you were able, hardly ever came home, hardly ever asked any of us how we were feeling. We were all miserable!'

There was a long silence. 'I didn't know . . .' said Laura at last. She sounded shocked. 'I'm sorry.'

'Don't be,' said Kate, the fight suddenly leaving her. 'Not your fault.'

'You should have told me.'

'I didn't know how,' said Kate. 'You were always so happy – I didn't want to spoil that. Everything always seems to go your way.'

'Well, it doesn't.'

Kate rubbed her forehead, feeling exhausted, regretting what she had said.

'I lost a baby,' said Laura. 'Back in the summer.'

Kate closed her eyes. 'You didn't say.'

'I didn't want to upset Mother.'

There was a long silence. 'I'm sorry,' said Kate at last. 'I really am. I wish – I wish you'd been able to tell us.'

She heard Laura sigh. 'We're all hopeless at communicating.' She paused. 'Are you going to stay in Birmingham?'

'I suppose so,' said Kate, her head in her hands. 'I haven't made many plans yet. I'm going to get my teaching certificate and then . . . who knows?'

She put her foot up on the chair beside her and examined the bruises on her thighs. The night before she had drunk too much, and once again had woken beside a man she didn't know and didn't much like.

'Kate,' said Laura, her voice soft, 'you are looking after yourself, aren't you?'

'Of course,' said Kate, and felt the tears trickling down her cheeks.

46

Tavoy, November 1942

The weeks passed slowly. Edwin knew that Rama was planning something, although he said little about it in case they were overheard. He knew what it was he felt for Rama, and knew that it was returned, but there was no way to be alone and no way to discover what was ahead.

He longed to be far away from the camp but felt a strange sense of fear for what lay beyond. The camp was predictable in its horrors, but who knew what awaited them outside? How far would they get in a country ruled by the Japanese?

The camp at Tavoy had been operating for some months and its inhabitants were starting to show signs of strain. They were all malnourished, the hospital ward almost always full. But even those who were not actually sick were weak from lack of food and worn down by the long hours of hard work.

Edwin, unskilled in any trade, was generally allocated to building roads. Other groups with more relevant experience were made use of elsewhere: gangs containing trained engineers were often sent off for days at a time, working on projects vaguely defined as 'construction'. Rumours flew of massive bridges being built, of the railway that was apparently edging through the mountains towards Burma, although no sign of it had yet been seen.

One day Rama was not at work on Edwin's stretch of road. This was not unusual; they couldn't always manage to work together. But Edwin was afraid, because that morning he had seen a truck arrive in the yard.

When work was over he headed back to the camp with the rest, his mind turning over all the possibilities. Perhaps Rama was being taken away. Perhaps he would never see him again. And he felt his heart clench, for in this desolate place Rama was the only thing that made him want to keep on living.

The truck was still in the yard but standing beside it were a dozen men. They stood in rigid lines, facing the side of the truck, and a Japanese officer paced up and down behind them.

Edwin scanned the rows; at once he saw Rama's tall silhouette and felt his stomach lurch. There was a shout from the sergeant and suddenly the men were being herded towards the back of the truck. Edwin fought the urge to run forwards, to shout something, to plead for mercy.

The man turned sideways and he saw at once that it wasn't Rama. The young man who was even now climbing into the truck looked quite different and Edwin found himself shaking with relief.

The man at the back of the group was white and for a split second he glanced towards where Edwin stood watching. The doors were slammed, then the truck moved off and the man was gone, heading off to some other bleak place of neglect and punishment, unlikely to be seen again. He had been thin, covered in dirt, his balding head bare to the sun, but Edwin was certain that it had been Daniel Haskell – the kindly, melancholy Jew who had once offered to let him an apartment in Rangoon, a lifetime ago.

✦

Returning to the sleeping quarters, early one evening, Edwin found a man from the cell next door, a young American, lying half-conscious on the floor. Another prisoner knelt beside him.

'What's wrong?'

'Charlie couldn't work today so they cut his rations,' said his friend, looking anxiously around. 'I didn't know or I'd have saved him some of mine.'

'I need to eat regularly,' said Charlie, his breathing shallow. 'I get – sick if I haven't eaten.'

'Sounds like low blood sugar,' said Edwin. 'You ought to go to the hospital.'

'No,' Charlie said quickly, his breath coming out in a gasp. 'They think I'm faking. Last time it happened they said I was just trying to get out of work. I'll be fine. I'll just have to wait until morning.'

'You won't make it to roll call,' said his friend. 'They'll beat you. Or worse.'

Edwin stood irresolute, wondering what he could do. 'I'm on water duty tonight. I might be able to get something.'

'What will you do? Steal it?'

'It's too risky,' muttered the sick man, but Edwin shook his head and hurried away.

He had noticed that the kitchen was sometimes left unattended for ten minutes or so in the evening, when the cook was taking food to Colonel Kojima in his rooms. There was usually a soldier on guard, but he patrolled up and down and it might be possible to slip in without him seeing.

I must be mad, thought Edwin, as he hurried along the path that led towards the kitchen area. This is absurd – I'll be caught! But something had gripped him, and he knew that it had been spurred by seeing Daniel Haskell and being unable to help him. Perhaps in some way, he thought, I can make amends.

Approaching the kitchen, he hovered in the shadow of a nearby building and watched the cook through gaps in the bamboo shutters. The guard was nowhere to be seen.

At last the cook emerged, carefully carrying a wide tray with a cloth laid over it. Even from twenty yards away Edwin thought he could detect a savoury smell and felt his mouth water as he wondered what delicacies were being served up for the Colonel.

As soon as the cook was out of sight he slipped into the low kitchen and felt the heat from the ranges rush towards him. A cauldron was boiling; sniffing it, he knew it was the same watery soup that was served up every day, sometimes with rice thrown in, sometimes not.

Flinging open boxes, his heart thudding, Edwin found sacks of dry rice, large unidentifiable vegetables, and in a cooler, a slab of raw meat, presumably destined for the Japanese rather than the prisoners. It was all he could do not to grab the oozing meat and eat it there and then.

At last he found what he was looking for: bread. A large hunk of hard bread, only a day or two old. Resisting the urge to eat any, he rushed out of the kitchen and came face to face with a Japanese guard.

He saw the machine gun in the man's hand at the same time as the soldier saw the lump of bread in Edwin's. They stared at one another. The guard was only twenty or so, and for the first time Edwin found himself seeing the Japanese for what they were: young men, far from home, fighting a war that they had no say in. He wondered if the man could see him with as much clarity: a thin, exhausted prisoner, stealing bread to give to a man who would otherwise die.

It seemed that they must have been there for some time, but afterwards he knew that it could only have been a few seconds. The soldier gave an almost imperceptible nod, jerking his head in the direction of the cells, and Edwin knew at once that he was safe.

He would never know what had made the guard let him go. He imagined that for one brief moment the man had recognised their shared humanity. Perhaps he, too, wanted the war to be over. Perhaps he had European friends. Perhaps he was just sick of the bloodshed.

After taking the bread to the sick man, Edwin went back out on his rounds, filling up buckets at the stream and carting them around the camp. He was still trembling, although he knew he had done the right thing, possibly for the first time in his life. Would the guard regret letting him go, and report it later? He thought not, although he could not have said why he felt so sure.

Passing the main courtyard, he saw another Japanese guard ahead, an older man, and walked faster, his head bowed.

'More water,' said the guard, pointing towards the main courtyard. 'Now.'

'Yes, sir,' said Edwin, and hurried along between the buildings until he came out in the courtyard.

In the moonlight eight naked men were washing hurriedly from buckets set out in a row. Most of the men were Burmese, slight and very thin now, their ribs protruding. On the end of the row was Rama, much taller than the rest, the scars on his back gleaming silver in the moonlight.

Edwin's mouth felt dry. His hands shook as he offered the buckets to one of the orderlies, who took them and thumped them down before the prisoners. The water was already brown and murky.

'Finish!' shouted one of the guards. Edwin saw Rama turn, his chest glistening, and he at once saw Edwin. Their eyes met and Rama's mouth curved into the beginnings of a smile as he scooped up water from the bucket and flung it over his head.

'Back to cells,' said the guard, and picking up their meagre bundles of clothes, the men filed across the yard, passing Edwin where he stood uncertainly, waiting to collect the buckets. The men dripped as they passed, leaving a trail of wet dust that turned to mud as they trod in it.

Rama brushed against him and whispered, 'Friday at noon. Watch for my signal.'

He was out of sight before Edwin had a chance to process what he had said, although his body was tingling. Picking up his buckets, he left the yard quickly and went to refill them, the words echoing in his head. Friday at noon.

47

Margherita, November 1942

At night the dead came as usual, making their sorrowful pilgrimage through Kate's dreams. She was no longer afraid of them. Now she just felt sad and guilty to be reminded again and again that she had survived.

She watched a corpse stagger past and saw that it was Edwin, his eyes blank, his body torn and bloody. Suddenly the silent procession was interrupted by shouts and it seemed that a dozen people were calling her name through the darkness, but it wasn't dark any more; the lamps were lit, the dead had vanished, and she was awake.

Christopher was at her side, Nurse Basu a few steps behind him, and he was calling her name and tugging on her arm.

'Kate, Kate! Come on, quickly!'

'What is it?' she said thickly, her mouth suddenly full of ashes.

'Fred.'

In a fumble of sheets, unsure whether she was still dreaming, she got out of bed, grabbing Christopher's arm to steady herself.

'Here,' said Nurse Basu, folding a shawl around Kate's shoulders as Christopher led her out of the ward.

'What's wrong with Fred?' Kate whispered as they hurried along the dark corridor.

'I think he's dying.'

Her bare feet were almost silent. There was a ringing in her ears and for a moment she was back at the airfield at Myitkyina, in the moments after the attack, dazed and uncomprehending.

They came to another room, where the letters on the door said 'George VI Ward'. The door opened and Kate saw one of the orderlies holding it, his dark face solemn in the half-light.

In the golden glow of an oil lamp Dr Choudhury leaned over one of the beds, looking up as they approached.

'How is he?' whispered Kate, going to the bedside. She looked down at Fred, who lay still, his eyes closed, his face flushed. She could see his chest rising and falling almost imperceptibly, and his moustache quivering a little each time he took a breath.

'He has had a heart attack,' said Dr Choudhury, turning to look at her sombrely. His glasses were askew and he looked drained. Kate wondered if he had been up all night.

She gazed down at Fred. He had been stocky when she first met him, but in the last few months he had become thin. Under the sheets his body looked bony and frail and utterly defenceless.

'Will he live?' she asked.

The doctor sighed. 'I don't know. I'm sorry. His heart is very weak. Has he had other attacks before? Collapses?'

'Not that I know of,' said Kate.

'I found him on the ground in the jungle once,' said Christopher suddenly. He looked at Kate anxiously. 'He said he'd tripped over a tree root and must have been knocked out. He told me not to tell anyone else as you'd all worry.'

'When was this?' asked the doctor.

'Oh, ages ago,' said Christopher. 'Before Shinbwiyang. Four months, or so.'

'Well, it's no matter,' said Dr Choudhury. 'His heart has always been weak, I believe. But the worry of your great journey, not to mention the constant physical trauma, must have put great strain on it.'

They were all silent. Kate took Fred's hand and squeezed it a little, hoping upon hope that he would open his eyes and tell them all not to fuss. She studied the kind lines of his face and thought of all that they had not said to one another.

'Can he hear us?'

'Perhaps,' said Dr Choudhury.

She perched on the chair by the bedside and leaned in towards him. 'Fred,' she said, speaking close to his ear. 'Fred, it's Kate.' He did not respond. But she felt – or was it her imagination? – a twitch in the fingers that lay within her hot hand.

'I'm going to get Mi Khin,' said Christopher and she saw him leave the ward with one of the nurses. The doctor was gone too, and suddenly she was alone with Fred.

'Kate,' said Fred, and she knelt at once beside him.

He was evidently fighting to stay conscious, his eyes blinking heavily and his voice thick. 'Forgive me.'

'There's nothing to forgive,' said Kate, pressing his hand between hers. 'I owe you my life.'

'Couldn't have got here without you,' he said slowly. 'I meant to get you . . . all the way.'

'You did,' said Kate. 'We're so close now. Whatever happens . . .' she gripped his hand tighter, 'I promise I'll look after the children.'

'In my bag . . . there's still about £50 in rupees. Take it.'

'Christopher and Mi Khin can have it,' she said. 'I don't want it.'

He was quiet for a moment and then said. 'I know it's been bothering you . . . Fielding, I mean. You did the right thing. Never regret that.'

'I won't.'

'And what I wanted to say yesterday – I wanted to tell you . . .'

'I know,' she said, lifting his hand and kissing it. 'I know.' His eyes met hers and she saw the yearning, the regret for all the wasted time.

'What will you do . . . after?'

'I don't know yet.'

'You want to be free,' he said. 'But there's – there's a home waiting for you somewhere. Find it.'

She saw Christopher looking hesitantly around the door. He brought Mi Khin into the room and she stood at Fred's side, her tiny hand in his. She was singing a nursery rhyme that he had taught her and Fred smiled up at her, whispering the words.

For a moment Kate could not bear to witness any more and walked away down the ward, passing beds occupied by sleeping figures. Breathing deeply, she went back, and saw Christopher crouched beside the bed.

'Your parents would be proud,' said Fred, patting the boy's arm. 'I'm sorry . . . that we couldn't save your mother. She deserved better.'

'Yes,' said Christopher, gripping the edge of the bedclothes, his face pale in the lamplight. 'But so do you. I'll be all right, Fred.'

'I hope you can put . . . all this . . . behind you,' said Fred. His voice was growing fainter, each word painful. 'There's a lot to look forward to. Out in the world.'

He looked around at all of them, swallowing, his dry lips moving, smiling a little as he caught Kate's eye. 'The shadows are closing in. Look after each other.' His eyes closed and he lay still, though his moustache fluttered a little now and then.

Dr Choudhury came unhurriedly across the ward and put a stethoscope to Fred's chest. 'His heartbeat is very weak.'

'Take Mi Khin back to bed,' said Kate, looking up at Christopher. 'I'll stay with him. Good night, sweetheart . . .' She hugged Mi Khin, who smiled sleepily.

Christopher took Mi Khin's hand. 'You'll be all right?'

Kate nodded. 'Go to bed.'

He leaned over quickly and kissed her on the forehead, then retreated bashfully, Mi Khin clinging to his hand.

Kate sat back in the cane chair, watching Fred's chest rise and fall very gently as it began to grow light outside. Two roads diverged here; she had hoped to have a choice, but now one was closed forever. There would be time tomorrow for making plans, for regrouping, for harnessing what energy she still had, but for now she felt dazed.

How do I go on? she remembered Christopher saying, and still she had no answer. She knew what Fred would say: we go on because we must and try to do what is right.

Kate fell asleep briefly and for once she did not see the armies of the dead. Instead she dreamed of Fred, younger, playing with a group of small children she knew were his, a pretty dark-haired woman waving nearby, the beautiful green mountains of the Shan State filling the horizon.

At dawn Dr Choudhury returned and told her Fred was gone. Her legs stiff, Kate stood, feeling tired and heartsick. She looked once more at his face, now peaceful, and kissed his cheek, then went out of the ward and walked across the grass, which was already warm in the early morning sun.

48

Calcutta, December 1942

It seemed to Kate that the culmination of such a journey should be marked by some sort of fanfare. Instead they arrived by train in Calcutta on a blindingly hot day in December, and all of a sudden the great journey that had begun for her nearly ten months before in Rangoon was at an end.

Fred had been cremated beside the river in Margherita, early one evening when the sun was setting and mist rolled over the tea plantations. She knew it was what he would have chosen and, despite offers of a plot in the Christian churchyard, they had flung his ashes into the river.

'Where does that river go?' she had asked the priest who supervised the cremation.

'It is joining Brahmaputra,' he said, gesturing to the east, 'one of the largest rivers in Asia. Eventually it is emptying into the Bay of Bengal.' He smiled, raising a hand to his chest. 'Heart of Asia.'

With nothing left to stay for, Kate, Christopher and Mi Khin departed for Calcutta soon afterwards. The journey was long and slow. Christopher, poring over a map, had measured the different lines they would take and looked up, astonished to find that there were over a thousand miles more to cover.

They had taken a slow train to Pandu, followed by a ferry across the Brahmaputra, then at last they had boarded the southbound service that took them all the way to Howrah Junction in Calcutta. They dozed through the long days and nights on hard wooden benches, watching the countryside roll by, getting slowly coated in red dust, living off the fruit and tea that was offered by hawkers.

'It's huge!' said Christopher, looking up at Howrah Junction as they approached through the suburbs. 'It must be a hundred times the size of Maymyo station.'

Kate led the way off the platform and onto the main concourse. All around the daily life of India danced: busy, dirty, poor, fascinating, alive. The children were excited to be in the city at last. Kate did her best to keep a cheerful face for their sake, but she knew that they saw through it. All her energy had been focused on getting them to Calcutta; now, the task complete, she felt as though she might crumble.

At the Evacuee Enquiry Bureau on Wood Street, which was staffed by efficient young Indian clerks and overseen by Mrs Sharpe, a formidable Englishwoman, they were given forms to fill in.

'Father's or husband's name?' said Kate, frowning at the sheet of paper. 'I can't see that my father's name will be much use here.'

'My grandmother's name is Diana Wilson,' said Christopher, after writing slowly on the form. He chewed on the pen. 'And there's Uncle Roderick, my mother's brother. But all I can remember is that they live at a place called Doddenham Hall in Sussex. Mother always called it Doddering Hall. Do you think they'll find them?'

'I'm sure they will,' said Kate. 'It might take a while, though.'

On Mi Khin's form she wrote the names Hla Pemala and Joseph Smith, noting that the former had died at Shinbwiyang. She wondered if anyone would claim the child.

'Where is my papa?' asked Mi Khin.

'He's not here, sweetheart,' said Kate, feeling wretched. 'We'll try to find him. I promise.'

'I thought he might be waiting for me.'

Mrs Sharpe took Kate to one side. 'Of course all efforts will be made to find the child's father, but I must warn you that it can take some time. There are hundreds of unaccompanied children looking for their parents and sorting them all out is the devil's own job.'

'What happens to them in the meantime?'

'Most of them are sent to children's homes until they are claimed,' said Mrs Sharpe. 'We'll find a place for the little girl.'

'A home? I ought to look after her.'

'She needs to go to school, Miss Girton,' said Mrs Sharpe firmly. 'I understand you want to do what's best, but supporting a child on your own would be a great strain and she needs to be educated. There are charities that will cover the fees. What do you plan to do?'

'I've no idea,' said Kate blankly. 'I suppose I must find a job. My savings won't last long.'

'I have a few contacts I can put you in touch with,' said Mrs Sharpe, shuffling the forms together. 'I'll send you some names and addresses next week. Do you have any experience of nursing?'

Quietly, when everything else was agreed, Kate asked Mrs Sharpe if she had any record of a man named Edwin Clear, who ought to have arrived from Burma within the last six or seven months.

After leafing through a number of ledgers, Mrs Sharpe shook her head and Kate's heart sank. 'Nothing, I'm afraid.'

Somehow, after everything, she had thought that Edwin would be here waiting for her, her dearest friend, with the same shy smile as always, ready to tell her what he had been doing since they last met. She, in turn, would tell him about her journey, about the horrors she had seen, and about the man she had killed and the man she had loved.

But Edwin Clear had not passed this way; there was no sign of him and nothing to say if he was alive or dead.

'Try the hotels,' said Mrs Sharpe, 'the army – the governor's office – we're not as joined up as we ought to be . . .' She supposed that the young woman was looking for a lost lover. It was a story she had heard again and again, people looking for husbands, fathers, brothers, wives, children. Thousands of fractured families, thousands of hearts broken.

✳

They were given temporary lodgings at Loreto House, a requisitioned girls' school close to the cathedral. The staff who ran the place were kind and gave them two small rooms on the top floor with a view of the nearby park. A few nights after their arrival the Japanese began to bomb Calcutta and the strange, quiet interlude of their months in the jungle came firmly to an end.

One evening, when the children had gone to bed, Kate took her towel to the shared bathroom. Undressing, she saw blood in her underwear, vivid red, and stood stock-still for a moment, staring at it. What a remarkable thing the human body was; you could starve it and abuse it, put it through hell, but it was capable of renewal. After many months without bleeding, her body at least was beginning to recover.

'The mental scars will take some time,' the doctor had said, and she supposed he was right. She still woke sweating and tearful from her dreams, and much of the time she was gripped by anxiety, as though an icy hand was squeezing her heart. Now, with Fred gone, she felt more alone than ever and afraid of the great emptiness ahead of her.

But this – well, it's a start, she thought, and throwing her towel to one side she stood under the tap that protruded high on the wall, feeling the cold water beat down on her skin, and watched blood and dust mingle in the suds on the floor before they were washed away.

49

Tenasserim Region, December 1942

Plunging down through the trees, tripping over roots and low shrubs, Edwin felt vines whipping his face and reached up to hold his glasses on his nose, terrified of losing them.

'This way!' shouted Rama, ahead of him, pointing between two trees. 'I can see a path going downhill.'

Panting, Edwin followed, feeling sweat pooling in the small of his back, his shirt clinging to him. In the distance he could hear shouting.

Rama had slowed to a steady jog and, looking back, he saw the panic on Edwin's face. 'It's all right,' he said. 'Just keep moving. No need to overdo it.'

'If they – catch us . . .' panted Edwin and shook his head. They ran on along the path, which sloped steeply away through the trees, winding down the hillside.

When they had covered half a mile or so, Rama stopped and Edwin did likewise, leaning over, his hands on his knees, feeling suddenly sick. He stared at the ground, focusing on a little patch of dry earth. At last his breathing and his heart slowed, the nausea retreated and he looked up.

Rama was listening intently. They both stood quietly. All Edwin could hear was the gentle rustling of the jungle in the breeze. The shouting seemed to have stopped, and here they were, away from their cells, away from the road, suddenly in unknown country.

'I think it's all right,' said Rama at last, relief etched on his face. He patted Edwin on the shoulder. 'Come on.'

This time they walked briskly downhill, following the narrow path that had evidently been worn by generations of Burmese villagers. It seemed to be rarely used and was overgrown with creepers and thorny bushes. He ran a hand over a bright red blossom and sniffed its sweet scent.

'Watch out,' said Rama. Edwin looked up to see a huge and intricate spider's web, glistening with the last of the dew, in its centre an enormous yellow spider.

'Poisonous?'

'Perhaps. Best to be on the safe side.'

Watching carefully for spider webs, Edwin squinted ahead of him as he followed the path. Peering through the trees, he blinked suddenly. 'I think I can see the sea.' He pointed to where a shimmer showed in the far distance, a slick of silver between the trees.

Edwin tried to picture the map of Burma. He knew that Tavoy was somewhere down on the tail where Burma narrowed and shared a long section of the Siamese peninsula. They were hundreds of miles south of Rangoon, and an unthinkable distance from India.

'It's such a long way,' he said, and heard the despair in his voice. 'Do you really think we'll get to India?'

'We can try,' said Rama. 'The only alternative was to stay in that camp for the rest of our days or until the war ends, and who knows how long that will be?'

Edwin walked on, following the path as it curved. 'It's so much distance to cross, and all of it Japanese territory now. I wish there was an easier way.'

'So do I,' said Rama. 'But we'll do our best. We'll keep moving, try to avoid seeing anyone, get food where we can. Perhaps we'll think of a better idea. But for now we have to just keep going.'

'I suppose people will try to turn us in,' said Edwin as they trudged on.

'Some of them, yes, I think so. Others – I'm not so sure. There is still affection for your people, even after all that has gone before. And the Japanese can be very cruel. There are many who will help us, I believe.'

Edwin hoped beyond hope that Rama was right. For now they were just walking through the jungle; that was all that was expected of him. There was a great deal of pleasure to be found in the simple act of walking freely among the rustling trees.

Late in the afternoon they saw a stone pagoda and knew that they were nearing a village. As they emerged into a meadow, Rama exclaimed and pointed up into the nearby trees. 'This fruit, we can eat it.' Edwin peered up and saw a bunch of small round fruits that looked like little potatoes.

'What is it?'

'It's a Siamese fruit, *longkong*. I didn't know it grew in Burma. I suppose we are very far south.'

Rama reached up into the branches and, breaking off a twig that held a cluster of fruit, handed one to Edwin, who sniffed it doubtfully. It smelled slightly smoky, as though it had been held near a fire. He tore open the yellow skin and saw shiny white flesh inside, the sweet smell immediately reawakening his appetite. He bit into the fruit and closed his eyes.

'Nice, isn't it?' said Rama, who was already on his second. He laughed at Edwin's expression and handed him another. They stood quietly under the tree, the juice trickling down their chins.

'I'd forgotten what fruit tastes like,' said Edwin, looking wonderingly at the tree.

'We'd better not overdo it,' said Rama reluctantly. 'We might get ill.'

'Let's take some with us.'

'Good idea.'

They picked dozens of the little fruits and put them into the sack they'd taken from the camp, which held their few belongings. The dry handfuls of rice they had brought from the morning's rations would not last long. As they finished, a shout came from somewhere nearby and quickly they darted back into the woods, ducking down behind a thick bush with sharp thorns.

A few minutes later they saw four or five young men crossing the meadow, all dressed in checked *longyis*. They carried scythes and other tools and had evidently been working somewhere in the fields. Their gossip and laughter carried clearly into the woods as they chatted happily, swinging their tools and strolling unhurriedly towards the village.

Edwin was reminded of the men he had seen in London coming off building sites on Friday afternoons, their boots dusty, their hands calloused, slapping each other's shoulders as they headed for the nearest pub. He had envied their camaraderie, in the face of poor wages and appalling conditions, and regretted that by class and by temperament he would forever be barred from such friendship.

'Let's go,' said Rama beside him, as soon as the men were out of sight. Moving tentatively through the trees they emerged again in the field and hurried across it. But they saw no one else that day and soon they were far away from the village, heading north, with the sea somewhere to the west. Dusk fell and they walked while the sky faded from pink to pale blue to darkest navy.

At last they found a stream, tiny and trickling, and stopped to drink deeply and to wash, kneeling on the dry earth. All around the jungle was quiet; nothing could be heard except the tinkle of the stream and the sighing of the trees.

They ate a meal of fruit, keeping the bulk back for the following day in case they found no food. When they had finished eating, Rama took the skins and flung them one by one into the undergrowth. With a sigh he lay down on the ground near Edwin and smiled up at him.

'You look anxious.'

'I'm fine.'

'Everything is going to be all right.' He reached for Edwin's hand and squeezed it, his touch sending sparks of desire through Edwin's body. He let go, and Edwin lay back on the jungle floor beside him, their arms touching.

'So many stars,' said Rama. 'Have you ever seen so many?'

'Never,' said Edwin, tracing the shapes that were both familiar and completely new. 'It's one of the first things I noticed at night in Rangoon. In London there are too many street lamps to see them properly.'

'Everything is different here.'

'It is,' said Edwin. 'I was lonely and grieving when I came to Burma, and yet somehow it has been one of the richest years of my life, despite everything.'

'Thanks to your friend Kate.'

'At first. Yes.'

'You care for her very much. What is she like? Tell me.'

And so he told Rama all about the girl he had known in Rangoon, about swimming at the India Club, sunrise at Amarapura, about Kate's father, about her yellow silk dress, about how lively and joyous she was despite her own sorrow and loneliness.

Rama listened, laughing in the right places, and Edwin knew he understood that she held a different place in his affections.

'I would like to meet her,' he said at last, pushing back his thick hair from where it clung to his forehead.

'You will,' said Edwin, and he suddenly felt hopeful about the future.

They were quiet for a few minutes, watching the universe as it sparkled above them.

'How long have you known?' asked Edwin, surprised by the question as it emerged. He heard Rama chuckle in the darkness beside him.

'Longer than you.'

'When you were a boy?'

Rama shifted so that his arms were folded behind his head. He was still looking up at the stars. 'I was twelve or thirteen, I suppose. I became aware that I was not quite like the other boys. They began to chase girls.'

'And you weren't interested?'

Rama laughed. 'Oh, I was. Girls are wonderful. And they liked me back. I listened to them, which none of the others did.'

Edwin felt a mosquito land on his arm and brushed it away. 'And did you ever . . .'

'I was sixteen or so. She was a little older and had already been with all my friends.'

'Isn't that frowned on in India? Before marriage, I mean?'

'Of course, but young people are the same in every country of the world. This girl was kind and gentle. I even fancied myself in love for a short time.' He laughed. 'It didn't last long.'

'What happened?'

'There was a boy. His father was a big landowner and they were wealthy and high-caste. He was twenty and much more experienced – he had had many lovers, boys and girls. He was handsome and dashing, very charming.'

Edwin listened. He wondered if he ought to feel jealous, but instead he was fascinated at this insight into a youth so unlike his own.

'I fell for him head over heels, spent all my meagre pay on gifts for him, almost abandoned my friends so I could spend time with him. He taught me a lot. We used to go to a place by a lake where the grass was long and the trees trailed down to the water.'

Edwin imagined hot nights in India, cool water, brown skin glistening as it moved, and felt a prickle of returning desire.

'It caused a rift with my family,' said Rama. 'Some rumour reached my father, I don't know how, and he wrote to me saying I was no longer welcome at their home. I haven't seen them for ten years.'

'What about your mother?'

'She writes to me in secret.' Rama frowned. 'At least, she did until I was captured. I didn't tell her anything about the boy, of course – or any of the others. She probably thinks I'm dead.'

'How did it end?' said Edwin at last.

'He got married,' said Rama, and laughed again. 'It's almost funny now but at the time it was a great shock to me. He'd never introduced me to his family or let me meet his friends, which was understandable because our backgrounds were so different. But it turned out he'd been engaged all along, to a girl he'd never met. The whole time he'd been – how do the Americans say – screwing around.' He shook his head. 'Poor girl. They had a grand wedding, I heard – thousands of guests, a great deal of food, dancing, no expense spared. She was from Jaipur, with strict parents. I doubt he stayed faithful for long.'

'Did you ever see him again?'

'Once. I was working as a waiter at one of the big hotels in Delhi just before the war, and I saw him come in alone. I was serving drinks in the foyer. He looked a little older and a little less handsome, but mostly the same. But he checked in under a name that was not his own. Who he was meeting I do not know, but it was not his wife.'

Edwin felt a pang of guilt. 'I behaved in just the same way. No one deserves to be treated like that.' He thought of Emilia sitting silently by the fire, trying to read a book as the clock ticked towards midnight. 'She was everything that is good and kind. I really did love her, in my way.'

He listened to the insects chirping in the darkness and remembered the smoke rising over Golders Green.

'You are thinking it was all a lie,' said Rama.

'Wasn't it?'

'Only you can know that. But what happened to her – it was not your fault.'

'But if . . .' Edwin had no idea how to finish the sentence.

'If she had lived you would not have come to Burma. You and I would never have met. Perhaps everything that happened was meant to happen. Who can say?'

He leaned over and brushed the hair off Edwin's forehead. 'All you have to decide is what you want here and now. Nothing more.' His brown eyes were kind and Edwin thought his heart might burst.

Rama pulled back for a moment and looked at him. 'It's all right to be sad still.'

'I'm not,' said Edwin, and the truth came suddenly. 'I'm happy.' And summoning his courage, he sat up and put his arms around Rama, tasting the sweet fruit on his mouth, and the ashes of his old life blew away on the warm breeze.

PART III

India, 1945

Three years later

50

Calcutta, September 1945

At the hospital, half of the beds at last lay empty. Kate stripped the linen from each one, throwing the white sheets into a basket, and wiped her forehead on the sleeve of her uniform as she progressed down the ward.

For more than three years there had rarely been an empty bed, and often men were brought in to lie on the floor until one could be found. The fighting in Burma had been fierce, wave after wave of soldiers sent against the Japanese, to return with mangled limbs or ravaged by disease.

But now the war was over and those soldiers who remained in hospital were being patched up before being sent home. The emptying wards echoed and Kate found herself walking aimlessly up and down between the beds, recalling the soldiers who had passed through her care, wondering what on earth she would do to fill the days.

'Look, nurse,' said Captain Howard, waving a photograph at her. 'This came in the post today.'

She went to his bedside and smiled at the photograph of three children, very solemn, sitting with a rather beautiful woman.

'That's my youngest,' said Howard, pointing at the little girl on her mother's lap. 'Edith. She turned two last month, and I haven't met her yet.'

'You will soon,' said Kate. 'It won't be long until you're out of here.'

'They might be afraid of me,' he said, suddenly gloomy. 'I shan't be much use with only one arm.'

'Children don't see these things,' said Kate, 'I promise. They might be curious but soon they'll stop noticing. They get used to things far more quickly than adults do.'

'You don't have children, do you, nurse?'

'No,' said Kate after a pause, and busied herself tidying his bedclothes. 'But my father came home from the last war almost an invalid when I was a child and it never occurred to me to find it strange.' She watched him cradling the photograph.

'I thought I wasn't going to get back to them,' he said, looking up at her. 'I thought I'd had it.'

She put his teacup on the trolley and picked up some letters that had fallen to the floor. 'Have you other family in the war?'

'My brother was killed at Monte Cassino,' he said, still staring at the photograph. 'And my sister Gloria was a POW, although she's on her way home now.'

'Where was she?'

'Malaya,' he said. 'Got caught in the first wave of the invasion. She says she's all right, but . . . well.' He sighed. 'Anyway, she's heading home. Going to live with Mother for a bit while she sorts herself out.'

'It won't be easy.'

'No.' He looked up at her. 'You were in Burma, weren't you, nurse?'

'That's right.'

'Came out through the jungle?'

She nodded.

'Then you know what it's like. When you've seen so much death and misery it's hard to imagine going back to normal life. I told Gloria not to worry about doing anything except relaxing when she gets home.'

'If she can,' said Kate. 'I find it's best to be busy – the busier I am the less I dwell on things.' She started to push the trolley away and then paused. 'What will you do when you get home?'

He waved the photograph. 'Play with my children. Get to know my wife again. Father wants me to join the family business but I'm not sure I'll be much use like this. I suppose I'll just try to put all of it behind me.'

'I'm sure you will,' said Kate, although she felt doubtful. Would anyone really be able to forget? Nightmares still plagued her – three years since she had arrived in Calcutta, three years since she had slept on the forest floor, three years since she had seen the remains of the dead all the way to India.

'I'm going to take some presents back for Edith and the boys,' said Howard. 'Get some toys before I leave Calcutta. I don't know what she'll like, though.'

'Anything you bring her will be treasured. It's you they want, really.'

'You're right, nurse,' said Howard, tucking the photograph carefully into the top pocket of his pyjamas. 'I must remember that. I've lost a lot of time with them over the last few years. Whatever I have left – well, I don't mean to waste it.'

Don't waste it, thought Kate, as she went about her duties, her heart still warmed by the love of the captain for his family. Who else had said that? Ah, of course. Fred had said it, long ago.

꙳

When her shift was over, she untied her rusty bicycle from the railings and pedalled slowly home across the city, taking the quietest route she knew. For most of the war a curfew had been imposed, but now the dark streets were buzzing with traders and traffic. She slowed when she reached Ashoka Street and stopped to buy a warm paratha from a man behind a stall. A lamp cast a gentle glow over his greasy pan as he slapped the dough back and forth.

'You are looking very tired, miss,' he said, and threw an extra paratha onto the banana leaf before tying it up for her. 'Time for sleep.'

Holding the parcel in one hand, she wheeled her bicycle along the alley with the other, stopping at last under a wooden staircase. She abandoned the bicycle and padded up the stairs to the room she shared with three other nurses. Pamela and Priya were out at the hospital, starting a night shift.

'There's a letter for you,' said Asanti, the youngest of the group, pointing to Kate's pillow. She sat cross-legged on her own bed in a long nightgown, brushing her long dark hair, and gazing critically into a little round mirror.

Kate picked up the envelope and saw her name and address printed on the front in neat capitals. She ripped it open.

Dear Miss Girton,

I do hope this address is still current. I wanted to let you know that our office recently received a request for information that may relate to you. I wonder if you might call at the Bureau one day this week and speak with me. I am here each day until six.

Yours cordially,
Eileen K. Sharpe
Evacuee Enquiry Bureau
12 Wood St
Calcutta

'Is it something serious?' asked Asanti, seeing her expression.

'I don't know. It's rather a shock, that's all.'

She sat down, reaching under the bed for the bottle of black-market whisky that stood on the floor and slopped some into a chipped mug. Sipping it, she looked thoughtfully at the letter once again. She felt the whisky spreading calm through her body.

Someone was trying to find her. She remembered the meticulous women at the Bureau who had taken down as much information as possible for each new arrival, cross-referencing it with enquiries such as this one. In the first year she had been there many times herself, asking for news, but none came and she had almost given up.

But now something was happening. Feeling elated, she drank deeply from the cup in her hand and read the letter once more, tearing strips from the greasy paratha that lay cooling beside her.

51

Calcutta, September 1945

Early the next morning Kate made her way to work, arriving at the hospital a little before seven.

What had once been a small teaching hospital now sprawled across several acres of dry parkland, forced by the war to grow swiftly to absorb the thousands of wounded being sent from across Asia. Dozens of rudimentary wards had been thrown up and scores of new nurses and doctors had been recruited. It was one of the biggest hospitals in India now and it made Kate feel pleasingly anonymous.

As she leaned her bicycle against a fence, she had the sudden feeling of being watched and swung around to look across the yard, but there was no one there, no one standing under the sad-looking palms or lurking in the flowerbeds. Apart from a few sweepers in the distance, there was no one to be seen.

She checked the rota and made her way to a distant ward, where she found Nurse Andrews coming off duty. She smiled wearily when she saw Kate and gratefully handed her the logbook.

'Any trouble?' said Kate.

'Very little,' said the nurse. 'Private Jamieson had a night-mare so there was a bit of shouting, but he's sleeping soundly now. Don't wake him unless you have to.'

'And the others?'

'Good as gold. Some fever still, and the usual dressings that will need changing. Nothing too onerous.'

Nurse Andrews patted her shoulder and departed, leaving Kate alone on the ward. It was silent; the men were still asleep. The only sound was the fan rotating gently overhead, pushing the warm, disinfectant-scented air sluggishly about.

She padded between the beds, checking on each patient.

'Nurse?'

She turned and saw Private Balewa, a Sudanese infantryman, blinking sleepily at her from his pillow. He was young, with wide eyes, and his dark skin glistened with sweat.

'Abdul. Are you all right?'

'I feel very hot, nurse. Feverish.'

'I'll bring a cold compress for your forehead in a few moments. It's still early, you know – try to get some more sleep.'

'How long till breakfast?'

'Nearly an hour.'

When she returned he was dozing again, and though she dabbed his forehead with a damp cloth he barely stirred. She perched on the bed next to him for a moment and observed how the blanket dipped in the empty space where his missing leg should have been. He had been shot by the retreating Japanese in the last months of the war, after nearly five years of combat.

Moving along the ward, she found that one or two of the other patients were beginning to stir and she chatted to each one, changing bandages where necessary, and tidied up their bedclothes.

At eight o'clock a bell tinkled and an orderly appeared at the entrance to the ward, pushing a trolley laden with bowls. 'Morning, nurse.' He lifted off the fly screen and gently stirred the large pot of tea.

'Thank you, Nikesh.'

He pushed the trolley around slowly, limping a little, and she helped him to distribute the bowls of porridge to the men. She hesitated at Private Jamieson's bed, but at the sound of someone's spoon tinkling against their bowl the Yorkshireman opened his eyes blearily and struggled to sit up. A wound inflicted at the Battle of Kohima had led to gangrene, but the danger had passed with the loss only of the toes on one foot, which he saw as a victory.

'I'm famished! Porridge again, is it, nurse?'

'Afraid so. It's good for you.'

'So I hear. I say, is that a newspaper?'

'Yesterday's,' she said, passing it over from the trolley. He seized it and read it from cover to cover during breakfast, balancing the bowl of porridge on his knees.

When she came back to collect his bowl the paper was lying discarded at the foot of his bed. 'Nothing?'

'What's that? Oh, no. No news.' He was lying back on his pillow, staring up at the ceiling unhappily. 'If my brother's dead I'd rather know for certain, but there's never anything, no hint. Mother keeps writing to me and I can't bear it.'

Kate picked up the paper, which was roughly folded over somewhere in the middle, and her eye was caught by a small photograph in the lower left corner. Two men in *longyis* were shaking hands in front of a crowd of people. In the background was a building she knew well, and of which she could have drawn a floor plan from memory: the Secretariat Building in Rangoon.

The brief article dealt with negotiations for a transitional government in Burma. Some of the names were familiar, but she could not see the one she was looking for. Instead she peered again at the photograph, scanning the faces in the crowd. For a moment she paused. There was a woman standing on the edge of the throng, her face slightly blurred, but Kate thought she was smiling. She held a child in her arms.

'Are you all right, nurse?' Jamieson was looking at her with concern.

'Oh – yes,' she said, putting the paper back on the trolley. 'I thought I saw someone I knew. It happens a lot these days.'

✦

Weaving through traffic on Wood Street, Kate arrived at the Evacuee Enquiry Bureau on Friday morning. She had come from a night shift and would be on nights for the next two weeks. Despite feeling tired, she was filled with nervous energy.

The waiting room already contained three other people, none of them talking. She pulled out the book she had brought, but she was too anxious to read and instead stared at the cover.

The minutes ticked past, and people went in and out of the main office until, at last, her name was called. 'Miss Girton?'

'That's me.'

'Mrs Sharpe is waiting for you. Her office is down the hall.'

'Thank you.'

Mrs Sharpe looked just the same as she had done three years ago, if perhaps a little more grey. 'Miss Girton, please sit down. How nice to see you again. Are you well?'

'I'm fine, thank you,' said Kate automatically.

'Still at the hospital?'

'Yes, for now.'

'I'm sure you're busy so I won't keep you,' said Mrs Sharpe, rummaging through a stack of papers. 'This was the letter we received that I thought might be about you.' She handed over a letter typed on thick notepaper.

Dear Sir,

I write seeking information regarding the whereabouts of a Miss Kate, an English Lady who was in Burma in 1941/42. I regret I do not know her surname or any further details except that her age is about thirty. We think she arrived in India in Spring/Summer 1942. We believe she is a teacher.

Any help you can give me with tracking down this lady would be kindly appreciated. I am working with a number of soldiers and former prisoners of war who are in the process of being repatriated.

Mr Shaji Acharya

'But who is Mr Acharya?' asked Kate, turning the letter over as though more information might appear.

'No idea, I'm afraid. He might be an agent or solicitor – I hear there's quite a thriving business in seeking out people who've been displaced in the war. The return address is a PO Box in Baranagar.'

'Well, as you may recall I have been waiting to hear from a man named Edwin Clear, but he knows my surname so I don't see how this could refer to me. And he's not a soldier.' She looked gloomily at the letter. 'How many other Kates are there on your list?'

'None that fit the description as well as you. A couple of Katherines but they are both older and married, an elderly teacher known as Miss Katie, a girl of fourteen who arrived in April 1942 – and you.'

'I can't imagine who else might be looking for me. And I was never a teacher.'

'Would you be willing to write a brief letter?' said Mrs Sharpe. 'Perhaps just giving a little more information about yourself and how you left Burma? Our mysterious correspondent might then be able to shed some light on the matter, if you are indeed who he's looking for.'

Kate felt suddenly deflated. She had been so sure that today was the day when she might get some answers. Now it seemed that there were only questions.

'Very well. I'll do it.' She scribbled a brief note, outlining her connection with Burma and asking, in turn, who was looking for her. It would all come to nothing, she was sure of it – but after three years it was the only lead she had.

Outside, Kate pushed her bicycle along the pavement, lost in thought. Two young men sitting on a wall muttered as she passed and turned to look at her, dislike etched on their faces.

'You are not welcome here!'

Resentment against the British in India had been bubbling for years, but the war had given it new fervour and she could easily imagine these men marching under the nationalist flag alongside Britain's enemies. They followed her for a while and her heart thudded as she glanced back, reluctant to give in to their intimidation by fleeing. She was used to being followed by strange men, but these two looked angry rather than lecherous.

'Miss! Excuse me, miss?'

'Why are you not listening? I am talking to you, please.'

At last they grew bored and stopped, throwing a few parting shots after her as she mounted her bicycle. 'Why don't you go home?' called the younger man, sounding frustrated.

Why indeed, she thought, as she pedalled away.

52

Calcutta, September 1945

'So who is he, this Edwin chap?' Pamela had asked, not long after her arrival in 1943. She had appeared at the digs one day clutching a huge suitcase and an absurd hat, slightly wilted after six weeks on a troop ship. 'Must be someone special for you to spend this much time on him.'

'He's just a friend,' said Kate shortly, wincing as she pulled off her shoes and sat down heavily on her narrow bed. She flexed her toes and looked critically at her swollen feet. She had done a full shift at the hospital before going to the government offices to make enquiries and felt exhausted.

'Oh, come on,' said Pamela, peering sardonically over her magazine. 'This isn't finishing school. You don't have to be coy.'

'There's nothing to tell.'

'You mean you didn't . . . you know.'

'No! It is possible to be just friends with a man, you know,' said Kate primly, feeling hypocritical.

'Don't be silly.' Pamela looked disappointed. 'Didn't you ever want to?'

'Not really,' said Kate, thinking back. 'It wasn't like that. He was kind and fun to be with, but in looks he wasn't my type at all. He was just sort of brotherly.'

'I bet he wanted to, though. They all do.'

Kate shrugged. 'I'm not sure he did. He'd been widowed and was grieving for his wife. And there was something . . .' She paused, trying to remember that sense she had had once or twice, something odd and confusing, something to do with the way he behaved with women and with men. But Pamela was looking eagerly at her, keen for gossip, and she found that she didn't want to share whatever it was.

'He was a good friend,' she said, rather lamely. 'I'd like to know where he is.'

Pamela had come straight out from England, and even though there were only a few years between them, Kate felt ancient by comparison. Pamela had worked as a typist at the BBC before the war and the wounded men who now passed through her care seemed to leave her untroubled.

I was once like her, thought Kate, as she waved Pamela off to a party, or, coming back from a night shift, saw her returning in the morning, the scent of cigar smoke and a man's cologne lingering in her hair. We would have been great friends.

In the early days in Calcutta she had made the effort, had gone to a few parties, had tried to behave like the old Kate. But the men who she would have flirted with once now bored her immeasurably, and the women were frivolous and dull.

Once a soldier just off active duty was present, and she spent the evening monopolising him in the hope that he might have a snippet of useful information. At the end of the evening he looked rather surprised when she turned down his offer to walk her home, and she felt a pang of regret. A few years ago she would have gone to bed with him just out of politeness; now she felt nothing.

Priya and Asanti, the other nurses who shared her room, were good Hindu girls, with little interest in parties, and occasionally she went to the pictures with them or shared a meal in the tiny kitchen. But the scheduling of their shifts meant that none of them had much time to spend together, and for this she was grateful. They were kind to her, but she had no energy for real friendship.

She preferred to work night shifts and sleep during the day, for the nightmares came less frequently when the sun was shining into the room. When this wasn't possible she drank late into the night, sipping whisky furtively as the others slept, and read a book until her head began to nod.

⁜

Kate woke with a shout, clapping a hand over her mouth at once, and looked around guiltily in the darkness, feeling thick sweat on her upper lip. She had been back in Shinbwiyang, with crowds of the dead pressing towards her, their mute faces accusing.

'What is it?' Priya's voice came sleepily from the other side of the room.

'Sorry,' whispered Kate, putting her hands by her sides, feeling her breathing begin to slow. In the darkness she could see occasional splinters of light reflecting off the ceiling fan. 'It's nothing.' She could hear the chirping of insects and the distant sound of traffic in the distance.

'You have nightmares,' said Priya quietly. 'I've heard you before.'

'Just bad dreams.'

'I used to have nightmares as a child,' said Priya, propping herself up on one elbow. 'I thought there were monsters in the dark.'

'Did you stop them?'

'Yes. I never get them now.'

'How?'

'It was a very poor village. There were no electric lights at all. One night my mother and father heard me crying and instead of bringing a lamp they took me outside, into the darkness. We walked for a long time and I was very scared, until we stood on a hillside above the village.'

'What did you see?'

'The stars,' said Priya, and Kate heard the longing in her voice. 'A million stars all gleaming high above me. We tried to count them and my father named some of them, and he said that if I was ever afraid I should think of the stars. No monster, he said, could live beneath such a sky.'

'And that was it?'

'That was it. No more nightmares.'

Kate was quiet, thinking of the sky. 'You can't see many stars in Calcutta,' she said at last.

'No. But I know they are there. I imagine them and think of my parents, my home.'

Kate pulled the thin cotton sheet back over her legs and breathed deeply, trying to calm her tense body.

'What are your nightmares?' asked Priya. 'What do you see?'

'The dead,' said Kate. She rolled over, pretending that she was drifting off to sleep, her eyes staring unblinking into the darkness. Eventually she slept and the dead came as always, making their passage through her dreams. But now above them shone a sheet of silver stars, and she recognised at once the beloved constellations that filled the night sky over Burma.

53

Calcutta, October 1945

As the hospital grew quieter, the nurses were given an extra day off each fortnight. It was a strange feeling, having time to oneself. Kate knew that staying busy was the only way to avoid succumbing to the worry and fear that dogged her footsteps. India was preparing for life after the war, and change was in the air, but she felt stuck; unable to consider the future when so much in her past lay unresolved.

She went one day to the great temple, walking there in the cool of the early morning as the city woke up around her. There were boys already sweeping the pavements and carts full of sacks of rice rumbling by. At the side of the road people were still lying in rows, wrapped in thin blankets against the cold pavements.

The poverty of Calcutta no longer shocked her. During the great famine of 1943 she had seen bodies being eaten by dogs on the riverbank and skeletal men fighting over scraps from a rubbish heap, their nails torn and their eyes desperate. Women had approached her in the street and tried to sell her their children for a few rupees. She gave them what she could and stumbled away.

The temple was still closed, so she sat at a stall outside the main gates and sipped a cup of sweet tea, lingering over it to make it last. The boy who ran the stall served her and then lay down again on the floor behind the barrow and went back to sleep.

When the temple gates opened at last, she went in and took off her sandals at the request of the elderly woman who was sweeping the steps. The woman was tiny and shrunken, her orange sari tucked up at her waist. Each time she leaned over to sweep, there was a flash of wrinkled brown midriff.

Kate wandered through the courtyard, feeling the cool stone under her feet. On all sides, archways led off to various chambers. She followed one of the passages and came out beside a huge statue of a goddess. Four-armed, three-eyed and wearing a necklace of skulls, she sat in a niche, her skin painted a dark blue-black.

Fascinated, Kate stared up at the statue, noting the corpse that she seemed to be standing on, a bone held in one hand and a weapon in the other. She was every inch the vengeful goddess, terrifying and powerful. Around her neck hung garlands of real flowers.

There was a sound behind her and Kate looked around to see an elderly priest closing a door nearby. He wore a white robe and his forehead was adorned with a dark red thumb print. He saw her and bowed low.

'Good morning, memsahib.'

She felt awkward, as though she was in the wrong place, although he looked kind. 'Is it – is it all right for me to be here?'

'Yes, yes,' he said, waving a hand. 'In there is for Hindus only, you understand? But here is welcome for visitors. You are Christian?'

'Yes, sort of,' said Kate, feeling cowardly. That was a conversation for another time.

'This our Goddess Kali. Beautiful, yes?'

'She is,' said Kate. 'I didn't know she was worshipped like this. Isn't she the goddess of death?'

The priest smiled, now gently dusting the statue's face with a small bunch of feathers. 'Death, yes, but also life. Kali is the mother,' and here he pressed his hand to his chest, 'the mother of us all. She is giving us life and taking away.'

Later, as she left the temple, Kate had that odd feeling of being watched again and scanned the street, hoping to see a familiar face. The crowd that swarmed on all sides was the usual microcosm of Calcutta's varied population: the small Bengali man in his white dhoti, carrying a plank on his head; the taxi driven by an aged Sikh in a turban; the veiled Muslim women who moved like black shadows; the low-caste sweeping girls who nevertheless were dressed in bright saris and whose arms were laden with bangles.

But no – she knew none of them, although she felt that she had come to know the people of this city well, had even begun, on occasion, to think herself one of them. They were all busy, filled with purpose, even the maimed beggar who sat patiently outside the temple gates. As she handed him a few coins to stave off her own guilt, she almost envied his serenity.

*

She walked along Chowringhee Road, where small, colourful stalls lined the street.

'For your children, madam?' asked a young man with floppy dark hair as he shovelled bonbons into a paper bag. 'They are how old, please?'

'She's almost nine,' said Kate. 'She's not mine, actually. Could I have a few of those humbugs, too? Three or four ounces, please.'

'Of course.' He weighed the sweets and then threw a handful more in. 'For the little one. I am having one girl same age. Oldest child.'

'How many do you have?'

'Five,' said the man with a smile. 'I am blessed. My wife is saying one more, that's it, absolute limit.' He wagged his finger, chuckling.

After accepting her coins and dispensing change, he wrapped the sweets up in a sheet of newspaper and handed them over. Kate breathed in the sweet, rich smell of the stall again.

'Thank you very much. I'll be back, I'm sure. My regards to your family.'

He waved and began topping up the jars that stood on his stall, pouring out bonbons and boiled sweets in a dozen bright colours with an ancient iron scoop.

Nearby she saw a mother and daughter and for a moment she could have sworn that it was Nabanita and Shreya, who she had last seen at Shinbwiyang. She almost called out, but they came closer and she knew they were strangers. Where is Nabanita now, she wondered. Did they ever make it out of the jungle? The hardest part was the realisation that she would probably never know.

✦

'For your little friend?' said Pamela, who sat writing a letter at the low table. 'What did you get this time?'

'Lots of sweets – of course. A couple of shiny bangles to wear on her wrists. A bolt of pretty cloth. And this rather peculiar clockwork turtle.' Kate laughed. 'I suppose puzzling over it will keep her occupied.'

'No sign of her father?'

'Not that I know of.'

'Why don't you go and see her?' asked Pamela, blotting the letter in front of her. 'Take a few days off?'

'Oh, I couldn't.'

'Couldn't – or don't want to?' said Pamela shrewdly. 'You know the hospital would let you have the time off now that things are so much quieter.'

'I'm not sure she'd want to see me,' said Kate. 'It's been so long. She probably feels I've abandoned her.'

'You should go anyway.'

Kate felt irritable and knew it was because Pamela was right. 'I'll think about it,' she said firmly.

That night she dreamed of Fred for the first time in a long time. He was on a ship, helping his brother to save people from drowning. It's not too late, he kept saying, it's not too late.

Kate awoke abruptly and stared at the dark ceiling. What would Fred do now, she wondered? She knew that he would go and see Mi Khin – would probably never have left her in the first place. I had no choice, she thought weakly, but it was a poor excuse. She had sent Mi Khin away out of necessity, but as time went by the harder it seemed to see her again.

54
Calcutta, October 1945

The inquiry at the Bureau had raised her hopes, but as the days went by Kate was forced to conclude that nothing was going to come of it. If Edwin was looking for her, why on earth wouldn't he have provided his name? Why the mystery?

Work had kept her busy throughout the war and it was still a safe haven. In the early days she had been so tired after a shift that she could hardly make her way home. Her muscles ached and her head throbbed from carefully repeating instructions to herself over and over again. Even the most injured men often wanted to talk, and staying cheerful and light-hearted was exhausting.

She had pushed herself on with the knowledge that it was just until the war was over, whenever that might be. There was no need to make any plans until then. But months had stretched into years and now, suddenly, it was over – and she was no closer to knowing what to do with herself when she was no longer needed.

She wanted desperately to know where Edwin was, to see him strolling towards her with a shy smile, to know that he was safe. Somewhere in this fantasy she had also tracked down Mi Khin's father and they were well and happy somewhere. Once that's sorted, she thought forlornly, then I can move on.

But it was not sorted, and she had started to realise that closure might never come. What then, she thought? Should I go home? I have been running away for too long.

'Nurse!'

Sitting in a dream one day in one of the half-empty wards, Kate heard a call from the corridor and leapt up, afraid of being caught slacking.

'They're bringing in a dozen men from the 21st General, nurse,' said Sister Melchett, hurrying past with a stack of sheets in her arms. 'Come and help me make the beds, please.'

'Of course,' said Kate, stooping to pick up a sheet that had fallen to the floor. 'I didn't know we were expecting anyone.'

'We weren't,' said the sister. 'They've had some sort of power failure, apparently – they're shipping patients out of some wards temporarily.'

Quickly they worked down opposite sides of the ward, Kate tucking and folding the sheets automatically. It was one of the first things she had been taught to do when she began training as a nurse in Calcutta, and she remembered how absurd it had seemed to be taking lessons in how to make a bed when she had spent months as an untrained nurse, assisting with the cata-strophic injuries caused by Japanese bombing and the climate of the Hukawng Valley.

'Has anyone here assisted with an amputation before?' the instructor had asked. Kate and two other girls put their hands up. The rest of the group looked anxious, knowing what was to come.

Asanti and Priya had been in her first training group and had offered her a bed in their lodgings. Asanti had gone against the express wishes of her mother and father in coming to Calcutta to become a nurse. For over a year they had sent her stern, disappointed letters, demanding she come home, even sending her brother to fetch her at one point. He had inspected their room, listened to Asanti's entreaties, given her a lecture about not going out to parties, and had finally kissed her on the forehead and gone back to their parents empty-handed.

'But aren't they proud of you?' asked Kate when he had gone, finding Asanti sitting mournfully in the empty room, plaiting back her long hair in preparation for her shift.

'I suppose they are, in their way.' She sighed. 'But this is a new world for them. It is hard for them to adjust and my father does not believe this is our war to fight.'

Kate had no answer to that. The Indians, like the Burmese, were caught in a war that they should never have been involved in, while their powerful masters fought for supremacy. When the war was over, the subjugated millions would demand their freedom. And who are we, she thought, to deny it?

Asanti's parents gradually softened their stance, sending food and clothing, even asking after Kate, who her brother had mentioned approvingly – she had been in a spell of numb depression during his visit, which had obviously been mistaken for timidity.

'Are you finished, nurse?' said Sister Melchett sharply, and Kate realised that she had been repeatedly tucking and re-tucking the last bedsheet.

'All done here, sister.'

In half an hour a stream of orderlies arrived. The first four or five patients were in wheelchairs, well enough to sit up and look around with interest at their new surroundings. The rest were brought in on stretchers and slid carefully onto the freshly made beds.

'Why, Miss Girton, isn't it?' said a bleary voice. Startled, she looked at the man in the next bed, who was staring intently at her. He was a stretcher case, but looked wide awake now, and suddenly familiar.

She stared at him, trying to place him. 'Tim? Good heavens.' He looked much older than he had been when he worked for her mother on the farm, only a few years ago.

'That's right, Tim Fletcher,' he said, a slow smile spreading over his face. 'Fancy seeing you in India, Miss Girton. And you're a nurse, now. What shall I call you, then?' His voice had the gentle country twang that she knew so well and it gave her an unexpected rush of longing for home.

'Just nurse is fine,' said Kate. 'What are you doing in Calcutta?'

'Oh, I've been all over, miss – nurse,' he said, closing his eyes for a moment as he tried to remember. 'I was in France at the beginning, then we were on the way to Singapore when it fell so we got sent to North Africa instead, and ended up over here in the last few months of the Burma campaign.'

'What was it like?'

He considered. 'Hot. Bloody. The Japs torched most of the towns as they retreated.'

'And the people?'

'Miserable. I don't know if they were pleased to see us, exactly – it wasn't the warm welcome you might expect. But they seemed glad to see the back of the Japs.' He looked at her curiously. 'I heard you'd come out East, now I think of it. Was that where you were?'

Kate nodded, thinking of all the people she had known. You do not understand us, Myia had said, and she was right. She had left them to their fates and knew nothing of the misery that they had endured in the years since the invasion.

'You got out, though,' said Tim. 'I'm glad to see that.'

I did, she thought. I survived. 'How did you get this?' she said, gesturing to the burn scars she could see inside the neck of his pyjamas.

'Wrong place at the wrong time. Got caught in an exploding oil depot a week or two before we took Rangoon. It was a native fellow who found me, as a matter of fact, and fetched my CO.'

'Does it hurt?'

'On and off.' She peered at the scarring, seeing how the skin stretched over his neck, mottled and dry.

'How's your mother these days?' he said. 'Seems no time at all since she was waving me and the lads goodbye.'

'I think she's all right,' said Kate. 'I don't write to her as often as I ought. I've been so busy here.'

'I'll always be grateful to her,' he said. 'She was a kind boss, and the moment I said I was signing up she did all she could for me.'

'I worry about her, rather.'

Tim smiled. 'Well, you'd know better than me, but I'd say she's a strong lady.'

'She is.'

'She was always very proud of you. When you went East she'd tell people about your adventures.'

Kate smiled, surprised but gratified. 'I've always felt that I let her down.'

He shrugged. 'It's not for me to say, miss, but I doubt she thinks the same. You were a great support with your father . . . and afterwards.'

With a jolt she remembered that he had been there the night her father died. Old Ben had found him in the barn and the other farmhands had rallied round, as much a support in their own quiet way as her mother's friends who arrived in droves with food and condolences.

'I was too late.'

He watched her curiously, then shook his head, and she felt a strange bond between them, though she had not seen him for years. He had been there, and she knew they were both remembering the farmyard, the police car, and the silence that had fallen.

His voice sounded as if it was coming from far away. 'It weren't your fault. No one thought that, not ever.'

She turned away and wiped her eyes, knowing that he had seen. She could not dwell on it again, not here.

'What about your parents, Tim – do you hear from them?'

'Aye, now and then,' he said, taking a sip from the cup of water she passed him from the trolley. 'It's not been easy for them. Nora – that's my wife – went to live with them, and she's a comfort to my mother.'

'You're married now?'

'Aye. Just before the war started.'

'Congratulations.'

He smiled wanly. 'She's a good girl. I can't wait to be home. We'd like to get a bit of land of our own, maybe raise a few pigs and cows, have a couple of kids perhaps.'

It sounded idyllic and Kate could see it at once – the little house that he would build himself, his wife sowing flowers that would bloom in the front garden, the children feeding pigs in the yard. While living with her parents, longing for adventure, she had found the locals dull and provincial, but suddenly their lives seemed richer and more real than anything she had achieved. Tim and his wife would be happy.

'I must get on,' she said at last, but turned back. 'Let my mother know when you get back, Tim. I think she'd want to know and help you any way she can. I'll write and tell her I've seen you.'

'Aye,' he said, and bobbed his head. 'Thank you, nurse. What will you do? Will you be going home soon?'

'I hope so.'

55

Bihar, October 1945

The bus up into the hills took most of the morning. Kate sat next to the wide, glassless window, watching the dry grass and ragged trees go by. Occasionally they passed through a village, where the bus would stop for a few minutes to pick up passengers and huge sacks of rice and bales of cloth.

Kate closed her eyes, leaning back against the hard narrow seat, and tried to shade her face until the bus moved off again. The air had been much cooler since leaving Calcutta, but the sun was still hot.

They went on, trundling around hairpin bend after hairpin bend. Sometimes in the distance she saw the road ahead, snaking up a sheer-looking hillside, and wondered if the bus would make it, but it always did, the driver grinding the gears lower and lower as they climbed.

The slow train had deposited her in Simultala, a small town a few hundred miles north-east of Calcutta. She had missed the only bus up into the hills that day, and the main hotel, a health resort, looked alarmingly expensive, so she stayed in a dak bungalow near the train station.

The caretaker, a wiry little man in a white dhoti, carried her bag into the bungalow, unrolling a sleeping mat and depositing a bucket of water. A little later he returned, carrying a basket that emitted savoury smells.

'Oh, thank you. How kind.' She went to help him unload, but he waved her away again and set down the contents of the basket on a low table.

'How much do I owe you?'

'Two rupees, memsahib.' He gestured to the bungalow and the food. 'For all.'

She handed over the money and he bowed deeply before slipping it into his waist pouch. 'You are going tomorrow where?'

'Dhanbasar. The children's home.'

He nodded and bowed before disappearing. A moment later he returned and said, 'Bus tomorrow nine o'clock,' and he pointed down the street to where a huge tree cast its shade. 'Beside tree. Nine o'clock.' After seeing that she understood, he withdrew.

She had brought whisky in her father's old hipflask, but for once she did not hear its siren call and it lay untouched in her bag as she ate and read a book on the veranda.

Later, emerging from the little hut that held the long-drop toilet, she caught sight of a brilliant moon, not quite full yet but radiant, and stood still, marvelling at it.

Afterwards, Kate lay down on the mat and listened to the silence. She had not heard quiet like this since the journey to India and she felt almost homesick for those nights in the jungle, surrounded by kind companions. She felt lonely, but somehow very safe, in this town where no one knew her.

The dead did not come that night. She woke to find her head in a square of sunlight, already hot, and realised that she had slept soundly through the night for the first time in years.

*

Dhanbasar Jubilee School was on a slope miles above the valley, about as high as you could go in this part of India. The bus dropped Kate off at the end of a long driveway, where an imposing set of gates stood open, flanked by two enormous stone monkeys.

Along the driveway were beds of flourishing roses and orchids, which were obviously carefully tended. A hose was coiled neatly next to an outside tap, and a steel watering can lay on its side. She noticed that the emblem on the base read 'HAWS – MADE IN ENGLAND'.

As she drew near the house, she could hear children calling somewhere nearby, and saw a sweeper busy on the steps outside the front door.

'Good afternoon. Where might I find Mrs Princeton?'

He showed her through to a small sitting room and she perched on a sofa, looking around at the watercolours on the wall and the lace antimacassars on the chairs, reminded irresistibly of her grandmother's parlour. Even the mournful china dog on the windowsill, she was sure, was the same.

Restless, she stood up and peered out of the window. There were five or six children playing a skipping game on the shaded lawn, two of them holding out a long rope. She peered at each of them in turn and saw a pram parked in the deeper shade nearby, accompanied by a nurse who sat calmly knitting.

'She's not there,' said a voice behind her and Kate turned to see a large-busted woman in a tweed suit.

'Forgive me, Miss Girton,' she said. 'I didn't mean to make you jump.'

'Mrs Princeton,' said Kate, holding out a hand. 'I'm glad to see you again. It's been a long time.'

'Do sit down.'

A maid arrived with a tray and carefully unloaded it, glancing anxiously at Mrs Princeton. She was a young Anglo-Indian girl who could not have been more than fifteen, her black hair pulled back in a tight bun. She took the tray, curtsied to both of them, and left as quickly as possible.

'Theresa is one of my recent graduates,' said Mrs Princeton, leaning to stir the tea. 'She's a good girl. She'll work here for a year or so until we can find her a place in a respectable household.'

'Where?'

'I hope to find her a position somewhere pleasant like Darjeeling. She's quite willing to travel to Calcutta or Delhi if necessary, but I prefer not to send girls to the big cities, for obvious reasons.'

'Of course,' Kate murmured. She took the cup of tea and allowed it to cool.

'I'll take you out to find Maria in a moment. But I must warn you, Miss Girton, that she is not herself.'

'How do you mean?'

'I'm sorry to say that she has been very badly behaved of late,' said Mrs Princeton, shaking her head. 'She has missed numerous classes and has at times been unforgivably rude to the mistresses. Miss Jones was quite hurt by her insults.'

'I'm sorry to hear that,' said Kate feebly. 'I suppose it's to be expected . . . she has suffered a great deal.'

'They've all suffered, Miss Girton,' said Mrs Princeton sternly. 'I'm afraid it's no excuse here. The staff all want the best for her and want to help her.'

'I should have come before,' said Kate. 'I meant to, but . . .'

'Perhaps you can speak to her,' said Mrs Princeton, sipping her tea. 'She won't listen to me. Explain to her that we are trying to help her. And how important her education is for the future.'

'I'm not sure she'll listen to me either.'

'Do your best, Miss Girton.' The older woman sighed. 'What news do you have from Calcutta? Have the soldiers all gone home?'

'Most of them,' said Kate, thinking of her half-empty wards. 'It's much quieter now.'

'How long do you intend to stay in India?'

'I don't know.' She frowned and drank some more tea. 'I'm still waiting for news of some of my friends. They may be dead but – well, I want to know. Either way. I don't know what else to do.'

Mrs Princeton looked at her sympathetically. 'It isn't easy.' Her voice sounded unsteady and Kate saw, in surprise, that her eyes had filled with tears.

'Are you all right?'

'Quite well. Thank you.' She paused and fiddled with her teacup. 'I lost my fiancé on the Western Front – almost thirty years ago now. The worst part was not knowing. Once I knew, I was able to pick myself up and move on. One never forgets, of course.'

✦

Kate followed a winding path between two walled gardens, pausing occasionally to sniff a rose or examine the fruit trees that grew espaliered against the crumbling red brick. On this Indian hilltop was a place that would be forever England.

The path went through a small orchard, where apple trees were mixed in with something more exotic, its fat, heavy leaves making the branches droop. She saw, in the distance, a small summer house, with a roof made of palm leaves. As she drew closer she could see someone sitting on the veranda in a rocking chair, but the girl made no move to greet her, simply watched impassively as she approached.

'They told me you were coming,' she said, when Kate was nearly at the steps. Her accent had faded and now she sounded almost English.

Kate observed her for a moment and noted the untidy plait in her dark hair, the scuffed shoes and the muddy knees.

'Hello, Mi Khin.' She sat down. 'I spoke to Mrs Princeton.'

'Did she ask you to come?'

'No.'

'Then why did you?'

Kate shifted uncomfortably and looked sideways at her. 'I know you're probably angry with me . . .'

'I'm angry at everyone.' Her dark eyes looked away and she rocked in the chair disconsolately.

'Mrs Princeton said you weren't happy.'

'She hates me.'

'Well, you're wrong about that.' Kate paused. 'She cares about you. She's worried about you.'

'They all say that. They don't like me much really, you know. I'm too much of a mongrel even for this place. You know what they call me? *Maria*. Like a nun or something.'

'I know. It's silly.' Kate was silent and looked out over the hillside that fell away before them.

Mi Khin looked sideways at her. 'You look tired.'

'Thanks.'

'You've been working hard.'

They were quiet again. 'Look,' said Kate at last, 'it's not an excuse, Mi Khin, and I'm sorry I haven't come before. I truly am. This is the first time I've had more than two days off from the hospital since I last saw you.'

'I understand. I didn't really expect you to come.' She hardened her mouth and sighed, fidgeting in her chair.

She expected me to let her down and I did, thought Kate. 'It wasn't just that,' she said. 'It was so hard – after what happened I could barely take care of myself. I thought seeing you again would open up all the old wounds, for both of us.'

'You were very sad,' said Mi Khin. 'I saw that.'

'Yes. But I was a coward. I'm sorry. I won't let you down again, I promise.'

Mi Khin nodded, but she looked less angry. 'I got your birthday parcel,' she said at last. 'Thank you.'

'It occurred to me afterwards that the turtle might have been a bit young for you,' said Kate. 'You were a little girl when I saw you last.' Mi Khin seemed far older than nine. It was as though the years in between had hardened her.

She shrugged. 'I liked it. And the little Indian girls enjoyed playing with it.'

'What did you say to the mistresses?' asked Kate. 'Apparently they were very upset.'

'Oh, that,' said Mi Khin dismissively. 'They don't like brown girls much, you know. I think secretly they all wish they were bringing up nice little white girls somewhere in England. Miss Jones got angry with me and said I would never be a respectable lady with manners like mine. So I told her that my mother was a Burmese princess and that one day I'd summon my uncles to raze this place to the ground and kill all the teachers.'

Kate snorted and shook her head. 'I'm not surprised she was upset.'

'I said I was sorry.'

'Did you? Out loud?'

'Not exactly.'

'I think you must apologise,' said Kate with a sigh. 'Learn how to play the game, Mi Khin. Be polite to your teachers, listen to them even if you disagree with them – and keep your head down. This isn't forever, you know. There's a whole world out there.'

'I'll try,' she said doubtfully.

'Is there anything I can do that would help? Anything at all?'

'Find my father,' said Mi Khin softly, gripping the arms of her chair. 'I know you've tried but – please – please keep looking. I'm sure he's alive.'

'I'll keep trying,' said Kate. 'But I've so little to go on. I sent off so many letters, filled in every form I could think of, but they haven't found any trace of him yet.'

'I had a dream the other night,' said Mi Khin, swinging her legs back and forth. 'I think it was about my grandmother – it was a little old Indian lady, anyway. She was calling to my father and she was saying, "Aditya!" But Papa's name was Joseph.'

'Aditya?'

'Do you think it's worth looking into?'

'Perhaps,' said Kate. 'All the forms I filled in just said we were looking for an Anglo-Indian man called Joseph Smith. If he had another name then it might explain why they haven't found him.'

'I never heard him call himself Aditya,' said Mi Khin doubtfully. 'But it's been so long and I was very little.'

'Some people don't use their first names,' said Kate. 'My grandmother was Doris Caroline, but she only ever went by Caroline as she didn't like Doris. Could be something like that.'

'It was only a dream, though.'

'It's something,' said Kate. 'We may as well try.'

They walked back down the path together and Mi Khin took her hand. Kate squeezed it.

'I miss Fred,' said Mi Khin with a sigh.

'Me too.'

'I had a letter from Christopher, though. He sent me some nice books and told me all about England and the strange food they eat. Merin-joos or something.'

'Meringue,' said Kate. 'It's a sort of crunchy pudding made of egg whites and sugar. Lovely with cream and raspberries. He wrote to me, too – I gather he's working for one of his uncles now.'

'He said he would come back to India one day for a visit.'

'I'm sure he will.'

Mi Khin looked up at her. 'Are you lonely, in Calcutta?'

'A little,' said Kate. 'But I work a lot and the girls I live with are kind.'

'You're not happy, though?'

'I'm alive and I'm healthy,' said Kate with a shrug. 'That's enough.'

56

Calcutta, November 1945

In the wide silence of the Imperial Library, only occasional footsteps intruded on the concentration of the scholars who sat staring at dusty tomes and occasionally scribbling on a scrap of paper. Most of them were university students; serious young men with self-conscious moustaches and round glasses who had been too young for the war.

Kate had noticed their polite astonishment at seeing her poring over books in the library; she suspected that they would be all the more baffled, and rather condescending, if they knew she had left school at fourteen.

Most of the books were old and of little interest, but occasionally she stumbled upon something vaguely appealing. Much of her time in the library was spent staring out of the window at the jute mills that lined the Hooghly River, and trying to write letters home.

Will is home at last from hospital, read the latest letter from her sister. Laura had been a diligent correspondent since Kate had made contact from Calcutta and wrote often despite her gruelling job in a London hospital. Kate felt guilty that she did not write nearly as often but it was hard to know what to say.

While she had clammed up, Laura had begun to confide in her. Perhaps due to the war, and the distance between them, she told Kate things that she could tell no one else. Kate was flattered and grateful for her trust, and felt deeply for her sister, even as she tried and failed to reciprocate with confidences of her own.

Laura's husband Will had been injured in Trieste shortly before the end of the war and had spent months moving between hospitals. Laura was caring for him now in a rented flat in London, and slowly adjusting to the reality that he would be an invalid forever.

One leg is all gone, Kate, it's awful to see. The rest of him – you must forgive me for such coarse talk – is intact. But so far he's in constant pain, so there's been no opportunity or desire to see if it still works. I've waited this long, God knows I can wait longer, but I'm terribly afraid. What if he's too damaged? I can live without THAT, though it wouldn't be easy I suppose, but what about children? How shall I have the children I want? He already feels that he's failed me. He won't talk about it but I can tell he's scared too.

Laura, dear Laura, who had talked of having children since she was a child herself. She was thirty-five. How would she cope if her last opportunity to be a mother was taken away from her? Would her relationship with Will survive? She would be condemned to repeat her parents' marriage, locked up with him as the world moved on outside.

Kate frowned down at the paper before her and stared around the library. There was a little old man who seemed to be there almost every day, sitting in a huge chair with a stack of books on the table. Sometimes when she looked at him he was dozing, and she smiled, knowing that like her he came for the atmosphere of the library rather than its contents.

A young librarian went past and as he did so he bowed his head to the old man, placed his hands briefly together, and then touched his forehead. The old fellow nodded regally and went back to his book. Kate wondered who he was, or who he had once been.

A shaft of sunlight fell across the marble floor, and suddenly she knew exactly what to do. She could not reassure Laura that everything would be all right, for it almost certainly would not be. But she could repay her honesty. Their mother had not pushed Kate to reveal what had happened on the journey out of Burma, and her letters were light-hearted and comforting, but she had suffered as much as either of her daughters. She, too, deserved to know.

Picking up the pen, Kate started to write. She would tell them everything. It would take more than one letter, but she would start today and eventually her family would know what had happened to her. One day when she saw them again, they might be able to grieve together for all that they had lost and take stock of what had survived.

✦

As she left the library and walked out between the great white pillars, Kate heard her name being called and swung around to see a man whose face she did not recognise at first. He wore a faded army uniform and carried a heavy knapsack.

'Patrick,' he prompted. 'We met in Mandalay.'

She stared at him. 'Of course! You worked with Edwin.'

'I wasn't sure if it was you,' said Patrick. He looked much older than the cheerful young man she had last seen nearly four years ago, his face lined and his hair speckled with grey. 'What are you doing in Calcutta?'

'I've been here for years,' said Kate. 'Ever since leaving Burma. Gosh,' and she put a hand to her heart. 'I feel quite shocked to see you! It's so rare that I see anyone from back then.'

'Here,' said Patrick, and took the heavy shoulder bag from her. 'Sit down for a moment.' They sat on a bench and Kate looked at him again with surprise.

'What brings you here? How did you get out of Burma?'

'Oh, it's a long story, I'm afraid. Edwin and I left Mandalay by car, I suppose it must have been a few days after you left.'

'You were with Edwin?' she said eagerly.

'On the day they blew up the Ava Bridge.'

'Do you know where he is now?'

Patrick frowned and shook his head. 'No. I'm sorry.'

She felt a stab of disappointment. 'But what happened? How did you get separated?'

'Edwin was captured,' said Patrick. 'By the Japs. We both were, actually. I don't have much time, I'm afraid, I'm taking the night train to Bombay and then a ship home.'

Kate sat still, trying to calm her thudding heart. Edwin had been taken prisoner by the Japanese. It was what many people had suggested to her, and what she had known was the most likely answer, but it was a wrench to hear it confirmed. Perhaps he was still alive.

Patrick looked up at the great clock that hung over the main library entrance. It was nearly five o'clock. 'Listen, my train leaves Howrah in two hours. I'll tell you what I can before then.'

'Of course,' said Kate.

'I hoped he might have got away somehow. You haven't heard anything?'

'Nothing. Do you suppose he's still a prisoner?'

'He must be,' said Patrick, although he looked doubtful. 'Unless—'

'Don't,' said Kate firmly. 'Just tell me what happened.'

57

Calcutta, November 1945

Late one afternoon Kate sat in the cathedral nave. It was quiet and cool, and in the transept a choir was practising hymns. Outside the merciless sun was glaring down, but here all was calm.

As a child she had gone to church regularly with Laura and their mother but after her father's death she decided that she no longer believed in God. It was not an angry parting, and she felt no anguish about it; it simply seemed impossible and absurd to believe in a God who had allowed such things to happen. I did not abandon God, she told herself – he abandoned me.

In India going to church felt very different. She had gone tentatively one Sunday afternoon, soon after her arrival in Calcutta, still raw with the pain of her journey, and found it almost empty. The place was big enough that she could sit undisturbed, dozing slightly and enjoying the cool marble on which she sat.

She had come nearly every week since, usually in the early morning or late afternoon, before or after a shift at the hospital. It had become a place of refuge, although God had never seemed further away. For I have killed a man, she thought, and knew she was beyond saving.

She now knew more about what had happened to Edwin, but Patrick's part in the tale cut off abruptly in May 1942, when he and Edwin had been separated. He believed that Edwin had probably been taken to another internment camp somewhere.

'I didn't see it myself but they put him in a truck with a few others and they drove off early one morning and that was that. Someone said they were going south.'

'And what about you? How did you get out?'

'I was put in another truck and taken west – odd, really. I can only suppose they were heading for one of the camps near the Chindwin to interrogate me further. But there was an accident – the truck went off the road, the driver was killed and the guard stunned. There were four of us prisoners and we hared off west for a few days and eventually met up with the British forces retreating over the river at Shwegyin. They let us tag along in their trucks to Imphal.'

She listened to Patrick's tale, trying not to feel resentful that he had made it out when Edwin had not. He had gone to war, she reminded herself; in the three years since his lucky escape he had probably seen unspeakable horrors. She wondered what sort of life awaited him at home.

He looked at Kate for a moment, and then said, 'It's quite possible that Edwin's still a prisoner, you know. Or he could have escaped. Or—'

'Or he might be dead.'

'Perhaps.'

The clock was striking a quarter past six when Patrick heaved his bag onto his shoulder. 'I must go. I'll just make the train if I get a rickshaw.'

He was already gone, she could see that; like the soldiers who had passed through her hospital, he had relinquished the ties that once held him here and was now pawing at the ground, impatient to be off.

Kate stretched out her hand and grasped his. 'Have a safe journey. And good luck.'

'I'll be fine. Go back to my maps, get a quiet job, forget the war altogether if I can. Look, here's my father's address – you'll let me know if you hear anything more of Edwin?'

'Yes, of course.'

He gave a half smile. 'Good luck.'

She watched him hurry away to the roadside, where he flagged down a rickshaw and slung his bag into the back before climbing in after it. The driver stood up on the pedals and it moved off into the crowd.

※

'Miss Girton?'

Kate's eyes flew open and for a moment she struggled to focus on the woman in front of her. She had fallen asleep on the hard pew at the back of the cathedral.

'Mrs Campbell! Good heavens.'

'So sorry to disturb you, dear,' said Mrs Campbell, fanning herself and looking flustered. 'I was just surprised to see you, that's all. I said to myself, now there's a familiar face.'

She looked hardly changed from how she had been at the Scottish party in Rangoon; winter 1941. Kate remembered, inexplicably, the beautiful gold trim that she had had on her dress that night. She was still a large woman, though her face was perhaps a little thinner, and her dress plainer. It was strange that she should appear so soon after Patrick, another ghost emerging from the past.

'It's quite all right. I'm afraid I was drifting off to sleep. It's so beautifully cool in here.'

'Isn't it?' Mrs Campbell hesitated. 'I didn't know you were in Calcutta, Miss Girton.'

Kate smiled wanly. 'I've been here since late forty-two.'

'Oh? You must have—' She looked flustered again. 'How did you come out?'

'The long way, Mrs Campbell. The Hukawng Valley route.'

'Good heavens.'

Kate took pity on her. 'You were sensible to leave when you did. How is Mr Campbell?'

'He's quite well. His business has taken a dent, of course, but it will recover soon enough now that the war is over. We'll be sailing for Edinburgh in the New Year.'

'And Mrs Hamilton – how is she? And the baby?'

Her face dropped. 'Oh, my dear,' she said, almost whispering. 'Such a sad story. They had a dreadful journey out. They got to India all right but the baby was sick. Mr Hamilton was a few weeks behind them and by the time he arrived little Sam was dead and buried.'

'I'm so sorry to hear that,' said Kate numbly. She stood to leave, feeling depression settling on her shoulders once again like an old winter coat. 'Please pass on my condolences to Mrs Hamilton.'

'I rarely see her,' said Mrs Campbell. 'I feel dreadful about it sometimes, but I'm almost ashamed to. We were the best of friends in Rangoon, but since coming here – well, it's not the same.'

'No, it isn't.'

Mrs Campbell pressed her hands together and looked pensive. 'There's too much of a difference between our experiences, Miss Girton. I'm not sure it's possible to bridge that gulf.'

Neither am I, thought Kate, as she left the cathedral, feeling the warm air roll over her, and the sound of the choir fading away. *Till we have built Jerusalem . . .*

She felt sorry for Mrs Campbell, and envious too. She had escaped unharmed, her family intact, but her life – most of it spent in the East – had been upturned and she would have to spend what remained of it feeling guilty for having survived. Much like the rest of us, thought Kate.

✳

The traffic on Kidderpore Road was even more congested than usual. As Kate walked towards the park she could see a long queue of cars and buses, could hear the deafening din of dozens of horns being leaned on.

A rickshaw wallah grew tired of waiting and mounted the pavement, pedalling furiously along, weaving in and out of pedestrians. Kate leapt out of his way and stood with her back to a wall for a moment, breathing deeply. This city!

There was a crowd gathering on the Maidan, and three black cars were pulled up at the roadside, half-hidden by the swarming onlookers. Someone bumped into a fruit stall nearby and the owner huffed irritably as he gathered up the guavas that threatened to roll away.

'What's going on?' asked Kate.

'Political delegation,' he said shortly, now piling the fruit back onto his stall. 'Conference starting today.'

'A delegation? From where?'

'Burma.'

'What conference?'

He shrugged. Standing on tiptoe she tried to peer across the crowd, but she could see nothing except a group of men surrounded by supporters, journalists and photographers.

Soon the photocall was over and they were being hustled back into the cars, which drove away and gradually disappeared into the traffic.

Kate saw a young Burmese reporter standing nearby, a notebook in his hand, and accosted him. 'Excuse me, can you tell me what's going on?'

'It is a delegation, miss, from Rangoon. Led by Thakin Than Tun. They are here to discuss the future of Burma with members of the Assembly.'

'Is there a man called Denpo among them?'

He scribbled something in his notebook and looked up at her distractedly. 'I do not recognise that name. Sorry, miss, I must go to my office.'

'Of course.' She watched him walk away and thought of Myia.

✳

At home a letter lay on her bed. She stared at it, knowing without a doubt that it held news of one of the two men whom she had been seeking since arriving in Calcutta.

She had spent years waiting for answers, for herself and for Mi Khin, and now she was almost afraid to open the letter. Was there even the smallest chance that they had found Mi Khin's father? Could Edwin really still be alive?

Quickly she ripped it open and began to read.

58

Calcutta, December 1945

'You look nervous,' said Pamela, looking up from the letter she was writing. She was lying full-length on her bed, nibbling at a bag of dried apple slices. Clothes were draped over the headboard and folded in precarious piles on the floor.

Kate shrugged. 'It just feels like a big moment.'

She smoothed down the smart linen dress she had borrowed from Pamela and adjusted her sun hat.

'Don't fuss,' said Pamela. 'It looks fine. Much nicer than any of your old things.'

Kate rolled her eyes. 'Nearly packed?' she asked, looking around at the chaos.

'Oh, there's plenty of time. You know this chap Damien I've been seeing? The one I met at Firpo's? He's promised to look me up in London. Apparently he's got a lovely sports car.'

Kate imagined Pamela being driven through the city in an open-top car, the wind in her hair, a handsome man at her side. She smiled but felt a small stab of envy.

Pamela surveyed Kate through half-closed eyes. 'What do you think he's like? This Joseph, I mean. Or is it Aditya?'

'Both, apparently, but he calls himself Joseph.' Kate stared at her reflection. 'I'm surprised he's here at all.'

'What do you mean?'

'Well, when they finally tracked him down I thought that would be it. He'd go and pick Mi Khin up and disappear and I'd never see her again.'

'He wants to thank you, I suppose,' said Pamela. 'You saved her life.'

'In a way,' said Kate, wishing that they had not started the conversation. Try as she might she could not get away from the journey out of Burma – at every turn it was waiting to remind her. 'I've been useless since we arrived in India, anyway. He's probably angry that I ditched her in a home.'

'Don't be silly.'

'The main reason—' said Kate, sitting down abruptly on the edge of her bed, 'The main reason I'm afraid to go is that I know this will be the last time I'll see her.'

Pamela sighed. 'You can stay in touch.'

'It won't be the same.'

'I know.'

✦

She went early to the appointed meeting place, a Burmese teashop, intending to sit for a while and calm herself. But she had scarcely set foot over the threshold when a familiar voice hailed her.

'Kate! It is you!' Mi Khin hurtled forward and clutched Kate around the waist. 'I'm happy to see you.'

'You look even taller,' said Kate, holding her out to look at her properly. Gone was the demure uniform of the children's home. She wore a new purple *longyi* and a white blouse, and on her wrist were the bangles that Kate had sent months before. Her hair was done in a new, grown-up style that reminded Kate with a pang of Myia, crowned with fresh orchids.

'Papa is here. Come and meet him!'

Kate followed her into the dark teahouse, feeling unaccountably anxious. She had always hoped that this day would come, but the reality of handing over Mi Khin's care to her surviving parent was very different to what she had imagined.

Near the back a man in a light suit waved and stood to welcome her. 'Miss Girton.' He was younger than she had supposed, no more than forty, although his hair was heavily flecked with grey. There was something in his bearing that reminded her instantly of Edwin. He was more handsome but had the same shy sweetness about him. He looked almost entirely Indian, and only his deep blue eyes spoke of his English heritage.

'You must be Mi Khin's father.' She shook his hand, reassured by his firm grip.

'Joseph. I am so pleased to meet you at last, Miss Girton.'

'Kate, please.'

He pulled out two stools, knocking one of them over in the process, and at last, after some rearranging, they sat down together, all speaking nervously at once.

Mi Khin beamed from one to the other, obviously delighted to have the two adults she knew best in the same place. Up close, she was very obviously his daughter; it was there in her nose and the dimples in her cheeks.

A waiter appeared. 'What would you like to eat?' said Joseph, looking from Kate to Mi Khin.

'Oh, anything,' said Kate. 'You order.'

He spoke to the waiter in Burmese and she listened to the familiar words with regret. She had tried to learn a little Burmese while living in Rangoon, but the prevalence of English, not to mention the difficulty of the language and the alien script – and my laziness, she chided herself – had made the project an uphill struggle.

'I'm starving,' said Mi Khin. 'We haven't eaten for ages and ages.'

'Since lunchtime,' said Joseph, laughing at her.

'It seems a long time ago.'

'When did you arrive?' asked Kate.

'Yesterday afternoon,' said Joseph. 'We came down on the train from Simultala and then booked straight into a guest house.'

'Papa came all the way from Bombay for me,' said Mi Khin proudly.

Joseph squeezed her hand. 'I would have come from the ends of the earth.'

'Your letter said you were in the army,' said Kate.

'I was in a barracks near Bombay, waiting to be discharged, when a telegram came last week to say that my daughter was still alive.' He looked intently at her. 'For more than three years I believed that I had lost her. I cannot express my gratitude to you for bringing her here safely.'

Kate shook her head. 'I did what anyone would have done. And besides, I was not alone. Mi Khin, have you told your father about our journey?'

'A bit, while we were on the train,' said Mi Khin. She fidgeted. 'It makes me sad to talk about it.'

Joseph stroked her hair. 'You don't have to talk about it yet if you don't want to. All that matters to me is that you are here.'

The waiter appeared again and began to set down large bowls of thick Shan noodles, and Kate breathed in deeply. The rich smell was instantly identifiable; with her eyes closed she might have been back there.

'You miss Burma,' said Joseph. 'I understand that.' He smiled ruefully, spooning up the broth from his bowl.

'Why did you leave?'

'I went to India on business in – I suppose it must have been early December 1941,' he said. 'I was only meant to be away for a few weeks.'

'You said you wouldn't be long,' said Mi Khin reproachfully. 'You said you'd be back soon.'

'I tried, my darling,' he said. 'I really did. But the Japanese joined the war and when I went to get a flight back there were none going.'

'You could have walked.'

'I tried,' said Joseph, running a hand through his hair. 'I got as far as the border. But the army stopped me and forbade me from going any further. The Japanese were everywhere by that point.' He sighed. 'Anyway, I went back to Calcutta and went every day to the refugee office. I telephoned friends in Burma – most of them were already gone. I sent letters, telegrams, but no news came. Finally, someone said that they had seen my family leave our town in a truck, but they never arrived in Calcutta. The more time that passed, the more sure I was that my wife and daughter must be dead.'

He rubbed his face, looking weary. 'So I signed up. I had hoped to be sent into Burma but the army were retreating and so I ended up going to North Africa and then Italy and Greece.'

'You were in Europe?' said Mi Khin, eyes wide.

356

'Yes, for a long time. We only came back a few weeks ago.'

'What was it like?'

Joseph looked thoughtful. 'Cold,' he said at last.

It was strange to discover that while Kate had been in Burma and India, taking care of Mi Khin as best she could, the child's father had been halfway across the world, closer to Kate's home in England than she had been for a long time. What had those years been like for him? Fighting for a country that was not his own, on an unfamiliar and hostile continent, supposing his family lost.

When Mi Khin disappeared to look for the WC, Kate put down her spoon abruptly.

'Mr Smith—'

'Joseph.'

'How much do you know?'

'About your journey? Very little.' He sipped slowly at the soup in his bowl, looking at her closely, and then put his spoon down.

'I was with your wife when she died.'

He nodded, frowning slightly. 'I did not know that. They told me that you found Mi Khin and that her mother was dead but I've hardly heard anything else, you know.'

'That's what I imagined.' Kate shifted in her seat, feeling overheated and anxious. 'I thought you ought to know.' She watched him chewing his lip. 'I'm sorry.'

'You have nothing to be sorry for.' He glanced around the teahouse. 'This is not a conversation for now, I think.'

'No. But – well – I'll tell you anything you want to know.'

'I'm grateful to you. Another time.' He looked up, smiling bleakly, and she remembered Edwin talking about the night his wife had been killed.

'How long will you be in Calcutta?'

'A few days,' he said, looking up as Mi Khin returned. 'We're going to do some sightseeing, aren't we?'

'And shopping!'

'More shopping? What else do you want?'

'Clothes. Sweets. Some paints.'

'Are you an artist, now?' said Kate. 'What kind of paintings do you do?'

'All kinds,' said Mi Khin, picking at the noodles in her bowl. 'The art mistress was cross at me and said I wasn't to paint any more.'

'What for?'

'She didn't like my pictures. She said they were too scary and that I ought to paint nice things.'

'We'll get you some paints,' said Joseph, his arm around her shoulders. 'And you can paint whatever you like.'

'I'm sorry the teachers did that, Mi Khin. They shouldn't have stopped you,' said Kate.

'It's all right. In the end Mrs Princeton said I was allowed to paint again.'

'Did she?' said Kate, smiling. 'Perhaps she's not so bad.'

'Ah, yes, the formidable Mrs Princeton,' said Joseph ruminatively. 'Quite a character, I thought.'

'She cried a bit when I left,' said Mi Khin.

'She's fond of you,' said Kate. 'It must be hard to say goodbye to the girls who come through her care.'

Mi Khin nodded. 'I'm glad to be with Papa, now, though.' She smiled up at him.

'You too, my darling.' He hugged her, and over Mi Khin's head Kate saw his tired, worried face. She felt apprehensive on his behalf about the great task that awaited him. He would have to get to know his daughter again after four years apart; pick up the pieces of an old life and remake it.

'Are you planning to stay in India?'

'Yes,' said Joseph, looking down at his daughter. 'We both thought – a fresh start – it would be very hard to go back to Burma now. My mother lives near Madras, so we'll go there soon.'

'What about the seaside?' said Mi Khin.

He laughed. 'Perhaps, little one. There will be plenty of time for going to the seaside. Don't you want to see your grandmother?'

'Of course,' said Mi Khin indignantly. She turned to Kate. 'My grandfather was a real Englishman, you know. Just like Fred.'

'She'll be so happy to see you,' said Kate, thinking of her own mother.

'I was three when I last saw her,' said Mi Khin. She looked up at her father. 'Do you think she's forgotten me?'

'No one could forget you.'

59

Calcutta, December 1945

Whenever she could find the time that week, Kate spent it with Mi Khin and Joseph, joining them as they explored the city. She did not want to intrude on their reunion, but they begged her to come with them and it was hard to resist. These extra days were precious and she wanted to make the most of each one before they left for good.

It felt like an atonement of sorts for the years that she had not been there for Mi Khin when she most needed her, although she could not undo what had been done.

Joseph was attentive and they talked more openly than she could remember doing with anyone for a long time. She felt relaxed enough in his company to tell him about things she had tried for three years to forget. She told him about his wife Hla Pemala's death at Shinbwiyang and how Fred was the one who had rescued Mi Khin. She told him about her father and how hard it was to go home. She told him about Edwin, her dearest friend. She even told him how she had killed a man.

'But I never see his face in my nightmares. Isn't that strange? I see all the others, but never him.'

They were watching Mi Khin playing with other children in the street during the Kali Puja festival, as elaborate statues were carried past on palanquins. Nearby, someone set off a firecracker, and people laughed as they drew patterns on the pavement in coloured chalk.

Joseph turned to her. 'You know, deep down, that you did the right thing. That's why. You saved my daughter's life. If you carry any guilt, please forget it now.'

'Can it be that easy?'

'None of this is easy.'

He, in turn, told her of the war, and how, in the battlefields of Europe, watching friends falling all around him and feeling utterly alone, he had often longed for death.

'I do not know how I survived,' he said.

'You survived for her,' said Kate, nodding towards Mi Khin. 'Perhaps you knew deep down that she was alive and needed you.' She saw his face soften as he looked at his daughter.

They walked home from the festival, Mi Khin holding hands with them both, her sleepy feet stumbling occasionally. Joseph was quiet and Kate felt a pang to think that he and Mi Khin would be gone tomorrow. The houses that they passed were lit with dozens of candles and sparklers twinkled in the distance.

They reached the guest house, where Joseph had rented a bungalow, and Kate looked at Mi Khin with a sigh. 'Well – this is it, little one. I must go. I'll get a rickshaw, I think.'

'And I think it's your bedtime, Mi Khin,' said Joseph.

'Won't you come in and tuck me in?' Mi Khin asked Kate plaintively. 'Like you used to? Just this once?'

'I'm sure your father wants to do that.'

'We can both do it. That is, if you don't mind. She's so thrilled to see you again.'

In Mi Khin's room, Kate pulled back the mosquito net and helped her into bed, laughing at the old-fashioned English nightgown that had been a parting gift from the school.

'Mrs Princeton says I'm too old for bedtime stories,' said Mi Khin, lying back. 'I suppose she's right.'

'Nonsense! Would you like a story?'

'Perhaps just one.' Mi Khin frowned and then sighed. 'I won't see you again after today, will I?'

'Not for a long time, I'm afraid. But you're going to have a wonderful time with your father, Mi Khin. You can't stay in Calcutta forever.'

'But you'll stay in touch?'

'Of course.' She kissed Mi Khin's forehead. 'What story would you like?'

'You choose.'

Kate dredged up a fairy tale from her memory and, as usual, it bore little resemblance to the version she had been told as a child – was it a magical hat or a shoe? – but Mi Khin didn't seem to mind, and she listened drowsily. Kate thought of the stories she had told each night in circumstances much less comfortable than these, shivering on a darkened hillside and listening to the rain falling all around. Three years and a lifetime ago.

Joseph watched from the doorway for some time and Kate was aware of his gaze. At one point she glanced at him and he looked away but kept listening.

At last, when Mi Khin was asleep, Kate stood and tiptoed from the room. Joseph smiled as she closed the door.

'Drink?'

'Yes. Thank you.'

He made her a gin and tonic, apologising for the lack of ice, and they stood by the window, looking out at the night.

'I've been drinking too much,' he said, swirling his glass in his hand. 'All of this . . .'

'How does it feel? Getting her back?'

'Bittersweet. I thought I'd lost everything.' He took a gulp.

'Not quite everything.'

'No.' He looked at her. 'And what about you?'

'What about me?'

'You've lost a lot, too. What does the rest of your life look like?'

'I can hardly remember what normal life is like,' she said quietly. 'I feel frozen. I worry sometimes that I'll never . . .' She felt tears starting and wiped them away.

He took the glass from her hand and set it down with his own on the table, and suddenly he was folding her in his arms, stroking her back, kissing her hair. She looked up and he kissed her, pulling her tighter to him.

Suddenly he stopped and pulled away. 'I'm sorry,' he said, running a hand roughly through his black hair, looking anxious and embarrassed.

'It's all right,' she murmured, and pulled him back towards her, feeling desire surging as she pressed against him. 'It's all right.' She could not remember the last time she had been held this way, feeling him cradle the back of her head, his lips warm on hers.

He pulled her into his room and closed the door. Silently, quickly, they undressed, hands fumbling. He looked at her intently for a moment, taking in every detail, and for once she didn't care about the scars and the stretch marks. After a moment he knelt down before her as she leaned back against the door and felt his breath on her thighs. Her fists clenched and unclenched and she could hear the blood roaring in her ears, filling the quiet room with noise.

At last she pulled him up and kissed him before pushing him onto the edge of the bed, lowering herself onto him. The frame creaked, making them both giggle. Joseph put a finger to his lips and looked towards the door, moving his hands to her hips, his breath quickening. He was flushed and looked wonderingly at her as she moved against him, bracing herself against the bed, his fingers tight on her skin. The world contracted.

At last she leaned against him and her breath became ragged, then suddenly she was holding him tight and kissing his face, his ear, the side of his neck, feeling her head and her heart pounding.

60

Calcutta, December 1945

Lying under a tree, Kate drifted. She could hear traffic in the distance and the shouts of people in the street, but it all seemed a long way away. She had been here for most of the morning, since waking early, and the shade was starting to move away from her. She could feel her feet and her face burning. A book lay beside her head, unheeded.

Suddenly the heat on her toes was gone and she realised that someone was standing nearby, their shadow falling across her feet. No one except her ever came to this quiet corner of the cemetery. She squinted, dazzled by the sky.

'They said I'd find you here,' said Joseph, moving so that his shadow covered her face. He sat down nearby, making sure to shade her face still, and watched her.

Kate closed her eyes. 'Where's Mi Khin?'

'Helping the landlady to paint a mural back at the guest house.'

'She'll like that.'

'Yes. Someone mentioned mango ices.'

Kate sighed and sat up, brushing the dry grass off her dress. She frowned and studied his expression. 'What are you doing here, Joseph?'

'I wanted to talk to you. Before we leave.'

'All right.' She folded her arms, feeling warm sweat in the crooks of her elbows.

'Don't do this, Kate.'

'Do what?'

'Close yourself off. I can see you doing it. Hardening your heart against me – and Mi Khin.'

'I'm very fond of you both,' said Kate stiffly.

Joseph shook his head, looking frustrated, and was silent. He pulled at the grass between his feet, and she saw again the callouses and burns on his hands.

'This is how I survive,' she said, although she no longer believed the words as she said them.

'By not trusting anyone?'

'I trusted Edwin,' said Kate. 'My best friend. On the way out of Burma there were others that I trusted – even loved. And they're all gone.' She shook her head, remembering Fred's stolid calm. 'I can't do it again. I can't.'

'So you do know why I'm here,' said Joseph, and he shifted closer to her, taking her hand. She felt his rough palm against hers and the sky seemed brighter than ever.

'Kate,' he said, 'why don't you come with us?'

'Come where?'

'Home,' said Joseph, and the word hung in the air, the past and the present and the great wide earth encompassed in one syllable.

'Where is home?'

'There's a little town on the coast, a few hundred miles from here,' said Joseph. 'I used to go there as a boy with my parents and I've thought of it for years. We're going there on the way to Madras. Ah, Kate,' and he gripped her hand tighter, 'you should see it. Long empty beaches, glorious swimming, and the sky . . .'

'The sky?'

'You can see a million stars,' he said at last, gazing off across the cemetery as though he was there, standing on the beloved clifftops, watching the night sky.

Kate was silent for a long time, feeling the pull of the tides that threatened to uproot her precarious existence. At one moment she wanted nothing more than to go with Joseph, and at the next she knew that she could not, must not. She had to find out what had happened to Edwin and to Myia. That was the path laid before her. Being alone had always been safer.

'I shall have to go back to England,' she said. 'Someday soon.' But she had been resisting doing so now for years, and her mother had never asked her outright to come back. My beloved mother, she thought sometimes, knows me better than anyone. Perhaps that's why I'm afraid to go home.

'Of course,' said Joseph, 'it's where your family are. I am longing to see my mother.'

'What is your mother like?'

'She's strong,' said Joseph, smiling. 'When she was a young woman her parents arranged a marriage for her, but she said no – she would marry a man of her choosing. Then she met my father, an English tea merchant, and they were very happy together for forty years. Now she volunteers in a hospital and helps my sisters with their children.' He laughed. 'She would like you.'

Kate imagined going with him to his mother's home, meeting this tough old woman in a white sari. 'What would I do?' she said.

'Whatever you want,' said Joseph gently. 'I would not expect you to play the role of quiet village wife any more than my father expected my mother to be an English society lady. We could live anywhere, go anywhere – you could work or do whatever you please.'

He paused. For a moment she pictured a railway station somewhere in Europe, Switzerland perhaps, with cool mountains in the background, and a family alighting from a train: herself, Joseph, and Mi Khin, dressed neatly in winter clothes and carrying umbrellas. The sound of bells and the smell of chocolate hung in the air, and for a moment she could almost reach out and touch the scene, before it vanished, and she wiped the sweat of Calcutta from her brow.

Joseph watched her and sighed. 'When I was a child my father had a parakeet that lived in a cage. It sang beautifully, but he worried about it all the time – whether it was happy. At last, one day he opened the door and it flew away immediately. But the next day we came to breakfast and found it perched on the cage, waiting to be fed. And after that we never closed the door again.'

Kate laughed despite herself. 'Are you saying I'm like a bird?'

'No! But I would never try to keep you if you were unhappy or stop you from doing what you want.' He put his hands either side of her face and kissed her, and for a moment the confusion fell away. 'I just want you.'

She pulled away and sighed heavily. 'You think you know me,' she said. 'Even *I* don't know me.'

'Perhaps it's easier to see from a distance. I see that you have been running away from your grief and that you've put up walls so that you don't get hurt again. Kate, if I thought for a second that you'd be happier to keep running then I'd let you go at once, without looking back.' He sounded passionate, and she knew he meant it. 'But you want a home, you want safety, you want love. I am offering just one possibility.'

'I used to wonder what it would have been like if my father had come back healthy from the war,' said Kate, pulling up tufts of grass. 'A sort of parallel existence – I could see it as if through glass, going on alongside mine. And Edwin: what if the bomb that killed his wife had not struck their house? Two ships sailing to different places.'

She took his hand gently, feeling her heart swell with love and sorrow. 'It's a sweet future that you have offered: you, me, and Mi Khin. But it's not mine.'

'Then what is?'

'I don't know,' she said honestly, trying not to weep in front of him. 'I don't have any answers yet.'

'Would it be different if you knew what had become of Edwin? If you didn't have all these questions hanging over you?'

'I don't know.'

'You can't spend all your life waiting and wondering,' said Joseph, and he looked so kind that she felt that she was making a terrible mistake. 'Whether or not you discover the truth, at some point you will have to choose a path.'

'I suppose I am choosing,' she said.

He stood, pulling her to her feet beside him, and she looked into his blue eyes, memorising the face before her.

'I hope you find what you're looking for,' he said, and she knew he meant it wholeheartedly, though the roar of misery and confusion in her ears almost drowned him out.

Kate watched him leave. She sat back on the rug and picked up her book, but the words blurred in front of her. She looked around the churchyard, surrounded by the graves of those who had come to India and never left. The merciless sun bleached their headstones. One day the English would be long gone from India, and all that would remain of them would be their churches and their bones.

61
Calcutta, December 1945

Kate bought a newspaper from the stand at the end of Ashoka Street as she arrived home from a night shift. Lying on her bed, she flicked through it until she found a small piece about the Burmese political delegation, which was still in Calcutta.

She thought of the Burma to which she had arrived in 1939. It was hard to imagine what the new Burma would look like. The men who had first betrayed the British and then allied with them to get rid of the Japanese would be in charge. Would they really do the right thing this time? It's none of my business, she told herself, but she had grown to love the country and cared very much what happened to it.

She wondered where Myia was, and what she thought of all this. Had she found Denpo? She knew that it was quite possible that they were both dead, and her heart clenched.

Pushing the paper aside, she rolled over and slept fitfully for a few hours. Myia and a man she guessed to be Denpo appeared in her dreams, followed closely by Joseph, who carried Mi Khin in his arms. It was better than seeing the dead, but she had lost them all, just the same.

Kate woke abruptly, caked in sweat and grime. It was early afternoon and the sun was pouring into the room. She noticed a letter beside her bed. Asanti must have left it there while she was asleep. On the envelope she recognised the handwriting of Mr Shaji Acharya but could not bring herself to open the letter yet.

She pulled off her uniform and flung it into the basket beside her bed. Bending under the tap, she washed her hair and thought about the article she had read. 'Members of the Burmese delegation are staying at the Royal Lake Hotel off Canning Street.'

Walking through the hot streets, she felt her hair beginning to dry. She heard a shout nearby. Two groups of young men were facing off against each other, the air crackling with tension, and she walked briskly past, averting her gaze. There were so many angry people in Calcutta, many of them justifiably, and she had no wish to be caught up in a riot.

She was in the part of Calcutta that some people called Little Rangoon, although it had none of the civic pride of Chinatown or Armenian Street. The buildings were tatty and even the temples looked neglected.

She passed the teashop where she had eaten with Joseph and Mi Khin, averting her gaze. It had been a mistake to meet with them at all, she saw that now. It would have been better to let Mi Khin go off without saying goodbye, without ever meeting her father. Joseph deserved a life with someone unencumbered by painful memories – he had enough of his own.

Tentatively, Kate approached the hotel. It was rather small and shabby, not at all the sort of place where one would expect a political delegation to stay.

She took a deep breath and approached the door. Two young security men questioned her briefly and then nodded her past. She went across the wide lobby to the desk.

'Can I help you, madam?' said the young boy receptionist, bowing.

'I'm looking for a Burmese man called Denpo. I don't know his full name. I believe he works for the new government but I don't know what his role is. Or what he looks like.' She stopped. 'I'm sorry, this is not very helpful.'

'It's quite all right,' said the boy, waving a hand, looking at the ledger in front of him. 'You are looking for someone in the Burmese delegation, yes?'

'Yes. Denpo. And there's a woman, Myia Win . . .'

He flicked through the pages. 'The names are not listed here. I will consult the manager and see if there is any information I may share.'

He vanished through the beaded curtain behind him, and she looked around. Incense burned somewhere nearby, making the air heavy, and tinkling music was coming from the back room. On the counter a statue of the Buddha stood beside one of Ganesha, and a wooden cross hung on the wall. Clearly this hotel liked to cover all denominational possibilities.

The boy returned, shaking his head regretfully. 'I'm sorry; only the manager is having the list of guest names for this party and he is not allowed to give it out. Security, you see.'

'Of course,' she said. 'Thank you anyway.'

She walked briskly back across the hall and out through the front door, feeling suddenly foolish. If Denpo had survived the war he was probably in Rangoon and she imagined him at the Secretariat, striding the corridors that she had walked down every day. As for Myia – she could be anywhere.

She wandered on for a while and found herself outside a crumbling building with a sign bearing looping Burmese writing. The place looked unprepossessing, but in English a smaller sign said, 'Burmese Buddhist Temple', so she went in.

For a moment she felt so strongly that she was back in Bagan that it took an effort to remember the distance that lay between here and there. At the back of the main chamber a great golden statue of the Buddha smiled slyly against an ornate gold screen and offerings of flowers and food were strewn around.

A monk appeared silently and nodded, seeming unsurprised to see her. 'Welcome,' he said softly. He turned away and busied himself with lighting new candles, then padded away.

Kate sat on a wooden bench and leaned against the wall, feeling the tiles cold against the back of her head. She watched the candles flickering.

Several worshippers passed in and out, prostrating themselves briefly before the Buddha and leaving a donation before moving on. She supposed they had been forced to leave Burma – it was written in the lines on their faces and their ragged clothes – and came to this temple to keep in touch with what they had lost.

At last it began to grow dark outside and, with an effort, she stood up, feeling calm. The Buddha sat serenely and she gazed at him, feeling as though she had spent time with an old friend. She rummaged in her bag for money and pushed a few coins through the slot in the lid of the teak collecting box.

She stood in the doorway, contemplating the fastest way home, watching people passing this way and that along the narrow street.

Visiting this part of Calcutta was probably the nearest she would ever get to returning to Burma. She knew that for the rest of her life her short time there would glow in her memory, and that even if she were to return one day it would not be the same. What was it that Fred had said about returning to England after the first war? *All of it turned to ash.* Burma would endure, her people would win the independence they deserved, and it would be a better place, but she could not help grieving for the country she had known.

The faces mingling outside were greatly varied and she marvelled at the range of nations and histories that were represented on the streets of Calcutta, many of them brought here by war and famine and disaster. She was just a tiny piece of a huge puzzle and suddenly her own small tragedies seemed unimportant. It was a strangely liberating thought.

Then she frowned and shook her head, for one face in the crowd looked familiar and the past and the present seemed very close together. The rest of the figures in the street seemed to blur around her and the only person she could see, making a beeline towards her as though they had planned to meet, was Myia.

She looked hardly changed, her hair pinned up as usual with a spray of jasmine, and she was beaming incredulously.

'Kate! I'm so happy to see you.' She ran the last few steps and threw her arms around Kate, the scent of the flowers in her hair almost overpowering.

'You're here! How?' asked Kate, holding onto Myia's shoulders and staring at her.

'I came to look for you!'

'What about your family?'

'My mother and brother are safe. They spent the war in Delhi and have just returned to Burma. My husband was sent to Calcutta on official business and so of course I asked to come too. I thought you might be in England.'

'No, I've been here all the time. Your husband?'

'Yes, and I have a son, too! He's almost two years old.'

Kate could hardly believe that it was the same woman she had last seen in Shinbwiyang three and a half years ago, debating whether to go back into Burma to be with the man she loved.

'I came looking for information,' she said, gesturing ineffectually. 'At the hotel.'

'I heard,' said Myia. 'The security men said a white woman had come to the hotel asking questions. Denpo's colleagues were a little suspicious but I knew it had to be you – I just knew it.' She smiled up at Kate, holding her hands tightly. 'I was making enquiries about you today. Denpo has a friend who works in a government department here and I thought they might be able to find your address in England. I never supposed you'd still be here!'

Talking rapidly, they went to a teashop nearby. 'What happened when you got to Rangoon?' said Kate.

'Oh, a great deal. I can't begin to tell you now. It took a long time to get back there, travelling from village to village, all the while terrified of the soldiers, and then I couldn't find Denpo for months because he had been sent elsewhere. By that time he was thoroughly sick of the Japanese but could see no way to get away from them. We married quietly and I kept my head down, working in a market. I had my son a year later – his name is Thagyamin.'

'What does it mean?'

'Change,' said Myia, smiling. 'Denpo's idea.'

'I've been following the news but I don't understand half of it,' said Kate, pouring out tea into tiny cups.

'It is quite complicated,' said Myia. 'They are trying to set up a new government but there is a great deal of protocol that must be followed – and of course there are many opposing factions. Denpo's old friend, Aung San, is the obvious leader but not everyone agrees.'

'I've seen his name in the newspaper now and then,' said Kate. 'I don't understand how he was able to switch sides. It must have taken a great deal to make him change his mind.'

'In 1943 the Japanese declared Burma officially independent,' said Myia. 'But it was a mirage, of course. That year Denpo told me that Aung San was planning to rise up and defeat the Japanese.'

'But what was it that made them come back to the British?' asked Kate.

'Aung San is a practical man. He would have risen up with or without help but knew that he had more chance of winning with the British on his side. It wasn't until May this year that they formally agreed to fight side by side. The rest . . . well, you probably know.'

'There was a photograph in the newspaper, taken outside the Secretariat. I thought I saw you in it.'

'I remember a day just after the end of the war when all of Aung San's men were asked to gather for a photograph with their wives and families. That must have been it.'

Kate shook her head. 'I thought you must be dead.'

'And I you,' said Myia, squeezing Kate's hand. 'I'm so glad you're here. But you're carrying a great deal of sorrow.'

'I don't know where to start. So much has happened. How long are you here for?'

'A few more days.'

'Then you'll go back to Burma?'

'Yes,' said Myia. 'It's time to go home.'

62

Calcutta, December 1945

Darling girl,

Your letter arrived on the coldest morning so far this winter. The sheep huddle together for warmth and the men are having to break the ice on the water troughs first thing. But it's beautiful – there are icicles in the wood and the sky is a pale clear blue.

I'm glad you felt able to tell me at last about the journey. You've been so brave, Kate – you won't like me saying it, but it's true. You have endured far more than you ever ought to have done. I know you feel that you've let people down, but don't think that for a minute. You have survived. You have saved lives. That is more than most of us will ever be able to claim.

I was never disappointed in you. You were the greatest comfort imaginable to me and to your father, and I know that we asked too much of you. The end was hard for all of us, but we find different ways of coping, and you did what was necessary. He was so proud of you, and would be even more so now, as I am.

Laura telephoned yesterday. She has some exciting news: she's expecting a baby. It's very early days but she asked me to let you know and said she would write soon. She and

Will are thinking about moving home, and I suggested they live in the little cottage, which is now empty. (Ben died last month, I'm sorry to say. He was eighty-five and quite ready to go, or so he said.)

The baby is due in the summer. Do you remember listening to the nightingales down in the wood? Every year I go back and think how lucky I am. I have been very happy here, despite everything, and there isn't much I would change.

You sounded unsure about coming home. You must decide for yourself, Kate, but you know that there is always a home for you here, and that we will be glad to have you back when the time comes. If there is something calling you to stay, then you must stay. There's no rush. Life is there to be lived. Grasp it with both hands.

The evening is drawing in and I must get the loaves out of the oven before they burn. It's beautifully warm in the kitchen when the range really gets going, but the rest of the house is chilly. When I'm making my hot water bottle I shall think of you roasting in Calcutta.

Sending all my love across the sea to my dearest Kate, and a very Merry Christmas.

Mum x

For a moment Kate could almost feel the frost on her toes and hear the cracking of ice on the pond. Winters on the farm were always hard, but so beautiful. She remembered bundling up in thick socks and a heavy duffle coat and trudging through snow to check on the animals. She and Laura had made snow angels in the meadow and old Ben had helped them to make a giant snowman.

'Look, Daddy!' Laura had called, aiming a snowball carefully at his window, and he'd opened it to peer out, wrapped in his dressing gown. The snowman was wearing one of his scarves and a pair of spectacles and he had laughed, even as he coughed and spluttered . . .

The ceiling fan juddered and Kate suddenly remembered where she was, looking around, startled, at the quiet room. Pamela's bed was bare, a set of clean sheets folded on the pillow. She would be halfway home by now. Beside Kate's bed was a basket of fruit that Priya and Asanti had given her as a Christmas present, adorned with a huge bow.

She blotted her shining forehead and looked again at her mother's letter, feeling a strange sense of relief. She realised now that her mother did not resent her for going away. She had been puzzled, perhaps, and a little hurt to find herself alone, but she trusted that her daughters knew what they were doing and had managed to carve out a life for herself. All she wanted was for them to be happy.

Perhaps I can be, Kate thought, chewing the end of the pen. I just wish I knew how.

She looked up at the clock, folding the letter over, and laid it down on her pillow. She would write a reply later. She had an appointment to keep.

✦

In Victoria Park the elegant European plants were wilting in the heat. In normal times a team of gardeners was busy every day, but these were not normal times. Kate had seen a troupe of sturdy Englishwomen pruning roses the week before, as well-equipped and as absorbed in their work as if they were at Kew.

At a quarter to four she sat on the bench nearest to the fountain and watched small children play in its feeble jets. Their parents perched on the stone wall that surrounded it, splashing them to uproarious laughter.

She remembered that Christmas in the park in Rangoon, four years ago to the day, when Edwin had played football with a horde of children, and for a few short hours she had almost forgotten the war. What a long way they had both travelled, she and Edwin, and what misery they had met along the road.

Autumn had turned into winter and Kate had been in India long enough now to notice the lowering of temperatures. The days were still hot, but at night she was no longer unbearably sticky, and the hospital wards were pleasantly cool under the ceiling fans. Nineteen forty-five was drawing to a close, and despite the end of the war she would be glad to see the back of this year. The patients on her ward were disappearing one by one, going back at last to their homes in Mysore and Manchester.

At home, England was starting to recover from the worst of the war's effects, but men were still coming back in coffins, and many of Europe's cities had been flattened. The war in Burma had been bloody and all-encompassing, for her and for millions of others, but it was a tiny part of a larger conflict and she sensed, with a sad inevitability, that it would soon be forgotten altogether.

For some reason Kate remembered the grand piano they had found on the way through the Hukawng Valley, sinking into the muck of the jungle as Fred played his lament, and saw that it heralded the end of an era. But the end of the Empire meant the start of something else, and it might be something extraordinary. *Don't waste it.*

As the clock struck the hour she looked towards the gate. In the glare of the afternoon sun she saw a figure appear between the gateposts, tall and thin, leaning heavily on a walking stick. He wore a pale linen suit and was almost invisible against the brightness.

Too impatient to wait, after so much waiting, she hastened towards him. He saw her at once and she knew that he had recognised her as she had recognised him, their faces strange but familiar.

'You're here,' said Kate, feeling suddenly shy, and studied his face. He smiled and held out a hand, and she grasped it.

'Hello,' said Rama.

63

Moulmein, December 1942

Somewhere near Moulmein, Edwin crept around the edge of a paddy field, trying not to crush too many plants and so give his presence away. It was early morning and the labourers had not yet emerged for their work in the fields.

He and Rama had been travelling north for what he estimated to be two weeks, although he had lost track of time in the simple repetition of the days and the glorious contentment of being together. In theory, they were travelling towards India, but it was a thousand miles away and somehow it seemed not to matter if the journey had an end.

Avoiding villages as far as possible, and foraging for food, they had several times taken a gamble on making themselves known to someone – a lonely farmer, a pair of women doing laundry in a river – and asking for food. The elderly farmer had shaken their hands and given them an armful of sugar cane; one of the laundry women had gone to her home and returned with a huge bag of cooked rice left over from breakfast.

'You're so kind,' said Edwin wonderingly, and she laughed.

'Japan soldiers not kind,' she said. 'Very not kind.'

Another time a group of adolescent boys had seen them on the outskirts of a village and shouted at them to stop, but they ran away and were not pursued.

'They might have been all right,' said Edwin.

'Or they might be working for the Japanese,' said Rama. 'Better not to take the risk.'

At night they slept in barns or under trees and made love in the darkness as the cicadas whirred in the jungle nearby. It was like nothing Edwin had known before, and for the first time in his life he felt sure that he was in the right place. Inexplicably, he had been granted a second chance.

'You said you came to Burma looking for a new home,' said Rama one day as they clambered over a crumbling wall. 'When all this is over, where do you think you'll find it? Perhaps you'll want to go back to England.'

Edwin shook his head. 'I can't imagine going back to England.'

'Then where? India?'

'As long as I'm with you, it doesn't matter.'

But it went further than that, this strange new feeling, this sense of completeness and detachment from the world, now that he had found this shared connection. Home is wherever you are, he thought.

'What about your family?'

Edwin was about to say that it didn't matter, but he stopped himself. That wasn't quite true. There were people he loved and who had been kind to him, though they were far away. His mother, his father – and Kate, he thought with a rush. Kate, who had been the dearest friend he had ever had.

He had promised to find her in India! He had been caught up in the excitement of being with Rama and had almost lost sight of their destination and what would happen when they got there.

They were approaching Moulmein, the first major town on their route. It had had a significant European population not so long ago, he knew; now, presumably, they were all flown, dead, or captured.

A few miles back they had passed an abandoned teak mill, the names of its British owners fading on the sign outside. Inside, massive saws lay rusting on the ground and ropes and pulleys hung from the rafters, creaking eerily. In the office they found mildewed photographs of the mill in its heyday, with a team of working elephants hauling timber into the yard. Now the place stood deserted and there was no knowing what had happened to the owners, the employees, or the elephants.

※

The mist lay low on the paddy fields, the cool wet drops brushing against Edwin's skin as he passed through it. The ground was muddy but he knew the sun would soon rise fully and dry the mist and the mud. It was his turn to forage and beyond the rice fields he could see the tops of what looked like fruit trees.

It was pleasant being out in the cool morning, watching the sky grow lighter. He had left Rama sleeping in a tumbledown hut, his chest rising and falling. He had not been sleeping well, a fever had been threatening, so it seemed kindest to leave him to get some rest.

Edwin passed the remains of a crumbled pagoda, the pale stones scattered into the trees, and saw a headless Buddha sitting impassively in an alcove.

He reached a high hedge, behind which he had seen the fruit trees, and moved along it looking for a gap big enough to scramble through. Instead he came suddenly to an ornate iron gate set into the hedge and he lifted the latch, feeling as though he was entering an English country garden.

Instead it was a small orchard filled with fruit trees, many of them thickly laden. He reached for the nearest tree, which was a papaya, and gently lifted three or four of the heavy fruit down into his bag, sniffing the warm skin. The next tree held ripening mangoes, and again he picked a few, trying to take them from different branches so that no one would notice their absence.

He knelt to tie the top of the sack. Then he stood and turned to leave, and found himself face to face with a nun. She was European and elderly, her crisp habit neatly folded around her shoulders.

'Good morning,' she said pleasantly, as though she found men stealing fruit from her orchard every day. Her accent was hard to place and her sharp eyes took in his ragged clothes and his thin frame.

Edwin had a frantic urge to run away but resisted. He felt dreadfully ashamed and lowered his bag to the ground. 'Look,' he said, 'I'm sorry . . .'

'You're very welcome to all the fruit you can eat,' she said, gesturing around the orchard. 'It's here for those who need it. But come, wouldn't you like a proper meal? I am Sister Caterina, the Reverend Mother here.'

Edwin had not spoken to another European for weeks, and he was so surprised that he found his mouth hanging open. 'What is this place?' he said at last.

'It's a convent. St Mary's Convent School, Moulmein.'

'What about the Japanese? Why aren't you prisoners?'

'Oh, but we *are* prisoners,' she said, shrugging. 'The Japanese soldiers check on us once a week. We can't go anywhere, but otherwise they leave us to ourselves. Where have you come from?'

'Tavoy,' said Edwin.

'The prison camp. Of course,' said the Reverend Mother. 'Look, do come inside. It's quite safe. We've got decent food – bread and so on – and can even give you a real bed for a night or two. You look dreadfully underfed.'

Edwin's stomach rumbled. 'That's very kind of you. I'm not alone, though. I'm travelling with a friend – I left him in the woods back there. We must keep going north.'

'Bring him here too,' said the Reverend Mother. 'We'll feed you up and send you on your way with whatever you need. We're rather poor but certainly have enough to spare.' She smiled and began walking back to the house. 'I'll put the kettle on.'

64

Moulmein, December 1942

Ten minutes later Edwin was tearing back through the jungle to where he had left Rama, his mouth watering at the thought of toast and tea.

'Rama!' he called in a low voice, expecting to find him awake, but he was still asleep, his black hair tousled across his forehead. He was curled up and looked suddenly vulnerable. I have never known love like this, thought Edwin.

'Wake up,' he said, kneeling beside Rama and putting his hands either side of his face, which felt hot and damp.

With a great effort Rama opened his eyes and peered blearily up at Edwin. His mouth tried to form words but it was too difficult, and he closed his eyes again.

'What is it?'

'I'm . . . not well,' said Rama thickly. 'Feel hot and cold.' He shivered suddenly and rubbed his arms.

Edwin gripped his hand, feeling how hot it was. 'Don't worry. Can you walk? Do try.'

With an effort he got Rama to his feet, where he swayed and looked dizzy. Flinging one of Rama's arms around his shoulders, Edwin leaned into him and took much of his weight. Rama was the larger of the two and Edwin was weak, but adrenaline and worry made him forget all that, and he supported Rama carefully as they walked across the fields back to the convent.

Passing through the orchard, they came to an open door in a stone wall. Inside was a garden, shady in the early morning, planted with neat beds that had once, perhaps, held flowers, but now grew mostly vegetables, although lilies bloomed here and there and a jacaranda blossomed on the lawn. In the shade of the grand stone house, the Reverend Mother stood by a table, pouring tea while a younger nun buttered slices of toast.

'Oh, heavens,' she exclaimed, looking up, and put down the teapot at once. 'He's sick. Sister Margaret, go and get some help.'

'Of course,' said the younger nun, who was Indian, and she smiled shyly at the two men as she passed.

'Put him in this chair for now,' said the Reverend Mother, and Edwin lowered the half-conscious Rama into a chair, feeling the sweat of his exertions sticking to him.

'I think he's got malaria,' said Edwin.

'We'll look after him.'

Sure enough, a moment later three other nuns emerged from the house and, with practised skill, loaded Rama onto a stretcher.

'I'll help you . . .' said Edwin, but the youngest of them, a cheery Frenchwoman, would not hear of it.

'Eat your breakfast. You'll do no good like that.'

He watched them carry Rama into the cool dark house and then sank back into his chair, accepting the tea and toast that the Reverend Mother was offering.

'There are eggs on the way,' she said, sipping tea herself and watching him.

'This is wonderful,' said Edwin, looking around at the house and the garden.

'You're not the first stray to come our way.'

'Did you say this was a school?'

'Yes. Much depleted these days. We had fifty children this time last year; then the invasion came and of course most of the children were retrieved by their parents. Those who are left are either orphans or their parents are missing.'

'And have the Japanese treated you badly?'

'Not really,' she said. 'My being Italian helped, at least at the start. Sometimes they get the urge to make us work and we all spend a couple of weeks chopping up fruit or sewing sheets for them and then they seem to lose interest. I suppose they know it won't look good if they harm a company of nuns and children.'

He told her a little about his history, but he found it difficult to reconstruct all that had happened, and the Reverend Mother did not push for information. She clearly saw it as her duty to help them, and it hardly mattered how they had come to be here.

Sister Caterina had come out from Italy nearly forty years earlier to join a convent in Rangoon and had eventually found her way to Moulmein. In its heyday the convent had had twenty nuns but over the years they had dwindled; by the time the Japanese marched into Moulmein in January 1942, there were just eight.

✳

'What will you do?' asked Edwin that evening as he dined with the nuns, revelling in the cleanliness of his clothes and skin. Rama lay asleep upstairs, the nuns taking turns to check on him.

391

For much of the day Edwin had watched the children playing in the garden. He joined in occasionally, but he felt very weak, and had at last to excuse himself and sit instead in the shade, laughing at their japes before dozing off. They were a charming bunch, clearly not much troubled by the war. Most of them were half Burmese, half English, and he wondered if any of their parents would ever come back.

'What can we do?' said Sister Margaret, placing a bowl of soup in front of him.

'I don't know. Escape?'

'This is our home,' said the Reverend Mother gently. 'We are blessed to live in this extraordinary country and we are blessed that the Japanese have been merciful to us. Oh, we've seen their cruelty, and they will be judged, but not by us.'

'So you'll stay here?'

'Of course. The occupation won't last forever. We hear rumours that the British are gathering their forces in India to strike back. One day the occupation will end and life will return to normal.'

Edwin wondered how long they would have to wait. It seemed very strange to be here at dinner in this country house with flowers on the table, eating with knives and forks and sipping glasses of home-made lemonade.

'What about you?' said Sister Madeleine, the youngest, who had a sweet round face. 'Where will you go?'

'We must get to India,' said Edwin. 'It's the only safe place.'

'It's too far!' said Sister Margaret. 'You will be caught.'

'Perhaps,' he said, rather helplessly. 'Since we escaped I dread all the time that we'll be captured. I can't fight or anything like that. In fact, I'm a dreadful coward.'

'God loves all his children,' said the Reverend Mother. 'You may not be a fighter, but you have a good heart. I see that you have loved very deeply and have also lost a great deal. God will protect you.'

As he was leaving the room a little later, the Reverend Mother called him back. She waited until the other nuns had filed out and then pushed the door shut.

'Mr Clear, I have a suggestion that I would like to share with you. An alternative to your plan to walk to India, which is reckless in the extreme.'

'An alternative?'

'There is a steamer captain who works out of Moulmein harbour. He is a Burman, certainly not a Christian, but a godly man nonetheless. He used to do the journey along the coast from Moulmein to Chittagong via Rangoon for the British, and since the Japanese invaded he has had no choice but to work for them, taking troops to Rangoon and the Arakan. He has several times intimated to me that he could take us – my sisters and I, and the children – to safety in India.'

'Why did you say no?' said Edwin, his heart beating fast.

'For my part, it is as I said earlier; this is my home and I will not leave it. Although it is a dangerous journey, I considered sending the children if they were in peril, but my heart tells me that they are better off here, waiting out the storm. You, however, are in real danger.'

Edwin looked at her. 'Do you think he would take us?'

'I believe so, if the request came from me. I will speak to him tomorrow.'

Edwin climbed the stairs to the first floor, which lay in darkness, and pushed open the door of the room where Rama lay. A cool breeze came through the window and, in a pool of candlelight, Sister Margaret sat in an armchair, reading a book. She looked up.

'I will stay with him tonight,' said Edwin.

'Are you sure? You need to sleep too.'

'I can sleep here,' he said, and pointed at the twin bed. 'Please. You've done enough.'

'Very well. There's a jug of water on the nightstand and clean cloths and towels over there. I've been sponging his face now and then; it seems to help a bit.' She went to the door. 'Do call if you need anything. I will pray for him.'

'Thank you.'

The door closed and he looked down at Rama, whose eyes fluttered open.

'You're here.'

'Yes,' said Edwin, grasping his hand. 'We're safe.' He kissed Rama's forehead and thought it felt cooler.

'How do you feel?'

'Strange. A little better, perhaps. Who are these ladies? They washed me and gave me clean pyjamas.' His voice was soft.

'Nuns,' said Edwin. 'They are very kind.'

'Are we staying here?'

'I don't know.'

He thought of the Reverend Mother's idea and was filled with conflict. If they took the boat they could be in India in a week or two. And what then? What kind of future awaited? Not for the first time he wished that time would stop, that this journey, these precious days, would go on forever.

'There might be a way,' he said quietly. 'A way to safety in India.'

Rama looked up at him. 'Another way to India?' His mouth was dry and Edwin reached for the glass of water on the cabinet and passed it to him. He sat up a little and sipped it.

'There's a boat.'

'You don't sound keen,' said Rama, lying back on the pillow and observing him with a smile. 'Oh, Edwin, don't you want to get to safety?'

'Of course I do.'

'It won't be the end,' said Rama, reaching out and taking his hand. 'I don't know what will happen, but it won't be the end.'

An hour later the Reverend Mother poked her head into the room to check on Rama and saw Edwin curled up on the floor beside his bed, still fully dressed and fast asleep. She closed the door quietly and went on her way. She had seen far stranger things.

65

Moulmein, December 1942

Two days passed in a haze of sunlight. The laughter of children rang through the house and good food was served three times a day. Edwin assisted the nuns in the garden, put up shelves for them, and helped the children with their schoolwork.

Upstairs Rama dozed, his fever receding, ministered to by the conscientious nuns. When he was well enough to sit up he peered out of the window and smiled to see Edwin deeply absorbed in a game of grandmother's footsteps with the younger children.

'He's good with them,' said Sister Madeleine, placing a tray on the table beside the bed. 'They do appreciate a change of company. It's been hard having them shut up like this.'

'It's good for him, too,' said Rama. 'I have never seen him so light-hearted.'

He sat back against the pillows and looked with interest at the tea and cake she had brought.

'What about you?' asked the nun. 'You look better.'

'I am much better. You have done so much for two perfect strangers.'

'Oh, you're not strangers,' said Sister Madeleine, now gathering up damp cloths from a basin by the bed. 'You are God's children as we are and that makes you our brothers.'

'I admire your faith.'

'It was never a choice.'

'Becoming a nun?'

She nodded. 'I knew from the age of ten, growing up in Marseilles, that I would give my life to God. I had a friend who knew she would marry a rich man, and she did. The convictions we have when very young are often correct.'

'Do you miss your family?' he asked.

'Yes. I have not heard from them for several years. When the war ends I hope I will have news and until then I must pray.' She hesitated. 'What about your family?'

'They are in a little town in the Punjab. I had a row with my father several years ago and have not seen him since. Unless he is dead I doubt I will go home, even if I get to India.'

'Wouldn't your mother like to see you?'

'Yes, I suppose she would.'

'Perhaps you ought to go anyway, for the sake of your mother. You should not punish her for your father's transgressions.' She flushed slightly. 'It's not my place, of course.'

'Sister Madeleine, your advice is very wise,' said Rama, smiling a little. He looked thoughtful. 'Perhaps you're right. I don't know what I can do about my father, though. He makes me so angry.'

'Forgive him,' said the nun, opening the door. She looked back. 'It's one of the most powerful things you can do. Then go home and be kind to your mother.'

⋆

Before dawn on the third morning Edwin was called down to the parlour, where the Reverend Mother stood looking agitated.

'You must leave immediately.'

'What has happened?' said Edwin.

'I have received a warning from a friend in town that the Japanese know we are harbouring Englishmen. Someone must have tipped them off and they will come here today, I'm sure of it.'

'We've put you in danger,' said Edwin, feeling the onset of panic. 'Forgive me.'

'There is nothing to forgive. But you must leave. I have sent a message to the captain. His name is Aung Pataya and he will be waiting for you at the far end of the docks, on a boat called *Golden Lotus.* He is due to leave for the Arakan today, from whence he is willing to continue up the coast to Chittagong. He will take you as far as he can.'

Upstairs, Edwin found Rama packing their meagre belongings into the sack.

'Must we leave?'

'Yes. We're in danger.'

Rama crossed the room and held him tightly, his strong arms reassuring. Edwin breathed in the scent of his neck and looked up at him.

'I'm a little afraid,' he admitted.

'Be brave. I am with you.'

'But you're not well.'

'I'm much better. I'll be fine.'

They went downstairs. The Reverend Mother stood by the open front door with a small wicker basket. 'Take this – food for the journey. And there are some rupees to give to the captain, to sweeten the agreement.'

'I will not forget your kindness, Reverend Mother,' said Rama, pressing his hand to his chest.

'Neither will I,' said Edwin. 'I wish you well in all that is to come.'

The old nun watched them walk briskly down the winding driveway. As they reached the edge of the paddy fields Edwin looked back and saw her raise a pale hand. Then the door of the convent closed and once again they were on the move, pushing along the overgrown paths between fields.

Soon the town of Moulmein was spread out before them, just visible in the first seeping light of dawn. In the centre the tops of pagodas were visible, as well as the slender spire of an Anglican church.

Before long they were on the outskirts of the town, padding along narrow, darkened streets. Few people were around this early, although occasionally they saw a boy on a bicycle, or a delivery driver with a cart in the distance. The ground began to slope gently away and soon they rounded a corner to see the black, shifting spread of the sea before them.

'The Gulf of Martaban,' said Edwin.

'It's a long way to India.'

'How long will it take, do you think?'

Rama shrugged. 'A week? Perhaps longer? It must be hundreds of miles to Chittagong.'

As they went downhill they could see the docks, with dozens of boats rising and falling quietly in the half-dark. In the distance they could see a few men unloading fishing boats and went quickly on towards the main jetty.

Rama kept a close lookout, twisting this way and that, as they proceeded along the jetty and Edwin checked the name of each boat. These were mostly sailboats and motorboats, much too small for the journey they hoped to make.

It was not until they were almost at the end that he saw in the dim light the words *Golden Lotus*, with a hand-painted lotus beside the name in Burmese. She was a compact steamship with two narrow funnels, her black mass rising and falling gently on the tide. The deck was piled high with cargo, covered by oilcloths tightly bound with rope.

'This is it.'

They waited beside the boat as the sky grew lighter. Edwin began to feel anxious again and wondered what they would do if the captain never arrived.

Finally a figure appeared from the shadows, a small, slim man dressed in the usual Burmese style, his *longyi* neatly knotted. He was near to middle age, his head shaved like a monk's.

'Gentlemen,' he said, bowing his head. 'Forgive my delay.' He looked around, ill at ease. 'I worry I am being watched.'

'I see no one,' said Rama, peering back along the jetty. 'But we should get away without delay.'

'Thank you,' said Edwin. 'We are grateful for your help.'

Aung Pataya nodded. 'I have much respect for the nuns. They help me many times over the years.' He gazed back at the town, now silhouetted in the half-light. 'These are evil times and all of us must do what we can.'

He bowed again and turned back to the *Golden Lotus*, which was rising and falling gently beside them. The captain leapt nimbly onto the ship and grabbed hold of a rope to steady himself. He fished out a narrow plank and flung it out towards the jetty.

'You first,' said Rama.

Edwin stepped tentatively onto the plank, reaching out for the rope that swung nearby. His foot slipped, leaving him dangling, and at that moment he heard the barking of a dog behind him, followed by shouts. He peered back to see men with lamps held high running down the pier towards them, only a hundred yards or so away.

'Quickly!' shouted Rama, pointing at the ship. 'Get on.'

'Not without you!' But Rama was already hunched low in a fighting stance, his breathing hard and his face beaded with sweat. He looked back at Edwin, who stood uncertainly on the gangplank, and jerked his head again.

'Edwin, go!'

Edwin leapt for the ship, feeling the plank slip sideways, but in the darkness behind him a dreadful crack rang out and he looked back to see Rama sprawled on the ground.

Aung Pataya looked out from the upper deck and saw Edwin swinging back onto the jetty; he shouted something down, but it was lost. He followed, leaping over the edge and landing like a cat with his knees bent.

'Get aboard!' he said. 'I must take you to safety.' He clutched Edwin's forearm with a surprisingly strong grip.

'Not without him.'

Rama had been shot in the leg and was bleeding heavily onto the wooden planks of the pier. Edwin could see uniformed men approaching along the narrow causeway while Aung Pataya untied the painter from around a thick bollard.

'Take him!' Edwin shouted to the captain, who began to drag Rama towards the ship. 'I'll delay them.'

He took a few deep breaths and stood squarely with his feet apart, expecting another shot to ring out at any moment. The first Japanese soldier was just yards away and lashed out at him, and Edwin, who had never fought in his life, found himself

401

ducking and flinging punches. He caught one of them full in the face and the man reeled away, clutching his bloody nose and looking angry. But it couldn't last for long, he was surrounded, and soon he found himself being dragged along the jetty, away from the ship, away from Rama.

'Stop struggling, Mr Clear,' said a voice, and he realised it was one of the interpreters from Tavoy, but he did not stop until they hit him hard in the face and he sagged, the adrenaline suddenly giving out.

Rama dragged himself into a sitting position and saw Edwin, in the distance, standing before three Japanese soldiers. Rama's leg was badly injured and he felt that he might pass out at any moment, but he held himself grimly upright. He could feel blood seeping onto the dock and knew that he would not be able to walk. Aung Pataya was behind him, trying to get him up and onto the boat.

Someone shouted and in a moment two more soldiers were marching down the pier, their guns trained on Rama. He felt rather than heard the captain behind him leaping for the boat, but one of the soldiers fired immediately and there was a splash as Aung Pataya hit the water. *Golden Lotus*, unmoored, began to drift away from the jetty.

'You are a fool, Mr Clear,' said the interpreter somewhere above Edwin. He could barely see; his glasses were gone and his eyes were full of blood. 'Trying to defend your friend. He's going to die, you know. He brought you here. He is – what do you say? Troublemaker.'

'No,' said Edwin, his breathing short and ragged. He had been kicked hard in the stomach and wondered if something had ruptured. Everything was painful.

'He's an Indian,' said Edwin, trying to sound disdainful. 'Do you really think an Englishman would take orders from an Indian? I needed a servant, so I brought him along, although he was reluctant. He wouldn't have the intelligence to plan something like this.'

'You English,' said the interpreter, sounding resigned. 'Such arrogance.' He shook his head and spat on the ground. 'You deserve everything that comes to you, you and the rest of your people.'

Edwin felt a surge of euphoria and knew that his lie had worked. He could feel the blood pulsing through his body and, knowing that the end was drawing near, he had never felt more alive. Will it be worth it? Have I done enough this time? And then, the astonishing thought: so this is love.

Rama, watching from a distance, saw the men talking as Edwin stood before them. Then suddenly Edwin was pushed down to a kneeling position. There was a little more discussion, and then a shot reverberated in the dawn, and Rama saw a figure sprawled on the dock.

66

Calcutta, December 1945

The sun was going down. A sweeper made his way through the park, dragging a hessian sack. He paused to pick up a banana skin and saw a couple sitting on a bench. The white woman was sitting very still, bolt upright, while the man beside her sat forward, his head in his hands. Unsurprised, the sweeper moved on. He had seen more illicit assignations and subsequent heartbreaks than he could count.

'Forgive me,' said Rama at last.

Kate shook her head, unable to speak. He looked despairing and impulsively she took his hand, pressing it for a moment. He turned to look at her.

'Did you know he was dead?'

Kate dropped her hands into her lap and stared at the fountain. 'Yes, in my heart,' she said at last. 'I knew that he had been taken prisoner and that many men don't survive.'

She had opened the letter containing Rama's brief request for a meeting and had known at once what it meant. But hearing it confirmed was quite another thing and she felt her chest tighten. She took short, fast breaths, trying to slow the pace of her thudding heart and quiet the sorrow that was roaring in her ears. They had been in the park for a long time.

The story that Rama had told her seemed quite incredible, but she had no reason to disbelieve him. That Edwin – shy, awkward Edwin – had escaped from a prison camp and had purposefully given his life to save someone else was startling; but she had seen his heart and knew that he was capable of it.

Rama had told her how he and Edwin had escaped, and how the Japanese had at last caught up with them, but there was a great deal that he had not said. He was protecting something precious and she had no wish to intrude upon his grief by asking. Perhaps he was afraid, even now, to be honest about who he really was. But it was clear to her, without the words being spoken, that he had loved Edwin fiercely, and that Edwin had loved him back. Questions that had hovered in her mind ever since she had first met Edwin now had their answers and it all seemed obvious. Of course he had loved this man. Of course he had died for him.

It was bittersweet that only after Edwin's death was she able to understand something so fundamental about him. He had told her a great deal but had held back this last piece of the puzzle, and now she would never be able to speak to him again, to tell him she understood.

She thought of the Japanese soldiers who had been responsible and wrenched her mind back to Rama. He was all that was left of Edwin. 'What did they do to you?' she asked. 'Afterwards.'

'They tied me up and took me back to Tavoy. They were very angry.'

'Did they torture you?'

He hesitated.

'You don't have to worry about distressing me,' she said. 'I've seen a great deal of misery.'

'They used water,' he said, 'poured water through a tube into my throat to make me believe I was drowning.' He paused and watched the life of the park as it undulated around them, listened to the sounds; the calls of children, the soft laughter of men playing chess on a stone bench, and the sharp thwack of a cricket ball somewhere in the distance. 'I wanted to die.'

'But you survived.'

'It was Edwin's loss that made me want to die, but somehow it was also what gave me the strength to live on. And I have, for three years,' he said. 'I was moved to another camp after a year or so, where we mostly worked on the railway. The camps were liberated by the army in August, although it has taken until now for me to get home.'

She looked at his thin face and his twisted, bony hands. Even now, months after the end of the war, he looked unwell. The physical and mental souvenirs of his time as prisoner would last, she supposed, for the rest of his life, and he had lost the person he cared for most.

'It must be strange for you to be back in India after so long,' said Kate. 'I still don't feel that I understand this place.'

'Will you go back to Burma?' asked Rama.

'No,' she said at last. 'I'm not sure I would be welcome.' She looked up at him. 'But my ghosts are quieter now.'

'Mine still clamour. But perhaps that's to be expected.'

'Where will you go?

'To the Punjab, to see my family. I have not always been a good son but it's time to make amends.'

'And what then?'

'The rest of my life?' said Rama, and he heaved a sigh. 'I have no idea. I will have to start again. What about you?'

'I'll work at the hospital until they no longer need me. Soon, I think. And then I suppose I'll take a ship back to England. I want to see my family, too.'

'Will you stay there?'

'I don't know.' She stared at the spray of the fountain, leaping high over the marble horses, drying almost before it hit the ground. 'I'm not sure I'll be able to, after all that has happened. Who knows?'

He smiled. 'You sound melancholy.'

'Shouldn't I be?'

'You have endured. I think that is rather extraordinary.'

'If anyone has a right to be melancholy, it's you,' she said.

He shrugged. 'I have mourned and raged for three years. But it grew quieter each day, and on the day the camp was liberated I felt a great elation. I have been granted another chance. I don't intend to waste it. He taught me that, in the short time we had together.'

He glanced up at her and she felt suddenly that they understood one another, that she knew everything that she needed to know. Though she had only known him for a few short months, Edwin had been one of the most important friendships of her life. At what might have been his darkest hour, he had found love and absolution.

Grant me the same courage, she thought.

'Edwin's parents ought to know what happened,' said Kate. 'I might be able to track them down.'

Rama was silent for a moment. 'I suppose they will also know where to find his wife's family.'

'I expect so.'

'He talked about her sometimes. He loved her. Does that sound strange, knowing what you now know?'

'Not strange at all.'

'He really did.'

'Emilia,' murmured Kate.

'I think they should know that he is gone,' said Rama. 'But also that as he approached the end she was in his thoughts. Perhaps it might bring them some small comfort.'

'It's kind of you to think of them.'

'I believe that regret is corrosive. Better by far to live well than to live in shame and melancholy. I will do what I can to become the man he believed I was.' He looked at her, his head on one side. 'I think you have allowed regret to direct you for too long. Let it go.'

She twisted her hands, feeling his gaze on her, and knew he was right. 'I don't know how else to live.'

'Let your heart guide you instead,' said Rama. 'Nothing and no one else can choose the right path for you.' He sat back with his eyes closed, feeling the sun on his face. 'Edwin talked about you, too, you know.'

'Did he?'

'He said you had a great capacity for love. He believed that you were destined for an extraordinary future.'

'He always saw the best in people,' she said wryly.

'He did,' said Rama, and they smiled at each other, pleased to have this shared affection.

There was something else that she couldn't put her finger on until later, when she was sitting on her bed with a letter from Joseph in her hand, scribbled on the train taking him and his daughter from Calcutta to a small town by the sea. It was an acknowledgement of a shared humanity; the acceptance that they were both human, with all the flaws and mistakes that

that entailed, and that Edwin too had been human, and that believing that was a way not of insulting his memory, but of honouring it.

Kate stretched out on the bench and felt a sudden weight lift from her shoulders. Edwin was gone and would not return, but his legacy was love. She had survived, though the road had been long and painful. She felt newly hatched into the world, fragile, unsure of what was to come, but certain for the first time that there was something out there, if only she had the courage to find it.

67

Calcutta, December 1945

Kate hurried along the dock. She heard the hoot of a steamer and walked faster, adjusting her straw hat. In the distance the sun gleamed off the water and for a moment she felt as though she was at the centre of a great web, with shining tendrils that stretched across the globe. From Calcutta Port ships went everywhere – even home.

She saw the steamer and hastened towards it. The gangplank was still down and goods were being loaded unhurriedly. The ship was due to leave at any moment, but time in the east was fluid.

A group of people were waiting on the wharf. Myia, turning, put a hand above her eyes to shield them from the sun and waved.

'You came!' she said, kissing Kate on both cheeks. 'Thank you.'

The young man beside her smiled, and the child in a sling on his back waved a chubby hand. Kate shook his hand and kissed the little boy, feeling unexpectedly tearful.

'Myia tells me about you,' said Denpo, lifting up an umbrella to shield his son from the fierce sunlight. 'I am happy to meet you.' Like most Burmese men he was slight, and his features were delicate. But he looked strong and muscular, and his eyes, when he looked up at her, were bright and fiercely intelligent.

'He is shy about his English,' said Myia. 'I have been teaching him.'

'It sounds perfect,' said Kate. She smiled at him, feeling real warmth. She had been afraid that she would not be able to see past what she knew about Denpo; that he had fought with the Japanese. Until yesterday she had not wanted to meet him. But talking to Rama had changed all that. Even though she now knew what had happened to Edwin, and knew that men like Denpo had betrayed him, she had also seen Rama's commitment to forgiveness and knew that it was time to look to the future.

'They did what they had to do to protect their families and their country,' Rama had said, shrugging. 'We all do things that we are ashamed of later. They will have to live with it for the rest of their lives.'

Denpo loved Myia. That was what she knew about him. The rest was in the past and would have to stay there. She watched him fussing over his little boy, Thagyamin – passing him a slice of pineapple, tweaking his bare toes – and felt a swell of mingled sadness and hope: for Denpo and Myia and their son, and for Burma.

There was no time. She and Myia had talked and talked, and still there would never be enough time. Their lives had briefly intersected on a difficult and extraordinary journey. Never again would they live in the same city, never again would they talk quietly in the darkness of the jungle as the campfire flickered before them. Myia was going home.

And so must I, thought Kate.

At last she embraced them both, then watched them walk up the gangplank together with their child. They turned at the top and waved, two small figures in bright *longyis*, and Kate stood alone on the dock, waving back and thinking of the great journey before them. In a few days they would be in Rangoon, and then the real adventure would start. The work of rebuilding Burma would take a lifetime, but they would be together.

With a long, low hoot the steamer slid out of the harbour and began to make its slow way along the Hooghly River, which would take it at last to the coast. From the top deck dozens of people waved and she waved back. When it was too small to see the passengers, the crowds on the dock began to disperse.

Kate stood irresolute for a moment, and then started back along the wharf. In several berths there were other ships preparing to leave, and some that had just arrived. All around families embraced one another while labourers loaded sacks and boxes onto ships. It seemed that the world was on the move.

By now, she knew, Rama would be starting his long journey to the small village in the Punjab where he had been born. She imagined him climbing down from a bus, dusty and travel-worn, and walking slowly towards the old woman who waited for him, her hair covered by a bright scarf. In the years to come Kate would think of him often, and however many miles and years lay between them she knew they were inextricably bound to one another for as long as they might live.

Reaching the end of the wharf, she stopped at the office where tickets were sold and stared up at the lists of sailings that were pinned to boards outside. Ships were leaving for Southampton every week.

She thought of a young woman, her mother, standing on the dock at Fishguard in the years before the first war, watching the ship steam away towards Ireland. Her hair is blowing in the stiff breeze and she licks the salt from her lips. She is calm. She watches until it is out of sight and then sighs, a long, low sigh. She has no idea what the rest of her life will be, or whether the decision she has made will prove to be correct. In this moment the future is tantalisingly empty . . .

'Can I help you, miss?'

Kate, lost in a reverie, heard the young man speak, and shook her head. She made her way through the port and out onto the main road, where she flagged down a rickshaw. As they moved off towards the city, the heavy smell of salt and fish began to recede, gradually replaced by the scent of rotting vegetables, petrol, frying dough, and the sweet bougainvillea that hung over the walls on all sides.

The rickshaw moved slowly through the traffic. All around the hordes of Calcutta walked and bicycled and drove in a never-ending stream, and looking out across the great seething mass she saw the city shimmer in the afternoon heat, like a mirage in the desert before it disappears.

Epilogue
Orissa, 31st December 1945

Wrapping her dressing gown around herself, Kate stepped out of the small wooden hut. In the evening warmth the jasmine that grew around the door was intoxicating and she pressed her face into a spray of flowers.

A number of other huts were dotted around and in the distance she could see fellow visitors making their way to dinner. An elderly Hindu couple emerged from the hut beside hers, the wife resplendent in a rich pink sari, her husband with a garland of flowers around his neck. They greeted her happily and pottered away arm in arm.

Kate picked up the towel that she had left folded outside the door and made her way down the steep steps that led away from the resort, following a winding path down the cliffs. The stairs were crooked and she descended carefully, pausing occasionally to look at the sea, which sparkled in the evening light.

As she emerged onto the beach she stopped and gazed out across the sand. The last few beachgoers were making their way back to the hotel, smiling as they passed her. They had that look of intense happiness and relaxation that can only be achieved by spending many hours baking on a warm beach and taking regular swims.

Finally the last family went by and made their way up the stairs, the sand-covered children scampering ahead while their parents wearily carried deckchairs and picnic bags up the cliff, obviously longing for a drink.

At last the beach was hers. The sun was setting, and with a pang Kate remembered another sunset and a golden stupa gleaming crimson, far away. The pink sky turned slowly to navy, and the year was almost at its end. At home her mother would be preparing gifts for local children and opening a barrel of cider for the farmhands, before the countdown to midnight and then the dawn of the new year, bright and full of promise.

Kate took off her robe and stood naked, relishing the balmy air against her skin. She glanced down, taking in the faded scars that crisscrossed her legs and feet, the callouses on her hands, and the stretch marks like a map across her thighs. Then she walked towards the sea, crunching sand under her toes, and felt the waves begin to lap at her ankles. The water was warm still and the white sand sloped gently away into the darkness.

Soon she was waist-deep and began to swim, rising and falling gently with the waves, feeling the currents shifting beneath her. She lay back and closed her eyes and floated on the surface, her hair splayed out around her head. The sea rushed gently on all sides and she could hear music echoing across the bay.

It was now almost completely dark, but Kate felt safer than she had done in years, lying here on the black tide, somewhere in the Bay of Bengal, a tiny piece of jetsam in an enormous ocean. The heart of Asia, she thought. She ran her fingers idly through the water and opened her eyes.

As her hand moved under the surface, a thousand tiny stars of luminescence burst and twinkled in colours too numerous to count, following the movement of her fingers. She swished her hands again, laughing delightedly, and thrashed her legs, and suddenly the whole dark ocean seemed to be lit with sparks of light, as if a new cosmos was being formed, and as if somehow everything that Kate had seen and done had brought her here, at this moment, to be present at its birth.

Acknowledgements

The seed for this book was planted in 2013 when I spent several months working in Burma (Myanmar) as a volunteer teacher. I am more grateful than I can say to the many people who showed me their extraordinary country, at a time of great upheaval, and were endlessly generous and welcoming. As I write Burma is once again caught up in a struggle for its future. I hope one day to return and to see their hopes fulfilled.

I thank my agent Charlotte Colwill, the Wilbur & Niso Smith Foundation, and everyone at Bonnier Books UK, particularly my editor Claire Johnson-Creek, for their encouragement and work on the book. After several years as an editor myself, being on the other side of the table has only reinforced my admiration for the huge amount of work done behind the scenes by many people in producing a book.

I am grateful to Kate Pearce, Ross Meikle, and my sister Daisy Blench, all of whom read the book in manuscript form and offered suggestions and advice. My partner Mark Wheeldon provided emotional and culinary support, always managed to look interested when I was bouncing ideas off him, and never doubted that I could do it.

I owe my parents, Pete Blench and Felicity Norman, a huge debt for their support and encouragement, and for always believing in me and my writing, as well as for reading the manuscript too and providing feedback. They have never once suggested that my ambition to spend my life writing and travelling was impractical, and I am very thankful for their steadfast love and support.

Thank you to everyone else who cheered me on – your enthusiasm and encouragement mean the world.

Finally, I must mention my maternal grandmother Mary Norman (née King), who went to India in 1942 with the British Army to nurse soldiers wounded in the Burma campaign and found her future waiting. Neither I nor this book would exist had she not taken that courageous leap into the unknown.

On 1 February 2021, the military in Myanmar (Burma) detained members of the country's democratically elected government and assumed power. A grass-roots resistance movement is fighting to restore democracy in the face of violent suppression. For information about how you can support the Myanmar people, including donating to charities and putting pressure on the international community, please visit: www.isupportmyanmar.com

THE WILBUR &
NISO SMITH
FOUNDATION

The Wilbur Smith Adventure Writing Prize supports and celebrates the best aspiring and established adventure writers today. Writers are recognised in three distinct categories with awards for published, unpublished and young writers.

The Long Journey Home by Cecily Blench won the Wilbur Smith Adventure Writing Prize, Best Unpublished Manuscript award in 2019.

Launched in 2016, the Prize is administered by The Wilbur & Niso Smith Foundation, a charitable organisation dedicated to empowering writers, promoting literacy and advancing adventure writing.

Find out more at www.wilbur-niso-smithfoundation.org